Francis Cowley Burnand

Very Much Abroad

Francis Cowley Burnand

Very Much Abroad

ISBN/EAN: 9783337416294

Printed in Europe, USA, Canada, Australia, Japan

Cover: Foto ©Andreas Hilbeck / pixelio.de

More available books at **www.hansebooks.com**

VERY MUCH ABROAD

By F. C. BURNAND

AUTHOR OF "HAPPY THOUGHTS."

WITH

Illustrations from "Punch"

LONDON

BRADBURY, AGNEW, & Co. Ld., BOUVERIE STREET

1890

LONDON :

BRADBURY, AGNEW, & CO. LIMD., PRINTERS, WHITEFRIARS

To

My Dear Old Friends and Colleagues

THESE VOLUMES

Containing the greater part of my Contributions to

MR. PUNCH'S PAGES

During the last Twenty-five Years are

Affectionately Dedicated by their Fellow - Worker

F. C. BURNAND.

May 31st, 1890.

CONTENTS.

VERY MUCH ABROAD.

THE BOOMPJE PAPERS.

BEING THE PAPERS OF THE BOOMPJE CLUB,

Collected by its Secretary.

PREFATIAL.

TO ALL and singular, individually and collectively, Boompje!

The history of the Boompje Club resembles that of most other great and flourishing institutions. It has been developed successfully out of small beginnings.

Such remarks as appear here are made in my capacity of Secretary, and on my own personal responsibility.

*   *   *   *

No man is a Boompje all at once.
This must be borne in mind, because we didn't, as a Club, begin

by being Boompjes. We, as it were, awoke one morning in a new country to find ourselves Boompjes. Of which word, it being double-Dutch, I will not take upon myself to guarantee the correct spelling or pronunciation.

One of our party—we started as a party and continued as a Club —looked out of the Hotel window at Rotterdam, by the river-side, and says he, gravely,

"Do you know where we are?" There was a pause, and he continued, "We are on the Boompje."

Thereupon, somebody said, "Let us be Boompjes," and somebody else said, "Let's," and the motion was carried *nem. con.*

[On investigation we found he was right. We *were* on the Boompje. "The steamers," said our friend, appealing to the infallible *Murray*, "land their passengers on the fine quay called the Boompje." * * * "The philosopher Bayle ended his days in one of the houses on the Boompje." This was enough.]

We find (so runs the extract from the Boompje diary of that memorable day) that we have hitherto been Boompjes without knowing it. This is evident on examining Boompje principles.

BOOMPJE PRINCIPLES.

Examples.—To say at ten A.M. "I'm off!" and to *be* off to Anywhere (America, for example), before eleven, is to act upon Boompje principles.

A man may act on Boompje principles, unconsciously, and without being a member of the society, as that gentleman did, who marched up and down his room for one hour and a quarter, overhead, while I was trying to write the first stanza of my poem, *The Fisherman of Scheveningen.* I had begun :—

> It was a Fisher of Schevening,
> Who went out in the evening,

but at this point one of our party (the names will be given soon) knocked at the door, on Boompje principles (*i.e.*, he did it so suddenly that I started up—boompje'd—from my chair), and informed me, when I asked him "if it wasn't pretty," that *evening* wasn't a rhyme to *Schevening,* because Schevening was pronounced Skayvening:" and then, having only come in to ask me what time it was (which I couldn't tell him), he walked out also, on Boompje principles, *i.e.*, banging the door violently. So, when I set to work again, I saw no prospect of a rhyme to Schevening, as pronounced, unless the poem could be supposed to be written by an Irishman, who would pronounce "evening" as "*a*vening," which I rejected, after dashing it off on one Boompje impulsive principle, and tearing up the paper on another.

> It was a fisher of Schevening,
> Whose . . . . ravening.

Something about "hunger" here. On second thoughts it occurred to me, that if you could talk of "stabling a horse," why couldn't a poet speak of "havening a boat?"

"Oho!" I cried, inspired, "the Boompje!!" and forthwith wrote:—

> A Fisherman of Schevening
> His little boat was havening,
> When——

And here the man above began to walk about. Then there came a banging of doors in the passage; then a creaking of *a* door, somewhere, at intervals. So that when the man didn't walk, the doors banged; when the doors didn't bang, *the* door cracked; and, when I was going to ring my bell violently, and say to the waiter, "For Heaven's sake, stop this inf——," the noises ceased, and, passing my hand through my hair, I once more set myself to find line No. 3 for

> A Fisherman of Schevening,
> His little boat was havening,
> When { a storm
> { a bell
> { a—a—

Arrival of a party, and "would I mind letting a lady see the rooms?" With pleasure: I'm going out. On with hat; off with self. Boompje!

Coming to think of it, I don't know anything more remarkable than the way in which we suddenly struck on the title. Came down, as it were, whop upon it, Boompje!

It's a wonderful word. Boompje !! If any one doubts me, let him try it as applicable to all sorts of occasions.

You talk of your acquaintance, the Duke of Upshire, as "Upshire" or "old Uppy," after being introduced to him, and saying good-bye to him at the corner of a street. This is Boompje.

You rise in the morning ; out of bed at last. Boompje !

You bound along the pavement, buoyant, light-hearted, and happy. Boompje !

See the rollicking carelessness of the porters in dealing with your portmanteau and trunks at Dover and Calais. Boompje principles. Boompje !

You are sad, despondent, and depressed. B-o-o-mp-je.

You are up again. Boompje !!

You go out for a ride, in Rotten Row, on a mettlesome charger, at so much an hour, and tell a friend that you are trying a horse with a view to purchase. Boompje ! Boompje !

You have all your electro-plate out and silver too (if any) for a leg of mutton and potatoes. Boompje !

In short, if the intelligent reader will but give his mind to it, and just try the word on *every* possible occasion, he will find it not only suitable, but exactly appropriate to *all* possible occasions.

In short, Boompje is everywhere in some form or another. In due course, as we proceed, I will give you the Hymn of the Boompjes.

*   *   *   *   *   *   *   *   *

NOTE POST-PREFATIAL.—The mystery or secret of the Boompje Association lies in the mode of pronouncing or giving effect to the word Boompje. It is two syllables ; the first (it is scarcely necessary to add) being *Boomp*, while the second (it is important to notice) is *je*. All that the present writer is at liberty to say on this subject to those whose destiny has not as yet led them to be Boompjes, is, that something of the force of the words may be gathered by coming down heavily, as it were, on the first, namely, the *Boomp*, and coming up, lightly and sharply, on the *je*. *Boomp* on one side of an ordinary see-saw, and *Je* on the other, will convey some idea of this mysterious word to the uninitiated. In any case the *Je* is to be *Je* up. *Allons !*

CHAPTER I.

THE TOUR COMMENCES—THE BOOMPJE PARTY PRIOR TO BOOMPJEISM.

ONE morning Bund comes to me and says, "I want to make a party to go abroad." As a commencement, we went out for a walk together, and called on Maullie, the eminent artist, who had just finished his great picture of *Home Again*—(subject: a young cavalier has rushed into an Elizabethan drawing-room to meet his wife or somebody—represented by nobody being there and through the door, which in his haste he has left open, are seen five interiors in perspective, one after the other, with the hall-door open in the distance, and a very little perspective man taking down a very little perspective portmanteau from a little perspective coach—sold for something over four figures, on the honour of a Boompje)—and was anxious to get away for a holiday. "Now," says Bund, who is an enthusiastic musician, and an amateur of the violoncello, "Here's the party: Painting, Music, and Literature." I was "Literature," and deputed to keep a diary. Somebody suggested that *Three* wasn't "company," and while we were debating this point, enters to us Dicky Gooch. "Look here," says he, "you fellars: if I come with you," making it a favour, "I *must* be back in ten days, because of the London season."

This being an imputation upon our social status, we all asserted that not only *must* we be back in that time or less, but that we experienced the utmost difficulty in tearing ourselves away from the crowds of parties, balls, concerts, teas, drums, &c., to which we had been invited at the rate of five a day for the next two months. (Boompje !)

[*Boompje note.*—Gooch had managed (I afterwards discovered) with some difficulty to get an invitation for a private operatic performance at the house of somebody whom he didn't know, and this represented *his* engagements for the season. But a genuine Boompje of London Society would rather die than own such a melancholy fact.]

CHAPTER II.

COMPONENT PARTS—THE START—LILLE—GHENT—THE BOOMPJE HATS

UND we elected Commodore, Commander-in-Chief, and President of the Travelling Society, whose object was to be the pioneer of civilisation to Dutchland. He wanted to bring his violoncello with him, but this was objected to by the entire party. There were still a few preliminaries to be settled. As to expenses, that is a matter generally ignored as "mere detail" on Boompje principles.

"Hallo!" says Gooch, "Who talks Dutch?" He generally prefaces a question or an observation with "Hallo."

It was explained to him, by the Secretary, that Hollanders generally talked Dutch.

"No, no," says he; "look here, you fellars" (another formula with him), "I mean which of you talks it. I don't."

No one did. Maullie thought it wasn't necessary. The Secretary thought it was; but suggested that French would do, to a certain extent.

Bund asked if he was Commander-in-Chief or not? Yes, he was.

"Very well, then," says he, "we'll have a Courier."

It was carelessly objected that this course might be expensive.

It was statistically proved by Bund that it couldn't be anything of the sort. His answer was, simply, "No, not a bit of it."

It was mildly opposed by the Secretary ; while Gooch, whose proclivities are swellish, but whose means are limited, halted between two opinions. Boompje, however, prevailed.

Maullie said that he'd once travelled with a Courier, and the plan was delightfully luxurious. He had just sold his picture, as I have already hinted, for a sum which would have purchased a wilderness of Couriers. (Boompje adaptation of *Shylock*.)

Bund offers to be Paymaster-General, and settle with everyone at the end of the time.

The Secretary and Gooch immediately agree to this plan, fore-seeing the convenience of a distant settlement, and place themselves entirely in Bund's hands.

Maullie yields, on condition that *he* is to map out what we *ought* to see.

Bund knows a Courier, and the thing is done.

Our reasons for going to Holland may be individually stated thus:

Bund goes because he's seen the picture galleries once, and forgotten all about them.

Maullie, because he knows all the pictures by heart, but has never seen them.

Gooch, because he has never heard of or seen the pictures.

The Secretary, because he has never seen the pictures, but heard of some of them vaguely.

The Courier, because he's taken.

Coincidence which I notice at Rotterdam after the Boompje title has been adopted, viz., that our Courier's name is Jömp, pronounced Jump ; and, therefore, the very name for a leader and guide of the Boompjes.

On we go to Holland, *viâ* France and Belgium ; and back again, *viâ* Belgium and France. Boompje !

"Yes," cries Gooch, as we were carrying it off jauntily on the quays of Rotterdam, with hearts both light and merry (with which "hey down derry" is to rhyme in *The Miller and his Men, vide* opening chorus), "here we are regularly out on the spree."

"No," returns Professor Maullie, sweetly rebuking his junior, "do not say ' on the spree ;' say that we are out on the Boompje."

Maullie is to meet us at Antwerp, which we are to pass through on our road to Rotterdam, but where we do not wish to stop, as three of the party "know it by heart." Maullie being of an independent Boompje nature, sets off by himself.

From the moment of our concluding arrangements with Jömp, the Courier, all trouble is supposed to be taken off our hands. We merely tell Jömp where we want to go, Jömp knows the place, of course, intimately, and he could find the way there blindfold. So Jömp arranges our route. We propose, Jömp disposes. Jömp gets all the necessary tickets, and we are to be oblivious of everything until we find ourselves at our first halting place, Ghent.

The only inconvenience about this plan, we find, is that *we* change our minds, and Jömp doesn't. *We* decide that we ought to go *via* Antwerp first. Then having decided that, we decide again that Antwerp oughtn't to be taken at all, but begin with Bruges.

Gooch exclaims, "Look here! you fellars! I say! Why not stop at Lille for a night?"

No one knows exactly why not, but it being discovered that there's nothing to be done at Lille at night, "except go to bed, that's all," says Jömp, disparagingly, the proposal is dismissed as unworthy of notice, and Gooch says, "Hang it: I think you might listen to some of my suggestions." As this looks like breaking up the party before it starts, we compromise by calling in Jömp (which would have saved us considerable trouble at first, as we now find he has taken all the tickets *via his own* route) and asking him if we go near Lille.

Jömp, when questioned, always gives one the idea of having been called out of bed at short notice, and dressed himself in a hurry. He collects his scattered senses by passing his hand forwards and backwards over his head several times, and murmuring something, partially unintelligible, still in his character of a man not quite awake.

"Lille," he is understood to murmur vaguely, "vell—um—um." It should be mentioned that Jömp is, it is supposed, of Swiss origin, and possesses such a knowledge of languages as is enough to render him generally unintelligible in any particular tongue.

"Lille," he replies, considering, "Lille—vell—um-um-um! Oh yes!"—this he gives in the tone of a permission—"Oh yes, you can go by Lille," wherewith he shrugs his shoulders, as if to give us to understand that such a *détour* will put the train to considerable trouble, not to mention the entire derangement of his own plans.

"Yes. But—" Bund puts it in a barrister-like style, "do we go there or *do* we *not?*"

"Vell," says Mr. Jömp, after polishing his head slowly, preparatory to taking his cap in both hands, and holding it behind him, "Vell—you can go by Lille—oh yes—de train pass true dere." Then he adds suddenly, as a conscientious afterthought, which is to take us by surprise, "If you go that vay."

It is finally decided that we won't stop at Lille. And the route is mapped out to the satisfaction of all parties.

Bund says confidentially to the Secretary, that he should like to have got down to Milan, or spent the time in Switzerland, instead of Holland.

Maullie takes an early opportunity (when we subsequently come up with him at Antwerp) of informing me that he gives way to the majority, but for his part he should like to have made Dort his chief place, and stopped *there*. Maullie's one idea is to go to Dort. Bund, who is always ready with an argument from *Murray*, points out that his authority says, "There is nothing to detain the traveller at Dort."

Maullie says that observation is only true *after* you've seen everything. He is sure that Dort is the most interesting place in Holland. Jömp says, "Oh yes, um—um—um, you can stop at Dortrecht—um—um." Then, as an afterthought, "if de steamer go dere." On the whole, we keep Dort in reserve for Maullie, if he won't go on without it. First Boompje sonnet by Maullie:—

> To judge by report,
> I always thought
> That we ought
> To stop at Dort.

Bund thinks it stupid! Gooch says that *Dort* doesn't rhyme to *ought*. Maullie likes it himself, and reads it to me privately.

Gooch hopes [before we start] that we shall push on to Brussels, and "see some fun." No one knows exactly what he means, except, apparently Jömp, who says, "Oh, yes—um—um, you can do something at Brussels," which is the fullest information he can offer us on the subject.

We start. A broiling hot day. Gooch thinks that there won't be a ripple on the water in crossing.

Bund is of opinion, having had something to do with nautical affairs in his time, that it may be "blowing freshish outside." The mention of "outside" exercises an unpleasant influence over Gooch. He stations himself as near the centre of steamer as possible, and won't rise from his seat.

Mr. Jömp, with admirable forethought, places the coats and bags on our seats, which he secures for us several minutes before the boat starts, in such a position that we get the sun in our eyes, the blacks from the chimney, and the heavy moisture from the steam valve pipe.

On being remonstrated with by Bund, who points out to him (Bund once had a thirty-ton yacht off Erith, which he thought resembled the French coast without the nuisance of having to speak a foreign language) that when the wind is SS. by EE., and the sun is at meridian, also when a boat is steering from SE. by NW. *then, if you want to keep out of the sun, you must get into the shade*, Jömp replies, with an admirable readiness, which shows him equal to any emergency,

"Vell, yes—um—um—you can move der tings."

Gooch, finding that there is no chance of being inconvenienced by the voyage, now becomes hilarious, and ventures upon pale ale and a cigar. He regales us with anecdotes of himself in various towns of Europe, chiefly Boulogne and Paris. He begins to air his French, and points out two or three people on board who he assures us, on his own experience, are "regular foreigners," and who turn out to be commercial travellers from Liverpool. Boompje !

At Calais he rejoices in being on the shores of France once more —"*la belle France!*" he exclaims—as if he'd been born or brought up there. He exhibits the soldiers, the *douaniers*, and the French people to us generally with this preface, " Look here, you won't see this sort of thing in England, you know. We can't do *that!*"— a summing up generally in depreciation of his own country.

CHAPTER III.

GOOCH'S DISTRESS—THE TOUR CONTINUES—THE INTELLIGENT JÖMP
—THE BOOMPJE LIVERY.

GOOCH, when on French soil, is very much annoyed at being taken for anything else but a Frenchman. Indeed this is Gooch's peculiarity everywhere abroad. He has no desire when in Holland to be thought a Dutchman, but he is immensely pleased when the Dutch waiters address him as "Moshoo," and flatters himself that there isn't a trace of the Britannic Islander in him. In Holland and Germany he is strong in his French, even to substituting it occasionally for English. But in Belgium he is more diffident of speech, excessively polite, and full of action.

Gooch calls the French language so "*expressive.*" His idea is practically illustrated by his seldom finishing a sentence, even if he gets half through it correctly (which is wonderful), but attempting to convey the remainder of his meaning by a shrug and a look. This is quite satisfactory to a foreigner, he says, who understands as much from this expressive pantomime as he does from the previous conversation. Bund and the rest assent to this as highly probable, seeing that, on one occasion, when Gooch returned from talking with a Frenchman with the intelligence that "he had found him (the Frenchman) a very pleasant fellow, full of information ;" and that he (Gooch) "had picked up a good many valuable hints in answer to his questions," we found the French gentleman in a state of utter bewilderment as to " what language your friend (Gooch) had been talking, *as he* (the Frenchman) *hadn't understood one single word he'd been saying.*"

Maullie is as decidedly English (which Gooch is perpetually deploring) as Gooch is undecidedly French. [*Arcades ambo—* Boompjes both.]

Gooch travels as if he were dressed for Regent Street, so as to be ready, he says, for the towns.

Maullie, who has started in advance of us, when he *does* appear bursts on us in a light check coat, check trousers, white waistcoat, and white wideawake. The English tourist complete. *Bradshaw* in a bag slung behind him, and a sketch-book and pencil in his off-hand pocket.

Gooch, not knowing Maullie very well, confides his misery to us in the evening. "I say," he asks, "can't anyone hide Maullie's wide-awake and burn his *Bradshaw ?* Or, look here, couldn't we subscribe and buy him a black hat and black coat for *towns ?* And (imploringly to us all) *do* talk French more. Hang it ; why shouldn't we all talk French ? And, then, we shouldn't get mixed up with these 'travelling English' everywhere." [Boompje.]

On account of that white wideawake and light coat of Maullie's, I know that Gooch suffered mental agonies.

One morning, Bund, the Commodore, exhibited a black soft felt hat, of a Tyrolean form, smashed. It had braved many tours, and was now produced by him to save his *other* hat and be comfortable. Gooch eyed it, and merely observed that it was impossible for him (Bund) to go out walking in *that* thing. Maullie was bad, but to be excused solely on the ground that he was an artist. But Bund had no excuse, and his hat was several times worse than Maullie's.

There is certainly a good deal of Boompje about provincial continental towns, perhaps not more nor less than in ours. But no matter, here, there and everywhere all is Boompje.

N.B. The careful and inquiring reader will be able to collect for himself, from time to time, such Boompje proverbs as embody most of the Club's leading principles.

1. Once a Boompje always a Boompje.
2. When with Boompjes do as the Boompjes do.
3. Here, there, and everywhere,—all is Boompje.

As to Lille and Ghent, this being previous to the great Boompje declaration at Rotterdam, suffice it to record the following facts :—

That being interested in the town of Lille, Gooch asks Bund, who passes it on to the Secretary, if Lille wasn't a very celebrated city.

The Secretary replies, "Yes."

Gooch asks, "Celebrated for what ?"

The Secretary passes this back to Bund the Commodore eating ices, who thinks it was something to do with wars, but he will tell Jömp to get his *Murray* out of the fly. Gooch implores him not to : he says it's so touristy : so English. Ask the waiter.

The waiter doesn't know that Lille is particularly celebrated for anything : except perhaps the shop where *he* is, and its ices.

" Fortifications ? " suggests Secretary.

" Yes, fortifications," returns the waiter, shrugging his shoulders depreciatingly.

" Thread ? " asks Bund.

" Yes ; it is celebrated too for thread," the waiter thinks.

" Lille thread," says Bund turning to us, and explaining.

We tell Jömp to let the coachman take us round the town.

We are passing a quaint old house ; gabled and carved all over.

" That," says Jömp, cleverly, from the box, " is the Town House."

We ascertain it to be the *Hôtel de Ville.*

We stop before a tremendous cannon, ancient and unwieldy.

Mr. Jömp, on the box, points it out to us, as if there was any possibility of our not seeing it.

Bund asks him if it's a gas-pipe ?

Mr. Jömp being taken aback, and having no invention ready to hand (it is the business of a Courier to be always ready with *some* story about an object of interest) replies, "Vell—um—um—yez —

perhaps," and we drive on. If Mr. Jömp ever takes another party there, he'll show that cannon as the first gaspipe ever laid down and taken up again in Lille.

We see an arch. "What is that?" we ask the intelligent Jömp. "That?" returns our inexhaustible courier, "um—um—um," he looks at it and thinks; then to us, as if astonished at our want of perception, "That is an arc,—an arch." With which explanation he expects us to be as perfectly satisfied as he is himself. We see Vauban's fortifications being pulled down. We view two churches, which are large and have fine windows. We don't know their names, but are as much pleased as if we had heard all about them.

Gooch says, "There! now we've done Lille, let's go back to the train."

We all feel the better for this episode, and presently, about four hours after, arrive at Ghent.

At the hotel and ready for dinner.

Ghent. Gooch asks, "*Qu'est-ce que vous avez?*" meaning for our dinner. The waiter is a little startled; but suddenly bursts out with "Roas beef, you can have, and mutton, and some plum puddang."

"Confound it!" says Gooch. "What's the good of coming abroad for *that?*" And forthwith, the table arrangements having been confided to him, he orders an elaborate *menu.*

At dinner Gooch, in his character of *un vrai Parisien*, insists upon having *hors d'œuvre.* But for these (which turn out to be radishes on one plate and butter on another) the dinner is served in purely English style : whereat Gooch is very angry with Jömp, who, he says, has told them that we are English and like this sort of thing.

Jömp denies this; but says he is very sorry.

"What for?" asks Gooch, brusquely.

"Um—um—um," replies Jömp, "vell—um—*I do not know.*"

But for a long time he doesn't get over the imputation of having betrayed the secret of our being Englishmen, and living only on "roas beef, mutton, and plum-puddang."

We apply to Jömp, as knowing all about it, to know what there is to be seen in Ghent.

Jömp replies, " Vell—um—um, you can see—um—um, a great many things." We wait to hear a few mentioned particularly. " There's " (it suddenly occurs to him by a sudden inspiration,) " vatever you like."

He says this as if Ghent belonged to *him*, and he was throwing it open gratis for our inspection.

" Aren't there some fine churches ?" Bund suggests as a leading question to freshen his memory.

" Oh, yez," he returns, shrugging his shoulders ; " there's, um—um—vell—there is churches."

" Hang it ! " growls Gooch, " go and ask somebody ; " and Jömp, more hurt than ever, in fact, almost shedding tears, quits the room, and we hear voices on the landing. Jömp and the waiter.

" He *said* he knew all these places," Bund explains apologetically. [Evidently a courier's Boompje.]

Jömp, the " intelligent officer," as the police reports say of a policeman who has done nothing but " receive information," returns, having ascertained (from the waiter on the landing) that there is a Belfry to see and a Church of St. Paul. He takes us to the Belfry, and tells us it is St. Paul's ; he takes us to St. Paul's, and tells us it is the Belfry. Both are shut ; but an old man, in his shirt sleeves, offers, instead, to show us the Gymnasium. Declined with thanks.

CHAPTER IV.

GOOCH TITLED—"WHAT, NO SOAP!"—MR. JÖMP, THE COURIER—IN
LIVERY—GHENT—ANTWERP—ROTTERDAM—THE BOOMPJE.

F COURSE, when we meet
the Great Boompje Maullie,
afterwards at Antwerp, he
exclaims—

"What! not seen the
Belfry! Not seen the
Gymnasium! Why, my
dear fellows, you've missed
the only things you ought
to have seen." But this
we set down (subsequently)
to Boompje.

Before Maullie and his
hat had appeared, Gooch
had been horrified at the
appearance of Mr. Jömp,
the Courier. He says he
doesn't mind it while travelling, nor when we were at Lille,
driving round the town in a fly, with Jömp on the box, in the
entr'acte allowed us (by Mr. Jömp's excellent management, who had
so contrived our journey that there was no station where we didn't
stop a quarter of an hour at least—with nothing whatever to do,
and no buffet—"Vell," said the inventive Jömp, "um—um—um
—*you can valk about.*") between the arrival and departure of the
trains; but now we are at Ghent, a *town*, and with a dashing
carriage (it certainly is that), and a coachman in livery, with a
new cockade, he must protest against Jömp being on the box,
unless he has a costume. "What sort of dress?" we ask.

Well, he has seen the sort of thing he means in the Bois, and
on a foreign ambassador's, or some foreign swell's, carriage in
Hyde Park. He proposes something military. (Boompje!)

First proposed dress—Rejected on account of being too much like a French *maréchal* on the box.

Second proposed dress—Rejected on account of its being painful to Mr. Jömp's feelings to appear in a footman's dress.

"But it won't be a footman's dress," explains Gooch, "when you *get the colours.*"

Thirdly—Gooch recollected a Polish count, whose servant used to appear at Baden in various uniforms. *Boompje argument:* "Why not be taken for Polish Counts?"

"The dress of a Chasseur," says Gooch, "would be *distingué*, and old Jömp wouldn't mind *that.*"

Old Jömp does mind it, however; but owns that his present appearance is not all that could be desired. "I voud vear anoder hat," he exclaims, "um—um—um—" and then adds, after carefully thinking it out, "*if I 'ad vun.*" Jömp can't say fairer than this, evidently. Even the philosophic Bayle, who died in a house on the Boompje, would have been satisfied with this as logical.

Gooch's opinion is, that Mr. Jömp resembles a travelling pedlar with umbrellas to mend. This comes from our having given him our umbrellas and our satchels to carry for us. The shape of his hat probably arises from its having been slept in for the greater part of the way, and sat upon during the remainder.

This is the compromise procured in Ghent at a tailor's. A livery coat, formerly the property of a duchess, but sent back because the family had gone into the deepest mourning. Black, with yellow facings, and black tags to shoulders. High black hat, with gold band: cockade, black and yellow. His (Mr. Jömp's) own collars and black tie, also, waistcoat and trousers *à discrétion.*

Sunday at Ghent.—First day of Courier in livery. We attend early masses at various old Churches; driving up in our carriage, and Jömp waiting at the Church doors (Boompje); Gooch and Bund behaving decorously, and *not* bringing Boompje principles into play while the people are engaged in their services; and finally after breakfast, we drive to the Béguinage, the College of Nuns who live in a little town of their own, take no vows, stay as long or as short as they like, occupy themselves in nursing and teaching, and so forth, and wear a white sort of towel on their heads, which, six hundred of them, as they enter Church, unfold and spread, one

c

after another, or several at a time, but all using one action, over their heads, and then they draw down the front to cover their noses, devotionally, retire to their seats.

We three, and four others of our sex, are the only men in the Church. We shrink into as small a space as possible, and keep near the door, with the view of retiring noiselessly should there be a sermon.

It is admitted on all hands, that, at all events, there is no Boompje here. "The Béguins are not the sort of people to put a Courier into livery," observes the Secretary to Gooch. Gooch objects to this, that they *do* wear a livery. This leading to no issue, the conversation drops.

Gooch presently says that up till this moment he had always thought the Béguins were birds.

Commodore Bund supposes he's thinking of Penguins. Gooch considers it not unlikely. Conversation number two dropped.

At Antwerp we see Maullie's hat in the distance, and, in three minutes more, we find Maullie under it.

Maullie is hearty and full of spirits. He stands at the door of the Hotel St. Antoine, and cries out, "Hooray! hip! hip! hooray!" (Boompje.)

"He might have said, 'Br-r-ravo,' or *à la bonne heure!*" Gooch grumbles, and expresses his wish that our meeting had been in a private room. This also is Boompje.

Gooch wants to know if dinner has been ordered. No, it has not. Well, then, what can we have?

The waiter answers promptly, "Roas-beef, roas-mutton——"

"And plum-pud*dang it!*" cries Gooch, in a rage.

Maullie says, good-naturedly, "Oh, anything for *me*."

This disgusts Gooch more than the waiter's announcement.

"Of course," he protests, "if you say you don't care; and hooray, and hip, hip on the steps of the hotel, of *course* they'll give you beef and mutton." And he boompjes out of the room, and comes against Jömp on the landing.

"Hang it, Jömp!" he says, "you ought to know. What can one get here besides this—this—beef and mutton?"

"Vell," replies Jömp, astutely, "um—um—um—" And we expect, by his considering so long, that we shall hear of some dish peculiar to Antwerp. So we wait while Jömp polishes his head with his handkerchief, and thinks it out. "Vell," he *says*, presently—"Um—um—*you can 'ave someting else.*"

Carried, *nem. con.*, that Jömp is an ass. This unanimity restores good humour; and the landlord is charged with the task of providing a *recherché* dinner on the distinct understanding that he is to avoid beef, mutton, and plum-pudding.

At Antwerp. We see all the great pictures and churches for the fifth time (for three of us) and assist at an *al fresco* concert in the Botanical Gardens in the evening. Here the best people of Anvers are present in grand toilette. Gooch hears Maullie, with Bund, discussing art in loud tones, and addresses himself to me piteously. "I wish," he says, "Maullie wouldn't come out in that hat. Hang it! you know, he wouldn't do it at the Zoo in London. And why *will* he speak English? Or, if he must speak it, why does he do it so loud?" Gooch, himself, is delivering all this to me apart and confidentially. What he *does* say aloud he says in French, and kicks me under the table impatiently if I don't answer in that language. Gooch points out to me, always in his character of *un vrai Parisien* (Boompje all over), that young Belgium imitates *jeune* France in dress. Gooch, wishing to be thought young France, or what he calls, a *petit crevé* the *haute gomme*, evidently thinks he is attracting the favourable attention of a young lady most elegantly dressed, who, he imagines, takes him for some leader of the fashion from Paris. He sees Maullie approaching. He foresees that that confounded hat and Maullie's loud and very plain English will destroy all illusion as to his being a French Count.

Henceforth we call him the Count.

Another thing very distressing to Gooch, is that Bund insists upon Jömp carrying for him a large bag, containing, among other things, *Murray* and *Bradshaw*. With this Jömp has to follow or lead us, as the case may be, and Bund stops him for reference, whenever he requires information. Maullie disconcerts him dreadfully by always wanting to stop suddenly in streets, and "take bits," in his sketch-book. He pulls up before an old gabled house, "There's a bit!" he exclaims enthusiastically, and out comes his sketch-book. "Hang it," says the Count aside to me, "you don't see foreigners doing that in London. *He* wouldn't do it in London.

If he did, the police would move him on. And then," adds Gooch, piteously, "he gets' all the little boys round him." Which is perfectly true, and they interest themselves as much in the Count as in the sketching.

And now by train through the flattest country; then on board a steamer, up a long, melancholy river, embanked by rushes. We are all becoming more and more depressed as we near our destination: at last, we see a terrace not unlike that at Southsea, or Littlehampton, with a touch of Ramsgate in it, too, and a dash of Chelsea, by the river-side. This is our first view of Rotterdam. After passing in front of a line of respectable red-brick houses, with little gardens (like those suburban houses on the western outskirts of Chelsea in the position above mentioned), we step at last upon

THE BOOMPJE.

There is elasticity in the word. Depression vanishes. In comes our luggage. Down goes Gooch's portmanteau. Whack. Boompje! Down goes Bund's on the top of it. Don't be annoyed, Gentlemen; it's all right—Boompje! Smash the carpet-bag heavily, bang the hat-box, mix our things up with somebody else's luggage—(Gooch asks if there wasn't a novel called, *Somebody Else's Luggage*, but receives no answer)—shovel 'em up, knock 'em down, stave in the side of that lady's box, drop the large portmanteau on to that evident bonnet-case,—whack, jerk, bang, anything you like; and here we are in the land of Boompje!

Down the passages; Boompje! luggage into rooms; on to the stands; on to the floors; wrong box in right room; right box in wrong room; bustle, bootjacks, and Boompje! Landlord apologises; but one hundred and seventy passengers have just arrived, and the house is full. Boompje!

Sorry he can't give us better rooms. There's one down-stairs : a sitting-room and a bed-room, with four beds in it. All for the Commodore.

The Count, Maullie, and the Secretary are distributed about the first-floor passages. Mr. Jömp follows everybody else's packages, and finally rescues ours.

Maullie, of course, has no soap. He is heard crying out for

soap loudly to the *garçon de chambre* (a Dutchman). "What sort?" asks the Waiter.

Maullie, busy unpacking, replies, "Any sort; only look sharp."

Gooch says, "Why on earth doesn't Maullie speak French; he'll never get any soap."

The Count is right. When we are nearly ready, Maullie is still ringing an electric bell in his room, and holloaing for soap.

To him the *garçon*, in a hurry, with a small tureen, a napkin, a spoon, and a large plate.

"What the Boompje's this?" exclaims Maullie. "I've been ringing for soap this half-hour."

"Could not pring 'em pe-fore; it take some time to hot." And therewith he sets it down on the table; and, whisking off the napkin, discovers a basin of hot Julien soup. Shouts from the Count, the Sec., and Mr. Jömp.

Maullie bawls at him—"Soap! not soup."

The Count (*with dignity*). "Le Monsieur veut dire 'savon:' comprenez, savon?"

Garçon. "Ah! vy he ask for soup?"

[*Exit Garçon with soup, and returns with soap.*

In a lofty room, with a painted mythological ceiling and carved mantelpiece, we sit down to dinner. Gooch has forgotten to inquire about the *menu*. It is brought in. Soup, roast beef, mutton, and plum-puddang!!! Boompje!!

CHAPTER V.

DEVELOPMENTS OF JOMP—ROTTERDAM—AT THE RESTAURANT—DUTCH
INSCRIPTIONS—WATER-ZOOTJE DINNER.

OUR order of proceeding through Rotterdam, is, Jömp first, with the Commodore's carpet-bag, containing (especially) *Murray* and *Bradshaw*. Then the Secretary, then Maullie in his celebrated hat with his weapons, sketchbook and pencil, in hand, "taking bits," lastly, the Count (Gooch) lagging well in the rear, afraid to lose sight of us entirely, but attempting to appear as if the assertion on our part of having any sort of connection with him were, as the advertisements say, "an untradesmanlike falsehood."

Our progress is slow, as we are pulled up every five minutes by Maullie, exclaiming, "Hah!" then he pauses, shades his eyes with his hand, compresses his lips critically, shakes his head at the antique house, as much as to say, "You're a sly old chap, *you* are, to be hidden away here in this manner;" then he opens the book and flourishes the pencil, and in another three minutes he has "taken the bit," and our halt has attracted a small company of little Dutch street-boys and a few loafers.

Gooch is utterly disgusted, and stands aloof, looking in at a shop-window.

Jömp has to clear away the crowd.

"Confound it," Gooch complains to me, "you know, they think we're going to perform, and do conjuring. It's all through

Maullie's hat,—and—hang it—they think all our tricks, and cups and balls are in that carpet-bag of Bund's. 'Pon my soul, it's too bad. It only wants a board and a bit of carpet to complete it."

Jömp, a perfect Irvingite in the matter of unknown tongues, somehow manages to explain to the little Dutch boys, that we are *not* going to give a performance of any sort, and we resume our progress.

The Commodore's one object in Rotterdam is to find out the statue of Erasmus. Gooch, who has dressed himself as if to walk in Hyde Park, and is suffering from the heat and the wretched pavement, says, "Hang Erasmus!" Maullie asks where the Picture Galleries are? These two questions being put to Jömp, that well-informed person stops, takes off his hat (the livery one, which is as hard as a policeman's, and as hot as the glazed one worn by *voituriers* in Paris) performs a sort of extempore shampooing operation with a faded brown cotton pocket-handkerchief ("Hang it," says the Count, "I'll get him a new one") and having "brought it out," replies deliberately, "Vell, um—um—um—oh yes—there's de statue of Rasums"—this is what "Erasmus" comes to in Jömp's dialect "Yes—oh yes—it's here," which we know, "but *where?*" asks the Commander, becoming a little irritable.—"Vell, I'll demand—oh, yes—*they'll tell me*"—as if this was a profound secret not generally divulged by the Rotterdammers, "and—de Picture galleries—oh yes—You can see dem—um—um—um,' here he thinks it out again, and makes a safe proviso—"*if dere are any.*"

"I thought you said," exclaims the Count to Bund, "that Jömp knew this place very well."

"He told me he'd been here before," replies the Commodore, evading the responsibility;—then to Jömp, "You *have* been here before, eh?"

"Oh, yes," replies Jömp, indignantly; "oh, yes—been here before—*but I never stop.*"

This confession compels Bund to have recourse to *Murray.* To get at *Murray* he has to open the bag, remove *Bradshaw*, two hair-brushes, an old comb, an eau-de-Cologne bottle, a pair of slippers, and a portable boot-jack. On the appearance of this last article, Gooch makes a final protest—"Out in the open air—oh 'pon my soul!—it's—it's"—and being unable to find words sufficiently strong to express his disgust, he walks away from us and saunters along, as if he were utterly *blasé*, and had seen it all scores of hours before.

At this rate we don't get on very fast through Rotterdam. Presently Bund cries out (he is sitting on a post, studying the *Guide Book*) to Maullie, who is taking a bit, "What do you think *Murray* says?"

"Don't know," returns Maullie, placing his pencil horizontally across the bridge of his nose, as, with a puzzled expression, he regards an imaginary vanishing point.

"He says," continues the Commodore, quoting—

"'*One day will suffice to see all that is remarkable in Rotterdam.*'"

"Oh," says Maullie, in a tone of utter indifference.

"Is there nothing to see!" says Gooch, who has sauntered back again on seeing *Murray* returned to the bag, and the bag once more in Jömp's hands.

"See? Yes!" cries Maullie, enthusiastically, shutting up his sketch-book with a click. "See? lots. I could spend weeks here. Isn't there a tower or something to go up and get a view from?"

If there are no picture-galleries, Maullie invariably wants "to go up somewhere and get a view." To boompje up a hundred and twenty-five steps gives quite a fresh lease of life to Maullie.

Gooch says, languidly, "Good heavens! if you want to do that sort of thing, why didn't you stop in London and go up the Monument." He complains (he is always presenting gravamina to me, privately) that to go up towers and belfries is "such a regular British tourist sort of thing."

"Let's go to a restaurant's," the Count proposes.

Compromise.—Tower first, restaurant afterwards. In the meantime (while we're up the tower) Jömp to go and order luncheon. "Not *luncheon*," says Gooch in despair, "*déjeuner à la fourchette, a bon filet, par example*, and be sure to order *hors d'œuvre, des radis, des sardines*, you know, Jömp; no confounded English things." And Jömp departs on his errand, taking with him, "thank Heaven," says Gooch, after he's well out of sight, "that boompje carpet-bag of Bund's."

On quitting the tower, from the summit of which we certainly have a wonderful view (about which Maullie minutely questions the guide who shows us over the place, while the Commodore, who will trust no information except *Murray's*, listens to him with the air of a man not to be taken in in this sort of way), we walk towards the restaurant, Bund stopping Maullie to draw his attention to what *he* considers picturesque (a tender of opinion immediately resented by Maullie who likes to choose for himself), the Secretary noting down the bright brass milk-pails, the Turk's heads, open-mouthed, over the druggists'-doors (as if always ready for physic), and the costumes of the women, with their wonderful spiral ear-rings, arranged on a startling boompje principle, apparently to shoot out suddenly and hit you, and looking very much as if the Dutch women had extracted the springs from small Palmer's patent candle-lamps, and polished them up into something resembling ornaments for their ears.

Mem. All Dutch children lovely; most grown-up Dutch plain.

At the Restaurant.—Gooch complains it isn't like Paris: more like Leicester Square. He hopes Jömp has ordered some dish peculiar to the country.

"Oh, yes," says Jömp, "I have commanded a—a—a——" (Here he thinks it out, and continues)—"a—a—*vot they 'are got.*"

Enter waiter with large dish, followed by another waiter with smaller dish. Cover removed. Exclamation (Boompje!) from Gooch,

"*A rumpsteak and potatoes!* Oh, confound it! Why the Boompje" (to Jömp, who stands by, smiling, with an air of intense satisfaction) "couldn't you order a dish of the country?"

"Vell," returns Jömp, hurt, "dis is from de country. *De cow is in the country, and de potatoes in de country.*"

Agreed *nem. con.*, for the fourth time, that Jömp is an ass. "And no *hors-d'œuvre!*" says Gooch, almost in tears.

"Oh, yes," says Jömp, triumphantly, "I command them, *but there are none.*"

Some capital light wine, and plenty of ice, restores us, and we again take to the Hoogstraat (High Street).

Note.—Dutch inscriptions. We notice "*Koffy Haus*" and

"Kaffy," too, as if they had not yet made up their minds how to settle the spelling. "*Slytery Tappery*" is very popular, and Hollandsche Spoorweg is far from occasional. It is satisfactory ("satisfactory" looks like a Dutch word, so do "lottery" and "pottery") to know that

"*Agentschasse der Sliedrechtsche stoorm sleep maatschaffij Haarsnijder Beschen 'en kleingoed.*"

Also,

"*Voor nat en drukken bewarren,*"

And

"*Het is verboden de lots of things.*"

"Heavens!" says Gooch. "Fancy being in a place where '*het is verboden to slytery tappery!*'" He makes this remark on seeing some notice not unlike the above, stuck up in a picture-gallery (not here, but at Amsterdam), which he subsequently finds means that visitors are requested not to put their sticks and umbrellas through the pictures. (At least we conclude that to be the idea.)

Dinner at the Hotel.—Bright idea of Gooch's. *He* knows what to ask for. Of course *the* dish of the country. What? Why—fancy not having thought of it before—of course, *water-zootje!* I suggest *souchet* or *souché*. The Commodore thinks it's *zouchy*. Maullie says he doesn't know, but should say *water-zootje*, inclining to Gooch's opinion. Jömp summoned. Does he know if there is any *water-zootje?*"

"Vell," says Jömp, "perhaps there is." He discovers his utter ignorance by offering to "find out for us vere it is."

"What do you mean—'where it is'?" says Bund, sternly. He is responsible for Jömp, and is beginning to feel that he mustn't be trifled with.

"Vell—um—um," Jömp explains, "vere it is—vot part of de town he is in."

"*Water-zootje* is something to eat, you—you Boompje!" cries Gooch.

"Ah!" returns Jömp, with an incredulous smile, thinking he is being chaffed, "*you can ask.*"

So the waiter enters. "Now," says Bund, shifting the authority on to the Count's shoulders, "*you* order what you want."

All eyes on the Count: the waiter deeply attentive.

"Have you," inquires Gooch, with the air of a barrister who'll get something out of the witness before he's done with him—"Have you any *water-zootje?*"

"*Vater——*" the waiter murmurs, puzzled.

"*Water-zootje*, you know," says Gooch.

"*Vater-zootje*," Maullie tries, with a feeble attempt at Dutch.

The waiter looks at Jömp. Jömp shrugs his shoulders, and smiles helplessly, as much as to say, "You see they *will* have their joke," which irritates Gooch almost beyond endurance. Then the waiter, evidently entering into Jömp's view of the matter, also smiles and shakes his head, as if we really were too funny for him.

"But, confound it!" exclaims Gooch, "don't you know your own dishes? Why, it's a regular Dutch dish—always have it at Greenwich——" (Waiter and Jömp shrugging and smiling; Commodore and Maullie anxious.) "Here, I'll write it down——" He writes it down. "Now," he resumes, triumphing in this effort of ingenuity, "what's that?"

The waiter inspects it, so does Jömp.

"Well," says Gooch, impatiently, "don't you know it? Haven't you got it? *Water-zootje*, eh? Your own national dish!"

The waiter, still under the impression that he is the victim of a weak practical joke, replies "*No, never 'eard of eet*," and retires with Jömp.

Agreed, *nem. con.*, stupid idiots! Don't know their own dishes. The usual foreign dinner follows—*roas* beef, &c. No *hors d'œuvre*, no salad. Capital champagne, however, well iced, restores equanimity. After dinner Gooch lights cigarettes. Maullie sleeps. Bund reads aloud extracts from *Murray*, and the Secretary makes notes.

Bund, finding it dull, regrets he didn't bring his violoncello, and requests me to note that there is no music in Rotterdam. If we stop any time in one place (Bund throws this out as a suggestion), he thinks he'll hire a violoncello.

CHAPTER VI.

STILL IN ROTTERDAM—GOOCH'S RAILWAY TIME—BOOMPJE NOTES—
FAREWELL TO THE BOOMPJES—THE HAGUE—THE GALLERY—
TWO FRIENDS.

GOOCH is peculiarly slow. It is through Gooch that we always manage to "run the starting rather fine," as *he* expresses it afterwards.

He is utterly unable to consider himself as a man slow in his movements. When he wants to give you an idea of his going to be some considerable time (during which, specially before breakfast, you are implored by him not to wait for him) he will ask you to "call it," or "say twenty minutes." This is how he wishes others to compute time, by "making it" or "calling it," or "saying" so many minutes. He seldom runs into hours. When he does this, if it's an appointment, you may depend upon either not seeing him at all, or on his turning up in a week or two, and proudly saying, "There you see, I *said* I'd *come*, and *here* I am!"

For instance, he is not out of bed, he has (by consequence) not had his bath, he has to pack his portmanteau, and have his breakfast.

"Well," says Bund, the Commander at the door, "how long will you be, eh?" "Oh," answers Gooch, from within, under the sheets probably, and the door craftily locked, "about a quarter of an hour, or," he adds, as if wishing to be particular to a second, and not inconvenience anyone by so much as a five seconds' delay, " say twenty minutes, and I'm there."

We say twenty minutes, and, of course, he is *not* there.

If he wishes to give us a notion of how quick he will be, when, for example, we want him to come and see some privately-collected picture gallery which is conveniently open at eleven and closed at twelve (on account of the private collector's family dinner), and Gooch has three letters which he has invariably got to " finish "— (not to *write*, oh no, that would be too long and tedious a proceeding,—he appears to keep a lot always by him half written, as Maullie has some three or four pictures always " on the stocks ") he says he will come " before you can wink your eye."

This is his formula for his own rapidity :—

He'll be dressed before you can wink your eye.

He'll put on his hat before you can wink your eye.

He'll come to you (he sends this by telegram a hundred miles off) before you can wink your eye.

After this, it is almost unnecessary to state that we find Gooch to be at least three-quarters of an hour dressing, and a trifle under that—not much—washing his hands.

Gooch's watch is invariably set by " railway time." This he will give with an air of authority, which is convincing at first. After missing the train on three occasions, in consequence of adhering closely to his (Gooch's) watch, we begin to mistrust him, and prefer Jömp's chronometer, which takes us down to any station at least an hour before the train starts.

Gooch's exclusive possession of " railway time " (no one else's watch ever coincides with his, and he generally manages to correct other statements and come in last, authoritatively) is peculiarly Boompje-ish. He announces it as a fact, by which you may take warning (or not), how it's for your own advantage (or not) ; but that's all one to him, and he pities you, if you don't. He is also consistent, a great point in Boompjeism ; for when we arrive at the station, hardly by *his* time, and the train has gone, he refers us to the railway clock as being in accordance with *his* watch, in which case he at first asserts that the train *can't* have gone ; and, on hearing that it has, threatens the ticket-taker in the pigeon-hole-that he will write to the directors ; or, if the station clock flatly contradicts him (which is very rare) he appeals to us (generally to me) to corroborate his statement of the agreement of his watch with that of the last station we were at yesterday.

After travelling with him for some time, we prefer Jömp's time to Gooch's ; but end by striking a balance between the two, and *then* generally having half an hour to the good.

Something Eccentric in Rotterdam.—I once saw a ballet, or musical piece, called *The Dancing Barber.* The chief character was dressed in a very closely fitting suit of sables, not a bit like a barber, and he wore a cocked hat. I mention this because Gooch reminded me of it in Rotterdam, where, when anyone is dangerously ill, the relatives send round a couple of these dancing barbers, in black, with funereal weepers to their cocked hats, who go about like two bogies, ringing at the doors, delivering cards, and frightening (I should think) little Dutch children into fits. (Boomp-je!)

Maullie proposes that, before going on to the Hague, we should visit Dort. The Commodore assures him that there's nothing to be seen at Dort except windmills.

Maullie retorts, that he likes windmills.

Gooch yawns on a sofa; and says, "Do let's go to the Hague. There's civilisation *there*. I say !" he exclaims suddenly, turning to Maullie, "there's a palace and swell shops there : *you might get a hat.*"

Maullie would prefer going without a hat to Dort.

Jömp settles the difficulty by saying, "Vell, you can see Dort if you like ; but—um—um—um—*ve don't go near there.*"

We take a final walk on the Quay called from the little boompjes on it "The Boompjes" (which, as a peripatetic club, we have long ago decided upon always writing as *we* pronounce it, Boomp-je), and depart for the Hague.

Note—I cannot again refrain from drawing attention to the ingenuity of the Dutch as to names. They call a river the *Rotter,* and they make a *dam.* It's a sort of charade. My first is Rotter, my second is Dam, and my whole is the name of a place. *Ans* Rotterdam. It is as clever as a riparian resident, who, having a house on a bank of the Thames, calls it "Thames Bank House."

They call a little tree a Boompje. They plant several little Boompjes on a Quay, and they call the Quay The Boompjes. There's a simplicity and a freshness about this which is quite enchanting.

The Hague.—Belle Vue Hotel. Very prettily situated, and first-rate altogether. Gooch, delighted, lounges out of window, smoking cigarettes. Maullie, in an arm-chair by a side window of sitting-room, commences "taking a quaint bit." There won't be much left for other artists after Maullie's visit. Bund is immersed in *Murray*, correcting his statements by *Bradshaw*, and Jömp is somewhere, asking what is to be seen.

I sit and admire the view—canal (of course), gardens, deer park, large trees—charming.

The houses of the Upper Ten at the Hague are generally situated on, as it were, square islands formed by stagnant canals. Smell delicious, naturally. *Query*, if the people at the Hague are no worse in health than at any other place—say, London—what's the use of attending to drainage, sewerage, and good supply of water?

This problem puzzles us.

Having walked about for an hour or so (without Jömp and the bag, thank goodness!), Gooch proposes finding out a restaurant, in order to provide for "*déjeuner*". He says this travelling makes him so hungry. We don't doubt him, seeing his appetite on every occasion. He is always proposing to sit down to a meal when Maullie wants to take us to a Picture Gallery. "Didn't we come to see the pictures?" asks Maullie, who is usually satisfied with what he calls "a snack."

"Yes," says Gooch; "but we can't see pictures without eating."

Decided : Gallery first, Hotel afterwards.

In the Gallery.—First striking notice :—

Het is verboden de schildengen Aanteraken,

which is, of course, highly satisfactory.

Gooch and self now taken by Maullie to see "a masterpiece, Sir, by Rembrandt."

Maullie walks straight into the room where it is, as if he'd been there every day of his life regularly.

"There!" he exclaims, triumphantly. "There's the *Lecture on Anatomy.* Rembrandt."

I see Bund surreptitiously consulting *Bradshaw* and a *Notice des Tableaux*, before committing himself to an opinion.

Gooch says, "Ah!" and looks round, to see if there are any other spectators besides ourselves.

I don't exactly know what to say. After considering some time, I venture upon a safe inquiry, founded upon Maullie's previous remark, "I suppose this is considered one of Rembrandt's finest pieces?"

"Certainly; yes," answers Maullie, and continues, enthusiastically: "look at old *Tulp*, there. Fine head, marvellous head."

I inspect *Tulp's* head critically; at least, the head of the man I take to be *Tulp.*

"There's character in that eyebrow!" continues Maullie.

I smack my lips, as if I were tasting it, and say, "Yes, indeed," (Boomp-je!) though I can't see that *my Tulp* has much in the way of eyebrow. Also, which eyebrow?

"Then, look at the hands!" says Maullie.

This decides me. *My Tulp is not his Tulp;* mine only showing one hand. Determine to find out which *is* "*Tulp.*" I ask, "Are they all portraits of celebrated people?"

"Yes," replies Maullie, who is well up in it.

"Their names are on a piece of paper, held by one of them," Bund informs us, quoting from *Murray*, which he has just put in his pocket, "and *Tulp* is lecturing on the body, in the centre."

(*To myself.* "Oh, *that's Tulp!*") *Aloud.* "Of course, that's *Tulp* in the centre."

Gooch gives it as his opinion, that it's "a doosid unpleasant subject." And, turning away, suddenly comes upon two friends (not in tourist suits) who are sauntering through the Gallery.

"Hullo!" exclaims Gooch, in that tone of utter surprise at anybody being abroad besides himself, peculiar to all travellers on meeting friends.

"Hullo!" they return, in precisely the same strain. Then they shake hands warmly, as if a quarrel had parted them for years.

They are introduced by Gooch as Muntley and Finton. I don't quite catch which is Muntley and which is Finton. I seem to have heard the name before, as a Company Limited, or, on second thoughts, in connection with candles and biscuits. No, that's Huntley and Palmer; Huntley for biscuits, Palmer for candles. Muntley is shortish and stoutish, his head generally a little thrown back, with the air of a man who is taking breath before making up his mind to tell you a secret.

Finton is a quick, sharp fellow, with a nervous sort of laugh, as if ready to turn off anything he might say too seriously into a joke.

Muntley (I discover) congratulates himself upon his conversational powers, and being able to talk to any one on any subject, specially Art. Being introduced to Maullie—whom Gooch takes care to describe apart to his friends as "*the* Maullie, you know, R.A.; you recollect his pictures?" to which they reply, "Oh, indeed, Maullie, by Jove, is it?" and they immediately overlook the hat and the tourist dress, which was the Count's object in playing such a flourish of trumpets. Muntley at once joins Maullie. "Very few good things here," says he.

"Um!" says Maullie, frowning at a jovial Jan Steen.

"They try to take one in with these catalogues," continues the knowing Muntley.

I ask how.

"Why," he informs me for Maullie's benefit, "they pretend they've got Rubens's pictures here, but they spell it 'Rubbens,' so as to do you. Look here: '122. *Venus et Adonis dans un Paysage.*'" This he reads with a real British accent, adding his translation, "'*Venus and Adonis in a Passage,* by Rubbens.' It won't do, you know."

I confess this *does* look like imposition.

"Then," he goes on, "here's 'Snijders' down for Sniders, and 'Wouwerman' for Woovermans; and who the deuce 'Vinkeboom' is, I can't make out."

Maullie is scowling furiously, but asks if Muntley has come across any Van Dycks.

"Not one," answers Muntley, ingenuously. "There's nothing about him here under the letter 'D.' There are some pictures——two Dijks—A. Van Dijk and Ph. Van Dijk;" (he pronounces these like "Dchick"); "but of course *they're* nothing particular."

Maullie has not stayed to listen. With a short "Ah!" he has passed on, and we find him fixed in admiration before No. 27—*Vue aux Environs de Dordrecht,* by Cuyp.

"I know," he says, "we ought to have stopped and seen Dort. I *will,* going back."

He *will.* Boomp-je!

CHAPTER VII.

AT THE HAGUE—AMONG THE PICTURES—ARTISTIC OPINIONS—JÖMP
CONSULTED—HOW WE VISIT A PRIVATE COLLECTION—RESULT.

OPPOSITE *Paul Potter's Bull.* Muntley and Finton in ecstasies.

N.B. Before a well-known work of art, safe to be in ecstasies.

Gooch exclaims, "*C'est magnifique!*" His friends, Muntley and Finton, being evidently of the same mind as himself as to the necessity of speaking French when abroad, reply in chorus, "*Oui! O oui!*"

Bund, who has got *Murray* by his side——

[*Note.* By the way, subject for one of the future Boomp-je Ballads—*Air,* "*With his Sabre by his Side*"—Boomp-je version:—

With his *Murray* by his side,
And his *Bradshaw* in his hand,

&c. &c., when the original words come to hand.

Maullie, R.A., shows me mems for various Boomp-je Ballads—"All among the Boomp-jes," a version of "*All among the Barley.*" I express my opinion that *his* notion is very good: he expresses his that *my* notion is very good. Like a fellow to be sympathetic and appreciative. Maullie, R.A., is.]

Bund, who has his *Murray* by his side (out of *the* bag) says, "Wonderful for its truth to Nature;" as if he'd lived among bulls

all his life ; and, " It's marvellous "—here he inspects the picture
closely, and then falls back a few paces,—" It's marvellous how
he has arranged his masses."

As this sounds like knowing something about it, we all (except
Maullie, who hasn't said anything as yet) agree with Bund, "that
it is, as a fact, wonderful how Potter "—a little too familiar, perhaps, but it shows a thorough knowledge of the artist—" how
Potter has arranged his masses."

[*Note.*—Consulting *Murray* afterwards, I find where Bund has
got his expression from.   Boomp-je !]

Gooch exclaims, after a minute's silence, "*C'est un tableau de
grandeur naturelle,*" on which he congratulates himself as being
excellent idiomatic French.

I join Muntley and Finton in responding "*Oui.*"

[*Note.*—Having purchased a catalogue, I discover that Gooch's
French is a quotation.   Also Boomp-je !]

Maullie says, " Yes, clever, of course, but uninteresting.   Very
much overrated ; " and he walks off to No. 125, *Le Confesseur de
Rubbens,* a portrait by Rubens of the cheeriest Monk possible.
" Isn't that the very fellow you'd pick out for jolly old Peter
Paul's Confessor, eh ? " cries Maullie.   We all agree, except
Muntley, who is a little bothered by the double *b* in Rubbens, and
inquires of Finton, in an undertone, " Peter who ? "   Subsequently
he evinces his knowledge of the subject by mentioning old Peter
Paul's Bull,—which sounds as if Peter Paul were a celebrated Pope.

Bund, who has his own ideas of art, professes intense admiration for the works of art painted by the Brothers Both.   He takes
us, one by one, into corners where pictures by these artists are
hung.   He fees officials to lower or draw up window-blinds
(the Boths are generally in the worst possible lights), in order to
show us the beauties of the Boths.   He doesn't ask Maullie to
look at them, but canvasses (as it were) for a majority in favour
of his (Bund's) opinion before appealing to Maullie.   Bund, being
our Commander, Commodore, and Paymaster-General, we agree
with him, to a certain extent, about the Boths, of whom we have
never before heard.   Muntley and Finton join us, and express
their sentiments, as far as to say, " Yes, very pretty."

"Look at the sunset," says Bund, pointing it out enthusiastically.

"Mustn't touch the picture!" says the official who pulled up the blind, translating *Het is verboden, &c.*"

"No, of course not," returns Bund; "but," to us, "isn't the sunset admirable?"

We think it is certainly. "It's so wonderful," continues Bund, "that the Boths, being Dutch, should paint Italian scenery."

We admit that it is *very* wonderful. Muntley, after some consideration, asks, slowly, "Why?"

"Why?" returns the Commodore. "Because,"—he begins as if he was answering a conundrum,—"Because—they never saw it."

This answer being satisfactory to all parties, we move on to another picture.

Note.—Bund's explanation, as above given, seems to be framed on the Jömp model. For the present we don't hear any more of the Boths, in consequence of Gooch's insisting upon our going back to luncheon. The Count says that having fed only two hours ago, he is so confoundedly hungry. Maullie remains in the gallery until, having been shut in by the doors being closed for the day, he is subsequently turned out by one of the officials, who finds him sitting solemnly before *La leçon d'Anatomie du Professeur Tulp*, No. 116. After this, he appears at the Hotel.

Jömp is now summoned. During our absence he is supposed to have found out all that is to be seen in or near The Hague. Muntley and Finton, as friends of Gooch's, have been asked to join us *pro tem.*

"Now, Jömp," says Bund, "what's to be seen next?"

"Vell," answers the intelligent Jömp, rubbing his head, as usual, and letting his eyes wander vaguely round the party, as if hoping that some one would suggest something—

"Vell—um—um—um—dere's de pictures." Thinks it out, and adds, "Ah, but you 'ave seen dem."

"Isn't there a celebrated town near here, eh? Leyden?" suggests Gooch, who thinks he's got hold of the place where *Le Prophète* came from.

"Isn't there a fishing-place—Scheveningen?" asks Bund, on *Murray's* authority, before Jömp can answer. Jömp, who has begun to think out the first question, turns his attention to the Commander's inquiry.

"Vell——" he begins, when Maullie jumps up from his seat (Boom-je !!) and interrupts.

"I beg your pardon," cries Maullie, apologising to every one in general, and only looking at Jömp, "but isn't there a private collection somewhere here?"

Muntley and Finton, together, say, "Oh, yes, lots."

Jömp becomes perfectly damp with agitation. He looks as if another question, put suddenly and sharply, would knock him down. A prisoner at the bar asked to plead "Guilty or Not Guilty" could not appear more utterly miserable than Jömp. He mops his head with the dull-coloured cotton handkerchief ("I *will* get him a new one," Gooch is heard to murmur), pockets it, puts his hands behind him, and having, so to speak, pulled himself together for an effort, says,

"Vell—dere is Schevening—oh, yes—you can go dere—oh, yes —and a private collection of pictures—oh, yes——"

"At Scheveningen?" asks Bund, thinking to kill two birds with one visit.

"At Schevening?" replies Jömp, considering : then, after cautiously thinking it out, he adds, "No; you can not see de collection *dere*—um—um—*because, you know, it's here.*" And he looks round to us as if for confirmation of the truth of his argument.

"Then where is it?" asks Maullie. "We're here to see the Dutch school, aren't we?" We nod our heads, as solemnly as the spectral skittle-players did to *Rip Van Winkle.* "Let's go there at once, Jömp ; " and he takes up his hat.

"But," exclaims Gooch, "it's a private house. You can't go, in that dress—and that hat."

"Pooh !" says Maullie, "don't come if you don't like. Now Jömp, you can show us where it is."

The Count makes one last effort. " Let's have a carriage, and drive there in style. Hang it ! don't let's walk to a private house like rabble—or bailiffs."

Jömp says, "It's not vorth vhile to 'ave a carriage.   It's only a few steps."

We set off: Gooch protesting to his friends, apart, that it's too bad of Maullie; and "Hang it!" he adds, "he's got an umbrella now as big as a clothes-bag.   It brings such a bad name on Englishmen.   Fancy," he goes on protesting, "a lot of fellows with bags, umbrellas, and wide-awake hats, calling on one of us in London?   Would we let 'em in?   Pooh!"

"A few steps," as represented by the intelligent Jömp, turns out to be half through the town, a distance doubled by Jömp's first forgetting the way, and then the name of the street.   Arrived at our destination, an elegant newly-painted residence of some municipal notability, Jömp knocks at the door, being induced to do so by the Commander.   ("He'll think we've all come to dinner," says Gooch, still protesting, "It's too absurd.")

A neat maid appears.

What she says, in Dutch, we don't know.

"Speak to her," says Bund to Jömp, with confidence in Jömp's acquaintance with the language.

Jömp appears to become suddenly bashful, and what he says to her is a perfect mystery to everyone, including the maid, who stares at him.

"Dash it!" says Gooch, "she'll think we're all drunk."

There does appear a probability of this, and of Jömp's being removed by some authorities as drunk and incapable, for he stands on the doorstep grinning and sputtering some unintelligible sounds which may mean something to *him*, but nothing to anybody else belonging to any known nationality.

Maullie begins something in French.

Gooch says, "It's no good, she doesn't understand that."

Bund, becoming very angry, swears at Jömp.   "What the Boomp-je did you bring us here for, if you can't speak the inf— Boomp-je language?" he asks of the unfortunate Jömp.

Jömp, in an agony and almost in tears, replies, "Vell, you *vould* come here.   I can't 'elp it.   I tought she'd know vy ve came." Then he turns to the girl, who by this time has become almost pale with fear, and with a gentle smile this time, tries some words on her which he believes to be very like, if not absolutely, Dutch.

This and his smile ("a confounded lunatic leer!" says Gooch, whose temper has quite gone) settles the question. She bangs the door, overturning Gooch on to Bund, and the next minute we see the family of the private collector at the windows, regarding us with horror and amazement.

"Vell," says Jömp, picking himself up from the lower doorstep, "Ve can't see dat if dey von't let us in."

"But you can't speak the language, confound you," cries Maullie, boiling over.

"Vell, um—um—um," retorts Jömp, hurt by this imputation; "she don't understand vot I say."

Carried *nem. con.* for the twentieth time, emphatically, That Jömp *is* an Ass. Also, that we'll get some one who *does* understand the Hague, and the language.

It is now four o'clock.

Proposed by the Commander, that we drive to Scheveningen. Seconded by Gooch heartily (he is always ready for anything in a carriage), with an amendment to the effect that we have a biscuit, or sandwich, and a glass of something first.

Generally agreed to. Carriage ordered.

CHAPTER VIII.

A TRIP TO SCHEVENINGEN—THE DRIVE—JÖMP'S INFORMATION—
MAULLIE'S JOKES—A DISCOVERY—A SKETCHING PARTY—BUND
AND HIEROGLYPHICS—THE ETABLISSEMENT.

SCHEVENINGEN.—
"Scheveningen," says Bund, authoritatively, " is a small fishing village three miles from the Hague, containing eight thousand inhabitants."

Gooch asks if he has counted them.

Bund, entering into the joke, replies that he has, and finds *Murray's* number exact.

Maullie, R.A., observes, " Exact ? I wonder at that : I should have thought you'd have *found several short.*"

This is Maullie's fun. It throws a gloom over the party for the remainder of the drive, which had begun very pleasantly. Gooch's friends (both in a rumble, hooked on specially for them, and evincing a strong tendency towards detaching itself from the main body of the carriage) beg that Maullie's joke may be repeated to them. It is repeated. *Consequence,* one short laugh, and then meditative silence and folded arms.

We take Jömp with us, because he has been instructed as to the beauties of Scheveningen by the landlord of the hotel, and we suppose that for once he is well posted up in the subject.

We see a large house, apparently of Italian architecture, among the trees. Bund attracts Jömp's attention by poking him in the back with his stick, much in the same manner as the keepers rouse the sleeping animals in a travelling menagerie, or a passenger wishes to intimate to the 'bus conductor that "he's a long way past where he ought to have been set down."

"Ask *him*," says Bund, meaning the coachman, "what that place is."

Jömp turns round again, and mumbles some soft, very soft, nothings in the coachman's ear.

The coachman makes some reply, evidently not understanding one word used by the intelligent Jömp, who tries again, going in at the conversation this time with his head and arms. The coachman nods, shakes his head, and laughs; then turns to us over his shoulder and, taking us into the joke, laughs again.

"He thinks Jömp mad," says Gooch, decisively.

"Hey? What?" asks Muntley and Finton, in the rumble.

N.B. The worst of having fellows in the rumble, who want to be sociable, is that everything said in the carriage has to be repeated to them, as if it were being interpreted. I give them, conscientiously, a sort of *précis* of the conversation and the circumstances leading up to what Gooch has just said, and they reply together, "Oh!" A sort of chorus in the rumble.

Bund says afterwards, "A rumble is only for servants." Maullie replies, "Yes, your *rumble* servants." Another gloom over the party. One laugh, and then gloom.

"What does he say?" asks Bund of Jömp, still bent upon knowing what the Coachman knows about the House which we've passed a quarter-of-an-hour ago.

"He say," replies Jömp, in despair of ever making any Dutchman understand him, "He say—um–um–um—he say it is nothing —um—um—he doesn't know."

"But you didn't explain," continues Bund, perseveringly.

"I explain," returns the unhappy Jömp, "but," he adds, shrugging his shoulders, as an expression of pity for the coachman's want of education, "he *vill* not onderstand vot I say: *he come from somevhere else.*"

This, henceforth, is Jömp's excuse whenever a Dutch person does not understand his (Jömp's) language: which case is of perpetual occurrence, the sole exceptions being when, by some lucky chance, the Hollander speaks English, or can interpret Jömp's Swiss-French. Jömp's theory (a Boompje theory) is that there is some part of Holland where a number of people come from, who neither understand nor speak their own language.

A pretty drive finishing with a newly-made road and young trees on either side, brings us to Schevening, or, as *Murray* will have it, "Scheveningen," throwing a syllable in for luck as it were.

We drive on until we stick in a sort of dry marsh of fine sand, into which the horses sink nearly up to their knees, and our wheels up to their axles. Further progress is impossible. An idea strikes the intelligent Jömp, who turns to us from his perch on the box and says,

" Vill you stop here ? "

Under the circumstances our reply is that we will, whereupon Jömp descends, opens the door, and we step as lightly as possible on to the sand.

Gooch and his friends being in low shoes protest in forcible language, and stand still, looking about for less sand.

Bund, preceded by Jömp with the bag and umbrella, ascends the hillock which commands the beach, and Maullic, after shading his eyes with his hand for a minute-and-a-half, as if looking about where to take Scheveningen unexpectedly, commences cutting a pencil by way of coming to the point as soon as possible.

"Coming to the point" was Muntley's joke, and would have been highly successful (as no doubt he has found it on several other previous occasions) but for the sand in our shoes, the unpleasant walking, the hot sun, the peculiarly strong odour of fish, (not unlike that of a poor quarter of London on a Saturday night) and the improbability of our being able to get any refreshment "except perhaps," says Gooch, in a tone of unmitigated disgust, "tea and shrimps." N.B. Always carefully select your time to be funny.

Jömp makes a discovery. He sees in the distance an *établissement*, and with a view to ingratiating himself with Gooch, points it out to him privately.

Gooch, Muntley and Finton are delighted.

"By Jove!" exclaims Gooch, whose mind at once reverts to Trouville, Dieppe, and Boulogne. "I dare say there's a band there, and a restaurant."

"And lots of people," suggests Muntley.

"And the French papers; the *Figaro*," suggests Finton, this being the only French paper he knows.

"Do you know," Gooch asks of Jömp, who has suddenly inspired him with confidence on account of his discovering the *établissement*, "if there is a promenade here?" Muntley and Finton both listen anxiously for the answer. A promenade to them means lounging about vaguely, examining the toilettes of the ladies, remarking upon "Doosid pretty girls those," asking one another, "Who's that? d'you know?" smoking cigarettes, settling their ties, coaxing their collars, and keeping their wristbands well *en évidence*, by dint of perpetual pulling up and shooting out their arms as if engaged in some species of gymnastic exercise. This last performance, by the way, Muntley terms "flashing his linen." As the Count and his friends would be perfectly happy to pass their afternoon in this simple fashion, they are all ears for Jömp's answer concerning the promenade.

"Oh yes," replies Jömp, with such an air of certainty as would make any one who knew him receive his information with a considerable amount of caution. "Dere is a promenade."

"Where?" asks Finton.

"Oh," returns Jömp, as if to put such a question was utterly absurd, "Vere?—'ere." He extends his arms on either side in the attitude of a street juggler chucking the balls and knives, and looks from right to left, and then from left to right, thereby taking in the whole line of the seashore of Schevening.

"But they don't walk about in this sand?" exclaims Gooch, who sees no sign, except the existence of the *établissement*, of anything like a fashionable promenade.

"Oh yes," retorts Jömp, "Dey valk in de sand." He thinks it out and adds, "*Dere's no vere else.*"

"I wish we'd known it was a fashionable place," says Gooch, "we'd have got Maullie another hat at the Hague."

Maullie is on the sands, sketch-book and pencil out.

Muntley and Finton go to inspect the *établissement:* they are to return and report to Gooch. Bund has followed Maullie, and is pointing out to him what he ought to draw.

Maullie is sketching one of the hundred and fifty picturesque fishing-boats which are waiting for the tide in order to put out to sea, and is carefully noting down all the details. Bund is pointing out a boy with a dog in a totally different direction from that where Maullie's eyes are engaged. "I say," exclaims Bund, who flatters himself on a great appreciation of the picturesque, "there's a bit for you to draw."

"Eh?" says Maullie, steadily continuing his boat.

"Boy with dog," Bund goes on, as if he was settling the name of the picture in next year's Academy Catalogue, "and fishing-basket. Just look what a quaint old fishing-basket."

Maullie pooh-poohs the suggestion, whereupon Bund sets to work to make what he calls just an artistic memorandum, which, he informs us, conveys more to *his* mind, subsequently, than any writing could do. What it may convey to *his* mind, it is impossible to say; but having seen the original of the sketch, it is quite certain that *this* is not conveyed to *our* minds by what may be called the Boompje hieroglyphic. The Commander, Bund, is always "dashing off," as he calls it, a little sketch.

"There's the basket; and boy; and dog," he exclaims, with an air of artistic pride, handing the fly-leaf of *Murray* (he generally does them in some odd corners of books, or on scraps of paper, preserved afterwards in his pocket-book) to us for inspection.

I say, "Yes," doubtfully; but add, "I suppose that'll recall to your mind the whole scene;" *i.e.*, Schevening, the sand, the one hundred and fifty boats, the crowd of costumes, the *établissement*, the huts, the houses, the carts, the sunset, the sea, &c., &c.

Gooch observes, "That it's a great thing to be able to sketch."

Our opinions are, perhaps, somewhat biassed by the remembrance of the constitution under which, as a Club, we are travelling; *i.e.*, that the Commander Bund is Paymaster.

Jömp, who is evidently trying to recover his position in the Commander's estimation, looks over his elbow at the drawing, and says, sagely—

"Ah, yes, um—um—um," he is considering the subject—"it is

very goot. Yes, oh yes—dere is de leetle dog," and he carefully points out what Bund intended for the basket.

Gooch and myself side with Jömp on this occasion only. We say, "Yes, the dog *is* very good; it's the animal itself in a few touches." For the matter of that, it's about as much like a bathing-machine as a dog, but Bund (who had intended it for the basket, or the boy, but certainly not the dog, there is no doubt about it, from the angry expression of his countenance, when he was going to retort upon Jömp) takes all the credit he can for the cleverness of the sketch, and to prevent any future mistakes, labels the thing, which we had settled upon as representing the dog, with a "D," and then, entirely mistrusting his own powers and intention, asks us knowingly, which *we* should say was the boy.

We choose, out of the two remaining figures, the boy (of course, it *is* the basket, though Gooch has some doubts upon the point), and Bund labels that No. 2, with a reference below: thus, No. 2, the Boy, and No. 3, the Basket, adding a line to the effect that the above is a *Sketch taken on Schevening Beach, Sunset.*

CHAPTER IX.

STILL AT SCHEVENING—ART IN DANGER—DRIVE HOME—AN INVITA-
TION—THE UNIFORM.

MAULLIE near the boats, and beckoning us to join him; his whole action is as stealthy as that of a deerstalker, or of a somebody who's found something dangerous asleep, and is going to take its head off. We join him. A fish auction is going on.

Carts, empty, are dashing down the beach, driven by boys in command of one, two, or three horses, and being dragged up again heavily laden. There is a fair sprinkling of men, but the auctioneering seems to be chiefly carried on by women. Children, apparently belonging to anybody or everybody, are running about and amusing themselves with fish. Dogs, with feline tastes, are growling over and munching fish wholesale and retail. Boys are throwing fish to one another. Men are bringing in baskets of fish, or taking out baskets of fish, or lading carts, or trays, with fish, or unlading other carts, or other trays, overladen with fish, or talking either about the fish they've got, or the prospects of catching more fish, and a few strangers are buying what is not already bespoke [*Mem.* "Bespoken" would be a good Dutch word], and everybody on or about the spot is doing something or other with fish, and the whole place smells of fish, and there are no meadows, nor grass-lands anywhere near, where you might get a third course of cutlets, or a *pièce de résistance* in the shape of a leg of mutton. But the fish have it all to themselves at Schevening, and the people make a perfect *jour maigre* of every one of the 365 days in the year.

"I've got something," whispers Maullie confidentially to me. He is dodging behind a fish-cart, with his sketch-book in one hand and his pencil in the other.

"What the Boomp-je is the matter with Maullie?" asks Gooch, whose sense of propriety here, with the chance of a promenade, is being utterly outraged by this eccentricity on Maullie's part.

"He'll attract a crowd," he adds, observing two or three little fishy boys already evincing an interest in Maullie's proceedings.

At last we discover what Maullie has "got." It is a very tall, hulking, gawky fisherman, in a costume composed, apparently, of various contributions most thankfully received by the present wearer. He is a difficult subject to sketch, as he won't keep himself in view (he can't help keeping his *head* in view, except when he disappears behind a fishing-smack, which he does occasionally as a short cut to some other crowd gathered round a fish auctioneer), and Maullie has to dodge him, in and out, between carts, to wait for him outside some small crowd into which he has plunged, and out of which he will struggle presently (his head being visible the whole time), when Maullie will follow him round a boat, he on one side, the tall fisherman on the other, like the pantomime business of the Clown and the Soldier round a sentry-box, until making a bad shot as to which way his unconscious model is coming, he and the tall fisherman bump up against one another face to face, that is, as nearly as possible, allowing for their respective heights. From this moment the situation is reversed. Hitherto it has been the Gigantic Model unconsciously escaping from the Artist, now it is the Artist, painfully conscious, escaping from the Gigantic Model.

"*Frankenstein*," says Bund, thinking the simile peculiarly happy.

"*Yah*," says Gooch, who imagines that Bund is saying something to him in German which he ought to understand. The Gigantic Fisherman, who really appears to have grown more grim and a foot taller, evidently suspects mischief. If Maullie retires behind a cart, just to "sketch in" the eye, or the nose, or a patch in his coat, the Giant is down upon him round the corner, with such a real expression of interest in *his* eye, as makes Maullie, as Frankenstein, shut up his book and walk off: monster following.

Maullie behind a boat: monster after him. Maullie, taking a flying sketch, retreating towards the hillock of sand near the town: giant after him, as if in seven-league boots. A stop. Maullie just sketching man's boots. Giant, scowling fiercely, advances.

Gooch's opinion: "There'll be a row. 'Pon my soul I don't wonder at it. How would Maullie like to be followed about if he was at home, and sketched and stared at by a stranger? If I was the man," adds Gooch, emphatically, as if with a view to preserve subsequent neutrality, "I should punch his head."

Jömp, sniffing, like the war-horse, the scent of battle, says, unlike the war-horse, that he'll go and see after the carriage; and instantly disappears. His reason, given afterwards is, to say the least of it, honest: "I tought," says he, "dat dere'd be a fight."

Cessation of hostilities in consequence of Maullie's pocketing his book and pencil. Gigantic man retires slowly, turning occasionally to look back at Maullie, evidently still uncertain as to whether he oughtn't to have punched his head, or got something out of him before leaving. They couldn't have "come to terms" in any language common to both, but fists are of universal application.

Muntley and Finton come back, disgusted. The *établissement* is closed. There is no one there. Jömp is (of course) wrong: there is no promenade, except in the season.

On our return, we find that Bund, who knows some people at the Hague, is asked to an evening party, and his friends are included in the invitation.

Gooch is delighted; he says he likes Continental dances, and immediately begins humming a *can-can*, and jerking his head with such a knowing air, as to send his friends Muntley and Finton into ecstasies. When he finishes,—which he does abruptly,—they all laugh together, as if over some secret reminiscence.

Maullie thinks the party rather a bore, but still he says it doesn't matter to him, as he has no dress clothes with him.

"You can't go as you are," Gooch protests, hastily.

Maullie replies, that if he wants to go he can borrow a suit from the landlord.

Bund wishes he hadn't met his friends, the De Wordes, who have given him this invitation, and to whom he couldn't say no.

The Secretary (myself) is pleased. There would be a mixed society of Dutch, French, German, and English.

After dinner I open my portmanteau, where I had expected to find my new evening suit, fresh from the tailor's on my leaving England, and still wrapped up in its brown paper. I open it. I only find a uniform, that of the Southwick Volunteers, which I had lately joined. The tailor had sent them home by mistake. The uniform is not unpretty, being grey with a gentle shade of blue (so as to mingle you with clouds in the distance, and make you a difficult object to hit) and trimmed up and down with a paleish canary yellow, with braided cord on the cuffs and shoulders, and wherever, in fact, there is room for it, and where there isn't a button.

" Go," says Gooch, " in the uniform."

I treat such a suggestion with contempt.

Bund thinks the idea is reasonable. He doesn't see why not.

Maullie thinks it would give a little colour to the scene. So do I.

Gooch says, " Why not ?" adding, that, if he were in my position, *he'd* go " before you could wink your eye."

Bund asks what rank I hold.

I answer that I don't know, but they've promised me a captaincy when I know my drill.

Maullie says that any English officer in uniform is received any- where.

I am doubtful of this. I am further doubtful as to whether I come under the description of " any English officer in uniform."

Gooch says, " Certainly, of course. If not, what are you ? Eh ?"

That's where it is—What am I ? What is a Volunteer ? When abroad ?

Boompje Riddle.—When's a Volunteer not a Volunteer ?—When he's abroad.

I try to turn it off with this. But they won't hear of it.

Muntley and Finton won't go if I don't go, and I don't go if my uniform doesn't go, with me inside it.

Gooch hopes I won't be selfish. Bund gives as his opinion that he's sure I won't. Maullie offers to do my portrait in colours, "as I appeared," if I'll only go.

I ask, do they seriously mean that I *can* go in this costume?

They say, "Certainly," of course; and Gooch brings in his eye-winking formula again, in proof of his readiness.

I agree, and promise to go.

Gooch announces that we ought to be "thinking of dressing" (another formula of his for expressing that it is high time to be actually getting ready, or for even being nearly ready), and gives us the railway time.

Jömp *has* ordered the carriage. We dress. While dressing, I have my doubts.

In the coat alone I feel I could go; it is decidedly handsome. The trousers I don't like. They are grey, and bear a decided resemblance to what I believe is the colour of a convict's costume. To go to a private ball, which is not fancy dress, as half convict, half soldier (of some sort), is not, it seems to me, to represent the English to advantage.

Then, again, I reason with myself, sitting on the bed, meditating, "They" (the Dutch) "won't know what I am"—like Watts's little star. The English *will*. Perhaps they'll sneer: if they don't, they may stick up for the honour of England, and Boompje a little about the Volunteer Contingent.

This name decides me. The "Volunteer Contingent."

Question.—What are you?

Answer.—An Officer in the Contingent.

I jump up from my bed. Boompje! I sat down, Myself, a Southwick Volunteer, and rise an Officer in the Contingent. The True Boompje Spirit does wonders.

With a light heart I dress.

I debate with myself whether I will or won't wear a white waist-coat, so as to show my watch-chain, and the coat open.

Question, then, how about collars?

If collars, sha'n't I look more like naval than military? Recollect dining at a mess once with Regulars. They wore collars. The more I think of this, the more uncertain I become.

I decide upon trying it, and asking Gooch's opinion. (He is a good hand at dress.)

He exclaims, "Pooh! collars and open uniform! They'll fancy you're somehow connected with the River Police."

Maullie, dressed in the landlord's clothes, which, he says, will allow for growing, is ready. He, speaking "as an artist," gives it against the white waistcoat.

"Button up," says he. I do.

At the House. I create a sensation in the hall, but do not seem to command respect. Am introduced to the lady of the house (an Englishwoman married to a Dutchman, and living at the Hague), and she welcomes me with a high-bred courtesy.

Shall I apologise, or not, for coming in uniform?

CHAPTER X.

AT THE EVENING PARTY (*continued*)—A PLUNGE—THE MAZURKA.

DECIDEDLY not. A uniform *is* something to be respected, like the British flag. (Boomp-je!) Let them find out what I am. (Begin to wish I was in bed.)

Gooch disappears. Bund is with people I don't know. Maullie has been introduced to some Dutch artists, and everyone else is either dancing, talking, or walking.

I fix myself by a door, and begin to indulge in bitter thoughts about the world at large. What an ass I was (I think to myself) to be persuaded to come in uniform. It's my confounded good-nature. Dear me !—two ladies from England, whom I've met before.

Miss Howker, quite the belle of the ball, and Miss Millar with her mother.

Miss Howker quite surprised to see me here. She is talking to a French gentleman with a red riband and an order in his button-hole ; she goes on talking after she has said she is so surprised. Can't enter into their conversation, as I don't know what it's about. All I can do is to smile on them patronisingly.

The distinguished foreigner is evidently puzzled ; so is she. I smile again ; I don't know why, but rather as if to say, "Isn't this funny, isn't this just like me?" That is *if* she views my uniform in that light.

I feel that many eyes are upon me, and eye-glasses too. The general opinion (I also *feel* this from little things I hear said in various quarters) is that I am an "*eccentric Englishman connected with the Post Office,*" and that the uniform is common enough in

London. One French lady explains to a German that I am an alderman. Muntley, who has been taking champagne, insists upon addressing me as My Lord Mayor, and bowing obsequiously. I beg him not to play the fool. He leaves me. I hope he won't go and spread it about that I'm the Lord Mayor.

There is an undoubted Englishman in the corner with large whiskers and moustache eyeing me indignantly. I return his look with indignation. We shall have words, " before," as Gooch would say, " I can wink my eye," if I don't take care.

I tell Miss Howker about the Contingent, which, I am bound to say, she does not believe, and I add that I am going to Aldershot to join the Rifles for drill.

Gooch, hearing this announcement of mine, says, " Do you all the good in the world, old fellow ; fine you down a bit."

I smile at Gooch, pityingly, to give Miss Howker the idea that I only tolerate him, and that I don't want " fining down." The *Mazurka* strikes up. Shall I (not knowing the *Mazurka* except by having seen it) risk it with Miss Howker, and so cut out Gooch, or not?

If I do, it will probably terminate amicable relations for ever between Miss Howker and myself. But still. . . . Boomp-je ! . . . Yes. I might boompje through it.

Just as the words are on the tip of my tongue, Gooch takes them, so to speak, out of my mouth, and says, " May I, Miss Howker?" and Miss Howker consults her card, and finding she has at least six names down for this one dance, settles the difficulty by accepting Gooch.

I smile disdainfully as they leave me, laughing. At what are they laughing? At whom? Muntley, passing me at this moment with a French lady on his arm, bows, and says, " *J'espère que vous êtes content, mi lord Maire.*" I frown. I hate such tomfoolery. Will speak to him alone, seriously. Besides, it is rather a liberty on his part, as I hardly know Muntley.

There are some moments when, if I looked in the glass, I should expect to see myself pale and haggard, with dark dank hair hanging about anyhow. I *do* look into the glass and I see—but no matter. " Time writes no wrinkle on thy something brow," as the poet says of the sea : and as he *did* say it of the sea, he might as well have written "winkle" instead of "wrinkle," a notion that I shall put forward in my earliest collection of Boompje Poems.

I watch the *Mazurka.* A great man has said, we can always learn something from somebody. This does not mean that we can always learn anything from anybody. Now here are a lot of anybodies and somebodies teaching me, unconsciously, the *Mazurka.*

It seems to me, observing this, that you must go a little back like a wave on the shingle with a view to coming well forward again like (also) a wave (same one) on the shingle. That you then hop—or jump—and then slide. Watching the different couples, I can't make out whether you hop first, or slide first. I feel an irresistible desire to dance it. I feel at the same time a shyness which whispers "Don't." I feel immediately afterwards a voice which says "This is pride, false pride. Dance! Boompje, dance!" Think to myself that I should like to try it alone in a side-room first. Of course to ask for this accommodation is out of the question.

I look around. Yes, there is Miss Millar near her mother. She is not dancing. "Come desperation lend thy furious hold." Faint heart never danced fair *Mazurka.*

Froggey would a-dancing go, whether Miss Millar's mother wouldn't or no.

All these quotations, adapted, oddly enough flit through my mind as I come up and say, "May I have the, &c. &c.," mumble, mumble.

She declines. I rush on my fate and exert pressure. She declines again. I become impassioned, nay, determined, as the chance of dancing becomes fainter and fainter. She accepts. [N.B. I must possess a wonderful dramatic power, facially, as it was my last look at her made her change her mind, and accept me. Must now use more facial expression, and look supremely happy.] She astonishes me by informing me that she can't dance the *Mazurka* very well, and hopes I won't be very angry with her.

I reply, encouragingly, that "*she will soon pick it up.*" I add that it isn't very difficult; and I sincerely hope it isn't.

We commence picking it up together. My sword joins the dance. I beg pardon. Must hook it up. Do so. Commence again. Sword too heavy. The start is a difficulty. Two steps totally unconnected with any known dance whatever, and a bump from a couple coming round. Apology from me. Stare from them. Two steps more. Another bump from somebody turning, apparently, the wrong way. Slight apology from me. Anathema I fancy from them. A couple starts behind us; their starting puts my starting out. I frown on them, and observe to my partner, that it is astonishing people can't keep out of the way in a ball-room. She says, "Yes, some people *are* so stupid." I agree with her. I propose going to another part of the room and commencing again. We go there. It is certainly clearer until we commence our steps, when everybody seems suddenly to arrive on the spot. I determine to start and go the whole Boompje, or perish in the attempt. We take two steps with *what* feet I don't know. I feel a sort of galvanic tremor, from my boots upwards. Then one foot will stick down, while the other comes up out of time. We do something which is intended for a hop, and turns out a jump. We struggle together, with clasped hands, somehow, as if we were trying the strength of our wrists, and we manage to turn round in a sort of uneasy jig, like organ figures with the machinery out of order, and then I come down with a decided stamp on somebody's train.

A sharp crisp sounding tear. I apologise with one leg in the air, having lifted it to do the hop. Apology scarcely acknowledged. I hear mumbled words like "*gauche*," "stupid," "doesn't know how to dance," and so forth.

Miss Millar thinks we'd better stop. I think so too, but I won't. No, we'll have another turn round. We try: and come sharply backwards on Gooch and his partner. They are laughing. At *me*. I know it. Should have done this turn well but for that. As it is I finish my next attempt at a hop and a slide by kicking Miss Millar. We stop. I beg a hundred thousand pardons, a million. Good gracious. I didn't mean—heavens——

"It doesn't matter—it was an accident," she replies, and asks to be taken to her Mamma. I protest against this. While I am protesting we are bumped three times in different directions, and are then cannoned into the crowd, where we do more struggling and tumbling, being finally landed near a sort of mantel-piece, on which we both lean, exhausted.

I apologise again for kicking her. Quite an accident, I say;

of course, she didn't suppose I only took her out to kick her. "Won't she have any refreshment."

No, she'll go to her mother, please.

I know, instinctively, what she'll say to her mother of me.

I take her back. She bows distantly, and I know that henceforth mountains separate me from Miss Millar.

I retire gradually, and join a convivial party (Maullie among the number) in the supper-room.

"Dancing, old boy?" asks Maullie.

"No," I reply, carelessly; "at least only just one turn. Too crowded."

We sup, and return to the hotel, where we discuss our next move.

CHAPTER XI.

"WELL, Jömp," says Bund, "have you ordered the carriage?"

"O yes," replies Jömp, deprecating the Commander's insinuation that he had allowed such a command as that to slip his memory, "O yes; the carriage vill be ready ——" He thinks it out; and, without committing himself to a positive moment for the appearance of the carriage, adds, "Ven the 'orses shall be in it."

"*Quel'espèce*—" begins Gooch, and then corrects himself, as if he'd really quite forgotten his native tongue, and run into French so easily that it was a difficult matter to get out of it again—"I mean, what sort"—he emphasises this, as his translation—"what sort of a place *is* Leiden!" Then, by way of a relapse, "*Triste, n'est-ce pas?*"

"*Bien triste*," answers Muntley.

"*Vous avez raison!*" says Finton. They are immensely pleased with themselves after this, which is what they call "airing their French for practice." When they want to keep up a conversation in this language, they explain their meaning to one another in English, and so get along excellently.

Jömp polishes his head with his handkerchief ("That — Boomp-je!—old rag!" growls Gooch, for the hundredth time, "I

must get him a new one !"), looks at Maullie, who is sitting in an
arm-chair at the window, " taking a bit," and replies,

" Vell—Leiden—O yes !"—here he ruminates, as if recalling
happy scenes of his childhood passed in Leiden—" Vell—um—um
—O yes !" Then, having thought it well out, he adds, " O yes,
you can go to Leiden," and looks round upon us with the air of a
man who has removed an almost insurmountable difficulty.

" *Murray* says," observes Bund, referring to his guide, as a
means of refreshing Jömp's memory, and rather as if Jömp had
written this portion of *Murray*, and was to be held responsible for
it. " *Murray* says—ah—where's the place?" Bund has got
about a dozen different markers in *Murray*, and generally exhausts
the Rhine before finding what he is really looking for—" Ah !
here it is ! Now—let's see. ' Leiden,' " he reads at intervals—
" was called *Lugdunum Batavorum.*' " Jömp smiles at this, as if he
didn't believe it. Bund proceeds : " ' There's a fragment of a round
tower '—hem—' Drusus '—yes—' Anglo-Saxon Hengist '—nothing
that concerns us particularly." Jömp looks on in an attentive attitude, but with the fixed inane smile of a big head in a pantomime.
Bund, having skipped over some paragraphs, as we suppose, con
tinues : " ' It stands in a tea-garden——' " Here he pauses, puzzled.

" What stands in a tea-garden?" asks Maullie, who is cross
because he considers that every minute spent out of a picture-
gallery is so much time wasted.

" What sort of a place is the tea-garden?" asks Bund of Jömp.

" *Une espèce d'un Jardin de Paris ?*" suggests Gooch.

" Like Mabille used to be, is it ?" inquires Muntley with the air
of a man who has been a *viveur* under the last Empire, when, by
the way, he was probably in the nursery.

Jömp thinks it out. " Vell—um—um—um—you can 'ave tea
dere, if you like." He shrugs his shoulders as much as to say
that he, personally, couldn't recommend it.

" But," urges Gooch, who sees a *café chantant* looming in probability, " is there any fun there?"

" Any band?" throws in the Commander, fondly thinking of his
violoncello at home.

" Vell," replies Jömp, considering his evidence in a way that
would drive a Judge and Counsel wild, and give a Special Jury

the fidgets ; " vell—dere's—dere's a—garden for tea, you know—-
O yes ! "

" Any pictures ? " demands Maullic, sharply.

" Vell—um—um," Jömp, becoming very warm from some interior conflict, mops his head with *the* handkerchief, and finally,
putting his hands behind him with the bearing of a man prepared
to die a martyr to his love of truth, says, " *I do not know. I 'ave
never been dere.*"

" Then, why the—Boompje !——" from everybody.

" Carriage ready ! " the Waiter announces, and Jömp escapes.

On the road to Leiden, Bund proposes to read *Murray's* account
of it to us. The country is monotonous, and the new entertainment of a reading from *Murray* partakes of the same character.
In half an hour we are all asleep. I employ the remainder of the
drive in making the following observations :

My impression of Holland—up to now (*N.B. Confirmed hereafter*).—From first to last all is Boompje, utter Boompje, unmitigated Boompje. Understanding that Boompje be always used in
our accepted Club sense. *Murray's* travellers, be they who they
may, from lucky Number One, who does all the good hotels, to
poor Number Five, who only lives to tell others what to avoid,
are all robustious, periwig-pated fellows.

Were I telegraphing my impressions to England, I should say,
economically, " Disappointed with Holland." Bund is not ; for he
believes in *Murray*, and the blameless *Bradshaw*. What *Murray*
says, Bund, our Commodore, sticks to. Muntley and Finton do
(in words) to Hollanders what the Hollanders did to their own
country when they made it what it is ; I need say no more.
But Maullic, R.A., is eager for pictures, and swears to see every
public and private collection in Holland ; even if he has to lug
out private collectors by the collar. As for Gooch, Holland is
not Paris ; and to him Paris is the Continent.

But why did *Murray* lead me to expect so much in Holland ?
Why does he say (quoting, perhaps, but no matter, he adopts it)
" that here the order of Nature is inverted." Here, in effect,
fishes swim into your bedroom window. That here you live two
thousand feet below the level of any known sea. Why am I
given to understand that my drives are to be under water. By

Murray I am led to expect that for the shooting season one must take out a licence to fire at red herrings, but sprats are vermin. Izaak Walton, if here, would have to angle for jackdaws, troll for cocksparrows, and bottom-fish for larks. We were to be in a sort of dry Red Sea land with water walls on either side. All the trees would be (I expected) of seaweedy character, and I was to be (I had fondly hoped) awoke in the morning by the piping of a fresh cock salmon on the upper branches. But what is the fact? Why simply that the country is flat, and canalled, instead of tunnelled, as it would have been if mountainous ; that in the towns you are as much above the canals as Londoners are when walking along the Harrow Road by the side of the canal, name of which I don't know, never did, and never shall, but it seems to me to commence in Paddington, to meander at right angles about the pleasant vale of Maida, to disappear somewhere at a small outpost of London (where mortuary stone works are made, suggesting the idea that those mighty efforts of the sculptor's art in the New Road had come down here for an airing), and to lose itself finally in the country, probably in the Uxbridge direction. This repeated, without any undulation of country, is Holland : that is, an eternal canal, and something to walk on on either side, with bridges to cross it whenever you want to vary the monotony of being on the left bank by changing it for the right one.

There is a good deal of bright polished brass about Holland, as you might expect in a Boompje land.

While writing the above, it occurs to me that a free translation of "*Boompje*," as settled and fixed by the Club Dictionary, would be "*Bounce.*"

Leiden at last.—What shall we do? Evidently, to begin with, wake up. We wake up. Here is Leiden. Ask the coachman. Can't, he's a Dutchman. Tell Jömp to ask Dutch coachman what we're to do here. No use. Jömp tries. As usual, Dutch coachman can't understand a single word. Jömp shrugs his shoulders pityingly.

We manage, between Jömp's Dutch (limited), and our French and English, to make an intelligent Baker understand us. The process is a long one, and all Leiden is out-of-doors to hear and see and, if possible, join in the conversation.

"'Pon my soul," exclaims Gooch, in a tone of unmitigated disgust, "We're being mobbed wherever we go. We might as well be a cracked Chinaman, or the Japanese ambassadors, in London. Confound it, it's too bad." He is very wrathful with Bund and Jömp, but settles down ultimately on Maullie. "If he was only dressed like a civilised Christian, and not in that Boompje hat and tourist suit, they wouldn't stare at us like barbarians. Hang 'em !"

"Are there not objects of interest here ?" asks Muntley, in the rumble. "Yes," growls Gooch, "*we* are : confound it."

We try to gather information from the intelligent inhabitants of Leiden. "Is there a church to be seen here ?" This puzzles them for ten minutes, during which time we repeat the question in all sorts of forms, and in ingenious variations of languages. The intelligent Baker, assisted by our intelligent coachman who rouses himself for an effort, suddenly grasps the meaning of our question. He explains to the populace (a crowd of about forty people of all ages and sizes), who take up the reply as a part-song for several voices. Hopelessly unintelligible. We demand a solo by the Baker, or the Coachman. They insist on making it a duett. (Gooch, writhing, says, "Boompje 'em—drive on : do !" but we don't stir.) From a solo by some one we are given to understand that there is no church open. ("It's not like Paris," says Gooch ; "they don't keep 'em open. Hang it ! let's drive back again." But we don't stir.) We insist that there must be a church worth seeing. The populace (after five minutes allowed to reduce this to intelligibility) ridicule the idea of our being driven over from the Hague to go to Church. ("They think we're mad. Do drive on !" says Gooch, piteously.) Maullie asks boldly for the Stadhuis. They don't know it. "Not the Stadhuis ?" reiterates Maullie, surprised. No : not the Stadhuis. "Then isn't the University worth seeing ?" Populace take this up as a riddle (it seems as if we are a travelling company for conundrums), and after considering it in parts as before, put the puzzle together, and desperately the answer is No. "O !" exclaims Gooch, "you be Boompje'd. Here, let's get out and walk about the town."

We discover the University at last. Down a street : very retired. It could be put into Trinity Hall's waistcoat-pocket. There are some comic drawings on the wall of the staircase, representing a scholar leaving home for the Academy, and his return therefrom. Dutch boy's humour. We yawn about the place. We ask about Jean of Leiden. We inquire for (*Murray's*) Botanical Garden, the Egyptian Museum, the Churches of St. Peter and St. Pancras. Nobody knows, nobody cares. It is vacation time. Leiden is asleep. Our conundrums are all given up, and we return to our carriage.

Dull road home. Bund reads extracts from *Murray* as to what we ought to have seen. Then he turns, angrily, on Jömp :

"You ought to have known all about it. It's your business. You said you'd been all over this country before. And if you hadn't been, you ought to have made all the inquiries, or sent somebody with us who could take us everywhere."

"Vell," replies Jömp, deeply injured, and almost shedding tears, "I say dat I 'ave not been in Leiden. I cannot tell you vot I do not know."

Finton, in the rumble, is humming the march from the *Prophète:* inspired by Leiden. Suddenly, he stops, and addresses us : "I say, what a capital match Jean of Leiden and Joan of Arc would have made ! Almost the same dress, too."

This induces meditation, and we wake up at the Hague.

CHAPTER XII.

THE CLUB VISITS THE QUEEN OF HOLLAND.

WHAT'S the time for seeing the Palace?" asks the Commander-in-Chief and Paymaster Bund.

"Four o'clock," Jömp answers, " vill be the best time for to see the Palace."

"*La Reine est-elle chez elle ?*" asks Gooch in his usual momentary obliviousness of his native tongue, adding his translation : " The Queen, is she at home ?"

Jömp believes that the Queen of Holland *is* at home. He has been all the morning making inquiries, and the above represents the result. Gooch thinks that, under such circumstances, "to call would be an intrusion." He emphasises "call," as if ours was going to be a visit of friends who had been hospitably asked to come in a general way when they liked, and who had (as is invariably the case) taken advantage of the invitation at the most inopportune moment.

"Pooh!" says Bund, fresh from *Murray*, "it's the regular thing to see."

Muntley, Finton, and Gooch, the Opposition, object to it solely on the grounds that, being the regular thing, it is so British-touristy and snobbish.

Maullie, who has been spending his morning in two private collections which he found out for himself without Jömp, votes for the Palace, with a view to probable pictures.

The Commodore has the casting vote, the Opposition gives in, and Bund, relying upon *Murray*, decides upon the visit of inspection.

"Not in that hat!" Gooch implores Maullie. "Not in that hat—to the Palace!"

Maullie, who has something of the rigid obstinacy of the Puritan in him, combined with his taste for simplicity in dress, replies that he doesn't intend to change it until he arrives at Brussels—"when," he adds, "I will astonish you in my Sunday best. I have," continues Maullie, proudly, "an Opera hat."

"French?" asks Gooch, anxiously, "silk, glossy, that you can wear in the day-time?"

To which Maullie replies that Gooch will see. As Maullie gets into the carriage, I hear Gooch telling his friends, *sotto voce*, "*Il a un chapeau*—he has a hat."

"You are sure," asks Bund of Jömp, "that the Palace is open at four?"

"O yes," answers Jömp, expressing by his manner that he is utterly astonished at Bund's doubting his accuracy even for a second. "O yes—um—um—um—it is open at four. O yes!"

We drive through an avenue—very pretty this—and enter the courtyard of the Palace. A pair-horse carriage, and a Victoria, are waiting. Some servants in Royal liveries are chatting with other servants (belonging to the aforesaid carriages) at the door.

'Some one's making a call," observes Gooch, pulling up his wristbands, and settling his hat, under the impression, apparently, that the Queen may be looking out of the window, and might be induced, by his distinguished appearance, to ask him in (not *us*, of course, and certainly not Maullie, except on sufferance in the character of "any friend of yours, Monsieur Gooch, of course," &c.), perhaps to dinner.

"It doesn't look like sight-seeing time," says Maullie. Even *he* is a little oppressed by the proximity of Royalty, and makes a concession to propriety by cramming his sketch-book into his pocket, and pulling his tie down under his coat, its tendency during a drive generally being to "ruck up" and obliterate his shirt-collar.

Bund bashfully produces black kid gloves, but as they have weathered several storms of rain, and the middle fingers are arranged on ventilating principles, this addition to his costume only induces Gooch to say, in a rapid under-tone, as we draw up at the portico, "Do put those things in your pocket, or you'll look like a respectable begging-letter writer." He casts his eyes up to the front windows, to see if, by any chance, the Queen is looking : but no one is visible.

Jömp, in his Boomp-je hat and livery, unintelligible to the servants, commands instant respect : at first.

Two servants in gorgeous coats and knee-breeches, six foot high each of them, let down the steps, and open the door.

A bell is rung.

Instantly we see the hall within lined on either side by tall servants, all in the same sort of costume, and standing bolt upright like theatrical nobles at a shilling a night in an opera chorus.

Muntley in the rumble leans over and says, "Isn't it just as if they were going to sing, 'Hail to the something or other,' eh ? "

Gooch silences him with a frown. We are all seated in the carriage, not liking to get out, as no one is certain what may happen next, and there is among us a latent, undefined feeling that the Queen is coming to receive us.

"There's some mistake somewhere," murmurs Bund, who has got his gloves out again, as if the display of these would rectify any misapprehension as to our being noblemen—"In disguise," adds Gooch, looking first at Maullie's hat, then at Bund's gloves.

Jömp is wholly incompetent, and utterly flabbergasted by the situation. He stands helplessly by the steps, staring at the tall men in liveries, but has nothing to say. Another five minutes like this would send Jömp to a lunatic asylum, where he would be shown as the "Idiot Courier" for the remainder of his life.

Two bells more. "Like on board a ship," says the Commodore, faintly, wishing he was at home with his violoncello.

In answer to these two bells appear two footmen in more resplendent liveries than the others, and about two inches taller.

They walk down to the door, and take their places, as if by clockwork arrangement or previous rehearsal, by the door. They don't notice *us*, except by a glance, having evidently enough to do to attend to their own deportment at the present juncture.

Another bell, this time more distant, as if some way down a passage ; a slight delay, and then one grander and more gorgeous footman, a sort of Swiss from a cathedral, topping by an inch all the rest, walks slowly forward, and approaches our carriage. He waits by the steps, inviting us (in Dutch we fancy) to descend. The Swiss gracefully removes his hat. The two by the door having a second before put on *their* hats, now politely, but stiffly, take them off. We all take ours off, and that part of the ceremony, whatever it means, is over.

Bund addresses Jömp. "Ask," he says, "if the Queen is in, and whether we can see the palace ?"

In such Dutch as he can manage, Jömp inquires as to Royalty being at home. The Giant looking down with some curiosity on Jömp, does not comprehend the question at first. Then on Jömp trying it again, he grasps it.

Yes, the Queen *is* at home. We will descend, of course.

Now comes a ticklish point. We have to explain what we want to see—not the Queen, but the palace. The Swiss cannot understand. "The Queen is waiting to receive us," he explains through Jömp, who gives us a very vague translation. Finding that we don't move ("There'll be a row," cries Gooch in despair, "and letters in the *Times* about Cockney Tourists. Let's go back "),

and being tired of standing with his hat off (all the other lesser
giants being fatigued too), he pulls a small door-bell, which is
responded to by a little wizened man in black, like the shade of a
departed butler. ("Good effect among the liveries," says Maullie
under his breath, making a mental note of it. N.B. He has
subsequently put the whole thing into a picture full of halls in
perspective, grandly costumed nobles with flambeaux in their
hands, and a secretary in black. He calls it Reception of the
Dutch Republican Ambassadors at the Court of the King of Spain.
All our likenesses are there, and it has been on his easel some
considerable time. Everybody says it's a very fine picture, but
nobody has bought it, as yet.)

The Butler's Ghost receives some information from the Chief
Giant. He glides towards us along the carpeted hall noiselessly.
He is at our carriage-door. He salutes Bund, fixing upon him
instinctively as the Commander, and ignoring Jömp altogether.

"Her Majesty," he says, "is within. Your Excellency——."
We look at one another. In an instant the Butler's Ghost sees a
mistake somewhere. Bund takes the opportunity, and informs
him that we wish to see the Palace.

The vision of greatness is dispelled. At a word from the Butler's
Ghost, three of the Giants replace their hats on their heads super-
ciliously, and disappear. After them disappear, in perfect order,
and without any show of confusion, their hatless but equally
gorgeous brethren-in-livery. Then we are all alone with the
Shade and one giant, the tallest. It is explained to us: this is
the time for private receptions. *Not* the time, oh, dear, no, for
seeing the Palace. *Up to four o'clock* the Palace is open to sight-
seers, but after that closed. Everyone here knows that. Jömp
wishes to make a personal explanation, but is called to order, and
stands by the carriage-door, discomfited.

Butler's Ghost declares that, the Queen being at home, sight-
seeing is *impossible—utterly out of the question.* Bund puts it to
him that we are going very early to-morrow, that he (Bund) has
only to call on his friend the Ambassador that moment, and he
would return (in effect) with orders to see every room in the
Palace, from the attics to the cellar. That he (Bund) and party
are most distinguished people, representing Literature, Science,

and Art (Science being, perhaps, Muntley and Finton in the rumble, who have been hitherto taken for our valets), and that, to sum up, if the Butler's Ghost will only break through rules, and show the Palace, the Butler's Ghost shall find that we will make "*it well worth his while ;*" and therewith Bund, having craftily got a large coin of the realm out of his waistcoat pocket, presses it upon the little man's acceptance, much to Gooch's horror, who exclaims, "I say! Hang it! You might as well tip the Lord Chamberlain at home," evidently under the impression that the Butler's Shade holds that office.

The *tip* has its effect. The Butler's Shade takes the giant into his confidence, shares (probably) with him, or makes arrangements for future sharing, and finally announces to us, after disappearing into and reappearing (for mere form's sake, I am sure) from, a dark passage, that the Queen has graciously permitted us to see the Palace.

I don't believe the Butler's Ghost ever went near the Queen. This is strongly borne out by his subsequent conduct.

He shows us through the rooms hurriedly, and as quickly as possible, as if he was doing something wrong. He stops now and then to describe, but his descriptions are abbreviated, and his eye wanders from one door to another as if to intimate at the shortest notice that, as the Pantaloon says to the Clown when he's stealing sausages, there's "somebody coming!" We're all, so to speak, stealing sausages, as Clown, and he's the Pantaloon.

We enter a drawing-room beautifully and curiously furnished with Japanese hangings and coverings. Jömp, who follows in our wake, and who has been rather snuffed out by our wizened little cicerone here explains to us that "Dese come from Japan," but on receiving a severe reproving look from the Butler's Ghost, he retires into himself (he can't go very far, I should say, on such a journey), and is satisfied with corroborating with gloomy nods the various points of our cicerone's information.

"Hush!" says the little man, suddenly stooping down, and looking through a keyhole.

We now discover that we are hunting the unfortunate Queen from room to room. Royalty flees before us. Royalty, for what we know, may be concealed behind a screen or a window-curtain, as we pass. A sort of hide-and-seek. The guide ascertains, as far as he can by the aid of the keyhole, that the Queen is not in her boudoir, and we enter. Evidently she has not long left it. There is her book open, and music on the piano.

A servant, in livery, suddenly appearing, motions to Butler's Ghost to pause before rashly visiting the next apartment. "It's too bad," says Gooch. "Hush!" says our mysterious attendant. We halt, looking dubiously at one another, and then, on a sign from our leader, who has again satisfied himself through the keyhole, we proceed stealthily, like conspirators in an opera. We only want daggers, to complete the resemblance. But our "sticks and umbrellas have been left" in the carriage.

We talk, when we *do* talk, under our breath. We hurriedly admire furniture and imitation bas-reliefs on the wall. We wonder at paintings on the ceiling, and we are hurried on to the ball-room, where, it being a very large place and only used on State occasions, we, as it were, breathe again.

The breathing time is very short, however, and we are once more hurried along a passage, then a corridor, where more pictures are explained to us, in a sort of patter-song, as fast as ever it can be given, by the Butler's Ghost, who, evidently very much to his own satisfaction, brings us out on a landing which leads by the back stairs and servants' offices to the front hall, and so we are smuggled ignominiously out of the building, and into our carriage.

Here we resume our dignity, and largesse is bestowed by Jömp (on our behalf, but we ignore the process, as not dealing in such dirty matters) upon our Guide and the tall Swiss.

Then we are driven through some lovely avenues, where all the peasants take off their hats to us ("They think we're the Queen, or something," says Gooch, much pleased), and at last we reach the hotel.

"Vell," says Jömp, perfectly satisfied with his arrangements, "you 'ave seen the Palace." And so we have; and agree that we won't see another in the land of Boomp-je.

"Dere is not another," says Jömp, which settles the matter at once.

CHAPTER XIII.

AT AMSTERDAM—THE BOOMPJE MOTTO—THE NEW GUIDE—AN
EXCITING PROSPECT.

EEMS to me, after visiting various Churches in Holland, that to take off your hat in a church is rather a sign of irreverence than otherwise. As the fashion-books would say, "Hats are much worn in church."

At Amsterdam.—New Grand Hotel some distance out of the town. We have it all to ourselves.

"Why," says our Commodore to Jömp, "we're the only people in the hotel. How's that?"

We listen; expecting to hear the cause of the conspicuous absence of visitors, something about dull season or want of funds, or whatever else may account for the emptiness of a Grand Hotel. We look for this, seeing that Jömp has been half an hour in the hotel, conversing downstairs with the proprietor and hall-porter.

"What's the reason," asks Bund, "of our being the only people here, eh?"

Jömp shrugs his shoulders. It is, evidently, to his mind, too absurd to put such a question. The fact, he thinks, speaks for itself. However, he replies, "Vell—um—um—you are the only people 'ere—O yes; because—you see — um—um—" here he finishes thinking it out as usual, "you see,—*dere is nobody else in de place.*"

Maullie delighted. Galleries of pictures. He spends his first day with Jan Steen, Rembrandt's *Night Watch* and Van der Helst's *City Guard of Amsterdam.*

It seems to me, speaking inartistically, that one doesn't understand what portrait-painting is until these marvellous pictures have been studied.

"Why," says Gooch, meditatively, "can't they paint groups of portraits now-a-days, this size?"

Maullie gives as the probable reason for there being so many grouped portraits, and so, comparatively, few "portraits of single gentlemen," that individually the Hollanders were not rich enough to have a picture every man of himself *to* himself, and so they clubbed together, "The artist," says Muntley, "making a reduction on taking a quantity."

We all visit Mr. Six's collection, and enthusiastically admire the pictures of Burgomaster and Burgomistress Six, painted by Rembrandt. Both equally good. Six of one and half a dozen of the other.

We drive about the town. The whole party, except Maullie, who prefers taking a sketch of the market-place from the carriage, visit the large church, *Nieuwe Kerk* (first cousin to Scotch Kirk, evidently), and on returning therefrom we find Maullie in a great state of excitement.

"Here! Hi!" he exclaims, vociferating and waving his umbrella and sketch-book.

"Good heavens!" says Gooch, considerably scandalised, "he needn't do *that.* We shall have a crowd round us again." And dreading this, he hurries on towards the carriage.

"Eureka!" cries Maullie, excitedly, which Jömp thinks is a real Dutch word, "I've got the motto for the Boompje Club. Look up there!"

With his umbrella he points upwards, towards the other side of the open Place. At first we see nothing except the tall houses closely wedged in between one another, as if they'd come late to see a performance and there was only standing-room for them.

"Don't you see?" he asks. We *do* see, but, clearly, not what he wants us to fix upon. "That inscription—there!" he urges, prodding the umbrella upwards always in the same direction, as if he could touch the spot to which he is drawing our attention.

There are names of shopkeepers, of trades, of houses, all in large letters, and we, more or less incorrectly, read them. "Now," he cries, "the next one," and Bund reads aloud an inscription, high up over the second storey of one of the tallest houses, the letters of which are painted in a decided undeniable black on a white ground,

"DAM No. 2."

"There!" says he, "isn't that the motto? Isn't the Boompje principle to take precious good care of Number One, and let Number Two look out for himself?"

We know by this time that the meaning of "Dam No. 2" is nothing more than, for instance, "No. 2, Portland Place," or "No. 2, Fleet Street," but the aspect of the words in this position, and their sound when given in the true Boompje-ish manner, recommend them at once to us as the motto for the Boompje Club.

When we separate and return to England, each member will take this motto back to his own house, and "when in doubt," as directions for whist have it, he will then act on the above Christian sentiment, and be a happy and virtuous Boompje.

We won't see the Palace, but we pass through its hall in order to ascend a tower (Maullie *will* go up a tower wherever there is one), in order to see the bird's-eye view.

"Now," says Bund, on the second day, "as Jömp never knows anything about any place, I have hired a regular Amsterdam Guide."

We applaud the Commander, and the Amsterdam Guide appears. He is a young man with a fresh complexion, and a Hebraic nose, dressed in a brown coat, bright check trousers, yellow waistcoat, blue tie, and a white wideawake, being the only living creature I ever remember to have seen in any way realising the coloured frontispieces of Music-Hall songs. If the Amsterdam Guide had suddenly thrown himself into an attitude, and announced himself as having been christened "Champagne Charley" by his godfathers and godmothers, none of us would have been more than slightly astonished.

After the following conversation, which I will here recount, we come to the conclusion that he is Jömp's nephew :—

Ourselves. Is there much to see in Amsterdam ?

Guide. Plenty. Full.

Ourselves. What is there ?

Guide. Vell (*uncommonly like* Jömp *this*)—'ave you 'zeen de Canals ?

As nobody could walk two steps outside any door in Amsterdam without seeing the canals, this question does appear somewhat pointless. We reply, naturally, that we *have* seen the canals.

Guide (*who, to our astonishment, is rather taken aback by our answer, pauses, and then resumes*). 'Ave you zeen de shoops (shops)?

Ourselves (*somewhat impatiently*). Yes, we've seen the shops.

Guide looks round at the party, as if we were evidently going to be one too many for him). Vell, den, you 'ave zeen the quays ?

Bund (*snappishly*). Yes, of course we have.

Gooch (*aside*). *Qu'il est bête !* (*kindly translating.*) What an ass the fellow is !

Jömp, in the background, watches the Guide with a patronising air, as much as to convey to us the idea that *he* could have done just as well as this Guide—"only you *would* have him ! "

Guide. Ah ! (*taking a new line*), den you must zee de tower. (*He is evidently prepared to hear us exclaim, rapturously, " Show us the tower ! "*)

Maullie (*shortly*). We've seen the tower ?

Guide (*faintly*). And de Palace ?

Muntley. Right through the Palace to the tower.

　　　[Jömp *smiles, and looks towards us, deprecating our engage-
　　　　ment of this Guide.*

Guide (*coming out with a trump card*). You 'ave zeen de Bazaar ?

Finton. No. We passed it yesterday.

Bund (*quickly*). And we don't want to.

Chorus. No. Hang the Bazaar !

Guide (*staggered*). De—de—Hôtel de Ville ?

Bund. Seen it.

Guide (*almost gasping*). De New Church ?

Maullie. Went all over it.

Guide (despairingly). De Jews' Synagogue?

Everybody. O yes! Yesterday in the Jews' Quarter.

Guide (tries to collect his thoughts, his memory fails him, he looks wildly round the room, then suddenly composing himself he shrugs his shoulders resignedly, and says) " Vell, den, you 'ave seen it *all.*"

Jömp, too, shrugs his shoulders and nods first at the Guide, then at us, as much as to say, "There, you see, I told you how it would be; better trust your own Jömp."

We have engaged the Guide, at least we suddenly discover that Jömp has engaged him, *for the whole day.* What are we to do with him for the twelve hours?

Gooch positively objects to walk about in company with a Dutch "Champagne Charley."

" Hang it," says he, " one can't go about with a sort of a ' Lion Comique.' Fancy, if we meet any one we know!"

Maullie wants to see a Private Collection. The Guide knows it, and offers to conduct Maullie thither. Offer accepted. We watch their departure. " Sure such a pair!" quotes Gooch.

" And when they return," says Bund, who is settling down to *Murray,* " we'll go to the village of Brock. It's *the* thing to see. A wonderful place." And forthwith he reads an extract from *Murray* concerning all the marvels to be met with in this unique village.

We all wish Maullie would make haste and return, so that we might hurry off post haste to Brock, where there are model farms, model dairies, model houses, model peasants, model roads, pleasure grounds, a mermaid, talking mechanical figures, temples, groves, and, generally speaking, it is a place where, apparently, wonders never cease.

" Hurrah for Brock!" we all cry, enthusiastically.

" Jömp," cries Bund; " isn't Brock well worth seeing?"

" Vell," returns Jömp, " O yes—um—um—it is vorth seeing—O yes!" Then he adds with his usual profound regard for the truth, " *I 'ave never been dere.*"

CHAPTER XIV.

A VISIT TO THE CELEBRATED PLEASURE GARDENS OF THE MODEL VILLAGE OF BROEK.

A DRIVE to Broek. Objects of interest, windmills, canals, ditches, flat country bearing a family resemblance to that cheerful swamp on either side of the line between Fenchurch Street and Tilbury, cattle, and peasants who touch their hats vaguely to any body in a carriage. This touching custom does not aim at the traveller's pocket, for there are no vagrant beggars in Holland. In the Jews' quarter, on our coming out of the synagogue, we were assailed, it is true, by a noisy crowd of female mendicants (why not say womendicants?), all daughters of Israel, or rather grandmothers of Israel, to judge by their appearance, who held out their palms and shrieked for largesse. Jömp, who was frightened by this demonstration, threw coins among them (to be charged to Bund the paymaster in a future account), and climbed on to the box of the carriage as quickly as possible. This was the only instance of begging that we encountered during our sojourn in the Land of Boompje.

Our driver, with whom we could not argue in any language, had us completely in his power on the road to Broek. A flourish of his whip and a jerk of his hand towards a turning to the right indicated that he intended leaving the straight road in order to drive through a pair of open iron gates.

"What's he doing?" asks Bund.

Jömp answers with his usual characteristic readiness and love of truth, "Vell—um—um—he is going through the gates."

"Where to?" inquires Maullie.

Jömp looks about him from his perch of observation, and having thought the matter out, replies, "Vell—um—um—I don't know," which, of course, is highly satisfactory.

It turns out, however, that we are being taken up to a Model Farm.

"Useful thing," observes Maullie R.A., "for Artists." He makes a note to the effect. I believe that when he returns to England he will propose to the Governing Body of the Academy the institution of a Model Farm, or a Farm for Models, where Artists shall be able to call and make their own selection.

The Model Farmeresses are at the door of their cottage. Two of them. There are no Model Farmers visible. Bund informs us (on what authority we do not know, as there is nothing about it in *Murray*) that the Dutch are very fanciful about their cattle, and decorate the cows' tails on Sundays and holidays with bunches of ribands.

The elder Model Farmeress shows us her neat dairy, the milk-pans, milk-pails, and cheeses in various stages. It is all scrupulously clean and tidy. She explains to us, that is, we imagine she is explaining to us, the process by which milk is made into cheese, and we are much obliged to her. We are led into the cowhouse, but the cattle are in the fields, so we don't gather much from this inspection. She then shows us the family beds. These curiously illustrate the semi-canal life of the Dutch, for they are berths made up in cupboards in the wall. Perhaps the house itself has no foundations, but only a keel, so that in case of unexpected inundation, the entire farm would rise from its moorings, and sail about doing business with other farms and villages (similarly provided), just as if nothing had happened out of the ordinary course of events.

Noah must have been a Dutchman; and if Ham hadn't gone as

a colonist to Africa, Van Ham would have been a peculiarly Dutch name.

After seeing Holland one prostrates oneself before that Grand Romantic Genius who could so far shake off the trammels of fact, as to conceive such an improbable character as the *Flying* Dutchman. The Swimming Dutchman, the Diving Dutchman, the Floating Dutchman, the Sculling Dutchman, the Punting Dutchman, all these would have occurred to the ordinary mind, but the Flying Dutchman is, so to speak, the result of such a flight of imagination as to command our admiration and excite our wonder.

The idea might have been suggested by the contemplation of the Flying Fish, which ought to be, if Nature were only consistent, a Dutch Herring.

Quitting the Models, we drive on to Broek. Gooch is looking forward anxiously to Broek, or "Brook," as it is pronounced. Bund quotes *Murray* about Broek. He says, "Such an accumulation of pavilions, arbours, summer-houses, pagodas, bridges, and temples —Gothic, Grecian, Chinese, and Rustic—are nowhere else to be seen."

"By Jove !" exclaim Muntley and Finton simultaneously. Bund tells us that here we shall see wooden figures moving by clockwork to a tune played by some invisible instrument. Here he pauses and sighs, for his thoughts are upon his violoncello at home, and he never ceases to regret that he did not bring it with him. He believes it would have enlivened us as we drove about, or, at all events, have kept us awake after dinner.

Gooch has a proposal for him. It is that he might have his violoncello made portable : the handle to take in and out, the back to open, and the inside might serve as a portmanteau, "from which," says Gooch, "you would only have to remove your stockings and things when you wanted to play."

The consideration of this novelty occupies us till we reach Broek. Our driver stops at an inn outside the village.

"Why doesn't he drive *into* the village ?" asks Gooch, who likes to make an imposing entry.

Jömp explains, "He cannot drive into the village—um —um — because dere is no road."

Bund corroborates this from *Murray.*

We enter the village path, paved in the centre with tiles, like a back kitchen. There is a row of little houses on either side, not very unlike those meteorological toy-cottages, in which the little old-fashioned lady and gentleman never could live together under any circumstances, except perhaps something going wrong with the pivot on which their lives turned.

We are pounced upon by an elderly syren lady in a satin dress (a "Mature Syren," article for *Sat. Rev.*) who with various blandishments induces us, all more or less objecting, to enter her abode.

In her front parlour the Lowther Arcade, the penny bazaar of Oxford Street, Margate and Ramsgate shops, and those unique emporiums on Brighton pier have poured out their choicest treasures. Here are "trifles from Brock" in Dutch, pen-wipers inscribed "Brock," views of Brock (Shanklin, Isle of Wight, I believe, with Brock written under them) in glass paper weights; knives with wooden handles, on which is carved the magic name of Brock, as if it was that of a Sheffield cutler. Japanese stores innumerable, as if Brock had once been to Japan, and brought all these things away; or as if the Japanese had fled from Brock, leaving valuables at hap-hazard behind them.

Then the old lady must needs show us her autograph-book and her photograph-book. The former contained the signature of the Emperor Nicholas, who seems to have visited Brock, and "expressed himself much pleased," as the visitors' books have it.

We escape from the elderly show-woman (leaving Jömp in her clutches) glad to get away from her at any price.

A troop of children follow us, most objectionable children, evidently jeering. Maullie injudiciously makes a face, and shakes his umbrella at their ringleader, and from that moment we are mobbed by the children of the Model Village.

Where are the gardens so celebrated by *Murray?* Jömp insists upon a turning to the left being the direct road. This induces us at once, and instinctively, to choose the right.

Jömp takes his road : we ours. The children follow us.

We find ourselves in a dilapidated ragged garden, cut up into various narrow paths, full of weeds, bordered by straggling bushes and exhibiting no signs of the gardener's care and attention for years past.

It depresses us. "This," said Maullie, "cannot be the garden."

"No," exclaims Gooch, with an attempt at assurance (all Boompje!) "didn't you say," referring to Bund, "that there was a mermaid here, and many swans, and mechanical figures, and a lake?"

Bund had ventured upon this, relying upon *Murray*. We stop in the middle of a path. The children behind us jeer. We are losing our amiable tempers. An old crone comes towards us, bent with age. She can only laugh and chuckle, and jingle some keys she has in her hand. From her signs we gather that she is the Guardian of the Art Treasures. Maullie makes a sketch of her for his new picture, *The Lancashire Witches.* She only wants a broom to be the very thing : only if she had a broom we shouldn't see any more of her, as nothing could prevent her flying away on it to a "Sabbat" somewhere in the neighbourhood.

She is full of chuckles, evidently at the idea of any party of people being such fools as to waste their time in visiting Brock.

She takes us to the lake, points out the pavilion, where a wooden man, sometime mechanical, is now lying on the ground with broken legs and arms, and the paint washed almost entirely off his face by the rain through the roof; and she points out the mermaid.

"That!" we all exclaim. Yes, there is no doubt of it. On the top of a ruined summer-house (everything is in ruins) is perched a little zinc or tin mermaid, about eight inches high, intended to serve as a weathercock, only (this being Brock) of course it is out of order, and won't move.

"Gentlemen," says Maullie, seriously, addressing us collectively, " we have come all the way from England to Holland, have endured much, and have travelled night and day in order to see a broken weather-cock in the shape of a diminutive mermaid ! "

The crone shows us two mechanical figures which *do* move on being wound up. The children follow us and are delighted. It is a melancholy performance, and only the model children of Brock could find pleasure in such an entertainment.

The two mechanical figures look as if they'd been rejected by Madame Tussaud's Committee of Selection for the Chamber of Horrors.

Finally, there is a cuckoo-clock, of which the old woman is very proud.

In fact, imagine our Golden Square in autumn unswept, and strewn with toys of children as at the seaside, the gardens of any seaside *Tivoli* on a wet Sunday in October, without tea and shrimps, waiters or visitors, the ruins of the once-famous Rosherville, people the place with a few old battered ships' figure-heads from the works by Vauxhall Bridge, throw in a tenth-hand rustic arbour or two from some suburban villa to be sold a bargain, and you will have some faint idea of the appalling desolation of the Pleasure Gardens of Broek.

Broek, to be true to itself, and to save travellers time and money, should be spelt and pronounced " Broke."

The immortal advice once given by *Mr. Punch* to mankind with regard to those about to marry, may be well repeated here :—

Advice to those about to visit Broek :—Don't !

CHAPTER XV.

BRUSSELS.

UNTLEY, Finton, and Gooch in their glory. Here is a town, a Paris in miniature, cafés, gardens, promenades, theatres, *opéras bouffes,* and everything in holiday trim.

We arrive dusty and tired. We all disappear to our rooms in the hotel. We reappear transformed. Gooch & Co. resplendent. Bund sedate and tidy, but his general effect marred by his *Murray* still in his hand, and *Bradshaw* (let, like the cat, out of the bag) protruding from a frock-coat-tail pocket.

Gooch remonstrates: dwells upon those blots as being a bad example to Maullie, who has not yet issued from his apartment. Gooch & Co. hope anxiously that Maullie will have some regard to social requirements, and not inflict upon us his "tourist's complete suit of dittos" and white wide-awake. Maullie enters. Grand and startling effect. Latest thing in summer clothing. Black frock-coat, white waistcoat, brilliant trousers, polished boots, check necktie, snowy collars, flannel shirt apparent beneath ("Why *can't* he go the whole animal?" complains Gooch, who is down upon the blot at once), disappearing behind his waistcoat and coat, and turning up again at the wristbands. Taken altogether, Maullie is in "go-to-meetin' costume," and is justly proud of the surprise which he has given us.

"Now," says Gooch, "where is your hat?" Then Maullie produces a "gibus," and exclaims, "There!" triumphantly.

" Put it on," says Gooch.

He puts it on, turning his profile, right side, towards us. Applause.

Gooch cunningly walks round him, and stops, in horror, on the left. He has found out the weak point of the "gibus." Maullie's countenance falls. " Yes," he admits, " the spring is a little gone on one side, but I don't think it'll be noticed."

" Not noticed!" exclaims Gooch, while Muntley and Finton laugh derisively.

" My dear fellow," continues the Count, " this is a *fête* day. There are two bands playing in the Gardens : *tout le monde et sa femme* will be there in the height of Parisian fashion. You can't escape remark."

Maullie thinks he can. He defends his hat. Bund, being impatient to go into the gardens, and hear the concert (he looks forward to something cheery on the violoncello), says, " O never mind his hat!—come along!"

Gooch sacrifices himself for the reputation of the Club's first appearance in Brussels. He announces his intention of walking with Maullie, adopting an idea of Muntley's (who knows something about theatrical effect), and keeping his companion with his bright side towards the audience (as it were), and his shady side towards himself.

The audience being seated in the gardens, this plan is found to answer; but Maullie, happening to get free for a few moments, takes the wrong side of Gooch, who, momentarily oblivious of the change, is talking to Muntley on his other arm, and at once becomes the cynosure of neighbouring eyes. " What a hat!" " Regard, my dear, that hat!" " How it is droll, that hat!" we cannot help hearing, and even Maullie is induced to recognize the fact that he is bearding Society to its very face. He joins Bund, who has found out a secluded restaurant in the gardens and is icing himself.

After two hours' promenade, Jömp appears at the gates with a gorgeous carriage.

" Is it," asks Gooch, who likes to do everything in its proper season, " the right time for driving in the Bois?"

" O yes," replies Jömp, " you can drive in the Bois—O yes!"

as if, after mature reflection, he, personally, knew of no just cause
or impediment to such a proceeding.

"But," persists Gooch (for Gooch & Co.), "is it the time when
all the swells—all the swell equipages—drive out? Eh?"

"Dey all drive out," Jömp returns. "O yes—um—um—dey
all drive out *now*—um—um—*as much as at any oder time*."

Carried, for the hundredth time, Jömp is an ass.

We drive into the new and unfinished Bois. It *will* be
undoubtedly very beautiful, it *is* certainly very dusty. So dusty
that after a time, and in one part of the drive, we cannot see
anything three yards a-head of us. All consequently in bad
temper, except Secretary and Gooch, who happen to be seated with
their backs to the horses. Jömp smothered; Bund and Maullie
as if they'd been left for months on a shelf without being touched;
Muntley and Finton, in the rumble, grimy and using strong
language, chiefly French, and very bad French too.

We encounter two carriages besides ours. This represents *du
monde* out driving in the Bois.

Gooch is very angry. "Confound it, Jömp," he exclaims,
"they *don't* drive out here at this time, you see."

"No," answers Jömp, shrugging his shoulders, "um—um—*dey
do not*."

"Perhaps," suggests Maullie, "we've come to the wrong place."

Jömp has nothing to meet this with, except another shrug, as
if acknowledging that this *may* be the case.

"Is there no other drive?" asks Bund of the Coachman.

"O yes, all round the town. Drive wherever Monsieur likes."

"Then," says Bund, resignedly, "drive all round the town." A
simple means of coming upon the fashionable rendezvous at some
point or another.

We determine (after our drive) to dine at the table d'hôte.
Gooch protests, but yields to majority. Places taken. Dinner
at a comparatively early hour, to allow of going to theatre. Gooch
selects two theatres: one where there is a Diableric piece
announced, and another where *Le Petit Faust* is being done, the
airs of which Muntley and Finton immediately commence to
whistle or hum, more or less incorrectly. In view of an *opéra
bouffe* and a French *melodrame*, they are in high spirits.

Bund hears there are concerts in the evening after the theatres, and foresees the chance of taking back some new solo pieces for his violoncello. Maullie visits photograph shops, and buys views.

Jömp, at liberty, employs his time in a manner most useful to a courrier. Being unacquainted with Brussels, he contrives to improve the occasion by standing in front of the hotel-door all day, doing nothing except joining in an occasional chat with the landlord.

"Why don't you go and see the town?" asks Maullie.

"O vell," answers Jömp, smiling at the absurdity of such an idea. "Derz is nothing here—um—um—all towns is de same."

And so they are—to Jömp.

CHAPTER XVI.

REASONS FOR THE BREAKING UP—JÖMP'S DESTINY—THE LAND OF
FATE—THE FUTURE MARTYR—THE BUMPER AT PARTING—
BOOMPJE FINISH.

THE musical Bund has received letters from London. He is in a great state of agitation. He is very sorry, but he *must* be off. They (who?) can't do without him. (Boompje!)

It appears that he has received an invitation from a quartette party in town; and he is to bring his own violoncello. Two violins, a piano, and a violoncello. The dinner is to come first, and afterwards the four are going to play Somebody's Something in G. Maullie says he should like to hear the tuning and screwing up.

Bund replies that the screwing will be probably done in the dining-room. But this is only his way of turning off the banter good-humouredly, as, if ever man was in earnest and bent on playing something no matter what in G, Bund is that man. He resolves to get the music in Brussels, and study it. Jömp having had a day with the Landlord, is expected for once to know something about Brussels. Bund asks him, "Do you know if there are any good music-shops?"

"O yes." Jömp, the intelligent, replies without the slightest hesitation, as if he'd been born among them. "O yes"—then, as usual, his sprightliness vanishes, and he begins to appear almost sorry he'd spoken, "Yes—um—um—dere are "—he admits it now as a probability—"dere *are* music-shops."

His tone implies that though there *are* music-shops, yet, he should say, they wouldn't sell you anything except ham sandwiches, or would sell everything except music.

"They ought to be first-rate music-shops," observes Maullie, "in this place."

Jömp rubs his head slowly, thinking this out, then shrugs his shoulders, and puts his hands behind him, resembling in this attitude himself (Jömp) in winter at a fireplace, or himself again (Jömp) in some celebrated impersonation of the first Napoleon deliberating. So far he *does* resemble the Great Emperor, he *does* deliberate. There the likeness ends.

"Well!" exclaims Bund, impatiently, to whom, now, minutes are crotchets, "where are these music-shops?"

"Vell," answers Jömp, deprecating the commander's impetuosity, "Vell—um—um—dese music-shops—um—um—*dey are 'ere.*"

"Go and ask somebody to tell you," says Bund, testily. Exit Jömp, in tears. The Landlord enters, and gives Bund the required information. Bund goes all over Brussels, and can only find Somebody in F. They're out of Anyone in G. So the Commander busies himself with *Bradshaw*, to find out the shortest and most convenient route back to his beloved Violoncello.

Maullie, R.A., has had his letters forwarded. Waterglass, the eminent dealer, wishes to see him at once: an enormous commission. We suppose it to be to paint the Norfolk giant in a series, with perspective background, and giants of various ages in the gardens. However, *he* must go, and as for Gooch, and Muntley, and Finton, finding that if they stop at Brussels they will be alone in their glory, and as, with the departure of Bund, the office of paymaster and commander is in abeyance, it does not take them long to decide on a course of action which will not precipitate the temporary separation of the Club members, a painful necessity which we agree to leave until we are once more upon the shores of Perfidious Albion.

"One Boompje bumper at parting " is Gooch's proposal, speaking

for himself, &c. Carried *nem. con.* And the proposition being duly
developed, takes the form of a dinner, and the presentation of the
Boompje livery, which he has worn so long and with so much
credit to himself, to the immortal and amiable Jömp.

We are astonished at finding that Jömp is most anxious to get
back to London as quickly as possible. On being questioned he
is somewhat reserved, but, as hitherto, so now, veracity itself.

"You want to get back quickly, eh?" asks Bund.

"Vell—um—um—yes—I should like to get back—um—yes,"
—after considering whether there is any other better form of expression, he settles in his mind that there is not, and adds, "Yes
—quickly—O yes."

"Why?" asks Maullie.

"Vell," Jömp returns, very slowly, and rubbing his head,
letting his eyes wander all over us, the walls, the looking-glasses,
and the carpet pattern, as if the reason he was going to give us
was written somewhere among these articles, like a revelation,—
"vell—um—um,"—fails to discover it in the carpet, and tries the
right-hand window pane over Bund's head,—"vell—um—um—I
wish to go because,"—another failure, he tries up the left wall as
far as the cornice, where he is stopped by some ornamentation,
which drives him to the looking-glass on the opposite side,—
"because—vell—it is nothing,"—here he smiles to himself rather
bashfully, and we begin to think that he is going to tell us of his
fixed intention of getting married,—"vell—only because,"—the
furniture failing him entirely, he settles on Bund's watch-chain,
and brings himself to bay as it were,—"I vant to go—um—um
—because—*I do not wish to stay here.*"

"Is there no other reason?" asks Gooch, inquisitorially.

"Vell—um—um," Jömp admits there is.

"What is it?"

"Vell—um. I vill tell you"—Jömp begins in a tone of most
abject apology, "I ave taken a—um—um—I ave taken a
Otel."

"A what?" we all exclaim.

He is as frightened as if we'd all suddenly forbidden the banns
of that imaginary marriage we had fixed on him.

"A Otel," he resumes. "O yes, I ave him. Vy not?" Then

warming with the subject, he continues, "Dere is mosh more money to be made as that, dan as Courrier, O yes, mosh. It is in a good place."

"Where?" we inquire.

"Vell," he pauses and looks round at us, to see how we'll receive the intelligence; "Um—um—um—It is in London."

He names London as if the idea of starting a Hotel in such a place was entirely novel and original, and calculated to make an unheard-of fortune from its taking the people so by surprise. He had evidently looked forward to every one saying, "Hallo! here's a hotel! Why it's Jömp's Hotel. Dear me, let's go in and sleep there, and dine there, and, in fact, live there. All, everybody; let us desert London and live in Jömp's Hotel."

We cannot discourage him, as he has taken the premises.

"A great place," he explains. "Make dee—two—tree—four—an twenty or tirty *Billiard Tables.*"

"How many beds?" was our natural question.

"O dere will be beds—O yes—plenty of beds. Enough for every one to sleep most comfortable."

Now what Jömp means by this is not to us distinctly clear: but it does seem that up till now sleeping accommodation has been a consideration of secondary importance by the side of Billiard Tables. Unless those who couldn't get beds, were to be accommodated with pillows and sheets on the billiard tables.

He goes on, evidently pleased, to give us particulars. "Vell den—dere is varm and cold vater always turn on—O yes—den dere is a large Organ dat play several tunes——"

"Good gracious!" exclaims Maullie, "what's the use of an Organ to a hotel?"

"Vell," Jömp returns, "he is no use, no. But I bought him at a sale. He plays," he adds, with pride, to show that he's not been taken in, "O yes, he plays."

"Any other curiosity in your hotel?" asks Gooch.

"Vell, no," answers Jömp, innocently. "But you must come dere von day. I shall be delighted if all de gentlemans vill come."

"If it's conveniently situated," cried Bund, "we might have a weekly Boompje dinner at your hotel, Jömp."

He is radiant. He would be glad, he would give us a dinner—O yes, we should dine.

"Where is it?" asks Maullie, pleased, as we all are, at the idea. "If it's in the neighbourhood of the Clubs, or about that part, it will suit us down to the ground."

"Vell," Jömp considers, "vell—um—um—it is not near de parks—no—vell it is—no," as if he were mentally calculating its exact distance in inches from the Marble Arch or Wellington statue,—"vell—no—it is not near de *Clubs*—no—but you can get dere—O yes—you can get dere."

This possibility is, we think, almost a necessity to the success of the hotel. However, where is it?

"Vell, it is—um—um—it is in SMITHFIELD!!"

"Is it!" exclaims Bund; "then, Jömp, you've made a martyr of yourself; your friends will roast you, and, 'pon my life, you deserve it. What on earth——" but Bund is so annoyed with him that we are obliged to come to Jömp's rescue, and start suppositions that he (Jömp) had some good grounds for thinking he should get business in Smithfield, in preference to any other place.

"O yes," replies Jömp, brightening up, as if anything like a tangible reason for taking this Hotel in Smithfield had never occurred to him before, as perhaps it hadn't—"It is a good place for a Otel. Dere are a number of——" "Farmers and Gentlemen Farmers from the Country on business," suggests Gooch.

"No—um—um—No." Jömp rejects this source of wealth, and we wonder on what vein, unknown to us, he is going to rely. "*No—dere are a number of Swiss Clockmakers living about dat part, and—um—um—I tink dey vill come.*"

Jömp's notion, fully developed, is that these Swiss Clockmakers, *firstly*, "must eat; vell—dey come to my Otel." In vain we point out to him that they'll probably continue to dine, as they are doing now, and have done for years, at home. He meets this objection by saying, "Ah vell—but ven dere is a Otel, dey vill come." *Secondly*, that the hot and cold water always on will be a great inducement to them; *thirdly*, that, their work over, they will be delighted to recreate themselves with billiards. Again, we point out that, being chiefly, in all probability, family men, they will prefer to do as they have done for years, the chances are, and stop at home.

"Ah," says Jömp, "but ven dere is a Otel and twenty, tirty, billiard tables, dey vill come."

We advise him to get rid of his speculation to anyone who will buy it, but he thinks we are wrong, and we hope he is right.

He says he must get back to manage it, as "it vill vant me to be always dere," he tells us.

The above explanation of Jömp's views stood in lieu of a speech from him at our dinner, where he waited on us, for not, let us hope, the last time.

Bund from the chair made a neat and appropriate speech. He expressed his pleasure at having been, conjointly with the present company (Muntley and Finton excepted, and welcomed as Junior Members) the founder of the Great Boompje Club, whose existence would be synonymous henceforth with that of Science and Art. They would all of them dine with him that day fortnight in town, and book it. "*Messieurs*," concluded our courteous and hospitable Commander and Paymaster (who has never yet sent in the bill, and never will) "*Messieurs, au plaisir!* Gentlemen, let us stand up and drink the Motto of the Club, which emphatically and concisely expresses our sentiments towards Number Two, and, at the same time, a long farewell to the Land of Boompje. Hip! Hip! Hooray! One, two, three,

'BOOMP-JEI'"

LA BOURBOULE.

NOTES OF A FIRST VISIT TO
LA BOURBOULE.

CHAPTER I.

EN ROUTE—TWO HOURS FOR REFRESHMENT—A FRIEND IN NEED—
MY TRAVELLING COMPANION—"EN VOITURE!"

ON the morning of the "Glorious Twelfth" (of August) I find myself not on the Moors and among the grouse and Gillies, but entering the *département* of France called the Puy-de-Dôme, *en route* for the *Station Thermale*, La Bourboule, whose rising reputation for curing all sorts of ailments has brought us, myself and Dudley Chivers, all the way from London (Chivers came *via* Dieppe, myself *via* Calais,

meeting at the *Gare d'Orléans,*—quite a historical event) to consult
La Bourboule's doctors, drink and bathe in La Bourboule's
waters, and in a general way do at La Bourboule as La Bourboule does; and we sincerely hope the young Lady with a rising
reputation,—for of course "La Bourboule" must be a feminine
personage,—will pay us every possible attention, treat us kindly,
and turn us out as "perfect cures."

From London (via Calais) to Paris.—Victoria early Continental
train. Who hasn't experienced this trying start! To bed early
the previous night, and in consequence unable to sleep. Very
wakeful up to midnight. Restless and feverish till about 4 A.M.,
"when daylight does appear,"—for of course the shutters are
open and the blinds up on this exceptional occasion, so that
darkness may offer no subtle inducement to take another turn
round and go to sleep again,—and, having given particular orders
about being called punctually at a quarter to six, and having
anticipated the arrival of this hour by jumping up hurriedly to
look at the clock three times already between four and a quarter
past five, I return to bed, and while congratulating myself on
having just exactly half an hour's more rest, I fall off into the
deepest, sweetest, and soundest sleep, from which nothing short of
shaking, rapping, hammering, and shouting can arouse me.

Then—every early *voyageur* is familiar with it—comes the
trying moment of "pulling oneself together," which is only
partially successful, and your glass shows you the ghastly
spectacle you really are in the very early morning,—an unhealthy, half-awakened sleeper, momentarily galvanised into unnatural life. At this juncture the idea will flash across you,
"Can anything be worth this thorough upset of my system?
Isn't this derangement of my natural night's rest quite sufficient
of itself to demand imperatively some medical treatment in order
to restore me *sain et sauf* to myself again?" Till this morning I
was (comparatively with what I feel *now*) well. But this restless
night, this anxiety, this unnatural early rising, this breakfastless
excitement, has utterly *bouleversed* me . . . . and—and—upon
my word, if I hadn't got two pounds' worth of French money and
my pink ticket to Paris in my pocket, I should feel strongly inclined to chuck up everything, so to speak, and—go to bed again.

But *Courage, mon ami!* my cab is at the door, and my barque (the steamer) is on the sea, and *faiblesse, adieu!*

From London to Calais.—Hungry and feverish. Is life worth living, Mr. Mallock? Why go abroad? why all this nuisance and trouble merely because three Doctors have told me that if there be a place on the earth to cure me "it is this, it is this" La Bourboule, whither I am now wending my way? Why not Harrogate? I don't know: but too late to discuss the subject now, and I have no one to discuss it with. Why aren't these sulphurous and arsenical waters in England? Naaman the Syrian asked, quite naturally, why the waters of Pharphar, which he could get at easily, wouldn't do for his complaint; and I put the question (not in the same spirit, but diffidently) about Harrogate adding *à propos* of Pharphar, why go *far-far*-farther, only, perhaps, to fare worse?

Calais.—This always excellent Buffet restores my equanimity. It invariably does. If it were only for this I would choose the Dover and Calais route. The *Calais-Doûvres* has taken us across beautifully. At the station there are scarcely any *voyageurs*, I am accommodated with a compartment all to myself, and begin to be a little, a very little happier.

Paris.—5·40. At the *Gare du Nord.* My old friend George Doe (no relation to the defunct Richard Roe) is waiting to receive me. He is the friend in need,—I mean I'm in need, and he's the friend. He is in Parisian summer suit, hot, of course, but fresh up and beaming. He knows everybody worth knowing in Paris, including the station-master and the officials of the Douane at this terminus. The result is that within ten minutes he is driving me in a cab, while his *Chasseur* Charles, in uniform (George Doe does the thing well), is on the box directing the *cocher* along the shortest and cheapest route to the *Gare d'Orléans*, and keeping his eye on the luggage.

Arrived, Charles, the *Chasseur*, takes all responsibility on his own shoulders; *he* will get my ticket to La Bourboule; *he* will pay the *supplément* for the *coupé toilette; he* will come to fetch me at the very moment when I ought to start; and, I believe, so actively obliging is Charles, the *Chasseur*, that *he* would actually go, instead of me, to La Bourboule, take the waters there, solely on my account, and would let me know by telegram when he considered I ought to look upon myself as thoroughly cured.

So, while the gay *Chasseur* is thus engaged, George Doe accepts my kind invitation to dinner at a small cleanly table, in the shade, outside the Station-Buffet. Yes, this is just one of the things they do manage better in France. The Buffet of the *Gare d'Orléans* serves up a very good repast; the small tables I notice are nearly all occupied, and not by *voyageurs* only. Our waiter is brisk and civil, and the *sommelier* is confidential, as, with a twinkle in his eye, he recommends a choice Burgundy. We have already had a remarkable Bordeaux, but as my worthy friend in need is very fond of Chambertin, I sacrifice myself to my friend, for I am not bound to undergo a course of sulphur (like the Ghost of *Hamlet's* Father) and arsenic, so what harm can just one glass of the generous, the too generous Burgundy, do to one who must suffer anyhow? This is George Doe's opinion, too; not perhaps quite disinterested. So we decide for the Chambertin, and, such is its excellent effect, a little later I find myself deeply regretting my having to quit Paris, and begging Charles, the *Chasseur*, to see that the change is all right in francs, as, somehow or another, what with the heat, the pleasure of meeting an old friend, the fatigue of the journey, and the excitement generally, my head is rather in a whizzle when I try to translate pounds into francs, and attempt the details of complicated calculations. After attempting it seriously with a pencil on the back of an old letter, I sum it all up in a generally convivial total of " All right!" and Charles, the *Chasseur*, leads the way to the platform, where he trusts me with my railway-ticket and luggage-number (which is only on a wretched thin slip of yellow paper—so easily lost), and is not satisfied until he sees me put them both, with the utmost care, in my watch-pocket.

At this moment it suddenly occurs to me that I have yet to meet my companion in illness, or, let me say, in getting-well-ness (that being our common object), Dudley Chivers, " who ought," I say to George Doe, " to be here by now, as Dudley is a man of business, a constant traveller, and——" Then I explain to George Doe that Dudley Chivers—the Honble. Dudley Chivers, with whom he may perhaps be acquainted. No? Well, he is an immense Swell, has been on several occasions accredited on "important Missions"—whereat George interrupts me to ask if he's a Clergyman, "because I used the word 'Missions,' you know," he says, apologetically, and I immediately emphasise "Diplomatic Missions;" whereat George seems a bit scared "And so," I add, noting an inclination on my present friend's part to decry my absent friend, "and so he will probably travel

FESTIVE SCENE À LA GARE D'ORLÉANS. *Dehors.*

Making the most of our time, or "One (or two, or more) bumpers at parting, fill fill for me," previous to going in for the waters of La Bourboule.

en prince, and be now saying good-bye to the President of the Republic, with the entire firm of Rothschilds taking farewell of him at the station door."

"There's some one waving his hat to you," says George Doe; "there, standing by that carriage—man in light shooting-coat and billycock hat."

"Ah, yes, I see!" It is—though I own I am surprised—it *is* Dudley Chivers. He is having a dispute with the ticket-collector about the *supplément,* and has stopped in the middle of the discussion to signal to me.

I have met him in gilded saloons, where he is the very pink of courtliness; we have dined together in the pleasantest company, he being an adept in the art of being agreeable to everybody: he has always been the youngest, the gayest, the most amiable, the most even-tempered of men, with an air of authority and mystery that at once convinces and commands respect.

But now—well, to begin with he isn't well, or he wouldn't be going with me to La Bourboule; and, secondly, he seems to be much exercised by having left most things that he requires behind him, including a servant.

I introduce George Doe to Dudley Chivers, who becomes suddenly as pleasant and agreeable as ever. I tell him I've got a *coupé* toilette for six francs extra. Will he change, and come to mine?

He replies, heartily, "I'll do whatever you like—my name's Easy!"—what a charming travelling companion!—adding immediately, "I've got all my things in here, and I've paid eighteen francs. Hadn't you better come into mine?"

Charles, the *Chasseur*, murmurs in my ear that I shall have to pay another *supplément* of twelve francs, and that then we shan't be so comfortable, as there is a washing-place in mine.

"But, my dear fellow," says Dudley, pleasantly, "you won't always want to sleep. You'd better come in here."

And so, yielding to the gentleman who has announced that "his name is Easy," I pay the extra amount, and Charles moves all my things—my "goods and chattels," as the little curate calls them in *The Private Secretary*, and mount into Dudley's *coupé lit*, in a corner of which he has already comfortably installed himself.

"It's fitted up with sliding-seats," says Chivers; "yours wasn't."

"No, but mine has a washing-stand," I return; to which he only replies,—

"Oh, pooh! What's *that*, when you want to sleep? I really don't care where I am when I'm travelling." He is at full length, and already turning over for a doze before we're out of the station, with his legs barring the *portière*, so that I cannot do more than stretch myself out at an acute angle to his prostrate form, and wave my *adieux* to George Doe, and Charles, the nimble and willing *Chasseur*. We are off by the 8 P.M. train to La Bourboule.

CHAPTER II.

DUDLEY CHIVERS has commenced the journey by saying pleasantly that he is "prepared to rough it," and that "his name is Easy." However, I soon find that his tone of mind belies the name which he has chosen for himself.

Dudley Chivers has become quite a changed character; that is, at the present moment *en route* for La Bourboule. Had I been asked at any time within the last twenty years to point out the man whom nothing could ruffle, I should, without hesitation, have named Dudley Chivers. Now, *à l'heure qu'il est* (one glides into French as *Wegg* did into poetry, and Chivers is *tout-à-fait le Français*—" Quite the Frenchman "), he is a grumble personified. I discover it at once. And the effect upon myself is curious; for whereas, up to now, I had looked upon this obligatory journey to undergo a course of water-treatment at La Bourboule as a purgatorial discipline to which only the prospect of a certain future and lasting beneficial effect could in the least reconcile me, now, owing to the wretched view that Dudley Chivers takes of everything and everybody, I am forced into so strong an opposition as to find myself becoming quite a *Mark Tapley*, every minute growing more and more cheery and sanguine, though occasionally shaken in my own beliefs by my companion's apparently well-founded scepticism.

"A long journey before us," I commence, pleasantly, " but the reward of returning quite well!—eh ?"

"Ah, that's it," growls the Gentleman whose 'name is Easy,' moving himself restlessly in the seat, where he evidently can *not* make himself comfortable. "What carriages these are! beastly! and eighteen francs *supplément!* What an infernal row that engine makes! Why the deuce can't the French start a train without all this confounded shouting, screeching, foghorn blowing, and bell-ringing? Ugh! the fools!"

"They are noisy," I reply, cheerfully, "but there's life in it."

Here the engine gives a series of screeches as if in extremest agony.

"Go it!" shouts the Easy One,—Chivers *nommé Facile,*—sarcastically. "Go it!—*allez!*—don't mind me!" This adjuration addressed to the Stoker, Driver, and Railway Officials generally, is perfectly unnecessary. They *don't* mind him in the least, and for a few minutes all attempts at conversation are rendered impossible.

Sharp, shrill, convulsive shrieks, answered by other engines in different quarters with similar sounds, make the night hideous.

"If this is to go on, we shall never get any sleep," growls Chivers.

"Oh," I say, to comfort him, and get him to be a little more agreeable,—otherwise I shall regret not having retained my own carriage, and travelled, 'for this night only,' alone—"this horrid noise won't continue when we're once clear of the station."

"How do *you* know?" he asks, discontentedly. I don't know; I only suggest it in the kindliest spirit. The shrieking ceases for a while, and then we talk.

"I expect it will be a beastly place we're going to," begins the Easy One.

"I hear," I return, "that it is dull, but very prettily situated."

"I shouldn't have been going there at all if it hadn't been for *you,*" says the Easy One, angrily.

"Indeed?"

"Yes—you gave such a glowing account of it when we dined together,"—(I remember I did; but that was when I was rather touting for a cheerful companion than speaking from absolute knowledge)—"that I at once asked my Doctor, and he strongly recommended me to come here, and wrote me a letter of introduction to one of the Doctors at the place itself."

"Dr. Probité?" I inquire, that being the name of the eminent practitioner to whose care I have been confided.

"Yes, that's it; Probité!" he replies, in a tone of the deepest annoyance. "Probité! what a name!"

"First-rate man," I say, at haphazard, and chiefly because I've been recommended to him. For surely my Doctor wouldn't send me to anyone but a first-rate man?

"Is he?" returns Chivers, in a sharp suspicious manner—(never saw a man so changed as Chivers!)—"I don't believe it. I believe the whole thing's a swindle."

"How do you mean?" I ask, for I am bound to expostulate with him, as, in bringing such a sweeping charge as this against the place, he is not only condemning the Doctors abroad, but the Doctors at home who have written on the subject, and setting down the experts and scientific men, who have published their analyses of the waters and their salutary effects, as all humbugs, everyone of them engaged in one grand conspiracy to beguile patients into going to La Bourboule.

"I mean," goes on the Easy One, with the brutal frankness of a man who having suddenly discovered that he has been a dupe, now wishes to undeceive everybody else, "I mean that the whole place is a humbug, a speculation. It was got up, it's a well-known fact"—(then how is it I've never heard of it? But I don't interrupt him—I want to hear all his startling revelations, and, if his facts are proved, back I go to London again, firmly resolved to burst the La Bourboule bubble)—"it was started by Dr. Schüssel,—a thorough speculator under the Empire,—and he got a lot of Doctors to form a Company, and work it."

"Well," I object, "but there must have been natural sulphuric and arsenical springs as a basis of speculation?"

"Not a bit," replies Chivers, with triumphant malice,—"ordinary mountain springs, doctored."

"What!" I exclaim, horror-stricken at the idea of such villany.

"Yes—doctored," he proceeds, with an air of being thoroughly well up in his facts—"yes, doctored. That is, the sulphur and arsenic are supplied every morning from Paris, and put into the wells and springs. Steam does the rest. The whole thing's a regular swindle."

"Then why go there?" I naturally inquire.

He shrugs his shoulders, and answers—"Well, you see, if the medicated mixture called 'the waters of La Bourboule,' produces the desired effect, what does it matter whether it's a swindle or not?'

I admit that this is true to the extent of individual benefit, at the expense of general and professional morality. To which Chivers simply replies,—

"Blow general and professional morality!"

"There's another thing," he continues presently—"the Romans were great chaps for baths." Chivers is a well-read man. "There's not a *Station Thermale*, as they call it, existing now but what was *exploité* by the old Romans originally. Take Aix-les-Bains, Aix-la-Chapelle, any of 'em,—Mont Dore,—beyond where we're going,—

La Bourboule according to Fancy.

and there is a Roman history to each of 'em, Roman ruins and Roman relics in every one of them. But at La Bourboule not a vestige, not a trace of a Roman having ever had even so much as a hip-bath there,—no Roman coins, no Roman ruins. If it had always had the present reputation, wouldn't the Romans have made the place? Bah! I don't believe in La Bourboule! I know it will be beastly! But mind," concludes the Easy One, as he turns on his side, away from me, and closes his eyes, "I'm hanged if you're not responsible for taking me there!"

I am now bound to tell him all I know about the place, its virtues, its benefits, its charming climate, its situation—high up in the mountains,—and its system of baths. I am going on in this strain when he looks round sharply and interrupts me with—

"Have you ever been there?"

I am compelled in truth to answer, "No, I have not."

"Very well," retorts the Easy One, sitting suddenly bolt upright,—"then, till you have, you don't *know* any more about it than I do. Your information is on hearsay,—so is

La Bourboule *not* according to Fancy.

mine. But when you spoke of the place at that dinner-party"—he is always twitting me with this, as if I were to be tied to everything being taken literally that I said at any dinner-party,—specially on an occasion when I naturally stretched several points in order to gain the one I had at the moment in view, that is of getting an agreeable travelling companion, who would beguile the weary hours of the night with pleasant talk and amusing anecdote—"when you spoke of La Bourboule at that dinner-party, you certainly gave me to understand you had been there yourself, and knew all about it. Oh yes, you did." And down he goes again on the sliding-seat.

Did I speak at that dinner-party about La Bourboule as if I had been there myself?

I'm really very sorry, but I don't think I could have,—at least I didn't mislead him intentionally. Besides, the conviction grows upon me that he could not possibly recollect, with any exactness, much that I had said at that dinner-party, because I remember his telling me that he was taking champagne, and smoking a big cigar, on that occasion only, *as an exception to his rule;* and then I remember distinctly that, on turning to ask him a question, I suddenly missed him, and, on subsequent inquiry, I found he had left comparatively early, but that no one had noticed the precise moment of his departure; insomuch that, on my asking for him, the wag of the company had at once pretended to look *under the table.* I am emboldened by this remembrance to affirm that I could never have said I had been to La Bourboule, as it would have been absolutely untrue, and therefore, &c., &c.

"No," replies the Easy One, who can't fix himself in a comfortable position; "I don't mean that I understood you to positively *say* so; but from your manner and way of talking about the place, anyone would have inferred that you had been there for several seasons."

Of course, I can't help what he inferred from my manner,—but here the engine re-commences shrieking, and brings this part of our conversation to an abrupt conclusion. After anathematising the noise, and once more preparing himself for repose, Chivers complains that he knows he shall be miserable, as he has left his valet behind him, and that in consequence he shall have to carry his own bag—(Does he throw this out as a hint that he wishes *me* to carry it for him?)—and he will have to unpack for himself, and brush his own clothes, and—O!—he knows he's going to be very wretched,—he has quite forgotten that "his name is Easy,"—and he does hope I won't trouble him any more with talking (here's a pleasant companion whose "name is Easy"!), as he wants to get to sleep, and he must request me not to get out at Limoges, or any other station, as he is lying just across the *portière,* in front of which his legs form a sort of bar, and I shall have to put him to all sorts of discomfort.

And this is the man whom, from knowing him for the last

twenty years in various circumstances, I have selected as the best
and most agreeable travelling-companion in the world! *Moral.*—
Take care how you tout for a companion for a journey; *stick
closely to facts when describing what you know nothing about except
from merest hearsay,* and don't be too expansive in manner at a
dinner-party. "What great effects from trifling causes spring!"

"By the way," he murmurs, before dropping off to sleep, "what
Hotel did you tell me to take rooms at?"

I tell him the name of the one where we are both expected.

"Ah!" he groans, "you've let me into a nice thing. My
friends in Paris, Parisians who know all these French watering-
places, tell me that the hotel you're taking me to is quite second-
rate. Ugh!" he growls, "I shall leave the beastly hole if I don't
like it. And, dash it, no servant! I shall have to unpack my
own things! and——Ugh!"

Why doesn't he get out at the next station, and take a return-
ticket to London? But *suppose what he says should happen to be
true?* Suppose we are the dupes of cunning and designing men
and that the whole thing *is* a swindle!! Suppose that we find
La Bourboule to be pretty much what *Martin Chuzzlewit* and
Mark Tapley found that Eden really was, after the American
agent's glowing description of the place as seen on the map?
What then? As they used to say in old melodramas, "The deadly
poison (of Chivers's conversation) has done its work,"—and *Iago*
(Chivers) has whispered into the ear of *Othello* (myself) his distrust
of *Desdemona* (La Bourboule).

This thought bothers me. The sliding-seat of the *coupé-lit* is a
nuisance; it slides when I don't want it to, and then won't be got
back again without much physical exertion, which is too fatiguing
this blazing hot night, only to slide out again when least required,
—and for this I have paid eighteen francs *supplément*, simply
because the gentleman who said he was going to "rough it," that
everything was "all one to him," and that "his name was Easy,"
would not move his things from his carriage into mine.

I cannot sleep. But . . . *the Grumbler can.* His name is Easy
at last. There he lies, extended on his sliding-seat, his feet
encased in natty slippers—"pumps," with striped socks just
visible, after the manner of the pantomimists, who in old pantomimic

days used to be down in the bills as "afterwards Harlequin"—an intimation scarcely necessary *then*, as the future Harlequin invariably played the Lover in "the opening," and was immediately detected by the least experienced *habitué*, on account of his pumps and silk stockings,—yes, there lies Chivers—as "afterwards Harlequin" —fast asleep, and no longer grumbling or growling, but snoring— but even in his snoring there is so strong a note of discontent that it only sounds as if he were still grumbling, in his sleep. At Limoges he *must* play the part of the "Sleeper Awakened," as I shall descend and seek the buffet, in search of a cooling draught.

Riddle composed, said to, and guessed by myself, while Monsieur qui s'appelle "Le Facile" dort en ronflant.—Why might I just as well have come to La Bourboule in a four-wheeled cab?—Because I have taken a growler.

Limoges.—No cooling draught. No ice. Nothing, except anathemas from Chivers, to which I pay not the slightest attention. On we go again, shrieking, whistling, and screaming without. Snoring within. "Sleep no more"—but I drop off about 5 A.M., and at 8·45 —just one tedious hour late—we arrive at Laqueuille, where we have to get into an omnibus to take us on to La Bourboule !

CHAPTER III.

NEARING LA BOURBOULE—OBJECTS OF INTEREST—EASY AND UNEASY
—ON THE ROAD—ARRIVAL—RECEPTION—FIRST IMPRESSIONS—
DIFFICULTIES.

ARRIVAL *at Laqueuille.* — Hot, dusty, dirty, weary, and not in the most angelic temper, either of us. Still, as Chivers sticks to it that but for me he would not have come to La Bourboule, I feel bound to make the best of everything for the sake of my own reputation as an adviser; besides, if we were both to succumb to melancholy, the very strongest waters would never do us any good.

So I begin, as cheerfully as possible, by pointing out that it seems to be a pretty-ish country.

"Pretty country be blowed!" growls Chivers, peevishly. "Why we can't see anything a hundred yards away from the station."

This is not strictly the fact, but I admit there is not much to be seen as yet.

"Wish to goodness I had brought a servant," exclaims the gentleman whose "name is Easy," adding, in despair, "I know I shall never get my things brushed. And then "—turning to me with an air of supreme dejection—"who's to unpack my confounded luggage?"

The Boots will do this, I suggest, or the Porter, or the Chambermaid. But he sneers at the mention of each one of these domestics separately, as if, though they might be good enough for the simple task of unpacking *my* luggage, or anybody else's, it would be utterly impossible for them, individually or collectively, to venture upon unpacking *his.* He speaks as if he were carrying dynamite. What *he* means by " unpacking" is not simply undoing the straps, but taking everything out, and laying each article, from the button-hook to the slippers, in its proper place. The fact is, that for seven or eight years of his life,—during which I had lost sight of Chivers, and it is only just at this moment it occurs to me that I *had* lost sight of him for so long,—Dudley Chivers held a supremely important post in the East, where he was waited on hand and foot by grovelling slaves, who, like sweet Alice in the song, "trembled with fear at his frown," and who "wept with delight" on the rare occasions when he deigned to "give them a smile." His every wish in that Oriental Palace was anticipated before it could be expressed, and, at first, before it could be even understood when it was expressed. And so, having been for eight years in the habit of clapping his hands as the signal for a hundred ebon slaves, more or less, to bring him his boot-jack, or his button-hook, or whatever it might be, it is no wonder that, in spite of his still affirming his name to be " Easy," he should be a trifle put out at having come on a long journey to a new place without any servant at all, and so find himself reduced to clapping his hands as much as he likes, without any immediate effect beyond that of making them very red and tender. Dudley Chivers is emphatically a man whom a Leader-writer in any paper would declare was "born to be a Ruler of Men." Quite so. Only he must have some one on whom to exercise this gift, and, at present, that one has been left behind.

" I shall *never* get anything done," he exclaims, wretchedly, and almost wrings his hands in the utter helplessness of his misery.

Pour le distraire un peu (as I have before remarked, one does drop into French as *Wegg* did into poetry), I direct his attention to the Station-master of Laqueuille, who is very much decorated, with about half-a-dozen silver medals hanging in a row on his breast, as if he had been convicted of uttering bad coin, and these were false specimens fixed on to him as a warning to others, just as a keeper hangs up stoats and weasels on a barn door, or a shop-keeper nails "duffer" halfpennies to his counter.

The appearance of this Station-master makes Chivers very angry. He says he hates officials,—specially decorated officials,—and, more especially, decorated French officials. He won't even condescend to obtain *renseignements* from him about the omnibus to La Bourboule. However, not much information is necessary, as here are the omnibuses all in a row, and, a little way off, some dusty, broken-down-looking two-horsed open flys, with very un-professional-looking drivers, dressed as ordinary peasants, in blouse and *casquette*.

The omnibuses have four horses each,—and such horses! They look as if another mile in any direction would shut them up alto-gether. The poor things hang their heads, as though ashamed of being seen by strangers in this miserable condition; and, if they cannot even "carry their heads," how they are going to carry their loads is a puzzle to any unprejudiced person, for the omni-buses are by this time choke-full inside and out, being apparently licensed to carry as many as can manage to seat themselves with out regard to personal comfort.

We debate whether it would not be better to take one of the open vehicles; but on being informed by a driver that his fare will be twenty francs, we determine to take out the money's worth of our railway ticket, which includes the 'bus.

Chivers is very angry. "Twenty francs!—a regular 'do!' just like 'em!" and he won't even make a bargain.

Ours is the last 'bus to start. We are on the roof of the omni-bus, on a seat of peculiarly ingenious open-work construction, warranted to keep the traveller awake, and prevent his falling over the side.

"What a beastly seat!" cries Chivers, wriggling. "What a wretched old omnibus! Ugh!" Then, as I really cannot help agreeing with him, though I still smile, and try by that simple means to put the best face possible on the matter, he goes on— "Did you ever see such horses! Poor devils! We shall never get to Bourboule. We're an hour or more late as it is! That's what comes of railways being under State control!" And for a few minutes he is buried in the deepest meditation, from which I would no more rouse him than I would venture to disturb the Poet's inspiration, for he is evidently revolving some tremendous scheme of European Railway Reform, which shall unite the Great Powers as one man, and be the inauguration of a new Golden Era for France, consolidating the Commercial alliance between the two countries, putting an end to State monopoly, and which, as an immediate practical but important result, will terminate the authority of the decorated Station-master at Laqueuille, and bring to an end for ever the wretched omnibus service between here and La Bourboule.

I am convinced that this is what is passing through Chivers' mind, but all he says, and herein he shows the caution of the true diplomatist, is, "What an infernally uncomfortable seat!"

Again I draw his attention to the prospect, which really begins to be very pretty, though not, at present, anything grand.

"I don't think it's a very friendly sort of country," he says. I subsequently find that the expression "friendly" goes for a good deal in Chivers's vocabulary, as he applies it, when in a better humour than at present, to everything and everybody.

"Ah! of course!" he exclaims, presently, jerking his head in the direction of the driver, "I thought so—I knew he'd do it! Just like 'em! Our stupid ass of a coachman has waited till all the others have gone on; and now he is sticking close behind, and we shall have all their dust. What a pig of an idiot! What a beastly drive!" And then comes the melancholy *refrain*, which is like the burden of an old song, "I wish to goodness I'd brought a servant; I shall never get my clothes brushed."

It is a dusty, up-hill journey. The sun has come out strong for the occasion, and the *rosses* (Anglicè, our *'osses*,—first symptom of an international *calembour*) have come out weak.

"Oh, the idiot may crack his whip, and shout as much as he darned pleases, but he'll never get 'em up this hill!" says Chivers, angrily.

This seems to be the universal opinion of the passengers outside, who begin to express great pity for the poor animals. But no one at present offers to lighten the load by descending. At last the horses come to a standstill. They don't stir, no more does anybody else.

"Dashed if I get down," says Chivers, The Easy, with a touch of the Oriental despot in his tone. "I didn't pay to walk. Let 'em get more horses, or stand us a fly."

However, half-a-dozen passengers do take to the road. I am too tired to walk. We have had no breakfast, and no refreshments except the abominably warm lemonade at Limoges, since dinner last night in Paris.

"Why," growls Chivers, "if one hadn't anything the matter

The First Example that catches my Eye of the Habitues who drink the Waters of La Bourboule.

with one, this infernal journey would make some sort of medical treatment absolutely necessary. Ugh! beastly!"

I point out the picturesqueness of the scenery,—it is for the most part a beautiful drive from Laqueuille to La Bourboule, with a good view of the Puy-de-Dôme itself in the far-off distance,—but he keeps his back turned on it. I point out to him the volcanic character of the rocks before him, but all he growls out is,—

"Bah! seen the same sort of thing in Devonshire. I believe La Bourboule's all a swindle. I believe the waters are doctored."

"And so will *you* be when you get there—at least you ought to be doctored, for you've got complaints enough," I retaliate, speak-

ing in defence of the beauties of Nature, and doing it as pleasantly
as possible in the circumstances. My chirpiness, however, is only
feeble just now, for hunger and heat and fatigue are beginning to
tell on my naturally fine constitution; and Chivers's complaints,
—I mean his persistent grumblings,—are really infectious. I am
positively beginning to disbelieve in La Bourboule. Where is it?
Up in the mountains? I don't see it. There are no snow-moun-
tains, too, as there are at Aix-les-Bains, and I am yielding to a
strong feeling of disappointment. I was told that one of the
advantages possessed by La Bourboule over any other sulphurous
and arsenical watering-place was, that it was high up and bracing.
Well, I don't see any town on a hill, except something on our left,
which we are leaving behind us, and the Puy-de-Dôme, kindly
pointed out to us by a fellow-traveller, in the distance. La
Bourboule at last!

"And a nice unfriendly sort of place it looks," says Chivers, in a
hopelessly dissatisfied tone, as we descend a steep incline, and enter
the village—or hamlet—or whatever it is, but certainly not a town.

On we go,—the horses pull themselves together, taking us with
them, and canter down-hill, with reins anyhow, bells ringing,
whip cracking, and driver shouting! Well may the driver be
triumphant! Well may he be proud of his gallant team, which
looks like a "forlorn hope" of horses, whose arrival here at all is
little less than a miracle. Hotel after hotel we pass,—all,
apparently, of a very second-rate character, and each one, as it
appears at this swift glance, styling itself "Grand Hôtel." We
are for stopping, but the Coachman and his wild horses won't hear
of it. They are all for urging on their wild career, and we can
only puzzle ourselves as to which is the hotel we ought to have
alighted at, and how we shall select our particular Grand Hotel
from all the other Grand Hôtels.

"I felt certain," says Chivers, sarcastically, "that your Grand
Hôtel was only a fifth-rate *auberge*. All right! Go on! Wish to
goodness I hadn't come to the infernal hole! And who's to unpack
for me?—who's to—— By the way," he suddenly exclaims,
"where *is* our luggage?"

I tell him that at Laqueuille I saw a *fourgon* being laden with
luggage, and among it ours. That it would reach this place some

time after us, was, I say to him, a "*fourgon* conclusion." But Chivers has no taste now for a specimen of what the *Calembour International Cie.* (Limited) can do, and the Oriental despot, whose name *was* Easy, can only unavailingly anathematise his own want of forethought, which has caused him so frequently to bewail "the *man* he left behind him." (Good notion for a song this. To be suggested to Chivers, and even sung to him, in happier moments.)

" What's all this crowd ? " he asks.

He may well ask. From every hotel, inn, and pension in the place,—and, apparently, it is a perfect rabbit-warren of hotels, inns, and pensions,—has trooped out a crowd of bare-headed *garçons* in white aprons, *commissionnaires* with labelled caps, chambermaids in costume, *gamins* of no occupation, touts, and porters. They are running after the omnibus like the gipsies on a Derby-Day after a drag, all chattering and shouting at once, and directly we stop, they form a *cordon* round the vehicle, so as not to let one of the *royageurs* escape, if they can help it. A *gendarme* in uniform stands by,—very much "posed" apparently, as he evidently has only come there by the merest accident, and as far as keeping order, or offering any assistance to the unlucky objects of this mobbing, he is perfectly helpless.

We elbow our way through the crowd, the Eastern despot carrying (much against his will) a heavy bag and an umbrella, with the air of a man who, if he liked, could suddenly pull out a warrant signed by all the Crowned Heads of Europe, and order off every one who dared to get in his way to instant execution. His autocratic manner is a little robbed of its impressiveness by his having to stop suddenly, put down the bag, and swear that he *never will* come out again without a servant ; at the same time regarding me reproachfully, to whom he attributes all his present misery, as much as to say that, as in his opinion I have brought him to this pass, I really ought to come forward and voluntarily relieve him of this intolerable burden. But my hands are full with a light waterproof, and a simple hand-bag that I can hang on one finger. My feeling is that Britons never *should* be slaves, unless somebody makes it very well worth their while.

"Where is your confounded Hotel ? " asks the Easy One, queru-

I

lously. I assure him that I don't know any more than he does, but I have the name of the proprietor in writing. I pronounce it aloud, and, as if by magic, a reply comes at once, " *C'est moi, Messieurs!* " from a respectably dressed, good-looking man, with a bronzed face, and a dark moustache, who is lifting his brown straw hat in the air by way of salutation. " Yes, perfectly—he has rooms for us in the Annexe. He will show them to us at once. Will we follow him?" We do.

"Come, this isn't so bad, eh?" I say to Chivers, who has assumed an air of gloomy power, quite out of sympathy with the anxious, hospitable, and cheery manner of our host.

" *Voilà!* " cries the *patron*, with some little distrust of our probable appreciation expressed in his countenance, as if he had expected persons of quite a different type to what we had turned out to be, and it had suddenly flashed across him that a couple of dark rooms in a back street, without any chance of a view, were not exactly the sort of thing we should have chosen for ourselves. We do *not* like them. Dudley Chivers won't give another look at them: in his character of Oriental Despot he refuses to listen to any explanation. " *Allons donc!* " he says, shortly and emphatically—" *Ça ne nous convient pas! C'est triste, sombre, mal aérée! faites-nous en voir encore d'autres. Allez!* "

Our host looks appealingly at me, but I endorse The Despot's verdict, and, finding that any attempt at compromise, in the way of a suggestion for temporarily rearranging the furniture, is only a waste of time, the landlord, rather disconcerted, takes us back to the hotel, and shows us a couple of rooms on the ground-floor, the only rooms at his disposition and ours. But they won't do; Chivers refuses them flatly; and, dreading a scene, for our landlord is evidently a very excitable person, and the blood is already rushing to his face, I try to soften matters, and to make the best of a bad bargain. Personally, for the sake of peace and quietness, I should yield; but the Easy One, appearing alternately as the stern, dogged English official, and then, as the Unspeakable Oriental Despot, is too much for the landlord, who is staggered into silence before his mysterious and impenetrable guest. Chivers condemns the apartments as if the entire wing of the hotel ought to be pulled down forthwith. "They're not healthy," he says, severely; "and, if you have nothing better than this, we'll go elsewhere."

I thought the attack on the sanitary state of the apartments would have aroused their proprietor, but it didn't; he only protests, more in sorrow than in anger, and informs us that he has nothing else to offer, but that if we will instal ourselves here, *provisoirement*, he will take care that we have the best apartments in a couple of days. No; The Despot is not to be cajoled. I, meanly I admit, follow his lead. No! I am not to be cajoled either. Seeing the innkeeper giving in, and that all chance of a difficulty, with perhaps a case in the local County Court, has blown over, I adopt Chivers's tone, and second all his resolutions with the utmost heartiness.

All this time I have been, as it were, playing *Jacques Strop* to Chivers's *Robert Macaire*. The landlord suddenly rouses himself, and makes an allusion to his loss. Chivers is down on him at once. "We can't take rooms that won't suit us," he replies, severely. The chance of a legal difficulty (with *Gendarmes*, *Avocats*, and *Juges de Paix* to follow) having again arisen, I go over, as it were, to the enemy, adopt the politest and most diplomatic (Chivers subsequently stigmatises it as "cringing") tone, and describe myself (omitting Chivers) as "*désolé*," adding "*c'est dommage, mais c'est une perte énorme pour nous, comme j'ai entendu parler tant de bonnes choses de votre admirable cuisine.*"

This sentence, being rather a long one, takes me some time to arrange and produce; but when the landlord has once grasped my meaning, he is disarmed. He bows, and he addresses *me* personally henceforth. "Your friend," he says, "is all very well—I do not care for *him*; but to lose *you*, *un Monsieur si distingué*, as a client, that is what distresses me so terribly." I am touched, and we are nearly weeping in each other's arms, when The Despot, at some paces off, and with a man to carry his bag, shouts out, brusquely, "Here! come on! Let's go and see the Doctor, and ask *him* what's the best hotel to go to,"—this is rather hard on the distressed proprietor, and I only hope he doesn't understand English,—"or else we shall lose a whole day, and shan't begin our *traitement* till to-morrow. We've got to have breakfast, too. Come on ! "

I obey. Having nothing further to say, I explain, in pantomime, to the landlord, that I am not my own master, and that I am torn away from his agreeable society, much against my will. I follow Chivers hurriedly, and am aware of the compassionate, almost contemptuous air of the worthy hotel-keeper, as he shrugs his shoulders, and turns to attend to his other customers, who are now thronging the door-step.

CHAPTER IV.

INTERVIEW WITH THE DOCTOR—DIAGNOSIS—NEW HOTEL.— JUST A-GOING TO BEGIN.

Étude de la langue Anglaise.

A COMMISSIONNAIRE conducts us to the residence of M. le Docteur Probité.

A pretty little house by the roadside, up-hill. Both of us, Chivers and myself, still unwashed, still grimy and dusty, fatigued, hungry, and thirsty,—two figures representing ourselves in disguise,—send in one card, Chivers's, with my name, in pencil, on it, and are then shown into the waiting-room. It is a quiet unpretentious apartment, with two portraits of medical men, signed by the originals, and presented to their " *cher confrère*, C. Probité," and a huge map of France, including a little bit of England, something of Germany, a morsel of Spain, and a trifle of Italy. Red lines marking the course of the railways to every part, convey the idea of Dr. **Probité** being summoned at any moment to any part of Europe, and hastily running his finger along the indications of rail on this map to see which is the shortest and quickest (but not necessarily the cheapest) *route.* Chivers is glancing at the journals on the table, and is beginning to be deeply interested in an article, when it suddenly occurs to him that he has read something like the special news contained in it before, and looking at the date, he finds it is *Le Monde Illustré* for *June*, 1882.

"Why do Dentists and Doctors always have these stupid old things on their tables?" asks the Gentleman whose name is Easy, and before I can provide a solution to his conundrum, the door is opened, and Dr. Probité himself appears.

Chivers, as the proprietor of the visiting-card, on which I had, so to speak, only figured as the "Co.," takes the initiative, and introduces me. Then I, in my turn, introduce Chivers. As an impromptu ceremony, got up and performed without any collusion whatever, the simple dignity of this presentation is most impressive.

In the Doctor's hand is Dudley Chivers's card, to which, after glancing sharply at us as if we weren't either of us at all like what he had expected—just the same idea as had evidently previously struck the hotel-keeper—he refers with the perplexed air of a man who has come upon two unnumbered figures in a Waxwork Exhibition, and is puzzling through the catalogue to discover who on earth they are. The unostentatious and effective ceremony above mentioned has somehow failed in its primary object. I should like to leave him alone, and see if he mistakes Chivers for me, and me for Chivers, but *politesse* forbids, and time is precious, so the Honourable Dudley, reproducing his courtliest drawing-room manner for the second time since we started, fifteen hours ago, and becoming his own polished self, in spite of all the outward grime and dust, and the inward pangs of hunger, steps forward, and, bowing gracefully, once more introduces me to the Doctor, whereupon I, following suit, smile sweetly, incline my back at an angle of twenty-five, and "beg to have the honour of presenting" —but before I have got it all well out in my stateliest French, the

Doctor, being a sharp man, with not much time to spare, has divined the situation, and with a marvellous command of logic, has deduced from the given premises, that, if I am not Dudley Chivers, Dudley Chivers must be the other fellow, and addresses him by his name accordingly.

Which will interview the Doctor first?

As I don't want to give too serious an aspect to my own case (for there's no knowing what a strange Doctor, and he a foreigner, might prescribe), I reply—

"*Permettez,—Je cède le pas à Monsieur Chivers.*" Somehow "Monsieur" and "Chivers" do not seem to go well together, and "*Je cède le pas à Chivers*" would have been *trop court.* Evidently I ought to have said *Monsieur Dudley Chivers,* or *Monsieur l'Honourable Dudley Chivers*—only, if the Doctor doesn't understand the title "honourable," he will either think I am chaffing, or, with his quick insight and logical French mind, he will deduce that we English bestow titles according to moral worth, and that Dudley Chivers is specially distinguished as a man of the most unblemished honour, *sans peur et sans reproche,* and that consequently, as I am *not* "the honourable," I may probably be the reverse.

However, the Doctor chooses Chivers as his partner, and, so to speak, waltzes off with him, while I am left meditating on what I should have said, and what I shall have to say when I have to state my symptoms clearly and intelligibly in French. The statement must be clear and intelligible, or the Doctor may treat me for something quite different. A wrong accent, the slip of a word, the substitution of a gender, might do it. After ten minutes' reflection, I determine to leave it to chance, and, to pass the time away, I resume my inspection of the Map of Dr. Probité's European Practice. By the way, I find one place in France—in the Auvergne district, I fancy, or rather more South—called "Le Gerbier de Joncs." I inspect it quite closely, and read it over half-a-dozen times, so as to make no mistake about it. It is in large type, and is evidently of importance, but whether as a *commune,* or a district, or a *département,* or other topographical division, I cannot make out. Suffice it that in the very heart of **France the family of Joncs has penetrated, and is commemorated**

on the map as "Le Gerbier de Jones." With a view to making
an antiquarian note, and publishing an interesting paper on the
subject of "Jones and Geography," I bestow on the name a yet
closer scrutiny, when I regret to find the "e" in what I thought
was "Jones" is only an imperfect impression of "c," and that,
therefore, the name is "*Le Gerbier de Jonc*," which is quite
another matter altogether, and so the result of my striking
antiquarian research is lost to the world.

Chivers takes a very long time to state his case. When a man
is talking about himself and his ailments, how the moments fly !
and how apt one is to forget the other fellow who is waiting for
us to finish, that he may have his turn ! How patients (every
one, except ourselves) will talk and chatter about nothing when
they go and see their Doctor ! It is too bad ! Ha ! he returns.
Chivers looks more cheerful : the interview has benefited him. *A
mon tour maintenant : c'est à nous deux, Monsieur*, as they say in a
Drama, an expression which is generally the commencement of a
row, but not in this instance.

Dr. Probité's social manner is charming, chatty, genial, and
pleasant—a man to be popular with everybody ; but his professional manner, when he once gets you inside his consulting-
room door, is something totally different. The geniality has
vanished ; he is the stern inquisitor, sharp, incisive, and decisive :
a manner that says plainly, "*Dis donc, pas de blague ! dîtes-moi
nettement, sans phrase, tout ce que vous avez.*"

At first, I am inclined to reply, *étant effrayé*, "*S'il vous plaît,
M'sieur le Docteur, je n'ai rien, je vous assure, je n'ai rien du tout*"—
then bolt out of the place, and never be seen again. But one
second's reflection tells me that I haven't been sent by the Faculty
(three Doctors, all friends of mine), to La Bourboule, merely to
tell a French practitioner that I've nothing the matter with me,
and run away again. No ! So, collecting my best and most
intelligible French, and, without any attempt at exaggeration,
which, I feel, with him, would only be an utter failure, I describe
my symptoms ; and I am really astonished to find, when treated
slowly, and cautiously, in this manner, how very few, and how
slight, they are. He listens attentively.

"*Bien ! très bien*," he says, when I've come to the end of it

"*Avancez un peu à la fenêtre—on y voit plus clair—et—tirez la langue, s'il vous plaît.*"

Now, though this operation is no novelty, yet somehow it is not what I had expected. That an English Doctor should ask me to show him my tongue, I should take as a matter of course. But, to have to show it to a foreigner . . . . well, I never knew before that my "insularity" was so strong, but I somehow feel that in my obeying his word of command,—for it is given in a sharp military tone,—I am lowering the British flag, surrendering my national independence, and putting myself at his mercy. Is there a more helpless spectacle than that of a man putting out his tongue to a Doctor? No. And if the patient be a Briton and the Doctor a Frenchman, then and there Waterloo is avenged,—terribly avenged. It seems so absurd too to have travelled hundreds of miles merely to put out my tongue. I could have put it out just as well at home. However, I comply, and do it, under silent protest. I open my mouth so wide, and he looks into it with such intense fierceness, that it seems at one moment as if he were going to put his hands together like a diver, jump right in, and down my throat.

"Now," says he, still in French, which delights me much, as it is excellent practice for me—(and, as a medical man, he knows what "excellent practice" means, only I can't put this *jeu-de-mots* into comprehensible, much less idiomatic French)—and is, *en effet*, a French lesson thrown in—*compris* in the consultation fee. "Now," says he, "I'll tell you exactly what's the matter with you." And he does so. No mincing the matter; plainly, straightforwardly, honestly. When he has summed it all up, the old once-popular nigger-phrase suddenly recurs to my mind, "Dat's what's de matter!"

I feel, from the expression on *his* face, that, through all my dust and dirt, I have, so to speak, shown my tongue in its true colours. *Il m'avait fait peur,*—and I tell him so.

"*C'est absolument nécessaire—il faut que je vous fasse peur,*" he replies, and sits down to write out the *traitement* to which, with such variations as he may choose from time to time to make, for twenty-one days I am to submit myself.

While he is writing, I make up my mind that I won't volunteer any further statements, that I am not bound to commit myself, and that I won't ask him any questions about diet and mode of living generally, as I am afraid he takes narrow views, and leans towards rigorous asceticism in his advice to patients.

He looks up from the paper, and says, brusquely, "*Je sais que vous fumez; il ne faut pas fumer.*"

"*Ne fumer pas!*" I exclaim, utterly taken aback.

"*Point du tout: et le café et les liqueurs sont également défendus.*"

"*Mais——*" I commence, but I get no further than "*voyons*" —"*Mais,—dites donc——*" and I am staggered.

I cannot realise it. "What! no smoke! So he died, and she very imprudently married the barber"—&c., for a new story of the Great Panjandrum. "What! no smoke! So he died——" No coffee! no Kümmel! What's the good of being abroad without smoking and coffee? And, hang it, if it's only to leave off smoking and coffee that I've travelled hundreds of miles, why I could have left them off just as well at home,—better in fact.

By the time he has finished writing out the *traitement* I have rallied my forces, and determine on making one last, but gallant, attempt.

"My dear Doctor," I say, still in French, and in the most dulcet and winning tone I can command, "I am accustomed to smoke every day, but very little—really very little—not three cigars "— I watch his face, but he isn't yielding, so I draw it still milder— "I may say, not *two* cigars "—he is still immovable, so I make one last reduction in my offer, with which I sincerely hope he'll close,—a *reductio ad absurdum*—"in fact, *as a rule,*"—(ahem!) "I *may* say," and on this occasion I *do* say it, looking him straight in the face, with an air of the most ingenuous candour and open confidence, "I only smoke *one* cigar a day—after dinner; and that,"—I put it humbly and plaintively—"it's not much, is it?"

"Better none at all," he replies, and for the moment I wonder whether he has heard the song, "*Not Much*—but it's better than nothing at all "—and has adapted it to his own sense of its fitness for present application.

"I only tell you," he says; "it's my duty to tell you." "England expects every man to do his duty" I have been well aware ever since I first heard "*The Death of Nelson*" sung, but that France was in the habit of making a similar demand of her Doctors I was unaware till now. Then this Medical Martyr to Duty concludes by giving me the encouraging example of the miserable end of a patient who wouldn't do what he was bid,—very much as, when I was a child, I used to be informed by my nurse how Master Don't-Care, who refused obedience to all legitimate authority, came to a bad end, and was eaten by bears, after which I never gave any buns to the bears at the Zoological, and always looked down into their yard, rather expecting to see some of the remains of the unfortunate "Master Don't-Care," in the shape of trouser buttons, or cap, lying about.

I am to a certain extent impressed by this story. I begin to see the errors of my way : and yet, after all, *I don't think he understands me.* By which (on analysing the basis of this opinion) I rather think I mean that I can't get him to treat me as I want to be treated. I can't get him to say, "Oh, do as you like, *voilà!* Drink the waters, take a bath a day, any time will do,—*massage* one day, *douche* another, *piscine* another, *pulverisation* when you like, drink what you fancy, eat what you like, *et amusez vous, mon enfant.*" And then to add, that, whatever may be the matter with me, I shall leave the place cured of it entirely.

But though I give him the lead, though I offer a compromise of one cigar and half a cup of coffee, and a quarter of a *liqueur*, he won't tumble to it. He has nailed his prescription to the mast, and he won't yield an inch. Stop . . . perhaps he treats everybody like this—perhaps there is one treatment for all, and he only looks on me as a body, and nothing more. My own medical men would treat me as a composite being, and would know my habits, my style of life, the necessities of my work, and could take all this into consideration when prescribing for me. But how can Dr. Probité know anything about me, the living, working, energising " Me," except as a body that walks into his room, and says, " I've got a pain in my jaw, in the left lobe of the ear, and an occasional shooting season in my great toe " ? Of course not : and so, oughtn't I,—I mean wouldn't it be fair towards him, as a Doctor, were I to take two chairs, and advancing towards the footlights (so to speak), request him to take one, while I, seating myself in the other, commence thus : " Doctor, I will tell you the story of my life. 'Tis now some twenty years ago, this very day, when," &c.

But, on second thoughts, I will defer this till my next visit, as, after all, isn't it better that a Doctor, on only seeing you once, should tell you everything that you feel instinctively to be true about yourself, should diagnose your case in two two's, and should say to you plainly, " Do this, and you're certain to be cured : don't do it, if you like,—only, in that case, why take all the trouble to

" His name's Easy."   Mine isn't.

come here and consult *me ?*" than that he should follow suit to your lead, return cigars when you lead tobacco, and give you *carte blanche* to do as you please ?

The *séance* being over, we return to Chivers, and both together take leave of Dr. Probité.

Outside, the Oriental Despot, whose name is anything but " Easy" at having been kept waiting, wants to know what the deuce I've been so long about, and then we compare *traitements*, and are annoyed to find that they are pretty much the same.

The Despot now proposes that we shall go to another hotel, close at hand, and see what rooms we can get ; that then we make ourselves tidy and clean, then breakfast, and that two hours after we take our first bath, and commence our "treatment" in earnest.

This is a good programme, and I agree. "Whatever you like," I say, "will suit me."

"My dear fellow," returns the Despot, pleasantly, "my name's Easy." I notice that this is always the title he assumes when nobody contradicts him, and when he gets everything entirely his own way. On such occasions, I mean when The Despot announces his appellation as "Easy," I know no more charming and agreeable companion than Dudley Chivers.

We select a hotel, pleasantly situated, with the short title of *Hôtel F. Sonnetton et des Anguilles Mécaniques.* The *patron* has some difficulty in suiting us. There is a room *à deux lits* in front, and a small bedroom round the corner. Both have good views.

The price of one is, of course, more than that of the other, but this is unimportant where invalids are concerned. One thing *va sans dire,* deeply as we are attached to each other, we *won't* share the *chambre à deux lits.* I have had one experience of Chivers in the train at night, and perhaps *I* have been asleep while *he* was awake, which may account for . . . . but in any case emphatically "*No!*"

"I have a lot of papers and books, and shall want to do some work," I observe, looking round the big room, and noting its capabilities.

"I like this room," says Chivers, going to the window, "it has a nice view. But my name is Easy."

"The small room," I tell him, "is a capital one. In fact," I add, "I am not sure if it isn't, really, better than this."

I have evidently overdone it by praise, and missed my mark, as Chivers closes with what he chooses to interpret as my offer, and replies,—"Well, *you* have the small room; I don't mind. My name's Easy. Here!"—to Porter—"bring in my luggage."

And before I have time to reconsider, Chivers has got his luggage deposited, has told the man to take my portmanteau to the small room, and while I am consoling myself with the thought that he will have to pay double for the accommodation, he has bargained with the landlord, and obtained a moderate abatement.

We are now settled, and within three hours more we shall have fairly commenced our serious *traitement* at La Bourboule.

CHAPTER V.

STARTING—CELLS—TREATMENT—COSTUME—PULVERISATION—
ANALYSIS.

"Gargarisme."

HAVING settled what is the matter, we (Chivers and myself) commence our *traitement*.

Chivers still doesn't entirely believe in it. Hopes for the best. He is, however, far better inclined towards everything than he was at first, and, while standing on one of the bridges, and surveying the scene, he goes so far as to admit that "it seems to be a friendly little country;" which, coming from him, is a great tribute to the local beauties of nature.

Dr. Probité has given me a letter of introduction to the Director of the Baths, who receives me with the utmost politeness, and puts me *au courant* with all the ways of the place.

We take our ticket. Being offered my choice of hours, I have to elect either 5·30 A.M. for my bath, or 9·30, or the afternoon 3·30.

I take 9·30, and a "*bain locale*," consisting of "pulverisation" at 9, to begin with. Chivers takes 3·30. But there being two baths vacant at the present moment, we commence at once, as the course is for twenty-one days, and we shall have saved a day by beginning immediately; "and then," says Chivers, astutely, "there will only be twenty days to work out." Committed, with severe treatment, for twenty-one days—that is our sentence.

The construction of the baths is quite different from that of the baths of Aix-les-Bains and Aix-la-Chapelle, where they are of a depth and size that you can stand upright in them, and very nearly have room to swim. Here it is an ordinary cell (quite in keeping with the twenty-one days' sentence), with a metal bath in it, somewhat of the shape of a boat that a child makes out of a newspaper, only without the peak in the middle. The accompanying sketch gives a fair idea of one of the *Cellules de Bain à la Bourboule*.

The Établissement des Bains is a very fine place, with three domes to it (out of compliment to the department where it is situated, the Puys de Dôme), bearing a strong family resemblance to those which are the crown and glory of the edifice in Trafalgar Square. From a distance the Établissement might be taken for a Cathedral; coming nearer, the traveller might possibly set it down as a *caserne*, or, if he were of a sporting turn, he would come to the

AT THE ETABLISSEMENT.

**Maître de Service, or Clerk of the Course (*traitement*), entering
the names of the Starters.**

conclusion that it was a pretty big training stable; and, having come quite close, he would feel certain that it must be an International Exhibition of some sort, until he found himself inside, and saw the industry practised there. No mistake as to what it is when you're once within. Notices to *Baigneurs* and *Baigneuses* everywhere: people drinking at a fountain; people waiting their turn for a bath; some coming, others going; some in corners, gargling; others disappearing into mysterious departments labelled " Pulverisation " and " Massage." The *Maître de Service, décoré*, serious, but courtly, at a table, entering names, and disposing of tickets. Everything done with military punctuality. You must be there exactly to your time, or you're out of it for the day, unless chance favours you. If you're a minute or so late, the *Maître de Service* shakes his head reprovingly at you; if five minutes late, he remonstrates with you on your laxity; if later than that, it is only by cringing and obsequious politeness that you can obtain your ticket. One hour is allowed you for a bath, undressing, drying, and redressing included. If you occupy more

Cell for the Bather at La Bourboule.

time than this, you must pay extra for it. A *Baigneur* can have a *Bain de luxe*, which consists of dressing-room, a bath-room, and, I believe, extra towels, and extra time. Some invalids are carried in sedan chairs to and fro; but these *chaises à porteurs* are not so *coquettes* as at Aix-les-Bains; for Aix is patronised largely by triflers who go there *pour s'amuser et pour se distraire:* but there's nothing of that sort *here*. La Bourboule is a *Station Thermale sérieuse*, and we are all very much in earnest. For amusements and distractions you may at first yearn, but after a while the patient succumbs to fate, and abandons all hope of amusing himself, content to take life listlessly so long as he takes his baths and waters regularly. A lotos-eater is a joker to a drinker of the waters of La Bourboule.

At La Bourboule.—Business is business here, and the Treatment is everything. At 6 A.M. I rise, and take my *chocolat complet.* Lovely air, fresh, coldish, and the mist disappearing over the tops of the mountains. Then I write till just on nine, when it is *l'heure du bain et je me rends à l'Établissement*, when I respectfully salute the *Maître de Service* at his desk, obtain my ticket for "pulverisation," and off I go to be "pulverised."

To undergo this, you have to put on a white robe, a napkin round your throat, as if you were going to be shaved, and then a waterproof "*bavette*," or baby's bib. Thus attired, you are shown

"PULVERISATION"—IS VEXATION.
Motto.—" Let us spray."

into a chamber fitted up with a series of little marble washing-places, in front of which are seated several persons arrayed similarly to yourself, all, apparently, waiting to be shampoo'd. It looks at first sight like a haircutter's establishment full of customers, but with no one to attend upon them. At the second glance, however, you see that each little marble division, which you had mistaken for shampooing places, but which you now see more nearly resemble the compartments in marble, and in minia-ture, of a telegraph-office, is fitted up with a small apparatus not unlike a microscope, only that as the persons seated at each marble desk is applying not his eye but his mouth to the apparatus, it suddenly occurs to the stranger that he is in a room full of lunatics who have gone mad about telephones, and they are being kept quiet by pretending to send messages. They are not lunatics, of course; and the apparatus is not telephonic, but is a small machine for shooting out a fine strong spray into the mouth and down the throat, or wherever you have to attack the local suffering. The sketches will convey some idea of the costume and the operation. Besides this, there is " inhalation," and there are "*bains locaux* " for all parts. There is the nose-bath, the ear-bath, eye-bath, thumb-bath, big-toe-bath, hand-bath, &c., &c. So that you can give any individual member of your corporation a dose of it without inconveniencing the others—which is a very just and proper arrangement, and one that might be well observed in various other corporate bodies.

For the drinking you go to the Fountain. You purchase your own glass, which is numbered and reserved for your own private use, and you take half a glass of the water of La Bourboule just ten minutes before the two principal meals. Those who do not believe in the merits of the *fontaine de La Bourboule* will consider all the accounts of the cures effected by these waters as merely new editions of *La Fontaine's Fables.* The motto of La Bourboule is " *Don't* leave Well alone."

This is not a Priest of some strange Rite in sacrificial vestments, but an invalid at La Bourboule, arrayed for Pulverisation."

For my part I hear so much, and have such convincing proofs of their efficacy—though at the early stage of the "*traitement*" I can't say I recognize any peculiar benefit, other than would be the natural result of living in the very purest air, rising early, going to bed early, getting sufficient exercise and plenty of rest, changing diet and habits of living, and giving up everything that would be likely to do one any harm— that I am hoping for the most beneficial results. So is Chivers. He eyes me suspiciously in the morning, when he comes down to drink his glass of water, as if I had taken some unfair advantage of him in the night, and had got ahead of him in point of health. He is not satisfied with himself until I have positively assured him that I don't feel any better myself, rather the contrary. " I don't know what the deuce the waters are doing to *me*," says Chivers, with the air of a man who has made an investment about which he begins to be a little uncertain ; " I don't feel so well. I'm languid, I'm weak." Then, turning to me reproachfully, he says, " *You* don't look weak ; *you're* not languid." He seems to resent this apparent want of sympathy on my part so much that I hasten to assure him that I *do* feel languid, that I *am* weak, and that I too am not satisfied with results so far. This pleases him, and for a time he is content. Given this "*traitement*," and where do the waters come in ? But

A Sweet Girl Gargler.

as we argue it out, Chivers and myself, if we hadn't come here we couldn't in London have gone in for the *traitement* seriously, and to the exclusion of every other consideration except that of health.

The various books on the subject give the analysis of these waters. I venture on giving my own idea of the *Composition de l'eau de La Bourboule : et la voici :—*

ANALYSE (TRÈS) ÉLÉMENTAIRE.

	Gr.
L'eau fraîche	. 5·678910
L'eau chaude	6·789
L'eau arseniqué (quand même)	. 4·1234
L'eau médicamentée de potass, soude, magnésie, acide sili-cique, et beaucoup d'autres choses au choix . . . }	10·123
Espérance	. 200·001
Foi	Indices forts
Confiance entière	Traces
Total	La Guérison

I think, when considered carefully, the above will be admitted, on all hands, to be a very fair analysis. Of course, it only applies to a first visit. If this is a success, then the grains of "*espérance*" are enormously increased, and "*foi*" and "*confiance entière*" are complemented to almost absolute certainty by "*expérience.*" "*Experientia dose it*"—and then you have no doubt as to the result of the treatment.

"Taking the Chair" at La Bourboule.

CHAPTER VI.

OUR DISTRACTIONS—THEATRE—GAMBLING—THE LEGITIMATE—GAIETY
AND GUIGNOL—CRITICISM—SUGGESTION—AFTER THE PLAY—
MELANCHOLY—SERIOUS WORK.

**One of the Water Nymphs
of La Bourboule.**

WE DINE at six, mixing our *ordinaire* with *eau de Vals*, having previously commenced with half a glass of the native arsenical waters as a *hors d'œuvre*, though if there be anything in the term, it is the dinner itself that is the *hors d'œuvre*, while the water-consuming is the *œuvre* itself. Cigars, coffee, and the comforting *liqueur* being interdicted during the treatment—I mean the special treatment to which Dudley Chivers and myself are patiently submitting, *and counting the days*—we have nothing to do but to stroll out, look at other people smoking, and congratulate ourselves on our almost superhuman perseverance in not yielding to the temptation of tobacco, and mocha, and kümmel, or other *liqueur*, which have, up to now, been a necessity of life. I protest that I haven't even brought my cigarette-case down from my room, lest the fact of having it in my pocket should induce me to give in just for once.

" Once can't matter," says Chivers, producing a silver cigarette-case, and regarding it fondly.

"No," I reply, doubtfully, "I don't suppose it can matter much."

" ' Not much,' " says Chivers, quoting the great Macdermott's song. Whereupon we both chant,—" But it's better than nothing at all," and then laugh. Still laughing, and, in moment of abstraction, Chivers opens the case, takes out a cigarette, and, after a short pause, lights it.

After all, a small cigarette is *not* a cigar, and it's only just the flavour of tobacco I want. If he hasn't got one to spare, so much the better. He has, however, and in another minute I am smoking and thoroughly enjoying it. Then we listen to the band outside one of the Casinos. At eight this band is summoned by a bell, to go inside the Theatre. We don't feel inclined for the Theatre, having assisted at a performance on the previous night, when, on a temporary stage, about the size of one that Mr. May or Mr. Nathan would bring with him and set up in a smallish back drawing-room, there we witnessed some indifferent acting, but heard some very fair singing, under difficulties created by the zealous, but slightly incorrect, musicians in the orchestra. On this occasion, Chivers, who had insisted on going in because they were playing some French Operetta that he had not heard since he was seven years old, was so affected by the music, or the heat, or the *traitement*, that, as soon as the piece had fairly started, and he had nodded to me his approbation of the commencement, he went fast asleep in his seat, and presently rivalled the violoncello in accompanying the performers. On my nudging him sharply, he awoke, with a start, looked round benignly, and forthwith began to hum and keep time with his stick, until sleep once more overtook him, and again his head fell on his breast, and again he started a harmonic match in which his nasal organ competed vigorously with the double bass, and won easily. When it was all over, he awoke, applauded vehemently, and as we left the house, declared that "it was really very well done," and that "he wouldn't have missed it for anything." Then he yawned, said "Good night," and went straight up to bed. This evening, therefore, not being inclined for the Theatre, we patronise the *petits chevaux*, which is being played out-of-doors, under the verandah of the Casino, and stake our money freely up to four francs, when, finding luck against us, we retire.

It is just 8·15. "The night is yet young!" we exclaim, gaily, as we eye the rather solemn promenaders, who are dividing their attention between *les petits chevaux* and another gambling table, where *La Mascotte* attracts a considerable crowd, the business done being chiefly in coppers. Here we watch the game, and see one pale and haggard man go in a regular plumper with a whole franc, which he throws down in a reckless manner on the table, and loses. He smiles defiantly, but returns to his former stake of a penny, and I hope won his money. There is a cadaverous, hungry-looking woman by his side, watching him eagerly; she is deeply interested in the fate of the *sou* he has just ventured,— and at this we leave them. But if there had been thousands on the turn of the machine; and if it had been *Trente-et-Quarante* or *Roulette* at Monaco, the excitement could not have been greater than at this Penny Pandemonium.

It is just 8·30. There is nothing to do out-of-doors, as we don't drink or smoke, and as walking is fatiguing. The music has retired, having been summoned by a bell to come inside the Theatre and be the orchestra; and so it suddenly occurs to me that during the day I have seen "Guignol" advertised at the other Casino, in the Parc Fenestre; and it stated that at Guignol's show, which he has set up under a tent, there would be performed a *féérie* called *Le Fils de Satan*, and a "burlesque drama" entitled *Roméo et Juliette.* This latter was to commence about 8·30. They had apparently taken a leaf out of the Gaiety programme at Guignol's, and Mr. John Hollingshead's sacred lamp was to illuminate the darkness of La Bourboule. Guignol set serious critics at defiance when he selected *Romeo and Juliet* as his subject for a Three-Act Burlesque.

We stroll up. We see the light from Guignol's tent. All else is deserted, but here, within and without, there is a crowd,—a dishonest crowd too outside, as they are trying to peep through the curtains, and see what's going on, without paying for the privilege. In this they are perpetually being baulked by a tall young man, of quiet exterior, with a remarkably quick eye, who is down upon them directly he sees the curtain of the tent moving surreptitiously, which occurs about every ten minutes. We pay our forty centimes a piece, and enter. It is full. We can only get seats at the back, just against the curtain that separates us from the troublesome amateurs outside, whose unprincipled curiosity is giving the afore-mentioned sharp-eyed young man so much trouble and anxiety.

There is a considerable delay,—perhaps the dolls are not dressed, or one of them has arrived late,—and considerable excitement among the audience,—so much so, indeed, that Dudley Chivers confides to me that he thinks "it must be a *première*," in which opinion he is subsequently confirmed by the freshness of the dolls' make-up, the smartness of their costumes, the occasional halts in the dialogue, and the somewhat undecided "business" in which the leading doll (Guignol himself, by the way, who is playing *Romeo*) indulges. But Guignol, being the popular favourite, can take liberties with his audience, and, as he has a very funny part, they shout at all his jokes, and all his lines "go" wonderfully. Chivers (whose "name is always Easy") is annoyed at the Curtain being down too long, and commences a vigorous protest with his stick on the *banc* in front of us. This process,—consisting of three raps, given one after the other in strict time, is taken up by the whole audience, who—the children being especially enthusiastic—take the measure at four in a bar, led always by Chivers—one, two, three, rest; one, two, three, rest—with the utmost precision. Then a bell rings, showing that Guignol has yielded, whereupon there is loud "Oh"-ing from everybody, led by Chivers, and, on the bell ringing again, considerable applause,—still "personally conducted" by Chivers,—which is increased when the Curtain rises, and discovers the exterior of *Capulet's* house, with gardens. Whereupon Chivers, the Eastern Despot of the iron will, turns towards me, and smiles triumphantly.

Judging the performance from a purely critical point of view, I should say that Guignol gave, with spirit and effect, his peculiar reading of *Romeo*. Even from a burlesque point of view, I should be inclined to question the correctness of Guignol's costume, until I have some unexceptionable authority for *Romeo* being attired in a square-cut plum-coloured coat—a sort of French *avocat's* cap, and a brown wig with a long pig-tail. Such a dress was evidently not intended as a caricature of anything in particular, and I rather fancy, judging from subsequent visits, that, when no special costume had been provided, Guignol, following Garrick's example of playing *Macbeth* in a Court-suit of the period, appeared in whatever costume he happened to be arrayed in at the moment. This primitive simplicity, I confess, delighted me. *Juliette* displayed a grace which is rarely met with, specially in her curtseys and her exits; while the scene in which she is whacked by her

father, and returns a box on the ear with interest, was worthy of
the best traditions of a Siddons or a Faucit.

The *Nurse* and the *Friar* were exceptionally good, showing an
intelligent appreciation of the text, which, by the way, is more
than I can say for myself, as, whenever Guignol appeared, he had
so many puns (his lines fell in pleasant places, and were stuffed
full of them), that, after a vain attempt to follow them seriously,
I gave up the *calembours* as a hopeless job,—but, to escape detec-

GUIGNOL'S THEATRE. NEW SCENE FROM
"ROMEO AND JULIET."

Guignol (as Romeo, addressing Juliet). "Ma Colombe! Je t'adore!"

tion, I hypocritically laughed rather louder than anybody else, and
only twice in the wrong place,—when, however, my lead was immediately followed by several people, and I also noticed that the
Ladies on my right and left turned away and blushed. What *had*
I laughed at? I asked Chivers, who had been laughing heartily,
what was the joke ; but as he pretended to be so deeply interested
in the performance as to be unable to answer my question, I concluded that he knew just as much about it as I did. From this
moment I begin to distrust Chivers as a perfect master of the
French language— that is, I doubt his being well up in *calembours*.
There is a Friar in the original piece, who comes in to tell his *con-*

frère, Laurence, the bad news about everything having gone wrong ;
in Guignol's burlesque version *Friar Laurence* loses his temper,
and belabours the unfortunate Friar all round the stage, and off
it, causing him to express himself feebly, but shrilly, in familiar
ecclesiastical Latin, finishing with "Amen!" after which he was
immediately knocked on the head, and finally disposed of. As
Friar Laurence was in black, and *Friar John* in white, this scene
might be taken as an illustration of the traditional rivalry between
the Black and White Religious Orders. Anyhow, the "treatment"

FRIAR LAURENCE, ONE OF THE BLACK FRIARS, DISPOSES OF
FRIAR JOHN OF THE WHITE FRIARS.

Friar John (crying). "A-men! A-a-men!"
Friar Laurence (unfeelingly). "Ainsi soit-il!"
[*Gives him one on the nob, and* **Friar John** *disappears.*

that *Friar John* received at Guignol's was found to be immensely
diverting by a crowded audience, whether historically or histrioni-
cally accurate being a matter of the very smallest importance.

Brilliantly and expensively as the piece at Guignol's was
"mounted," and excellent as was the general performance, yet
truthful criticism compels me to state that there were evident
signs of either insufficient rehearsal or indifferent stage-manage-
ment. No doubt in a night or two, I say to Chivers, they will be
more perfect. The piece, however, was well received, and rapturously applauded by an enthusiastic audience, who, at the end,

joined Guignol and his Company in a chorus expressive of thorough satisfaction.

What a cheerful finish! How genial if universally adopted! Suppose Mr. Henry Irving stepping forward at the end of *Much Ado* or *Twelfth Night*, or *Hamlet*, or anything, and singing or chanting—

> Ladies and Gentlemen, now we've done,
> We hope we *have* pleased everyone ;
> So give us your hands, and the moment seize
> To start a chorus, if you please.
> > Ri tooral looral looral looral
> > Tiddy fol looral
> > Ri tol looral li-do !

Actors and Audience (rising in their seats all over the house, and beating time with their hands while singing heartily). Ri tooral looral, &c.

Loud applause. Mr. Henry Irving *bows.* *Curtain.*

Well—why not? Isn't Guignol's plan Shakspeare's, after all? How does *Twelfth Night* end? With a song by the Clown. Isn't there to one of his plays an Epilogue "spoken by a dancer"? How about " Rumour painted full of tongues"? The fact is, the song at the close of every performance in Shakspeare's time was no innovation ; and probably the audience, who were both on and off the stage, joined in chorus as *chez* Guignol, and went away delighted with themselves and the entertainment. For what puts a set of people in better humour with themselves and everybody than joining in a chorus, be it "*Auld Lang Syne*" or "*He's a Jolly Good Fellow !*" or "*With our tol de rol tooral looral !*" or any other recognized *refrain* of English minstrelsy? Would there be so many harsh criticisms next day if critics were only to join in a final chorus with the rest of the audience on a first night? Wouldn't they all go away delighted? But, by the way, why doesn't Mr. Cremer, or some other purveyor of dolls, start a series of these Guignol Shows for Home amusement? What an admirable way of inculcating Shakspeare in the nursery ! A Doll's Edition of the most popular of Shakspeare's plays ; a condensed acting edition, a sort of Punch Show, with the chief scenes painted to let down and draw up like blinds, and to each set a box of dolls representing all the characters of the play. Each child could work two or more dolls and learn their parts. Capital hint for a Crystal Palace Show at Christmas. *Vive* Guignol !

Guignol's show being over, Chivers and myself find that we have reached the hour of 9·30. *Que faire ?* No smoking, no drinking. Yet we are thirsty after Guignol, and, from ancient habit, we feel we must have something in the way of refreshment, on returning from the Theatre.

" Why can't we bathe now, and go on with the cure," grumbles Chivers, " instead of wasting our time ? "

I have no answer for him. I agree with him—I wish he could always be progressing. But I am thirsty, and I propose convivially that, ere we go to bed, we should sit down in the hall of the hotel, we two gay dogs, and crack a bottle of mineral waters between us.

We agree to this—and do so.

It is a melancholy sight. We two—*viveurs*—in that hall alone, at 9·30 P.M., having just returned from witnessing a sort of Punch-and-Judy Show, sitting at a table, with two tumblers, and a bottle of *Eau de Vals.* We try to be jolly, but it won't do. . . . We give it up . . . and, having "cracked the bottle," however, we mournfully ascend the stairs together, and, as we part on the landing for the night, we say,—

" Only nineteen more days of this, and then we go home."

We shake our heads dismally, and glide down the dark passages, each going hopelessly, miserably, to his cheerless couch.

Thus ends one of our merry nights when we go in for the distractions provided by the public enterprise of La Bourboule.

CHAPTER VII.

TAKING   PLEASURE   SADLY — CONTRIBUTION   TO   NEW   FRENCH
GRAMMAR—OUR   POLICE—ARRIVAL   OF   THE   SERPENT—OUR
FIRST FALL.

M. Tirard, the French Minister of Finance, honouring a draught.

YES, La Bourboule is decidedly *une Station Thermale très sérieuse.* If you come to be cured, La Bourboule must be endured. But no one stops here for pleasure.

M. Tirard, the French Minister of Finance, is here. He takes his waters seriously, and rides with determined regularity. Otherwise he is never seen amusing himself, though I fancy I once caught a glimpse of him studying the doctrine of chances at *les petits chevaux,* but it was only for a second, and as his face was almost hidden entirely in a wrapper, I may have been mistaken.

No — *à La Bourboule soyez Bourboulais* — I should say "*quand on est à La Bourboule, on bourboule.*" I do not know whether there is a French verb "*bourbouler*"—but, if not, I here invent it, patent it, say it, write it, and present it with my compliments to the French Academy. It is *not* an irregular verb; nothing can be irregular that is connected with La Bourboule. It is a verb active.

INFINITIVE.

PRESENT.	PAST.
Bourbouler—to go through the treatment, and do all that is to be done at La Bourboule.	*Avoir bourboulé*—to have gone through the treatment at La Bourboule.

INDICATIVE.

PRESENT.	PAST.
Je bourboule—I am going through the, &c., &c.	*J'ai bourboulé* — I have gone through the, &c., &c.

And so on.

The "Conditional" must depend on the patient's health and temper. The "Imperative" is the Professional or "Medical Mood."

SUBJUNCTIVE (IMPERFECT).—*Que je bourboulasse*—that I might go through the treatment, &c. (This is the expression of a fervent hope ; or the consideration of a Doctor's doubtful permission : *il avait dit que je bourboulasse*).

On Sunday evening the place is quite *en fête*. But the Eastern Despot, whose name is no longer Easy, and myself have no right to be *en fête*. We feel that we are robbing the Casino by occupying a table when we can neither drink nor smoke.

For us even *La Mascotte, c'est-à-dire le jeu au Pandemonium à un sou la mise*, with its *Baigneuse qui perds*, its *Chinois qui gagne*, offers us no enticement, and the proximity of *les petits chevaux, série jaune ou verte, courses à un et à deux francs*, does not make our hearts beat one throb the faster, nor set the blood coursing through our veins.

I hear of complaints being made, at other places, against the patronage extended to the *petits chevaux*, and of indignant questions (probably put by losers) as to why the police do not suppress the game of the Little Horses. Here, at La Bourboule, not only does the game attract everybody, but it is even regularly patronised by our solitary representative of the police, a jovial-looking Gendarme, who comes out on duty in full uniform, and is generally accompanied by his admiring wife and family, to the youngest of whom (not the baby) he gives francs to play for him ; and I notice that the lad, who can scarcely reach up to the table, is usually a winner, and honestly hands back the gains to his papa, who smiles on his spouse and pockets the francs with an air of considerable satisfaction.

Suddenly the situation is changed. Our Evil Genius, in the form of Tom Spicer, has arrived. Chivers and myself are obeying the Doctor's orders steadily, but Tom Spicer only considers his Doctor as a guide to the manners and customs of La Bourboule. He breakfasts with us, and—confound him! he takes everything and anything! So he does at dinner. Hitherto, on the appearance of a beautiful melon, or a nice fresh salad, Chivers and myself have regarded one another mournfully, but have felt that we were doing our duty in ordering the waiter at once to *enlever cette chose,—pas de ça.* But Spicer exclaims, " What! not take melon ? My dear boy, the finest thing in the world for you !" And he consumes two slices before we have got over our fit of astonishment. We almost expect a sudden and awful punishment upon him for his rashness. Not a bit of it; he beams upon us cheerfully, pushes away his plate, and drinks off a bumper of the generous *vin rouge.* Still nothing happens to him, and we breathe again.

" But the Doctor !" we commence.

" Doctor be ——" but here comes in a dish of fish, with butter sauce, which puts us on common ground again.

Then there is a *filet de bœuf,* and again we are with him. Then there is *jambon sauce japonaise,* and we daren't.

" *Comment!* " he exclaims, " *pas de jambon !*" And before we have time to shake our heads wearily, he has helped himself freely, and is enjoying it.

Once more we watch him with painful interest, and again nothing happens. A bowl of *haricots verts au beurre* appears, and we are all " on in this scene."

Then the *entremets.* " *Comment !* " he again exclaims, as we refuse slices of open jam-tart—" *pas de pâtisserie !* It's the most wholesome thing in the world, and a *spécialité* here."

Chivers regards me curiously, and then he eyes the jam-tart affectionately.

" Is it good ?" he inquires, hesitatingly, of Spicer.

"*Très bon*—first-rate!" replies Spicer, who likes mixing his English—"*ça ne vous fera mal à la tête, et vous en avalez un tonneau.*"

One cloud of mistrust crosses Chivers's face,—if his "name is Easy" *now*, will it be afterwards?—one second of lingering conscientiousness, one brief thought of the past, one doubt of the future, one wistful glance at the pastry, and then—all is over—the toothsome slice is on his plate, and the next instant in his mouth. Suddenly he has brightened up; and with the air of a man determined to be satisfied with the rash step he has taken let the consequences be what they may, he exclaims, nodding to Spicer,

"You *are* right. It is deuced good!"

Then he turns to me, as Eve might have turned to Adam, and says, persuasively, "Have a bit. Do!" adding, *d'une gaïeté folle*, which cannot deceive *me*, "*La conserve est tirée, mangez-la.*"

No. I refuse resolutely.

I am sorry for him. I regret his backsliding from the paths of virtue. Spicer, of course, takes dessert, cheese, and *petits gâteaux*. Then we rise from table, and Spicer is again going to have his cigar and coffee.

"*En aurez-vous un?*" he says, tendering me his case.

"*Merci non*," I reply, in excellent French.

I cease to be Adamite, and am once more adamantine.

"Does your regular Doctor in Town forbid it?" asks Spicer, carelessly, as he lights up.

"No," I answer. "None of my Doctors have ever forbidden it in moderation."

Spicer makes no observation on this, but smiles sarcastically. At once a light breaks in on me. Yes—I see his drift—of course—if none of what he calls my "regular Doctors," who know me, have ever forbidden it, why should I have such a great regard for the *ordonnance* of a Doctor who doesn't know me, and who by comparison is only "an irregular Doctor" who has only seen me four days ago, for the first time in his life? Clearly absurd. Still, if he should be right and the others wrong? If they didn't like to tell me, and sent me here to learn the truth? Oh, no! that's impossible.

So. . . . I'll . . . . well—I'll just smoke a little bit of cigarette to-night, and to-morrow, *perhaps*, I'll try a cigar.

"I should take a cigar," says Spicer. "Cigarettes are injurious."

Yes; I *have* heard that cigarettes are injurious. Therefore, in for a penny in for a pound—in for one cigar in for a pound of 'em—and I smoke a cigar.

Chivers appears with a cigarette—a large one.

"Hallo!" he exclaims. "What, *you* smoking! Oh!!"

Our Local Gendarme on Duty.

CHAPTER VIII.

MORE BACKSLIDING—THE SERPENT AT LA BOURBOULE—WE DON'T
"DECLINE," AND DO "FALL"—NERVOUS ANTICIPATIONS—
RESULTS.

THE Mephistophelian Spicer has done it. He is the Serpent who beguiles us into making a *détour* into flowery paths away from the narrow way of obedience to Doctor's orders. He insinuates distrust of the *traitement* while artfully extolling the virtues of the waters of La Bourboule.

His argument is, "It is absurd to lower yourself." In one sense we admit it is worse than absurd, it is absolutely wrong. But Spicer is serious and he won't be put off. He says, "Take the waters by all means, but don't suddenly give up everything. Look at the people who are at the Casino here. They'll all be drinking coffee and *liqueurs*, and smoking. Well, aren't they all invalids, and probably invalids of some standing, who have been here before, and know the place?"

I venture to remark that I've seen very few taking coffee and smoking.

His reply is, "That's because you've not been out at the right time. Look here! Chivers is low, very low,"—this is true, as the treatment has unaccountably told on Chivers, whose name has now become "Uneasy," as he can't make out whether the waters are doing him any good or not.

"Now," continues the insinuating and jovial Tom Spicer, "you" (to Chivers) "have a bottle of good wine, and we'll help you. *Dis donc, garçon, apportez-nous une bouteille de Château Palmer.*"

L

C'en est fait de nous. Spicer's done it. The bottle is brought.
'Tis excellent wine, but it does not come from the hotel cellars,
having been presented to Chivers by a charitable friend who has
brought his own private supply with him (an excellent plan), and
who can spare us this bottle as he is off to Paris in the morning.
We enjoy it, that is Chivers and myself, as if we had been two
Crusoes found on a desert island by Spicer, the gay mariner, who had
brought us a bottle of rum from the ship's stores. It is excellent.

"Of course you feel better already," says Spicer heartily; and
we swagger—or stagger—for a couple of glasses of Château Palmer
have already done their deadly work, and we are merry and ready
for anything. Doctor be blowed! *Garçon, du café!* First-rate
cigar. Good music to-night, too. And, dear me, yes, the place
is crowded, and all the people taking coffee, *liqueurs*, and cigars.
Let us risk at the *petits chevaux.* Chivers does so, and at once
wins seven francs.

"*Voilà! la bonne chance!*" cries the Demon Spicer, more Mephistophelian than ever. "*Le Château Palmer porte bonheur.*"

Capital game, *les petits chevaux.* I lose three times, and don't
think so much of it. Chivers proposes *La Mascotte.* We enter
the tent. We get seats. Spicer, however, prefers the theatre,
the admission to which is six francs to-night, because a M. Fusier
is giving an entertainment.'

On the *La Mascotte* board there are painted pictures of *L'Ama-
zone, Le Chinois,* he is called *Le Coquin Chinois* this evening—a
political allusion—*La Baigneuse, La Princesse,* and *Le Petit François.* I back *Le Petit François* and the white. There is immediately a run on *La Baigneuse,* the *Coquin Chinois* turns up
occasionally, and the *rouge* about six times out of eight. Consequently I am not a winner. Suddenly it is the turn of the *Petit
François,* the wand in the hand of the figure of an angel blowing
a trumpet stops at the picture of the *Petit François,* represented
as an effeminate youth in Watteau costume, and touches number
cinq. The colour on which my little friend's picture is painted is
white, and so, having backed *blanc* and *le petit,* I have a good
time of it, and receive five francs in all; as, so strict are the
conditions of the game, your stake is counted in as part of the
winnings, *c'est à dire "la mise compte au jeu,"*—an excellent arrange-

ment for the table, but hard on the *joueurs.* After this I pause for a second. Fatal loss of time! for while I am thinking on what I shall stake my money, the *croupier* calls out, " *Le jeu est fait—rien de plus,*"—it is too late for me to back the little Watteau-esque youth and white again—nay, it is any odds against their winning twice running—when suddenly the wand of the winged Fortune stops in precisely the same place, and ticks off exactly the same number! Ah! *miséricorde!* had I but . . . . Too late! I will encourage the *Petit François.* I will back him through thick and thin. I do so, but the chance for to-night has come and gone. The Angel of Fortune blowing the trumpet favours *Le Coquin Chinois* (*absit omen!*) and the red, gives an occasional turn to *La Princesse,* and something else, I forget what, but the stupid little *François* passes by, turn after turn, cutting me dead every time. I put my last half-franc on *Le Petit François,* but he takes no notice of me, and the little man, in his courtier-like attitude, his pearl-grey satin square-cut coat, and his background of garden-landscape *à la Watteau,* turn slowly away from me, as I rise from my seat, and go out into the star-lit night. Chivers has vanished: he lost on *La Baigneuse,* and retired early.

It is half-past eight! the night was yet young. I can go no-where, for I have no money. What must the ruined gambler feel? Yes, there is one place to go to,—bed. *Entrée libre. J'y suis.*

If the Demon Spicer's *traitement* is better than the doctor's, *va pour le Démon* Spicer! If not—then back to asceticism *et le traitement du célèbre Docteur Probité. Nous verrons.*

Le matin après.—Levée à six heures. Droit comme une trépied. The Doctor comes in unexpectedly, when I am in my bath. He takes me by surprise. I take him by surprise. I am so well. Dr. Probité is so delighted with me up to this moment that I feel bound to confess the enormity of last night. " *Voyons!* " I say cheerily. "Guess what I did last night!" He looks *at* me, and through me—right to the other side of the bath, and he says, sharply, "Smoked?" "Yes. Only one cigar."

"One too many," he replies; but he cannot find it in his heart or his head to say anything in the face of facts.

The *traitement,* then, *à la Bourboule* comes, I think, to this:

Use the waters till they disagree with you; then leave 'em off for a day or so, and then recommence. This is not a bad rule any-where. *Bourboulez comme à la Bourboule : et ayez confiance en votre médecin.* To adapt Monsieur J. L. Toole's phrase, "*Tenez l'œil sur votre Docteur et votre Docteur vous en tirera net.*"

Chivers is better. Spicer is about the same, but delighted that his *traitement* of us has succeeded so well. Taken altogether I should say we arrive at the Probité-Spicer philosophy, "If you want to enjoy life, live by rule, and prove the truth of the rule by the success of the exceptions."

Our *Rosses* at La Bourboule, and the Jolly Young Cocher who " ' drives '
along thinking of nothing at all."

The horses and flys are all out on "the Place;" and the flies, swarms of 'em, are all there, too, you may be sure. I wish I could draw a horse as well as a horse draws me, as these "moun-tain ponies *Anglais*" are worth the trouble of mounting (on card-board), but not the cost of a ride, about ten or twelve francs, except as a *dernier ressort pour se distraire.*

This pretty well sums up the distractions of La Bourboule. Outside La Bourboule, at seven kilos distance, there is Mont-Dore; but in this place, which, because it is higher up in the mountains, and of more ancient reputation, professes to look down upon La Bourboule, I have no sort of interest. Its Établissement looks

like a gaol, and its bathing-cabinets like condemned cells,—ex-
teriorly, at least. Mont-Dore is bigger, but not better even for its
own *spécialité*,—you see I am a partisan,—as La Bourboule is little
and good. But for La Bourboule, as for *La Périchole*—"*elle
grandira.*" And there will be bigger and grander hotels, more
lodging-houses, larger stakes at *La Mascotte*, fortunes lost and won
at *les petits chevaux*, splendid stables and equipages, and a magni
ficent church, of course. But the simplicity, the seriousness, the
tranquillity, and the piety of La Bourboule will have disappeared,
just as even now the peasant's Bourboule has disappeared, and
the oldest inhabitant no more recognizes the La Bourboule of his
childhood's days, than would a present Bourboulais, going up into
the mountains and returning, like *Rip van Winkle*, twenty years
hence, recognize the La Bourboule he had quitted in the Year of
Grace Eighteen-Eighty-four.

CHAPTER IX.

A RIDE—RESULT—LAID UP—SNATCHES—OPERATIC—A HISTORY—
ORIGIN—THE RECKLESS ONE—ANOTHER REAL INVALID.

SPICER and myself having nothing better to do, on a fine
afternoon after the rain, hire horses, ten francs the pair, for
two hours, the cheapest thing of the kind I've yet come across in
La Bourboule, where the simple Auvergnat does fleece the tourist
lamb to any extent in the matter of *promenades en voiture et à
cheval.* Mine is a wonderful pony; and the saddle and the
stirrups were apparently originally intended for a rocking-horse.
However, both the beasts are "*solides*," specially mine, and away
we go up a mountain-road, which serves as a water-course in
Winter, at full galop, without a stumble or a slip, until we find
ourselves in the high road, and close to a picturesquely-situated
village, *en route* for Saint Sauves.

There we descend : the view is beautiful, reminding Spicer of
Surrey considerably enlarged. It reminds me of Surrey and
Devonshire mixed, with a little bit of rocky Cornwall thrown in.

Quite a fancy-sketch. Our horses descend with perfect ease and safety. We are back by dinner-time ; and—we go to bed very early.

The next day I am laid up with a severe cold—the waters are knocked off, and the *traitement* interrupted. Chivers looks in to sympathise with me. I say that I could have caught this cold at home—there was no necessity to come all this way to do it. Chivers doesn't know what the waters are doing to *him*, but he is of opinion that they're all humbug ; and he reminds me that it was I who induced him to come here. "I'm getting worse instead of better," says the Gentleman whose name is Easy, as he strokes

Open-air Livery Stables. Horses waiting to be hired at La Bourboule.

his nose reflectively ; "and if I had only got a servant here to pack up, I'm hanged if I wouldn't go at once. But the packing up!"

The prospect of this exertion, and the impossibility of getting the work done by deputy, is too much for him. He sits and stares blankly at the window. Then he hums snatches,—they are never more than snatches, taken at haphazard, and violently torn away in a maimed condition from the original melody, whatever it might have been,—and marks what he conceives to be "the time" with his stick on the floor. I try to stop him by inquiring where one of the fragments comes from ? He doesn't exactly remember ; but, to aid his memory, he repeats it over again, adding some other "bits," which he says he *thinks* come from the same Opera. I devoutly wish he had left them there, and not "brought them away with him."

After this entertainment has lasted about twenty minutes he rises, observing, as if pressed for time (the idea of being busy, or pressed for time, at La Bourboule!)—that "he really must go," and then he kindly asks if there is anything he can do for me; whereupon I request him "to go and see the Doctor for me," which, including having his pulse felt for me, he at once undertakes to do, and, with a snatch of melody still on his lips, he leaves me.

Sleep, gentle sleep! I am just dozing off when the Easy One returns.

"I say," he says, tapping on the floor with his stick, "you asked me what it was I was humming just now." I reply that I did, and try to evince as much interest as circumstances will permit. "Well, I've just remembered it—part of the march from *Fidelio*—or else it's a bit from *La Gazza Ladra*—it goes like this" —but, just as he is making a dash at the melody, he alights on the wrong note, puts himself out, and, after several vain attempts at recalling it, gives it up, and as he goes out he observes, "I'll come back directly I've caught it, and tell you what it is. I *never* forget a tune." Much annoyed with himself for the slip of memory on this occasion, he once more leaves me, and I hear him, his humming getting gradually fainter and fainter, trying to recall the lost tune as he walks slowly down the passage to his own room.

While laid up with cold, I commence notes for a short history of La Bourboule. The materials being scant, I apprehend that it will be a very short history.

It was built by Balbus, who was always building walls by way of taking Latin exercise. Hence the first origin of the name. After the death of Balbus and Caius his partner, the place gradually fell into disuse. It was not heard of again till, oddly enough, tradition associates it with England and the name of Cromwell.

The Lord Protector has to go through the *traitement* at La Bourboule in order to get rid of the wart on his nose, which was always annoying him, as the Poet Milton would ask him pointedly every morning, "Wart's the matter?"

But as the *traitement* didn't do him any good, the Protector,

being too impatient to stay out the twenty-one days, flew into a
passion, and, adapting his original and striking phrase, which had
made such an effect in the House, exclaimed—

"*Enlevez La Bourboule !*" and hoped to see the town razed to
the ground.   It wasn't, however, as La Bourboule is gifted with
everlasting youth, or at least with a perpetual Spring.

I don't get any further at present with my short history.

The place is rapidly emptying.   The Easy Eastern Despot, the

"Take away that Bourboule!"

Reckless Spicer, and my miserable self are the only English
patients left.

Spicer thinks he will go out and make a sketch of La Bourboule.
He takes a small portfolio under his arm.   Being the only stranger
visible, his movements attract attention.   Nobody is doing anything at La Bourboule now, and the news soon spreads about that
an Englishman—an eccentric Englishman—is absolutely going
out to amuse himself.   *How* he will set about it is a matter of the
intensest curiosity to the crowd, who for the first time in their
experience have ever heard of anyone attempting to amuse himself

at La Bourboule, which, as I have before remarked, is essentially a serious place.

Later on the Reckless Spicer returns. Where has he been? He doesn't know, and he can't give any particulars, as he has been taking a draught of mountain air, has caught a severe cold, and entirely lost the use of his voice. In pantomime the Reckless One expresses his determination to retire at once to bed. It has been

LATE IN THE SEASON.

The only remaining Visitor announces his intention of "going out to amuse himself." Curiosity of the Inhabitants of La Bourboule to see how he will achieve his object.

glorious summer up to four o'clock ; now it is chill October, and, interpreting Spicer's signals, we order logs to be brought, a good fire to be made, *tisane* boiling to be followed by hot grogs every half hour, and three blankets on the bed. Finally, we all have fires, and all retire early. Such are the delights of La Bourboule in the first week of September. This, as they say in novels, is "The Beginning of the End !"

CHAPTER X.

STILL WITH COLD—NO MORE WATERS—NOTES FOR FUTURE GUIDE.

MY room in our hotel is situated *au seconde* over a murmuring stream and a howling dog. I don't wonder at the stream murmuring; when the dog howls, it's quite enough to make one murmur. But when the dog is silent, the stream, from some unexplained cause, murmurs louder than ever, and, at first, the noise of rushing water being continuous, it seems to me as if I were trying to sleep with my head against the cistern of a London house, in some district where either the Turncock had gone mad, or the Water Company had become recklessly prodiga .

La Bourboule is a great place, as I have already said, for infantine maladies. It is, therefore, a great place for children; I may say, distinctly, a very great place for children. I never met so many children with noisy toys as at La Bourboule. They have cow-horns, tin-trumpets, imitation pistols and cannons, which go off with a startling bang, un-musical carts, drums, and so forth. But of all things. the little cow-horn is the worst. It is the curse of the place, and the worst of it is you can never find out where the deuce the little boy is who makes the noise. If you have a headache, this invisible "Little Boy Blue," or "Little Boy *Blow*," with the juvenile cow-horn, will worry you until you feel inclined to out-Herod Herod, and run a-muck for all the children in the place.

The dogs of La Bourboule are another nuisance; they bark and they howl as no other dogs do, and are evidently irritated by the children and the trumpets. Sometimes at night the owners of the howling dogs are aroused, and then the noise is redoubled. But, if you are snugly tucked up in bed, it is some consolation to reflect that the dog is punished for howling, and that the master, who is beating it, is probably catching a severe cold. When the toy-cow-horn is not in full blast, the real instrument of torture is being blown by the *conducteurs* of the omnibuses touting for customers to Laqueuille, Mont-Dore, Tauves, and other neighbouring places. This lasts for about an hour at a time, twice a day. A fourth trouble is the bell-ringing at the various hotels, to announce the preparation for the different meals, and then the hour of the meal itself.

There are also bells to announce the *clôture* of the *établissement* twice a day. Bells are rung on every possible occasion. The rule at La Bourboule appears to be, "When you've nothing else to do, ring a bell."

The greatest nuisance of all, against which, as being a public matter, affecting nervous invalids, I wonder the fourteen Doctors forming the Medical Staff of La Bourboule don't protest, is the firing off of some infernal machine several times a day, for no other object that I have been able to ascertain than that of startling the pigeons, and making them fly madly about. It is quite enough to cause all the invalids to fly, and never return. On a nervous individual (and there must be many here), specially if partially confined to his room, and for whom perfect tranquillity is abso-lutely necessary, this explosion, which is a perpetual surprise, is quite enough to produce most serious results. The only time I witnessed this performance, the actual perpetrator was a dirty little boy, who came down from the Casino with something under his arm, which, at a distance, seemed to resemble an old-fashioned hat-box. To this he applied a fusee, when it at once went off with a tremendous detonation that sent the pigeons (which, one would have thought, might have been accustomed to it by this time) whirring up and circling about in the air, while several ladies started up from their seats, and the young Dynamiter having accomplished his fiendish purpose, retired giggling. Where was our one Gendarme?

Before the term of my sentence has expired, I find myself asking if a great many of the cures with which the springs of La Bour-boule are credited may not be classed among the *Fables of La Fontaine?*

A Conversation-book for La Bourboule would be useful. I shall here merely hint at it, reserving all my rights as the discoverer of La Bourboule, comparatively little known to my suffering compatriots, for my forthcoming *Guide à La Bourboule.*

Morning Dialogue.—How is (*comment se porte-t-il*) your thumb (*pouce*), Sir (*Monsieur*),—your big-toe (*orteil*), your little-toe (*petit doigt du pied*), your nose (*nez*), your right ear (*oreille droite*), your left (*gauche*) ear, your knee (*genou*), this morning?

Your nose (*nez*) is not so red (*si rouge*) this morning as usual (*comme ordinaire*)—your nose is much redder (*beaucoup plus rouge*).

Morning.	Midday.
Bathing Costume.	The Lightest Summer Suit.
Flannel. With Wrapper.	95° in the Shade.

My thumb pains me—Oh!—(*mal au pouce—Ah!*)—I have shooting-pains in my head.

I will not take any more of these beastly waters (*eaux affreuses*). You must see the Doctor (*il faut passez chez M. le Médecin*). The Doctor be —— (*que le Médecin soit béni*). I think I shall go away (*me sauver*) to-morrow (*demain*). No—stay, and go through the course (*traitement*). I am better. I like the place—I like the waters. It is the tenth day I am here. I shall be so well when I get back (*quand je reviendrai chez moi*). When I return I shall go in for champagne, hooray! (*à la bonne heure*), and smoking, and coffee, and *liqueurs.*

With the Doctor.—I am better. I have a sore nose (*nez douloureux*), a pimple (*bouton*) on my lower lip (*lèvre inférieure*). It is nothing. What! (*comment*) give up (*renoncer*) the waters? Why, I've come thousands of miles to take them! Oh, for one day only (*ne que*). Very good (*très bien*), and put off (*remettre*) the spray (*pulverisation*), inhalation, gargle (*gargarisme*) till the day after to-morrow. Good! (*très bien*). I will observe (*obéir*) all you tell me. Eh! No smoke, no *liqueur*, no coffee (*pas de café*)! Ah well, then (*eh bien alors*). no fee (*pas de récompense*)!

Dinner Suit,
known as
'The Compromise.'

Evening from 7 P.M.
Must be thoroughly
wrapped up.

To a Friend (*à déjeûner*).—Look! (*regardez*)—that nose—that ear—that cheek—how red—it is less red (*moins rouge*) than yesterday (*qu'hier*). Your nose looks beautiful (*beau*) this morning; how does mine look? Will you have some eggs? I have had two eggs—a bad egg and a good egg. Is this chop (*cotelette*) cooked (*cuite*) with tallow candles (*bougies de suif*) or only with bad butter? I do not know. I will have some of the good red wine (*du bon vin rouge*), while you have the nasty water. I cannot get (*trouver*) any good red wine. The wine of the country (*vin du pays*) must be made out of old boots (*vieilles bottes*). Then (*alors*) the grapes (*raisins*) must grow on boot-trees. I shall have the red nose (*le nez rougi*), while you will have the beautiful complexion (*la peau claire*). I will smoke the great and good cigar, and drink the strong black coffee (*café noir*), while you will have nothing to do (*rien à faire*). You who have just arrived (*venez d'arriver*) are thin and vigorous; but I, who have been through (*passé par*) the course (*traitement*) am fat (*gros*) and feeble (*faible*). He is happy (*heureux*) because he is well. I am unhappy (*malheureux*) because I am unwell. You will have the big pimple (*bouton*) on your tongue (*langue*), and I shall be quite well and happy.

Animated Appearance of La Bourboule.

CHAPTER XI.

LAST CHAPTER (BUT ONE) THAT ENDS THIS STRANGELY UNEVENTFUL HISTORY.

WE THREE, Chivers, Spicer, and myself, are almost the last roses—or noses—(for, with all our other ailments, that is a sore point with us) of Summer. "All our bloomin' companions," as the song says, have packed up their traps and gone. Guignol still plays *Roméo et Juliette* and *Lucie de Lammermoor* to crowded audiences, but the Theatre is closed, the attendance at *les petits chevaux* is meagre, and around the Mascotte are gathered quite a little family party, with twenty sous each time on the table, the circle diminishing as one after the other reaches his limit of five francs.

The Band still plays, but there is no heart in the performance, and the Conductor is listless. A few adventurous spirits, well wrapped up, make a bold attempt at sitting out at the tables under the verandah of the *Café*, and try to appear as if they were enjoying their coffee and cigars. Some Ladies in thick mantles lend their aid in this ghastly attempt at galvanising the moribund season into a temporary life. It is useless. The Band shivers, and retires. The Waiters regard their customers with compassion. One after another the tables are left bare, and the chairs are empty. Then the wind and the Waiters have the *Café* all to themselves. The lights are gradually extinguished, and, the Waiters having departed, only the wind remains whistling round the corners, having all its amusement to itself, and enjoying it as only the wind can. But the tables and chairs have been removed, so even the wind, finding it has nothing to play with, drops off to sleep, or goes somewhere else,—for which I, personally, am profoundly thankful, as now my wood-fire will burn without filling the room with smoke, and compelling me to open the window, and risk another severe cold.

Cold! Ah, it is a place to catch cold in is La Bourboule! Never was a climate so variable.

If you walk, you must take care not to walk too fast, and not

to stop and sit down ; if you drive, you must have plenty of wraps ;
if you ride, you must keep on at an even pace.

Fortunate the invalid who at the end of ten days can walk or
ride, the effect of the waters of La Bourboule (as far as our experience goes—I mean that of Chivers, Spicer, and self) being to
make the patient fat and feeble, increased in weight, and indis-
posed to anything remotely resembling activity.

The invalid's appetite will be pretty good, but he is unable to
gratify it to any great extent, the food being of an inferior quality.
The *spécialité* of the La Bourboule *cuisine* seems to me to be a peculiar way of cooking everything with bad butter ; its *chef d'œuvre* is
a dish of tough mutton cutlets, gently grilled over a fire, which,
judging from the flavour of the meat (when you *can* get one of the
chops to yield to the pressure of a strong knife, used with all the
muscular force of which an invalid is capable), must have been
mainly composed of tallow candles.

After nearly three weeks of constant companionship our conversation is exhausted.   Chivers makes a few attempts at repeating
some stories which were excellent when we first arrived, but which
have now lost their first freshness.   On the third repetition of one
of his best, both Spicer and myself stop him.   After this, as newspapers are the only substitutes for conversation at breakfast, each
one brings his own journal or letters.   We take no interest in anybody or anything.   We are Lotos-eaters.   We should like to break
with La Bourboule, but haven't the energy.   Spicer, who came
last, and was the blithest and gayest of the gay, is now the most
melancholy spectacle.   He really ought not to be out of bed.   The
fact is that we are now really ill.   We are down.   I am suddenly
aged ; Chivers has the Eastern Despotic temperament quite taken
out of him ; he is humble, meek, mild, and no longer bewails the
absence of a servant.   His name is indeed Easy now.   He is indifferent.
Only let him sleep, and don't talk to him, and he is happy.   He
wakes up occasionally to discuss the politics of the day, but, as a
rule, news from the outer world has ceased to have any effect even
upon him.   Only one thing has any real interest for him now, and
that is the left-hand side of the tip of his nose, which, considering
all he has done for it, is not behaving as it should.   The lobe of
my right ear is causing me also some considerable trouble, and

as to my nose, I am beginning to be thoroughly annoyed with it.

We stand before the glass ; then we ask one another what each thinks of the other's nose. This is a prelude to breakfast, and it is the only semblance of conversation that remains.

Two mornings out of three I prefer Chivers's nose to mine. I tell him I think *his* nose is getting on admirably. How's mine? I ask. Oh, he is enchanted with my nose ! he only wishes his nose were doing anything like as well. But surely, he says, reproachfully, I must be flattering when I tell him his nose is so much better.

I reply, rather indignantly, protesting that on such serious subjects I am not given to flattery, and that the last thing I should flatter would be anyone's nose, and I assert, honestly, that his nose is making great progress, is in first-rate condition, and is just the sort of nose that he, with his peculiar constitution, ought to expect it to be after using the La Bourboule waters up to this point. But, I add, whatever he may say to the contrary, I cannot accept what he has told me as to the appearance of my own nose in such satisfactory condition as being any index as to its real state.

" But, my dear fellow," protests Chivers, " your nose is—I give you my word of honour—your nose is twenty per cent. better than when you came."

Secretly, I am delighted to hear this, but I will not let my joy be seen, lest the delight of the morning may be turned into the grief of the afternoon. All I permit myself to reply is that, and I say it in a sad tone, I am glad to hear what he says about my nose, but he must allow me to know best about my own nose, not as to how it looks, but as to how it feels.

That it looks well, I admit—fairly well, at all events, the sunset hue having yielded to a delicate salmon pink—but that it feels better is what I cannot allow any man to be a better judge of than myself.

Here Spicer, who has got no nose to speak about—I mean that it is his throat and not his nose which is his weak point—throws in the apt quotation of—

> "Says Aaron to Moses,
> Let's cut off our noses.
> Says Moses to Aaron——"

Chivers interrupts him with the air of a man inspired, and who can't wait to be asked, as he'll lose his inspiration for ever,—

> " Says Moses to Aaron,
>   Let's go to La Bourboule."

And then it occurs to him that the inspiration has deceived him, that a false voice has spoken to him, and that " La Bourboule " does not rhyme with " Aaron." " But no matter," says Chivers— " the idea's all there, and the rhyme will come afterwards. My name's Easy."

Spicer has developed into a walking cold. His nose doesn't trouble him—that is the exceptional thing in his cold. It is the gigantic cold of a man without a nose, or of a man to whom the medium of a nose affords no relief. He has become so hoarse as to be almost unintelligible, and so husky as to suggest that he must have been eating a pound of nuts during the night. What an occupation! Unfortunately Chivers has developed deafness; and so when Spicer, having addressed any remark to him, has to repeat it, not once or twice, but three or four times, the last time causes him a great effort. How Spicer keeps his temper and loses his voice, is wonderful to me. For instance, Spicer asks, huskily, something, which, to Chivers, sounds like nothing at all, and to me sounds as unintelligible as this sentence, which will carry some sort of idea of my meaning (but not of Spicer's) :— " Havellrcl Glallstulspec shesday ?"

Chivers, awaking to the fact that an observation has been addressed to him by Spicer, turns suddenly to him, and asks,

" Eh ? What ?"

Spicer, with an air of fatigue, repeats the above sentence, when Chivers turns to me, as if asking me to interpret.

I can't.

" I'm very sorry," says Chivers, with the forced politeness of a man who has been disturbed in the perusal of a deeply interesting article, as he puts his hand up to his ear, " but I really don't catch——"

Spicer rolls in his chair, as if working up steam for the next effort, leans over towards Chivers, and placing his hand to his mouth as if he were hailing somebody a mile off, shouts, more hoarsely than ever—the voice coming up as if through a hubble-bubble pipe when you blow down it instead of drawing—"Have you read Gladstull's speech yesterday?"

But Chivers is horribly deaf. "Eh?" he says, looking up at Spicer as if to gather from his expression of face what he has been saying, and so save him the trouble of repeating it.

Spicer is perspiring—he can't stand the exertion—he mops his face, and is preparing for a supreme effort of bawling, when I inform Chivers, in a mild undertone, that what Spicer wants to

Reflection at La Bourboule. The Last Nose of Summer.

know is whether he (Chivers) has read Gladstone's speech of yesterday.

Chivers regards me with a puzzled expression, and says, "Eh? What? Gladstone?" Then, when the question asked five minutes ago suddenly dawns upon him, he becomes as radiant as if he had guessed a difficult acrostic, and nodding pleasantly to Spicer, to intimate that all's well that ends well, he repeats, "'Read the speech of Gladstone?' Oh, yes. Wonderful, wasn't it? Eh?"

And there the conversation ends, Spicer lying back in his chair, wiping his forehead, and too exhausted to utter another syllable for the next quarter of an hour.

Then Chivers takes up his *Gil Blas*, and I take up the *Gaulois*, and so we merrily pass half of our breakfast-time.

I feel that there is no encouragement to get up a conversation with two companions, of whom one is deaf, and the other very nearly has a fit whenever he tries to speak plainly.

Thus it is that we are getting down, depressed, low, disappointed with everything. The diet is not exhilarating. Of the *vin du pays*, which we call "the Generous," the only thing to be said is, that there's not a headache in a bucket of it—mind, I distinctly emphasize *head*-ache.

We have no general conversation, for the reason above stated; and the only topic of interest is our health. Spicer hasn't even got this, as his health seems to have completely broken down, and the *traitement* with him is absolutely a failure. He has to give it up, and directly his cold is better, and he can render himself intelligible without too severe a strain, he will go away from La Bourboule "for ever!"

THE LAST CHAPTER.

"OFF! OFF! SAID THE STRANGER."

THE view we individually take of the *traitement* here is this, that "it is good for the other fellow." For example—Chivers thinks that the waters suit *me* perfectly, but that they don't suit *him*. For my part I hold conscientiously that the waters don't suit *me*, but are evidently benefiting Chivers. Spicer is of opinion that the *traitement* suits us both, but that *he* ought never to have been sent here. We tell him that he is vastly better for the course.

Chivers returns to his first opinion, and exclaims, "I believe it's all humbug. Look at my nose!"

I do look at his nose, and affirm—*je constate*—that it is distinctly better. It is a wiser and a better nose than when it came here.

"So is yours," says Chivers, as if he were uttering a retort.

"But," we all three put it, "if the waters can be bottled and sent to England, why not go through all this at home?"

The only evident answer to this is, that there are fourteen Doctors at La Bourboule. And the fourteen Doctors of La Bourboule must live. At least, *they* think so; that is their opinion, as Doctors.

This is in our minds and on our lips as we sit down to our frugal dinner, when suddenly there enters Dr. Probité to see his patients.

Now, a Doctor should never come, professionally, to see his patients at meal-times. It is unfair. It is the Schoolmaster paying a visit to his young friend during the holidays. If the Doctor comes, it must be as a guest. He accepts, with pleasure. "Lesbia hath a beaming eye"—but not so beaming as Dr. Probité's, when he consents to join his three patients at dinner, and goes out to hang up his hat and coat in the outer hall. While he is away, we say, as by one inspiration, "*Now* we'll get out of him the truth about La Bourboule."

In a *moment d'égarement* we expect to hear him laugh outright under our very noses, to see him throw himself back in his chair (after the tenth bottle of "the Generous"), and exclaim "La Bourboule be blowed! *Entre nous,* and not letting it go beyond this table, La Bourboule is humbug, and the *traitement* bosh!"

Then shall we pulverise him? No. He is our guest, and the laws of hospitality will have to be respected.

We are looking forward to Frightful Revelations about the La Bourboule Swindle, when our Doctor enters, merrily rubbing his hands.

But—shall I reveal the secrets of the dinner-table? Never!

What if our Doctor gave us a dispensation for once and away? What if we availed ourselves of it to any extent under his able advice and distinct encouragement? Is it for me to "split" on my brave companions? Perish the thought! And suppose I cannot remember one quarter of the good things said—or what time we retired to rest—or whether the Landlord looked in to say that everyone had been in bed for hours, and that nothing more could be had, not even Vals Waters? and suppose that even now, in trying to recall the events of that night, I have some vague recollection of how we all wanted to sally forth to find the real, unadulterated, original spring of the La Bourboule waters; how we thought we saw before us a new Company to be started, which should deal with this real spring, wherever it might be; and how we were for arguing the legal points as to who was the real owner of the waters of La Bourboule, and whether, being a natural product, and for the benefit of mankind, it ought to be in the hands of anybody in particular, except ourselves; and whether we could cut the La Bourboule water off and take it somewhere else ; and how the Landlord reappeared, and said he must put out the gas, and how he was dubious about trusting us with candles ; and how he saw us safely to our rooms ; and how we didn't know exactly when the Doctor had left us,—whether he had gone out by the door or had disappeared under the table,—suppose, I say, that all this were so,—what does it prove ?

I think it proves that we were very much better.

Chivers is dismayed at the prospect of having to pack up for himself. "I'll never come out again without someone to pack up

The "Traitement;" or, Theory and Practice.

for me," he says. Spicer suggests that he should be accompanied by Eastern slaves. Why not by "Packer's Band?" His name is Easy, but his task is difficult.

We all start for Paris. Charles, the faithful *Chasseur*, is at the P. L. M. Station (we have returned by a different route, and have seen Royat in passing, which is a charming place we all agree, as far as we can judge of it from our carriage-window, and we regret not having been there instead of at La Bourboule), and he has taken my room for me at the Grand Hotel, which I reach at about a quarter before midnight. At the last moment I catch sight of the Gentleman whose name is Easy having a row with a porter and a cabman, while Spicer, whom the waters of La Bourboule have quite deprived of his voice, is gesticulating to an amiable coachman who, apparently, doesn't or won't understand him.

The next day—oh, the comfort of a good breakfast at the Grand! It is in the off-season, yet it is a breakfast worth eating, and the dishes are not cooked *à la mode de La Bourboule* with bad butter or tallow-candle grease.

In the evening Chivers and myself appear, after our long absence, in the character of *deux viveurs attablés chez Bignon, et après le dîner, buvant le café en fumant de bons cigares,* hearing from the head-waiter Henri how dull everything has been, and is; and how the foreigners have been scared away by the report of cholera, and *habitués* have departed for the *chasse,* or are still disporting themselves on the sea coast. We drink Dr. Probité's health (at a distance—bless him!) in a couple of bottles of Pontet-Canet, and, for the first time for nearly a month, are able to enjoy what it is just to Bignon's to call an extra good dinner—for which it is equally just to Bignon's to add we pay an extra good price. A couple of quails—excellent, I admit—cost us ten francs, and this in the first week of September. A peach,—Chivers said "anything would do for him," and insisted on having a peach,—was half-a-crown. *Mais, que voulez-vous?* We don't escape from the prison-fare of La Bourboule every day,—thank goodness! After this light entertainment we visit the Eden Théâtre, where *Excelsior* is still going on, but sadly shorn of its first glory.

There we meet Spicer, who has already partially recovered the use of his voice. He is full of regrets; his chief regret being that he did not go to see Guignol at La Bourboule. He has half a mind to retrace his steps. In this state of indecision we leave him on a wet night at the corner of the Rue Scribe, and, wishing one another farewell, we separate, each one taking his own way, as he has done before the treatment of La Bourboule had brought us together for three short weeks of our life. And so ends our trip to La Bourboule, where, as far as I can say at present, it seems to me I have been "very much abroad."

ROYAT.

SOME ACCOUNT OF
A VISIT TO ROYAT.

CHAPTER I.

HOW IT CAME ABOUT—WHO ADVISED IT—WHO AGREED TO IT—
WHO WENT—WHO DIDN'T GO.

ROYAT

EVERYBODY— that is everybody to whose friendly judgment I submit my intention of going to Royat-les-Bains — says, "What on earth are you going to Royat for?" Which question only proves how little they know of me, physiologically, and of Royat, medicinally.

I could write a philosophical treatise on this inquiry of my friends. When they say, "What on earth do you go to Royat for?" does it mean that they will provide me with something better if I don't go? Does it mean that they are going to stop in town, and are so anxious for my society that they can't spare me? A hundred similar queries suggest themselves to be summed up in one very simple one, which is, "Do they mean anything at all?" and, "Do they care one snap of the finger and thumb " (to put it classically) "where I go to, as long as I don't bother *them?*" Friendship has its limits, and its seasons.

The foregoing is merely a hint as to what variations I *could* play on such a theme.

My immediate answer to my friends is that " I am *ordered* to go there." This sounds better than "recommended," as implying that my departure for Royat is a matter of vital importance to myself and also to my friends. So I speak as if I were a soldier, " ordered off at a moment's notice, to take the field,"—a phrase which is more suggestive of the betting man than the soldier—and I expect my friends to accept this as sufficiently explaining why I choose Royat in preference to Vichy, Aix-les-Bains, La Bourboule, Mont-Doré, Homburg, Luchon, or any other watering-place. They have, all of them, the air of resenting my choice of Royat as a personal affront to them individually and collectively ; or if not exactly as a personal affront, at least as showing on my part a want of consideration for their feelings. If they do not mean this, why does my old friend Holdum, lunching at his table by the Club window, exclaim with an appearance of surprise, and in an injured tone, "Why Royat?" and turn away to look out of the window, as if my conduct was too painful for him to trust himself even to regard me one moment longer without weeping.

Why does Tom Underleep, whom I only see to speak to for a few minutes on Tuesdays and Wednesdays, when he is waiting furtively in the Club hall to waylay the new number of the *World* or *Truth*, and, so to speak, get the first cut at it before it has become as stale as the *caviare* which was opened for some one a fortnight ago; why, I ask, does Tom Underleep, to whom it can matter nothing where I go or what I do, suddenly take upon himself to look up from his *Truth* or *World*, and growl in a discontented manner, "Why do *you* go to Royat?" as though he had already made up his mind to go there himself, and was afraid there wouldn't be room for both of us? That those of my medical acquaintance who are interested in other health-resorts, should strongly advise their particular fancies, was to be expected ; but that my familiar friends should be hurt by the announcement of my resolution of visiting Royat, seems to call for some preliminary explanation of my apparently, to them, strange conduct; for they look askance at me as if, when I am out of the room, they will tap their foreheads significantly, muttering, " Poor chap ! something wrong in this quarter" (meaning my head)—"going to Royat ! Must be off his nut !" and so on. Well, this is my explanation :—

Happening one day to be having a scientific chat with my friend Dr. Putteney—Hammond Putteney, M.D., the well-known author of that *brochure* which created such a sensation in society about three years ago, entitled *How to get Fat in Two Minutes*, and even more celebrated in the medical and scientific world through his learned treatises on *The Unnecessary Fabrication of Vital Tissue* (25th Thousand), *On the Treatment of Vehicular Disease on the Lower Lugnosis* (50th Thousand), *On Vicarious Phiningitis of the Assimilated Cuticles* (with Diagrams in Colours—8th Edition, Revised and Corrected by the Author), and, I should add, famed in the French, German, and Italian Schools of Medicine, for his brilliant discovery of the *Clignotic Movement of the Nervous Tegocular Membrane*, which has already revolutionised the treatment of this mysterious mechanism in the human frame, which is now known among the Faculty as " Putteney's Membrane "—happening to be chatting with Dr. Putteney about his own state of health, which was puzzling him considerably, and, incidentally, about my own, he suddenly looked up, and said with an air of the deepest conviction, " There's only one place for you,—Royat !"

When Dr. Hammond Putteney, sitting easily on a garden-chair, —that is, as easily as it is possible to sit on a garden-chair,—enjoying a big cigar, suddenly brings his knees sharply together, jerks his body bolt upright, adjusts his spectacles with his left hand, while in his right he takes his cigar (which he thenceforth uses as if it were a piece of chalk, and he were a lecturer drawing a diagram on an invisible black-board, and emphasising his discourse with it), he is immediately transformed from a round-visaged jolly-looking person, a compromise between a young English Squire and a superior German Student (after a series of soap-and-water baths) who was wearing his Professor's gold-rimmed spectacles for a lark, to the respectable English scientific, professional practitioner of several years standing.—and, I am bound to say, the metamorphosis is as astounding as it is complete and entire.

His manner is earnest, his action energetic, and his speech determined, a combination which would give a tone of severity to any other man, but not to Dr. Putteney, whose hair, what there is of it, is very light and thin, and whose features, guiltless of any sign of moustache, beard, or whiskers, more nearly resemble those of the conventional cherub than any other variety of the human physiognomy with which I am acquainted.

There was "once upon a time," a learned person, a Doctor, not of medicine, but of divinity, who was distinguished as "The Angelic Doctor." I feel inclined to borrow a hint from this title, and christen Dr. Putteney "The Cherubic Doctor." I would not wish it to be thought that I adopt all the consequences of this simile, as Cherubs are usually represented on tombstones as blowing trumpets, presumably their own; and I am bound to say that this is a sort of thing Dr. Hammond Putteney never does. If he blows trumpets at all, they are not his own instruments, but those of his friends, and these he blows loudly. To-day,—the day this dialogue takes place,—he sounds the Royat trumpet, and plays upon it a marvellously fascinating tune; so much so indeed, that my Cousin Jane at once agrees with him, that Royat is the place for me, Dr. Putteney having long ago settled that she, as his patient, was to go there before the London season was over.

"You must go," cried Mrs. Dinderlin, enthusiastically. She is also under Dr. Putteney's orders. "It has done *me* such a lot of good every year." She is a pale diaphanous lady with a rather high-pitched voice, and quick incisive manner of speaking that will not brook contradiction.

"It does everyone good," cuts in Dr. Putteney, authoritatively, evidently not wishing to go into such useless details as to the nature of the ailments from which his various patients, for whom he has prescribed, or is prescribing, Royat, are suffering. "It does everyone good, and," turning to me, "it'll do *you* good especially—and so you'll go—and I'll get your rooms, and see you all through your treatment, and you'll start with your cousin, who is off next Saturday, and I leave to-morrow. So that's settled;" and, dropping the character of the Cherubic Doctor, he proceeds to throw himself back in his chair, kicks up his legs on to another chair, lights a fresh cigar, and with his face wreathed in smiles, he is once more transformed into the hearty, boyish young English Squire, who has been spending a year among the German Students, and is wearing, always for a lark, his Professor's gold-rimmed spectacles.

I have one short interview on our way home from the Richmond Club; it is in that garden the memorable conversation takes place

The Cherubic Doctor.

which decides me. To Royat I go. And so I sing with Cousin Jane the duet from *Manon*, which I adapt to the occasion—

> " À Royat
> Nous irons,
> Tous les deux, tous les deux ! "

The second line is, curiously enough, very suggestive of the waters of Royat, if "irons" were pronounced as in English. There is plenty of "irons," not "in the fire," but in the water of Royat. For the rest of the week we have "Waters on the brain," and we cannot quote the line as applicable to our case (mine and Jane's)

"*Eaux !* no, we never mention them !" for we are perpetually

talking about them. Either Cousin Jane is calling on me, or
I on Jane. Her husband can't go with her, but he holds
out some hopes of his just looking in, that is if, as I understand him, he finds Royat is on his way to Scotland, where
he has to go on particular business, not unconnected (I fancy,
though I wouldn't make mischief for the world) with a
fishing-rod and gun. But no matter. I am to take care of Jane
(who, between ourselves, is of an age to be perfectly able to take
care of herself), and her husband has only to see her off at the
Station, confide her to my care (why can't he come himself? he
had said he would, and then changed his mind) and that of Dr.
Puttency as medical attendant at Royat, and pay the bills. So
Dr. Puttency precedes us with some other patients, including
the diaphanous Mrs. Dinderlin, giving himself a week's start in
order (it is very kind of him) to have everything ready for our
reception.

CHAPTER II.

PRIVATE REASONS FOR GOING TO ROYAT—START—WHAT IS IT?—
MY PRETTY JANE—THE BAGGAGE—A FRIGHT—NO INDICATEUR
—WHERE?—GREENGAGE—QUALIFYING FOR ROYAT—PARIS—OFF
—NO INDICATEUR—ON THE LINE—CLERMONT-FERRAND—
ARRIVAL—REJOICINGS—DRIVE—ON THE ROOF—IN OUR ROOMS—
A DOUBT.

The Colonel.

WE START. Cousin Jane's husband sees us off by train, and then
leaves her to me and the Doctor who has
charge of her health at Royat.

Never in the long water-course of my
unhealthy experience have I ever visited
a *station thermale* under such favourable
circumstances as the present. For to be
in company with an English Doctor who
has several patients under his care, and
who is on the spot to appeal to at any
hour of the day, and in your own language too, whatever sudden change may
happen to you, is not this to be under
the eye, as it were, of a Special Providence? And then Dr. Putteney is a
personal friend; he will not look upon
me as a strange Doctor would, as a mere
body, which means a no-body, but as a
somebody. At the present moment I am
bound to say that I feel, and look, uncommonly well.

Jane is rather *poitrinaire*-ish and what *she* calls "rheumatic," but I'm sure that *her* symptoms are simply gouty. However she'll soon know the truth at Royat. She won't believe
me, though I've told her over and over again that she has incipient
gout.

N

Certainly, as far as I am concerned, there *are* symptoms—but surely these *may* be rheumatism or overworkism, but quite impossible that a shooting pain down my foot, and a red-hot twinge in my right toe, can be gout! Absurd!

I admit that, in any other person, such symptoms would be decidedly and unequivocally demonstrative of gout. But in myself—oh dear no—perish the thought! Still I should like to know exactly what it is; only let my doctors thoroughly understand this beforehand, that *whatever it may be, it isn't gout.*

Dr. Putteney has said, "We will find out what it is when we get you to Royat." So to Royat I go on a sort of voyage of discovery.

"We fly by night." Lovely weather. Bad crossing for many people, including Jane, for the sea is decidedly rough, though the Heavens above are clear, and the moon and stars shining brightly. I am well; yet I feel that any injudicious movement on my part, or two extra careless lurches finishing with a going-any-how sort of roll on the part of the steamer, would destroy the balance of comfort and number me among the victims of sea-sickness. The sensation caused by this dubious sort of all-rightness, the reason of which I can't understand, is so peculiar that there are minutes when I almost envy the sufferers.

We arrive at Calais: Jane a mere wreck, myself still in an abnormal state of all-rightness. Not being famished at the moment, we purchase a little refreshment to take with us. I find time hanging rather heavily on my hands; the train is pretty full, but we have secured our seats. Our companions are three grubby-looking Englishmen, who would not be useful as advertisements for any soap.

I wonder (to Jane) why we do not start. Jane wonders too; but being sleepy, she is indifferent to all that is going on, and to all that is not going on, including our train. A bell rings: "*En voiture—pour Paris—en voiture!*" Jane from her dim and distant corner faintly inquires, "I suppose our luggage is all right?" This is her fixed idea: that in travelling abroad, your luggage must go wrong. I reply of course it's all right, and am explaining that when once it is registered *through*, you need not trouble yourself about it till you reach your destination "—when it suddenly flashes across me that I had been strictly charged, on starting, to remember that *all luggage for Royat would be examined at Calais, and not at Paris.* Heavens, there are two minutes! As if struck by an electric shock, I jump up, safely accomplish the difficult feat of letting myself down from the carriage—which is as if I were escaping from an attic-window —(why are all these French compartments such a height from the ground?) rush across the line, on to the platform, and excitedly demand the *douane.*

In a tone of utter indifference two officials pause in their conversation to ask me what I said, to which, when repeated with an adjuration for pity's sake to stop the train, they reply by pointing out the office "*au bout,—là-bas*"—and I run to the extremity of the station, burst in among the *douaniers,* claim our *bagages* (there are no others), swearing by everything I hold sacred that there is nothing contraband in any one of my pieces, pointing out that if they stop to examine any of them I shall lose my train,—the train that is going to Royat,—that it is not a matter of smuggling, but that it is *ma santé qui est en jeu,* that on them will be the responsibility if . . . when the *chef* (bless him!) accepting my assurances, goodnaturedly passes them, tells off a couple of porters to place them in the train, and grateful beyond expression, except in bows which are rapid but profuse—for never did man make so many obeisances or do such wonderful things with a hat in one second, as I do on this occasion,—I return the way I came, and forgetting to remunerate the porters, rush back to our carriage—there is no difficulty in finding it, as Jane's head and shoulders are leaning out of the door, and her looks are as distracted as *Sister Anne's* must have been when she didn't see anyone coming—scale the dizzy height, not without injury to my trousers, and once more take my seat, telling her that it is all right.

Scarcely are the words out of my mouth, when up come two guards and address me brusquely, as if obeying such a word of command as "Up, Guards, and at 'em!" "What do they say?" asks Jane. *That we are not in the right carriage for Royat!* No, I know we are not; but we intend, I inform them with the air of a traveller who knows his way about, and has done this sort of thing before, to drive across Paris, and not go by the *Ceinture*; and so, Misters, you see we are in the right carriage for *that* anyhow. "Guards," baffled, retire. Then suddenly Jane produces a paper-bag full of greengages. She has bought them at the station, because it was better than getting anything to drink. Well, it's not a bad idea.

Fruit is always wholesome. I try one. Only one is possible: all the others are as hard as their own stones, and have to be thrown away scarcely indented. Indented!—Ah! that greengage . . . . I bit it. I partially ate it . . . . it was sweetish . . . . it was sourish . . . . it was bitter . . . . and "this indenture witnesseth." . . . . . But never again, a greengage ripe or unripe, when travelling. The next thing (which I do not attribute to the greengage) is that I sneeze three times, and find that I have caught cold. Already I am qualifying for Royat.

Whenever I go abroad again (I made this Mem. mentally some time ago) I will on arrival buy an *Indicateur des Chemins de Fer*, which is the French *Bradshaw*, and most useful not only for the time one is away, but also, as they do not alter the hours of their trains very much, whenever one wants to sit down comfortably at home and map out a trip from place to place in France.

At Calais there is no bookstall open. Cannot procure the *Indicateur*. Perhaps at Boulogne. Boulogne no stoppage to speak of. All very dark. No sign of bookstall. Consequently no *Indicateur*. Can procure one somewhere along the line. Bookstall at Amiens; no *Indicateur*. Never mind; sure to get one at the Nord or at the Paris-Lyon Station.

Journey as usual. Alternately sleepy and wakeful. The Three Dirty Men fast asleep, and breathing heavily, but not snoring. Two of them become quite disjointed, and tumble up against each other like badly-packed sacks. I envy their deep sleep. Whenever I wake up and look at them they seem each time to have become hotter and dirtier, but faster asleep than ever.

At Paris, my trusty friend, George Layzo, has sent the invaluable Commissionaire David, in full uniform, at 5·50 A.M., to take charge of us, see us across Paris, secure rooms where we can get "a wash and brush-up," then breakfast, when David produces to-day's *Matin*, and gives me all the latest, or earliest, news of Paris. With nearly another hour to spare, we saunter about, buying books and papers, while David secures for us a *coupé à réculons*, in which we place our small *impedimenta*, and then we see the carriages, which have taken all this time getting round Paris by the *Ceinture* line from the Nord station to that of the Paris-Lyon, where we are now, coming in slowly, and being joined on to our part of the train.

Just as we are leaving I remember that I haven't bought an *Indicateur*. We are actually moving. Through the noise of bells and steam-whistles I call out to David, "*Indicateur—il me faut un Indicateur! Vite! vite!*" David nods amiably towards me, smiles, takes off his cap, salutes me, and evidently hasn't an idea of what I have been shrieking out to him. Never mind. Some-where along the line I can get one. Certainly at Nevers. Nevers for Ever! Not a bit.

Owing to a break-down on the part of the engine—very volatile conduct of an engine doing a "break-down," but perhaps it is its way of letting off a little of the superfluous steam—our stoppages at the stations are so uncertain, that it is very risky to leave our carriage at all. In some places, where an official tells us we are to stop two minutes, we remain very nearly ten, though it is impossible to foresee this, and as far as appear-ances go,—Guards in their places, doors shut, man ready with flag, telegraph bell ceased—we are ready to start at any moment (and here is the danger to the unfortunate *voyageur*), and at the shortest possible notice. At other stations, where they profess to stay ten minutes, they give us scarcely two, and I am actually on my way to a bookstall to purchase an *Indicateur*, when I hear "*En voiture, s'il vous plaît!*" and I hurry back again just in time to climb up into the carriage, grazing my knees in the effort, and to throw myself at the feet of Cousin Jane, who is almost in a state of collapse at the idea of my being left behind with the tickets, and the luggage ticket too, in my pocket.

So I give up my search for an *Indicateur* until I shall arrive at Clermont-Ferrand.

Cousin Jane's anxiety is still about the luggage. She does not

believe that it can get on by itself, but is of opinion that it ought
to be somewhere within reach of the eye, at least. This disturbs
her equanimity,—what disturbs mine is that early greengage. As
the time goes on, and as we go on along that apparently inter-
minable journey, I am becoming more and more the invalid at
every station, until we arrive at Clermont-Ferrand, when I am
prostrate. What I feel fit for is to be carried to a dark room, to
be laid on a sofa, to be covered up, and to moan and groan till
I'm better. At all events, to suffer alone, and keep my misery to
myself.

As it happens I am compelled to keep my misery to myself, for
here, on the platform, is Dr. Putteney, looking the picture of
health, and more jovially cherubic than ever, lifting his white
hat on a stick with one hand, and waving a white and yellow
handkerchief furiously with the other, as if he were a bookmaker
on a race-course anxious to indicate the precise spot where
he is to be found. It really expresses his delight at our safe
arrival.

Near him is Mrs. Dinderlin, telegraphing to us with her sunshade, while a stoutish, elderly gentleman, of decidedly foreign appearance, in straw hat, coloured shirt, big white tie, knee-breeches,
and riding boots, and carrying under one arm a very small toy Skye-
terrier, is moving towards me (I say " me," for I have lost sight
of Cousin Jane in the crowd), gesticulating with a whip, his face
(which I seem to recognize, but without being able to associate it
with a name or a place) beaming with smiles as he cries,—" Allo !
Allo ! Here they are ! Kom tis way—I show you. Here—ter
Arnspektur, he will take your teckets,"—and before I have time
to ask anything, or to explain quietly how unwell I feel, to Dr.
Putteney, who will insist on still continuing a kind of savage war-
dance while waving his hat and stick—much to the astonishment
of the natives, who set him down as an eccentric Englishman, but
of course haven't a notion that he is a medical man—fortunately
his practice is in London and not here, or such conduct would ruin
his chances—I say before I have time or opportunity to say a
word to Dr. Putteney privately, the excited foreign gentleman in
sporting costume has snatched the tickets out of my hand, handed
them to the collector, and is lugging me through the crowd,

saying, " Eet is all-right. Tis man here, the Commissionnaire, will see to all your baggage." It is booked for Royat, I say, and this station is Clermont-Ferrand. *Ça ne fait rien,—même chose.* You go by road—drive more quick as the train, and we will be at ter Otel before the baggage. *Allons!*

We have come at such a pace, by the force of my foreign friend's energy, through the station and out into the road, that I have been unable to look round. Now I see before me a landau with two horses, and a driver in a blouse (this reminds me of La Bourboule), and in the carriage is seated Cousin Jane (how on earth did she get there?), Mrs. Dinderlin (who, a minute ago, was on the platform), and another lady, *petite*, handsome, dark, with very bright eyes and a lovely complexion, while Dr. Hammond Putteney, white hat in hand, and still in the highest possible spirits, is holding the door open for me to step up, and addressing me with great glee as "*Altesse.*" He says, "*Montez, Altesse!*" in the hearing of the crowd of porters and omnibus-conductors, travellers, idlers, and railway officials.

The Commissionnaire of the Hotel grins from ear to ear. He knows that it isn't an *Altesse;* and even the idlers in the crowd are too busy to trouble their heads about anyone's affairs but their own. So Dr. Putteney's joke falls a little flat except as regards himself, with whom it is a great success and "goes" enormously.

The bright-eyed lady is Madame Leverriez, to whom I am at once introduced by Mrs. Dinderlin, and I am preparing a few casual observations in my best French, when, addressing Cousin Jane and myself, our new acquaintance says, in excellent English, "You must be very tired after your journey, but really you both look quite fresh."

It is disappointing, when you expect French, to be addressed in English. For a moment my command over my own native tongue seems to have left me, so completely had I made up my mind to reply in a foreign tongue.

Colonel Leverriez puts the very small dog which he has been carrying on his wife's lap, and says, " My dear, take Lili back wit you. She will be lost in ter crowd, and tere are so many leetei dogs and poppies about. Ter Docteur and myself, we will go

witter baggage; it is registered for Royat, and we will be at ter
Otel as soon as you. *Allons! Docteur!*"

The Cherubic Doctor has been standing by, gaily beaming on
everything and everybody through his gold-rimmed spectacles,
with the air of a man who has done his duty with the happiest
possible results. He is awoke from his ecstatic day-dream by a
smack on the back from Colonel Leverriez, who, in spite of his
slightly grey moustache, has more the air of a big boy out for a
holiday than of a dignified warrior. However, as everything
seems for the best in this best of all possible watering-places, the
Cherubic Doctor only utters a gentle remonstrance, expressed in
the words, "Oh come, I say," when the Colonel, taking him quite
affectionately by the elbow, and bending his head over him
as if he were imparting to him some amusing information of
a strictly private and personal character, walks him off, and
they disappear in the crowd which is still swarming about the
station.

Through Clermont-Ferrand. Even at a first visit, and coming
from the train as we are, tired and dirty, and more inclined to
shut our eyes than open them, it strikes me as a very remarkable
old town. As we leave it, I see the beautiful towers of the
Cathedral, which, like the Crystal Palace, are visible from everywhere; and they have certain advantages over their lofty rival the
Puy-de-Dôme, which is some ten miles or so higher up in the air,
perpendicularly, inasmuch as they can be seen in pretty nearly
all weathers, while the Puy is frequently in difficulties, that is,
"under a cloud;" they can also be mounted by the curious
traveller in search of a view for considerably less than it costs
to ascend the competing mountain; and the city being situated
in a plain, the Cathedral towers are, so to speak, within
everybody's reach.

I look forward to revisiting Clermont-Ferrand, where there are,
the ladies inform Cousin Jane, excellent shops, and a really very
good dress-maker (only away twenty-one days for a water-cure,
and they can't do without a dress-maker!) and I see at once
that Royat, which is to Clermont-Ferrand what Kensington is to
London, is far superior in the resources of civilisation to my old
friend La Bourboule.

When we are well on our way to Royat I suddenly give a start —I can't help it—and Mrs. Dinderlin anxiously asks me if there's anything the matter.

"I've quite forgot——" I say.

"The luggage!" cries Jane. "I knew it! I felt certain——"

"No, no," I hasten to reassure her. "The luggage is all right. You'll see it at Royat. But—I've quite forgotten the *Indicateur!*"

"Oh, well," says Jane, who always likes to offer consolation, "you can easily get one here, or on our road back."

Yes; I will. I must get one here, in case we want to return by some other route. But it is curious that during so many hundred miles from London to Clermont-Ferrand, I have not been able to purchase an *Indicateur des Chemins de Fer.* So strongly am I bent on procuring an *Indicateur*, that for the moment all other considerations of health seem to have been put aside, and my one object in coming to Royat appears to have been (unconsciously to myself up till now) the purchase of a French Railway Guide, price seventy-five centimes.

Up-hill all the way, under a viaduct, past some gardens and a stand of *voitures* on our left, past hotels, shops, and booths, post-office, more hotels, round a corner, up-hill again, and into a sort of tea-garden, where there are tables and seats under the trees, which is the court-yard of our hotel, the Hotel Continental. This court-yard adjoins a terrace, which I ascertain by walking to the balustrade at the edge and looking over, is actually the leads of the Premier and Splendid Hotels, commanding one of the finest views in Royat of the park below and of the distant country. In point of fact we have driven upstairs, and alighted on the roof of the hotel where we are going to stop. This is astonishing, but true.

A sharp-eyed, pleasant-faced young man steps forward. This, says Madame Leverriez, is Monsieur Bachl the Manager. Once more I am preparing my best, or second-best, French for Monsieur Bachl, and once more I am disappointed.

"Your rooms are ready, Madam," he says politely to Cousin Jane, in English which scarcely betrays the accent of any nationality. "You would like to see them? This way, I will show you."

And so he bows us pleasantly off the roof, and we find that we have only one short flight of stairs to descend in order to reach our rooms on the top floor of the hotel below. And so here we are at Royat! Charming rooms!

"And the luggage?" exclaims Jane, looking blankly at me.

"It must have arrived," says M. Bachl, reassuringly, and so he conducts us back again to the court-yard on the roof.

CLERMONT-FERRAND.

CHAPTER III.

ARRIVAL COMPLETED — REMARKS ON SITE — DINNER — COMPANY —
RESTRICTIONS — CASINO — LITTLE HORSES — RISKS — AN INTRO-
DUCTION — RETIREMENT — NIGHT — MORNING — THE FIRST GLASS.

One of the gracious Nymphs
of the Eugénie Fountain.

THE luggage has arrived. The Cherubic Doctor and the Colonel have been carried up with it by the omnibus, and the whole lot, consisting of the two men and the four boxes, have been safely deposited on to the roof of our hotel.

"To what address shall we have our letters sent?" I ask M. Bachl.

"Oh," replies our obliging Manager, "it is all the same. We are five hotels, one on the top of another, the Premier, the Splendid, the Continental, the Chabassière, and the Annexe. Address which you like, Sir: the letters are sure to come safe."

"Pairfaitly," says the Colonel. "Tere ees er man who cannot read: he sort all ter letters, and tey are delivered all right. Vonterful!" And he smiles encouragingly on M. Bachl, as if he had been bestowing the highest praise on the method adopted.

Three of the above-mentioned hotels seem to have been built in the lower part, and the two others are built against the upper part of a rocky mountain side, an advantageous site, probably the result of a prehistoric volcanic eruption—(which could not of itself have thrown up a whole collection of hotels from the depths of its own inner volcanic consciousness)—and from the garden-court-yard, where the *salle à manger* is situated, and which therefore is the centre of attraction to all the visitors, are various flights of steps leading down to mysterious-looking door-ways and passages, so that this garden resembles the feeding ground of a human rabbit-warren, and we are the bunnies who at stated times come out of our holes, run up to feed, and, having finished our meal, we pop back into our holes, not to be seen all together again till next feeding-time.

"Now," says Dr. Hammond Putteney, "we give you twenty minutes to prepare for dinner. We are already late," and his face actually assumes a look of severity, which is probably not entirely unconnected with an interior appreciation of the emptiness of most human organisations at a certain fixed hour.

None of us require any further hint, the Colonel and Madame Leverriez are already disappearing down into a hole on the left of the warren, we catch a glimpse of the last of Mrs. Dinderlin's skirt as she vanishes into another hole opposite, Mr. Bachl retires into his bureau hole, the waiters, who have come out to take stock of the new arrivals, are scampering back into their *salle à manger* hole. Dr. Hammond Putteney runs down an incline, and apparently goes head-first into his own particular hole. The Concierge, in blue and silver livery, appears out of a sort of game-keeper's hut on the premises (and perhaps it is at the sight of him that all the rabbits have scuttled away frightened), the Chamber-maid and Boots belonging to our *étage* appear on the steps leading to our rooms, and following their lead, we also vanish to our holes under the roof—which sounds more like starlings, or mice, than rabbits—and I find myself overlooking a most beautiful view which tempts me away from my sumptuary preparations for dinner. When I emerge and come out into the upper air, there is no one on the garden-roof. The Concierge (who most annoyingly will insist on speaking English, but whom I persist in answering in French,—his nationality being Swiss and his native tongue princi-pally German,) informs me that they have all gone in to dinner; and at an oval table, private, and out of reach of the noise and rattle of the *table-d'hôte*, from which we are divided by a temporary screen, I find seated Madame Leverriez, Dr. Hammond Putteney, the Colonel, Mrs. Dinderlin, Cousin Jane, and next to her a lady with whom Cousin Jane seems already on terms of the closest intimacy, and to whom she immediately presents me. She is a Mrs. Toffam, a sparkling-eyed American, speaking with just enough accent to give her remarks a certain piquancy which arrests attention. I have often remarked that a commonplace observation about the weather, a request to pass the salt, or an inquiry as to the state of your health, if given with the least American intonation, will be received by an ordinary English audience with a broad grin; and an obvious repartee, similarly delivered, will be the signal for almost inextinguishable mirth.

Dr. Hammond Putteney at meal-times is more cherubic than ever, as, metaphorically of course, he "sits up aloft to keep watch for the life of poor Jack"—poor Jack representing in this case the

PERFORMANCE OF "DRINK" AT ROYAT. Act First.

Early Spring-time at the Fontaine Eugénie.

patients generally, who, while feeding, are under the lynx-eye of Dr. Putteney.

Never have I seen the proverb that what is one man's meat is another's poison, so perfectly illustrated, as in this dining-room, and at our particular table, where Dr. Putteney, with his watchful eye, not only on us, but on the diners at many other tables, partakes heartily of everything, as he is out for a holiday, and "treating himself handsomely"—and I must say he treats himself very handsomely. On the table, with the costly wine of the

country, of which, as at La Bourboule, the Hotel is so lavish that
as much as each person can drink of this rare stuff (thank goodness, very rare !) is included in the price of the dinner, and so we
call it "the generous,"—a name by which it is henceforth known
to the waiter who serves our table,—there are all sorts of the
waters of the place, César, St. Mart, and Fonteix, which, as the
Irishman said of the whiskey, "take the cruelty out of the water,"
—only, in this case, it is the water which takes the cruelty out of
the wine.

As everyone at our table is taking baths and waters, we have
plenty to talk about, the main subject at every repast being our
progress, our symptoms, and ourselves generally since we were last
together round the festive board.

None of us ever meet without comparing notes of new pains and
fresh symptoms.   When undergoing a treatment, the knowledge
that others are having, or have had, all the pains which have so
taken oneself by surprise on their first appearance, is a great
solace and encouragement to persevere.   It is comforting to be
assured that your particular pain in your particular toe is not the
only pain in the world ; that others are suffering equally in
corresponding toes, and that others have suffered it, and have got
rid of it—"it may be for years, it may be for ever."   And let me
add, with all my heart and toe, another question, "If for ever,
then for ever fare thee well ! "

The night is lovely.   We take our coffee and cigars—Dr. Putteney permits coffee, cigars, and *liqueurs,* and I hope Dr. Rem, to
whose care he will resign me to-morrow, will be of the same
opinion—out in the garden of the Casino Samie, and once more,
after an interval of two years, I see my old friends, the *petits
chevaux,* with their *petits jockeys,* going round and round with the
same provoking uncertainty ; and, as if they, too, were glad to
welcome me back again, they allow me to back the winner twice
out of three times.   Cousin Jane, becoming rash, ventures two
francs, and retires discomfited.   She says she was not made for a
gambler, and thinks that as early hours are to be our rule, the
sooner we go to our rooms and "couch ourselves" the better for
health.

Just as we are leaving, Dr. Rem enters the grounds, and Cousin

Jane and myself are introduced to him. Slight, above the middle height, is Dr. Rem, with a countenance expressive of the utmost benevolence, and clear bright eyes which regard you straight in the face, as much as to say, "Yes, I am benevolent and kind, but don't you attempt to presume on these qualities, or you'll find yourself considerably out in your calculations, my friend." Dr. Rem, like Sir Pen Oliver, Grand Master of the Knights of the Octave Table, is not only a distinguished physician, but a man of letters, an enthusiast in every department of science, something of an artist (as indeed his name indicates), and as devoted to music

as is Sir Pen to etching and painting. He is an Englishman, though his name is foreign, and, if there were another syllable to it, he would have been able to claim descent from one of the greatest of the Old Masters. I am to begin by taking one glass at the Eugénie Spring to-morrow morning, and then I am to call on the Doctor, when my real serious Water-Course, under his orders and the personal supervision of the Cherubic Doctor, is to commence in earnest.

My window is open all night. I look out on to the park, where the lights are glittering among the trees, and where the little horses are still playing, *à deux francs* the course, and then I look up at the woods, the vineyards, the near hills and distant mountains. The entire country is volcanic; in ages gone by it has been in a frightful state of eruption; then suddenly the mysterious arsenical, ferruginous, and potassian waters sprang up and cured the eczema on Dame Nature's face. This is my history of Royat. Balmy air; no flies; no mosquitoes, but no sleep—to speak of. Very restless. Up betimes next morning. Air balmier than ever. Room faces nearly due North—perfectly cool. Dr. Putteney, looking even more cherubic than usual, and finishing a cigar after his first *petit déjeuner*, calls to take me to Dr. Rem's room, where we are to hold a consultation, and decide on what is to be done with me. On our way we make a slight *détour* and call at the Eugénie Source, where at the hands of an elderly buxom nymph with a huge pink bow above her cap, I receive my first glass of the Waters of Royat.

CHAPTER IV.

A CONSULTATION—A BODY—THE PRISONER—BODY AGAIN—ANXIOUS MOMENT—DECISION—REHEARSAL—LAUNCHED.

Dr. Rem.

WHENEVER I call upon a Doctor professionally, with a view to consulting him about my own health, I am invariably diverted from what ought to be the all-absorbing subject of my visit by an overpowering interest in *his* health. It seems,—that is, so it strikes me at the moment,— so dreadfully selfish and egotistical when two men are together for one of them to have no other subject of conversation but himself, his history in the past and his manner of life in the present, and so I cannot avoid discarding my own health, putting that topic aside as one which we can take up at any moment when we've exhausted others of more pressing importance; and the Doctor, specially if he be one whom I am consulting for the first time, becomes at once the object of my sympathetic curiosity. I want to know all about himself, first; and when we've done that, then we will take myself up as a secondary consideration. If the medical man is an old friend, we have so much of common interest between us that it is a long time before we get at the special object of my visit. On this occasion, however, I am taken by the Cherubic Dr. Hammond Putteney to see Dr. Rem of Royat; and as they have to discuss me as a "case," it is for me to listen, and, if necessary, answer questions. Once in Dr. Rem's professional *sanctum*, Dr. Hammond Putteney ceases to be cherubic, puts on his gold spectacles (both doctors wear gold-rimmed spectacles) in a way that gives him a grave and anxiously scientific air, and seats himself at such a distance from me, as conveys the idea that from this moment until the close of the interview we are no longer on our ordinary equal and friendly footing, and his entire manner gives me clearly to understand that for the time being I must look upon himself and Dr. Rem as two super-human intelligences, and myself as a mere passive body, conscious, but in a state of suspended animation. Then, as Dr. Rem seats himself at his desk, with pen and paper before him, the scene seems to undergo a change, and it occurs to me that he looks like a benevolent country Magistrate hearing a charge in his own private room, and that Dr. Hammond Putteney figures in the scene as the constable who brings the charge, keeping an eye on me, who am, as it were, the prisoner.

"Now!" says Dr. Rem, taking up his pen, and looking in the direction of Dr. Putteney. Whereupon Dr. Putteney, in his character of constable, commences his charge against me, giving his evidence "from information received," *i.e.*, from myself. I listen calmly, and, as he is stating the case fairly and succinctly, I see no reason for interrupting or contradicting him. Occasionally I nod affirmatively, or put in an adverb intended to qualify, or intensify some of his statements.

His whole testimony he delivers with an air of deference due to the presence of the elder Doctor, and yet with something of the

o

pride of a discoverer. It is in this latter vein, that having finished his evidence, he ceases to appear as the constable, and resuming his original character of scientific Doctor, gives his own opinion on the case, which he announces as something that will take Dr. Rem by surprise, and ultimately astonish the faculty generally.

" You examine him yourself," says the Cherubic One, nodding in the direction where I am seated, but not otherwise recognising my existence as a body ; " you'll see he's anæmic."

Dr. Rem professes himself sceptical, but at once puts the assertion to the test.

" Well," he exclaims, drawing a long breath, after having satisfied himself by a thorough examination, during which I simply remain a body, offering no resistance, making no remarks. " Well, I own I am astonished. Yes," he adds, emphatically, and yet with a slight indication of unwillingness at being compelled by truth to corroborate Dr. Puttency's assertion, "he *is* anæmic."

They do not talk *to* me, but *of* me, and an expression of surprise escaping me, which is an attempt on my part at joining in the consultation, passes as entirely unheeded as does the clock striking the quarter.

Mentally I say to myself, "So I'm an *anémique*, am I ! I see— no man's *anémie* but my own. Good ! What next ? Go it, Gentlemen ! "

But Dr. Puttency having already scored, has nothing more to observe, and waits with a self-satisfied and critical air to hear his senior's verdict.

Dr. Rem asks me a few questions, but as my answers only confirm Dr. Puttency's previous account of me, they fail to throw any fresh light on the subject, and Dr. Rem enters the whole case in his notebook, considers it carefully, closes it, pushes it away as though its presence bothered him, sits back in his chair, and, after an awful silence of at least half a minute, during which I begin to wonder, rather nervously, whether he has hit upon something so fatal in my case as to render any treatment whatever utterly useless, and whether he is only meditating how best to break this unwelcome intelligence to me, he turns to Dr. Puttency, and, to my infinite relief, observes that he has every hope of putting me all right—ultimately, and states what his plan is to be. Dr. Putteney ventures to suggest some alterations, but as he has had his turn, and played his part, Dr. Rem only courteously considers his propositions in order to as courteously dismiss them, preferring his own "*traitement*," the particulars of which he will let me have a little later this morning, when he will introduce me to the Director of the Bath Establishment, and put me *au courant* with everything necessary.

Rehearsing the Douche Nasale.

We are on the point of being bowed out, when Dr. Putteney smoothing his hat in a nervous manner, asks diffidently, "Don't you think he may take the *douche nasale*?"

Dr. Rem hesitates, and regards me dubiously. This part of the interview reminds me of the time when a relation used to come for me at school, and ask the Head Master, if, always supposing I had been a good boy, I mightn't have a half-holiday. How anxiously I used to await the master's answer, and how tremblingly I noted his hesitation, as he looked in my face inquiringly, as much as to say, "Shall I recall the fact that you were not a good boy yesterday—that you were punished the day before—that you put jam in another boy's hat last Thursday—and for these courtesies, am I to grant you a half-holiday ?"

That I am to take an ordinary bath every day, and to drink so much water regularly, seems to me to be so monotonous an affair that I shall really be glad if the Doctor will vary it with a *douche nasale.* From my former experiences at Aix-les-Bains, Aix-la-Chapelle, and La Barboule, there is nothing so wearying as the mechanical order of the treatment, and it is therefore quite a little holiday for the patient to be prescribed a *gargarisme,* or a *douche,* or a *vapeur,* or a *massage.* So when Dr. Rem's eyes meet mine, I am conscious of a beseeching look in my own, as if imploring him not to condemn me to a terrible unbroken monotony. With joy I recognise a gleam of pity in his glance as, with a benevolent smile, he turns towards Dr. Putteney, and says, " Yes, he may take the nasal *douche.*"

" And," inquires Dr. Putteney, with increasing diffidence, as if he feared the result of his temerity in asking too much all at once, but he'll risk it,—just as my relation coming to fetch me at school having gained a half-holiday, would request the Master to stretch one point more of discipline in my favour, and allow me to return after the hour of " lock-up,"—" Mightn't he take the *pulverisation* later on ? "

Dr. Rem regards me thoughtfully. He evidently considers we are presuming on his previous concession : besides, if he agrees to this addition to his original prescription, it is no longer his treatment, but his in collaboration with Dr. Putteney. He is on the point of refusing (I am sure of it) and the Cherubic Doctor is already beginning to be sensible of having gone a little too far, when a brilliant idea of a compromise strikes Dr. Rem, who quite brightens up as he says to the Medical Cherub, " I'll tell you what he shall do ! He shall take the *douche nasale* and the *pulverisation* alternately," and thereupon he sits down triumphantly, and makes a note of this in his book. The Cherubic Doctor beams on me through his spectacles, as much as to say, " There ! you wouldn't have got all these luxuries if it hadn't been for me ! " I feel immensely relieved and satisfied with the prospect of a pleasing variety in the treatment, and Dr. Rem who has several patients

waiting in the ante-room, bows us out so courteously, and says
"*Au revoir*" so reassuringly, that I already feel more than half
cured of whatever is the matter with me. I differ from him as to
the symptoms being at all gouty, but I keep this opinion, being
an unprofessional one, and not asked for at the consultation, to
myself.

The Cherubic Doctor, who outside Dr. Rem's, and away from
business, becomes at once the gay young Anglo-German student

M. Le Régisseur l'Exploitation des etablissements thermaux (or " Commander
of the Bath ") de Royat, receives us Royat-ly.

out for a holiday, is in ecstacies of delight at the permission
granted me to take a *douche nasale* and a *pulverisation.*

" Do you know how to manage them ?" he asks.

Yes, I am on friendly terms with "*pulverisation*," but to the
douche nasale I am a stranger.

" Come along, then, I'll show you," he exclaims joyfully, and,
as if he were off for a real good lark, away he hurries me to the
Etablissement.

We enter a room, the aspect of which is familiar to me, as it is fitted up like the *pulverisation* department at La Bourboule, and he introduces me to the attendant nose-doucher, who fits me with a small glass tube all to myself (I thought he was going to measure my nose for it, but he guesses the size, and has one ready to hand), ties on a waterproof bib, and I take my seat at a tap.

"Can you play on this pipe?" asks the Cherubic Doctor, in the character of *Hamlet*.

"My liege, I can," I reply, rashly presuming on my acquaintance with the *pulverisation* process. In another minute I have douched my eyes, sent the water with four-horse engine power up my sleeve, into my mouth, and everywhere but up my nose, and in fact made a nice mess of it. The Cherubic Doctor watching me, now steps forward. "This is the way," he says, and guides my hand with the glass tube in it, "and don't forget," he adds, "to keep your left hand on the tap, so as to regulate the force."

For awhile I remember the injunction; I turn it on full; it operates wonderfully, and I feel as if I had filled my head with water, and would have water on the brain in another second, but for its running out as quickly as it has come in. Dr. Puttency, being near-sighted, has put his head down over my shoulder to see that I am carrying out his directions exactly, and at this moment pausing in the operation to tell him my sensations, I remove the pipe, but forgetting to turn the tap, the water goes without the slightest warning with full force right at the Cherubic Doctor's spectacles, and gives him such a startlingly unexpected douche as knocks him back into the arms of the attendant. There is no harm done, however, and here ends the first lesson on the *douche nasale* pipe.

Coming out on our road to breakfast we meet Dr. Rem, who introduces me to a most courteous gentleman, M. Chassan, the Acting Director of the place, or Commander of the Bath, who welcomes me to the Baths, and presents me with the freedom of the Casino. Now I am fairly launched on my Water-Course.

CHAPTER V.

CHIEFLY ON THE DIFFICULTY OF BEING "UP TO THE TIME OF DAY"
AT ROYAT.

**At the Fontaine César. Miss César
giving instructions to Pumpey.**

ON RETURNING, I find that Cousin Jane has been ordered César Water and César Baths.

"Doesn't he say your symptoms are gouty and not rheumatic?" I ask.

"No," she replies, "he only says I'm anæmic."

This is rather provoking. If Jane is anæmic, and has to drink César Water and take César Baths, why do I, being also anæmic, not have the same treatment? No; it is clear to me that, judging from the difference of treatment, Cousin Jane is gouty, as I have always told her she was, only a polite Doctor doesn't like to say it out point-blank.

It is so odd to me how some people will flatter themselves they haven't got gout, when every symptom proclaims most plainly to their friends what their real complaint is.

Happy-Thought Proverb.—Lookers-on see most of the gout.

The day goes wonderfully here. Rising early, drink from Eugénie or sources, then bath, then *buvette* again, then short walk, buy French papers and sometimes an amusing illustrated local journal called the *Royat Bijou*, in which the pictures of the place are really excellent. After this, first breakfast and rest in room, listen to band, write letter, or part of one feebly, and, at 11·30, second breakfast, *i.e.* early lunch.

As everything is done methodically here, to ascertain the correct

time, and to set your watch by it, is a matter of the first importance. But the Royat clocks, like the Rule of Three in the old
schoolboy rhyme, "they bother me." The timepieces, or the out-
of-time pieces, cannot agree upon a decided policy; they cannot be
unanimous—no, not for an hour. The visitors are implored by
the Hotel proprietors to be punctual in their attendance at the
table-d'hôte. A prayer to this effect meets the eye on every
landing, on every staircase, in every passage, until the visitor gets
it impressed upon his brain; and if he be of a truly sympathetic
nature, he will put himself to any temporary inconvenience rather
than that his unpunctuality at the *table-d'hôte* should in the
slightest degree distress the humble and beseeching proprietor.
He will do so once or twice, not more; and only this during the
time of his inexperience, which will not last beyond a couple of
days. At the *Etablissement* the tone taken is quite different.
Here the bather is peremptorily informed by printed cards which
he cannot possibly avoid seeing at every turn, and on the wall of
every cabinet, as well as by his bath-attendant—I am in the care
of the *doyen* of them—that, if having once fixed his own time, he
doesn't stick to it, he runs the chance of not getting a bath at all;
and if, being once in, he doesn't come out to the very minute, the
Administration will, to put it colloquially, know the reason why.
Consequently, what strikes you forcibly, at first sight, is the strict
punctuality of Royat. So you at once look about for the exact
time. Where are you to get it? The Church Clock? There is the
parish church—a marvellous old castellated church—up a hill, a
good, or, rather, a very bad quarter of an hour's toil, on a Royatly
hot day, and, when you reach it, well worth seeing in itself, but
no clock. You decide on setting your watch by the clock at the
Etablissement. You do so, and on returning to the hotel, you find
that either your watch has gained a quarter of an hour in less than
five minutes, or that the Hotel time is not in accord with the
Bathing-house time, and so you make a calculation, and take the
Hotel time.

At eleven, by Hotel time, you, as a novice, present yourself at
the *table-d'hôte.* It is the hour fixed by the Proprietor. The
tables are laid, but—*personne?* Not a soul! From behind different screens in various parts of the very long room a few waiters

appear, coming out as if they were playing a game of hide-and-seek, or rehearsing an entertainment. They give some finishing touches to the tables, and whisk off a fly or two with their napkins, as is the custom with waiters when they have an idle moment. The punctual visitor asks one of them, if it is not the hour of breakfast. Perfectly. Will Monsieur be seated? He can be served at once. No, thank you; Monsieur would rather not begin until there are some few to keep him company, as it looks

Mr. Baehl, of the Five Hotels at Royat, and a few more elsewhere.

Day Companion of the Bath. The Doyen of the Ministers, or Dean of Bath and Wells at Royat.

so greedy in a *table-d'hôte* of one hundred and twenty to be the only one feeding when the other hundred and nineteen guests arrive. They will be here soon. They come in gradually, and by 11·20 the room is full, and the breakfast has seriously commenced. From this the novice deduces that "eleven" punctually means a quarter to half-past eleven. But by which time? The clock on the stairs, the clock in the passage, the clock over the Post-office, or the clock at the Baths? There are other clocks in the village of a perfectly free and independent turn, and one on the basement of the Splendid Hotel of so feeble a character that it has given up the struggle altogether, and stopped dead with its two hands helplessly pointing to eleven, as if it had been within five minutes of finishing the day, but hadn't strength left to struggle up to twelve.

The force of all this bad example on my watch is that one morning it suddenly stops, and for one quarter of an hour with mule-like obstinacy refuses to go on. Now whether this course of conduct was adopted by my watch out of a mistaken sense of politeness towards the other clocks, in order to let them come up with it—it had been fifteen minutes in advance of most of them—or whether it thought it ought to start fair, or whether it was from sheer cussedness, or the effect upon its works of Royat temperature, has ever since remained a mystery to me, which Time may or may not explain. Just as I was on the point of taking it to a watch-maker's, its state of suspended animation came to an end (which looks uncommonly as if it had been attempting some deception, and was afraid of professional investigation), and not only did it go on again as briskly as ever, but, as if to make up for lost time, it shot ahead of them all, and kept the lead by twenty minutes in front of the fastest of them, up to the end of my stay at Royat.

True there are bells to summon you; but if you attempt to check the time by the bells you will be "quite at sea." There are all sorts of breakfasts everywhere about, for all sorts and conditions of men. And there are bells to each meal; the first to inquire "Are you ready?" and then after waiting some twenty minutes for an answer, the second bell says "Off!" The Band is advertised to play from 9·30 to 10·30. But personally I have never been able to fix it to a particular time. I can say it will play about 9·30 and leave off about 10·30, but this is the nearest approach to certainty at which I can arrive. When it does start, the Band, which is excellent, keeps admirable time, though it never indulges its audience in any selection lasting more than two minutes, and the duration of its *entr'actes* is quite out of proportion to that of the *morçeaux* it performs. The exception is when they play as a *finale* the Overture to *William Tell*, or when a clever flageoletist—an artistic Whistler—gives us his peculiar views of how the "*Carnival de Vénise*" ought to be played if he could always have his way.

My conclusion is that a well-regulated healthy appetite is the best clock. I charitably allow for the difference of clocks, which are of all shades of opinion, and my advice to the visitor is, that he should daily regulate his own watch by the Bath-house clock. This is the only thing necessary, the appetite will do the rest.

Anyhow the day goes very quickly here, and, as the lively little

The Clockless Parish Church. "Time no object."

gentleman who has his shop next door, and acts as our Universal Provider—there is nothing he is not ready to get for you—observes, "All times are good at Royat," and he refuses to believe that an Englishman, coming here from his own land of fog, can possibly have any complaint to make. Does he not come here to get rid of his complaints?—and of his money too? The visitor is good for Royat, and Royat's good for him. "*Allons donc!* what matters the difference of clocks? You are hungry—good!—you go to breakfast. Nothing more to purchase this morning? Hair cut to-morrow? Perfectly—*à demain alors.*" And he laughs and nods as he re-enters his shop, and goes to his own *déjeuner*, after which he will reappear in his shirt-sleeves, enjoying a briar-root pipe.

Dr. Rem has hinted that the most useful guide for his treatment is a record of health kept by the patient himself. The "Treatment" is going on. So I am noting all pains and penalties. I am watching myself with a most vigilant eye. Not a twinge escapes me. If there's a sudden shoot in my knee, I spot it at once, and down it goes in my diary. If, on seating myself, there's a pain in my left shoulder, up I get again, out comes the diary, and time, place, and duration of pain are accurately written down. If I am out walking, and my foot hurts me, out comes note-book and I put my foot in it. If I am comfortably in bed, and feel sort of cramp all along my left side, out I roll (not jump), seize diary, record the fact, and back again to bed. By the end of four days—if I am only able to read what I have written—my diary of sensations will be by that time quite a sensational work.

Our "Lively Neighbour."

CHAPTER VI.

THE BAD PATIENT'S DIARY—JANE'S PROGRESS—OYSTERS—THEORY
—FACT—AT DOCTOR'S—THE STRANGE CASE—HALVES—CON-
SULTATION—NOVELTY—SENSATIONS—RESULT—PUZZLED.

WHEN you once get into the swim, so to speak, in a water course such as this, then, whether it be at Royat, or Aix-les-Bains, or Vichy, or Homburg, or even at La Bourboule and Le Mont Doré, the stream is very strong, and you are carried on rapidly to the end of your stay. The first week is exciting, if the place is itself a novelty; if not, it is only less exciting; we walk up into the pine woods,—"when," as Dr. Putteney says, "we pine for air"—(this is the effect of the place on him), and we take the week to settle down. The second week is generally dull, yet at the end of it the time seems to have flown. Third week begins slowly; but as the climax of the twenty-first day approaches, when the course will be over, then the time and money go with startling rapidity.

By my Diary of Pains and Penalties I find I am at the end of the first week. What is the result? Well? No, decidedly not well; that is, according to my Diary, which records a variety of alarming symptoms—sleepless nights, sleepy days, troubles in toes —where the shooting season has commenced before the Twelfth—pains in the nose, limp legs, wrestlings with sciatica, and what the meteorological reports term "Disturbances" generally, resulting in "Depression."

An annoying circumstance is, that Cousin Jane, who has not been strictly ordered here, as I was, but only "recommended" to the waters, is becoming better and better every day. I cannot help remarking it. The improvement in her health is so marked that it forces itself on general observation. She takes a bath of César water every day, into which she goes like cold lamb, and out of which she comes like boiled lobster, and is all the better for it. She is able to walk about briskly; she doesn't hesitate as to taking a *liqueur* with her cup of coffee after dinner; she insists on venturing at least four francs on the *petits chevaux*, and in her manner

there suddenly appears something of the effervescent and sparkling character which is, she informs me, the peculiarity of the
Source César. The Romans discovered these baths, and this particular spring may have been the source of Cæsar's greatness.
The question—

> "Upon what meat does this our Cæsar feed,
> That he is grown so great?"

is, as it is termed in theatrical slang, "a little bit of fat" that
would never have been put into the mouth of *Cassius*, "lean and
hungry" as he was, had Shakspeare only known of the waters at
Royat, which Cæsar used to drink, and in which he used to bathe;
and out of which, after a few dozen oysters,—for they find heaps
of oyster-shells here among the Roman remains,—he used to come
out re-invigorated.

By the way, although I am considering Cousin Jane's case, and
have so got back to Cæsar, to whom historically she owes her rapid
improvement in health, I cannot help diverging on the subject of
Oysters, to note down, for some future work of my own on Chris-
tianity in Britain, the theory, which is strongly supported by
facts, that Britons, who never would be slaves (except when they
couldn't help it), owed their conversion entirely to Oysters. I
am not going to discuss this further or to commence the first
chapter of my history now, but before the thoughtful reader
I place facts and theory:—1st. It is undeniable that the Romans
loved oysters: 2nd. That directly they heard of oyster-beds
they went to them: 3rd. They found the beds ready-made
for them, and originated the old riddle (which occurs in the
works of Josephus Millerius) about taking the oysters out of
their beds and tucking in themselves: 4thly. The Romans
became Christians without ceasing to be oyster-eaters,—in fact it
is probable that they practised oysterities — and consequently
the British oyster-openers, and oyster-bed-makers, were the first
to encounter the Christianised Romans, who lost no time in
converting the natives, and thus the British became Christians by
the dozen.

From the oysters, *à nos moutons;* second course. To resume.
Naturally Jane's progress is annoying to me, but politely and

cousinly, I am delighted. I complimented her, she is looking so well. But I cannot compliment myself. Do *I* look well? Jane says I do. But I don't believe it, and I'm sure I don't. A high colour isn't health : it may be "the picture of health," but health isn't a question of the picture, but of the frame.

Whatever was the matter with me before coming to Royat, I am quite sure as to there being plenty the matter with me, and to spare, now, after just a week of the treatment.

My Sensational Diary is assuming formidable proportions. If I neglect it for half a day, the next morning I set myself to work to remember all the sufferings of yesterday afternoon. If you do not jot down pains at the moment, as they occur, when you can really feel what you are describing—the secret of all truly graphic writing—you are apt to describe the twinges, the smarts, and the aches coldly, as if you were writing the history of somebody else. You are likely to take a very different view of a pain you suffered several hours ago, from what you will take of the pain which afflicts you at the time of writing, and which itself is the immediate cause of your putting pen to paper. In a retrospect of pain you are inclined to philosophise and probably attempt to trace its cause. In a description of a pain, making its presence felt as you write, you do not stop to pick and choose your words, but your style is short, sharp, jerky, powerfully graphic, and minutely accurate.

I determine not to disturb Dr. Hammond Putteney, who, not taking the waters in any form, eating and drinking everything, and smoking all day, is in the enjoyment of most perfect health, and apparently of a thorough holiday, but to go quietly to Dr. Rem, show him my Diary, and astonish him.

I call upon him. He is within. I wait : at last I usher myself into his sanctum. Will I be seated. I will. So will he, at his desk, and once more he pulls out his note-book and refers to my particular case.

Before he can ask any questions, I produce, with quite a professional air, my analytical summary of my own state of health. I am very glad I have noted it all down so carefully, because, as this is a peculiarly fine morning and I am feeling uncommonly well, my view of the past few days, had I left my pains to verbal description from memory only, would have been necessarily coloured by my healthy, happy, and perfectly satisfactory state at the present moment, and Dr. Rem might, under a false impression, write down "cured in five days' treatment," or order me to go on as I had begun, a treatment that might be exactly contrary to what I ought to do. As it is there is my plain written statement which I can neither explain away nor contradict. *Litera scripta manet*, and this diary is produced by myself as evidence against myself. It is a *précis* of my pains and penalties, and, considering that after all it is the work of an amateur, I really am quite proud of it as a scientific treatise written by myself, Dr. One-Half, as an impartial observer, on myself, Mister Other-Half, or patient, merely taken as a body.

Everyone has read the *Strange Case of Dr. Hyde and Mr. Jekyll.* (By the way it may be *Dr. Jekyll and Mr. Hyde*, but that's of no consequence, and I haven't the book by me.) Well, here is the story very simply exemplified in Me. I am compounded of two halves : *Dr. Hyde* one half, the scientific medical man ; *Mr. Jekyll*, other half, the patient. As *Dr. Hyde* I call on Dr. Rem, to inform him how poor *Mr. Jekyll* has been getting on with his treatment. *Mr. Jekyll* the patient sits in the chair : *Dr. Hyde* is represented by the diary containing the scientific analysis of the "strange case," which Dr. Rem has now under his eyes.

Dr. Rem is reading *Dr. Hyde's*, *i.e.*, my, scientific analysis, most attentively. I, *Mr. Jekyll* the patient, am watching him anxiously. I expect him to raise his eyebrows at certain points, and exhibit surprise. I expect him to purse up his lips, and mutter to himself "Dear me !" or "Bless my soul, is it possible !" I expect him to rise in an agitated manner from his desk, go to his book-case, and bring out big volumes, over which he will pore, from time to time comparing what he is reading with my strange narrative of the past week. I expect him after this to sit down and rest his aching head on his hand thoughtfully, as if this extraordinary case had fairly perplexed him, had upset all his principles, all his practice, and had compelled him to own himself beaten. Should he disappoint me in exhibiting any of the above-mentioned emotions, I

certainly look forward to his throwing himself back in his chair,
drawing a long breath and regarding me with an air of mixed
wonder and admiration, when he comes to that touching, but
forcible passage (which I have underlined) about the perfectly
unaccountable pain in my left leg.

But he does none of these things: he reads on calmly and quietly,
as if my remarkable statement were a conventional letter from a

Peu de Cheveux aux Petits Chevaux.

distant relative, or an ordinary leading article in an English newspaper during the recess. Sometimes he nods towards the diary,
either as if he were agreeing with it, or going to sleep over it, and
occasionally, he smiles slightly; but what he can find to smile at
in an analytical account of pains during the past week, I cannot for
the life of me make out. Evidently I have been too considerate
for his feelings, and in recounting my sufferings I have not been
sufficiently harrowing. However, he turns over the second page,
and reads on. I watch him closely as he comes to the point about
a sudden and excruciating twinge in my left knee, and in my ancle.
He doesn't move a muscle of his countenance, I know *I* did when

P

I felt it. Clearly, I couldn't have put it strongly enough. He turns over to the fourth page: again I watch him narrowly. Surely the recital of crackling pains in every joint, and a kind of catherine-wheel in both great toes, ending in a coruscation of fireworks of pain all over my body, ought at least to make him gravely shake his head. But it doesn't.

He has reached the end of my piteous narrative, he has read the exhaustive analysis, he sees sitting before him, "the subject of the present memoir," feverishly awaiting his verdict, and after folding up the paper and handing it back to me, he adjusts his spectacles so as to focus me thoroughly, and take me in, as it were, all at once, and then with a smile,—actually with a smile, and of the utmost benevolence too,—he says, "Capital !"

I am so astonished, I can only ejaculate gaspingly, "Eh ?" as if I hadn't heard aright.

"Capital !" he repeats, smiling more radiantly and more benevolently than before. Then tapping his hands gently one against the other, as if he were playing "pat-a-cake Baker's man," with an infant, he adds, "Just exactly what I had expected."

I am so utterly knocked over that I can only stare at him vacantly, as if wondering which of us two had temporarily taken leave of his senses. Coming to the conclusion that I am still in possession of mine, I rouse myself for an emphatic protest.

"But," I say with animation, so that he may understand that I am really in earnest, "surely it isn't right for me to have a pain in my knee every night," here I rub my knee, where there is no pain at present, "so that I can hardly sleep."

"Perfectly right," he says with composure.

"And the day before yesterday," here I refer to my notes for corroboration, "I had such a pain all down my left leg, I couldn't move for ten minutes."

"That's just what it ought to be," he replies, nodding complacently.

"But that pain in my elbow," I point to a passage in the diary where it is graphically described, "I never had that before I came here. It was really—most—most—" I am drying up for want

of words,—all my epithets are in the diary, and it seems weak to
repeat them—"it was most aggravating."

"Oh yes—no doubt," returns Dr. Rem, still nodding at me
encouragingly, "but it couldn't be better. Indeed I should have
been sorry if you hadn't had it. I should have been afraid the
waters weren't doing you any good."

"What?" I exclaim. Then, as if I were trying to bring him to
reason, I expostulate calmly with him, and, adopting a conciliatory

Source au Toe-martyr.

tone, I attempt to demonstrate to him that at all events a pain
right across the forehead can't be a good sign.

"On the contrary," he replies. "Excellent."

"And my sleeplessness?" I ask.

"Perfect," he answers, briskly.

"The pains in my ancles?" I go on.

"First-rate," he says, rubbing his hands gleefully.

"And in my toes?"

"Just where it ought to be," he returns, highly pleased.

"And in my back, and wrists, and—so that I can't walk—and over my knees, and such a cramp at night that I have to jump out of bed and stamp in agony?" I ask, piling up all the symptoms together in my despair.

"It's splendid!" says Dr. Rem, perfectly beaming with rapture at what he immediately explains to me are certain and unmistakable signs that the Waters of Royat are really doing their work on me in the most satisfactory manner possible. "You will continue," says Dr. Rem, dipping his pen in the ink preparatory to entering the *ordonnance* in his own note-book, "you will continue as you have begun, only varying it with an increasing dose." And then he amplifies his former instructions.

While he is writing them out, I am meditating on the unexpected turn events have taken. I shall give up keeping my Diary of Pains and Penalties. If I am to go on suffering them, where's the use of mentioning my sufferings? If, on the contrary, I am entirely free from any pain, then I should have nothing to write down, but the sooner I saw the Doctor the better. As Dr. Rem hands me the prescription I say, dubiously, "Then, in fact, the worse I am, the better I am. Is that so?"

"Quite so. You're going on admirably. Come and see me again in four or five days."

On the threshold I pause for a last question—"But if within the next two days I am absolutely free from any pain, shall I come to see you at once?"

"Yes, certainly. Do so by all means. Good morning. *Au revoir!*" And still nodding and smiling encouragingly, Dr. Rem bows me out, and, having concluded my visit, I find that Cousin Jane is waiting for me to take her into breakfast.

"You feel quite well, and have no pains?" I say to her.

"No; none. Why?"

"Well——" Then I tell her the result of my interview, and deduce therefrom that she must be in a parlous state to feel so perfectly well, and that the sooner she consults Dr. Rem the better.

But she only laughs, and says she shall "leave Well alone, and continue the Waters."

And the Waters have made her quite sprightly. I've never

heard her make anything resembling a joke before, and this is uncommonly like one. But if everyone acted on the principle "let Well alone," who would go to Royat or Aix or anywhere where the Springs of life are? Somehow I am depressed. The Colonel will cheer me up. To breakfast!

"Whene'er we take our walks abroad"

CHAPTER VII.

THE COLONEL AT OUR TABLE.

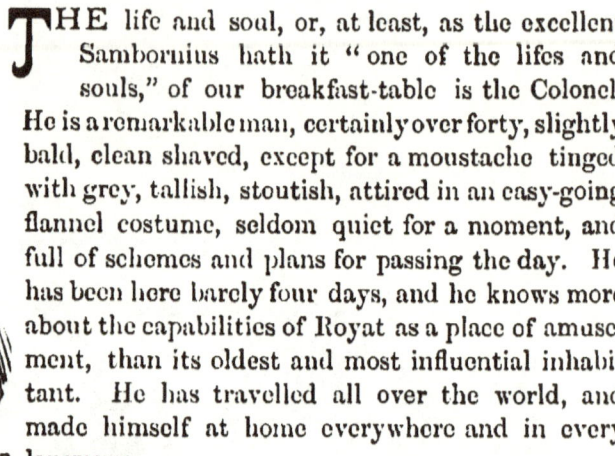

"I'm not an Eton Boy."

THE life and soul, or, at least, as the excellent Sambornius hath it "one of the lifes and souls," of our breakfast-table is the Colonel. He is a remarkable man, certainly over forty, slightly bald, clean shaved, except for a moustache tinged with grey, tallish, stoutish, attired in an easy-going flannel costume, seldom quiet for a moment, and full of schemes and plans for passing the day. He has been here barely four days, and he knows more about the capabilities of Royat as a place of amusement, than its oldest and most influential inhabitant. He has travelled all over the world, and made himself at home everywhere and in every language.

His nationality, I believe, is Dutch; he speaks German thoroughly, French well, English fluently, having, as I understand, obtained his military rank in the American army. He possesses a smattering of Italian, in which country he met a young English lady, who having made a successful *début* on the operatic stage, consented to become his wife on condition that she should not abandon her profession for at least five years. As her engagements soon compelled her to travel all over Europe and America, nothing could have better suited the Colonel's roving taste: but besides this, he was devoted to music, for which he possesses a quick but inaccurate ear, and a memory wherein is stored up any amount of plots of Operas, their titles, the names of their composers, of the singers, and the points of the leading dramatic situations,—only all so mixed up that, when he wants any one scene, air, name, or situation in particular, he has to rummage about in his memory-box, whence he produces a medley, from which, after a considerable time spent in sorting, he extracts the required material, whatever it may happen to be.

With a special liking for artistes and artistic life, he has dabbled in journalism, and has on two or three occasions acted, in an

amateur way, as "Our Own Correspondent Abroad." Nothing
gives him so much pleasure as composing newspaper paragraphs,
except subsequently seeing his compositions in print, when he is
in a state of the most gleeful excitement. These paragraphs are
a matter of considerable expense to him, as on the appearance of
any one of them he at once purchases an extensive number of
copies, which he posts to friends all over the world.

He is already on the friendliest terms with the journalists of
Royat, and on the second morning of our arrival he comes into
breakfast flourishing one of the local papers, and exclaiming,
" Look ! see ! what tey say in ter paper," and then he reads out
a flaming paragraph, in which after introducing all our names
among the "distinguished arrivals," a graceful compliment is paid
to the eminent Dr. Hammond Putteney, on his great wisdom in
selecting Royat, above all other *Stations Thermales,* for the
sojourn of his patients.

"Who on earth put this in ?" I ask, innocently.

The Colonel chuckles with delight, but shrugs his shoulders and
professes to be absolutely ignorant on the subject. As, however,
his thorough acquaintance with phrases in the paragraphs is remarkable, and as he knows so precisely where to put his finger
on the passages which, as he considers, constitute the beauty of the
work, I cannot help expressing my opinion that their inspirer, if not
their actual author, is not two hundred yards from our breakfast-
table.

"Ah !" cries the Colonel, in a perfect ecstasy of shrugs and
winks fraught with unutterable meaning, " I cannot tell ! I do not
ask. But tey get tese things in somehow. See ! " he cries out to
his wife, who just then enters the room, " See, my dear, what they
say about you ! It is nice ! Very nice ! I must send it to some
friends."

Though his English is generally delivered with only the
slightest possible accent, our " th," being an occasional difficulty,
yet on the whole there are peculiarities of manner, intonation and
emphasis, which are evidence of his foreign origin.

Then the Colonel has a few more papers to show, journals from
other localities, with longer accounts of Madame Rosetta's (her
professional name) triumphant career, and a sonnet addressed to

her, not only as a genuine tribute of admiration for her talents, but even more for the use to which she so frequently puts them, singing for local charities which benefit largely by her unvarying good-nature. The Colonel is radiant, as he draws our attention to the first verse :—

> " Quand vous chantez, Madame, on accourt, on s'empresse,
>   Fût-ce même à l'église, on vous aime, on vous suit,
> Vous forcez le sceptique à se rendre à la messe,
>   A défaut de la foi, le charme l'y conduit."

" *Regardez !* the heading ! " says the Colonel, and then we notice that most of this information contained in the journal of another water-cure place not Royat, comes under the title of " *Le High-Life.*" But this is of the past, and just now the Colonel's chief delight is in our own local paper, where the writer of the paragraph felicitating Royat on our arrival, finishes with " *Et remercions encore une fois,*"—" You see, tey've done it before," says the Colonel, who, in the exuberance of his enjoyment, is nodding and winking at everybody round the table and at friends seated at a distance, for whose benefit he waves aloft the journal and goes through a variety of pantomimic action—" *le Docteur Hammond Puttency de nous avoir amené de si charmantes clients,*" —— the " *charmantes clients* " are Cousin Jane, Mrs. Dinderlin, the American lady (also under Cherubic care) and myself, who have all of us arrived within the last week. It is a great morning for the Colonel.

He professes extreme devotion to the fair sex, which he expresses in phrases and in action—specially in action—of a most exaggerated character. On the entrance of the ladies of our party into the *salle-à-manger,* he rises from his seat, bows at an angle of ninety, places his hand on his heart, at the same time shaking his head, as if disavowing all individual importance on his own account, and in a general way going through the sort of performance to which Harry Payne, at Christmas time, is accustomed to treat us in the comic Bed-room Scene, when exhibiting the effect of a suddenly-conceived passion for a truculent-looking landlady in long black corkscrew curls, whom, so fickle is man's attachment, he will, within the next two minutes, send flying out of the room with a few delicate strokes from the warming-pan ; though, of course, this particular portion of the entertainment does not form part of the Colonel's programme.

To Cousin Jane—who has led a country life, and whose knowledge of pantomimic politeness is not extensive—the Colonel's movements, performed with the utmost gravity, are at first considerably embarrassing. But she sets it down to foreign manners, and accepts his homage with an air of serious courtesy that would do honour to the most stately Duchess. Mrs. Toffam, the American lady, puts out her hand, which he immediately kisses in the most respectful manner possible. At this she looks across at Madame, as if expecting some interference from her, which, however, Madame being perfectly accustomed to these eccentricities on her husband's part, only occurs when the Colonel's humour is of a more exuberantly rollicking character than usual, when she says, in a warning tone, and equally emphasising both syllables, " Al—fred ! " whereupon he immediately abbreviates the performance, whatever it may happen to be at the moment, and coming round to his wife's chair, insists upon taking her hand, and kissing it in the most respectful, and at the same time the most profoundly apologetic manner ; then, after Madame has given him a playful tap on the head with her fan, saying, " Alfred, you are a great big boy—do sit down, and behave yourself properly," he returns to his seat, and for a short time, during which he employs himself with his breakfast, he is comparatively quiet.

He has a quick eye for ladies' costume.

" Ah, permit me to say it—you do not mind ? "—he says, addressing Mrs. Toffam, " but what a beautiful lace you have ! "

" You think so," returns Mrs. Toffam pleased.

" It is—is it not, my dear ? "—this to his wife, who also expresses her admiration of it, and smiles on Mrs. Toffam. " It ces pretty ! But—you permit me ?—you do not mind ? "—

" No, certainly not—what is it ? " asks Mrs. Toffam.

" Well—I notice you have always a lit-tel pin sticking out where it should not—permit me——"

And then he suggests to Mrs. Toffam, first, and afterwards to the other ladies, such improvements as would revolutionise their entire costume. He directs their attention, too, to the visitors.

"That one is new—she has just arrived yesterday. She is an Actress at the Gymnase. That lady there, with the gray hair, is her mother—How do you do, Madame?" He rises, and bows to her across three or four tables, causing every one to turn in that direction, which confuses the unfortunate Madame Chose considerably. But this is of no consequence to the Colonel, who has discovered other celebrities, whom he is now pointing out to us. "That old man there, *décoré*, like Napoleon Third, he is a rich banker; that is his daughter, the Countess—I forget her name. How do you do, both?—and those who are just taking their seats are a Spanish family. There is a Prince somewhere—of Portugal —but he breakfasts in his apartment—ah! look at that little fat man with moustache and green riband—he is his secretary"— he salutes him with a friendly nod.

"Ah, I must not forget my family! I must feed my family!' cries the volatile Colonel. Cousin Jane who doats on children, looks immensely pleased, expecting to welcome the Colonel's children.

Madame observes this, and smilingly explains, "Alfred is so silly. You see that box?" the Colonel is now putting bread and bits of meat, and vegetables into a small silver box, on the table by his plate. We reply that we do see that box, and I remark that I had thought it was a snuff-box, which amuses the Colonel immensely. "Well," continues Madame, "that carries the food for his ' family,' as he calls it. His 'family' consists of his Parrot Lili, and his little dog Mimi, which he carries about with him everywhere."

"There!" says the Colonel, "there is the family's breakfast, and ah!" he cannot be quiet for a second, but as he turns round, he sees a bright-looking little French boy, in very wide collars, who has paused in his walk up the room to where his parents are breakfasting, in order to watch the Colonel filling the box. "Ah! here is a dear little Eton boy!" Any small boy less like an Etonian I never saw. "How are you, my little Eton boy?" says the Colonel, assuming an expression of fatherly benevolence. "How are you; and tell me which beat this year, was it Harrow or Eton?"

For a second the little boy is quite taken a-back.

"Alfred!" remonstrates Madam, sympathising with the situation of the little French boy, and fearing lest his father and mother, who are a few tables off watching the proceedings, should rise up in wrath, and object to the Colonel taking such an unwarrantable liberty with their offspring.

"Ah! The dear little Eton boy, he does not unterstant! He does not know what 'Eton boy' means, eh, *mon petit?*"

But the *petit* having quite recovered himself, replies briskly and with complete self-possession, "Yes, I do. I'm not an Eton boy. I'm not old enough to go to Eton yet. Eton beat Harrow this year. Were you at Eton?"

"No, I was not," answers the Colonel, for once utterly taken a-back and striking his flag before the little gun-boat.

"I thought not," the sharp little chap continues, speaking English perfectly, "because you would have known that Eton boys don't dress like this. This is French, not English style. I must go to breakfast. My papa is there. Good morning." With perfect manners, he salutes our party collectively, and leaves the Colonel utterly discomfited.

"That will teach you, Alfred, not to be always chaffing everybody as you do," says Madame. "It is the

The Colonel keeping the Ball a-rolling.

biter bit;" and we rise and leave, for once, without the Colonel's usual pantomimic performance of bowing to the ladies, fetching their sunshades, and kissing the tips of their fingers as they retire from the scene. The interview with the little Eton boy, who delivered his sentences as if he were repeating off by heart an Ollendorffian exercise, has made him thoughtful, and, with his silver box in his hand, he disappears to solace himself by feeding his family, and having an interview with the parrot, who will cheer him up by joining in the air of "*Coming through the Rye,*" of which the

Colonel sings the five first words, and the parrot the last one. " If a body meet a —" sings the Colonel. "Body," sings the parrot, through his beak. " Coming through the ——" sings the Colonel. "Rye !" sings the parrot,—and so on until the verse is concluded, when the bird, having sung for his breakfast, duly receives it.

Within ten days the Colonel knows everybody in the Hotel. At the end of the first week he has got up a dance, which is patronised by Dr. Rem, without whose presence, as imparting a sort of benison on a form of entertainment that is certainly not included in the ordinary *traitement*, the patients, when indulging in the delightful dance and the dangerous draught afterwards, might feel somewhat guilty. The Colonel, on this occasion as self-appointed Master of the Ceremonies, is all in his glory ; and those ladies who have brought ball-dresses are so grateful to him for giving them a chance of wearing them, that the next day a petticoated deputation formally thanks him on the roof—everything takes place on the roof—for his exertions on their behalf, and he is thenceforward the most popular man in the five hotels. Afterwards, when, somehow or other, in the local journal there appears an account of the " *soirée dansante* "—" *exquise* "—" *ravissante* "—with a full description of Madame Rosetta's charming costume, and so forth, the Colonel, who, like the immortal *Mr. Crummles*, "cannot imagine how these things get into the papers," is radiant, and spends his entire afternoon in sending copies to his friends.

Cousin Jane and myself only literally " look in " at this gay affair, which begins at an hour that we religiously consecrate to retiring to rest. " What is the use," says Cousin Jane, very sensibly, " of being here for health, and then sitting up and going to parties, and taking supper, just as if we were in London for the Season ? "

I quite agree with her. She is absolutely right. " Besides," I add, " I haven't brought any evening dress with me."

" And," says Jane, as she takes her candle, and opens her door, " I haven't got anything I could go in. *I wish I had.* Good night."

CHAPTER VIII.

EQUESTRIAN EXERCISE—MY FIRST RIDE ON UNTAIRE.

First appearance of Untaire.

REMEMBERING that the Colonel was in full equestrian costume the day of our arrival, I ask him if the riding is good about here.

"Eh?" he exclaims, putting his hand heartily on my shoulder, "Eh, dear boy, you ride? We will go together. The country is superb. I will take you. To-morrow? *Soit*: good. I will order the horses of M. Detaché. Two, good, dear boy, not much to look at, but to go—eh—first-rate, all right, dear boy! I will order Risette for me, and Hunter—they pronounce him *Untaire*—for you. I'll take ter tickets of M. Detaché, and you can buy them of me—joost what you want."

As I do not quite seize the plan, he explains to me that M. Detaché's method is to sell so many tickets at eight francs a-piece, representing so many rides, and you return a ticket after each ride. I see: perfectly. I take two tickets for Untaire, as if he were an entertainment.

In the afternoon they arrive. No, they are not much to look at. Risette is the better in appearance, a bay of about fifteen hands, and Hunter, or "Untaire," is about fourteen one, with a weary expression in his eye, a drooping head, an unkempt dirty mane hanging raggedly about a neck so curiously indented as to suggest the idea of his having been, at one time or other, decapitated and imperfectly refitted. His bones are everywhere visible; he is rather down in his shoulders, as apparently he is on his luck, but his hind-quarters are peculiarly strong. His feet are broad, and his legs certainly warrant his owner's description of him.

"*Il est bien solide*," says M. Detaché, the proud proprietor of Untaire.

So on the solid Untaire I mount. Until I am on his back I am convinced that Untaire is fast asleep. He wakes up however on his girths being tightened, and looks round with a shrug of his thin shoulders, as much as to say, " Hallo ! Another two hours ! Ah well ! Risette's going, so that's company at all events." By the way, this affection for Risette is most remarkable. Untaire at first refuses to turn round to the left in order to go out of the gate, because the movement involves losing sight of Risette for an instant. I am determined that the affectionate Untaire shall go

The Proprietor of Untaire.

the way I want him. He sulkily yields to a sharp touch of the spur and a tug of the left rein, and, catching sight of Risette's tail, he decides that for once *my* way shall be his, and consequently comes round to my way of thinking.

From this experience of Untaire I draw two conclusions ; first, that the characteristic of his temper is obstinacy ; secondly, that he possesses a mouth about as impressionable as a flint wall. My stirrups, which are small and slight, strike me as having been originally made for a rocking-horse : so do the reins. The saddle, also made for a rocking-horse, is fairly comfortable. We are starting at half-past three, and the heat is tropical. I am waging a continuous war against the persistent horse-flies that fasten on to the solid Untaire like so many leeches. Any other horse would have been driven mad long ago, but Untaire seems accustomed to it. Sometimes he shakes his head as if gently remonstrating and saying to some flies more pertinacious than the rest, "Oh, really now this is too bad ! You might leave me alone, some of you !"

The high roads are hard as granite, with a soft powdery dust on each side. The short cuts, originally used only by pedestrians, but which the Colonel, as guide, selects in order to show his thorough knowledge of the country, are rocky, stony, and uneven, having been formed during many winters by the mountain torrents.

"Look here, dear boy," says the Colonel, with all the enthusiasm of an explorer, or an Indian Pathfinder, "you follow me. I find a lovely road. We must ride pretty quick at first, because it is all up-hill, but, after, it is all down, and we shall have to walk much. *Allons! Tchk!*" and, without waiting for a reply, he dashes off up the road, and is suddenly lost to sight round a sharp corner.

I follow at the same pace : that is when I say *I* follow at the same pace, I mean that Untaire does. For, immediately Untaire sees Risette go off at a gallop, he pulls himself together and starts after her at such a pace, and in so blind and reckless a manner, that I am brought within measurable distance of a collision with a bullock-cart which is advancing towards us, and then, after scattering a crowd of terrified pedestrians, and so startling an old gentleman, who is reading, that he clasps the book to his breast and makes precipitately for a heap of stones, Untaire skirts an open drain and dashes round the corner where the Colonel has just disappeared. Then catching sight of Risette in the distance, where I can just see the upper half of the Colonel—above a low wall—careering at full gallop, Untaire redoubles all his efforts to come up with Risette. Heavens! What a ride! Rocks, actual boulders, sticking up in the middle of what they call a road—loose stones as big as your head—ruts—gutters—I shall pull up,—that is, if I can. "Hi! Stop!" I shout to the Colonel. "Let's go quietly over this nasty bit——"

No use my shouting, he is half a mile off, and if I lose sight of him I shall have to go back again, that is, if Untaire will consent to return, and give up my ride. Untaire hasn't fallen on his nose yet—perhaps he is accustomed to rocks, and knows how to get over them without falling . . . it's up-hill, that's one good thing, and it's no use pulling at him, I might as well tug at a milestone. . . . Now between two vineyards and a mountain-side covered with pine-trees on my left—I wish the Colonel would stop to admire the view, instead of galloping on at this Headless Horseman sort of pace—hah! a big rock in front of us—and the end of the road?—no—it's a high bank and a sharp turning to the right—I pull Untaire's left with all my might to steer him well away from the wall—I just manage it—we are round it sideways like Mr. Batty, at full speed on his bare-backed steed in the Circus, and on we go again. *Mazeppa* isn't in it with me, mounted on Untaire the wild horse of Royat. Up a mountain. . . . At the top. . . . Colonel already nearly half-way down on the other side. . . . More rocks, more stones, more boulders—and then a small mountain-stream and two roads. Here the Colonel has pulled up—thank Heaven!—and is considering which way he'll take.

When I have recovered my breath sufficiently to make an observation, I say, sarcastically, "This is a nice sort of a country."

"Isn't it?" returns the Colonel, delighted at my approval, and in the highest possible spirits. "We must get to Charrade—that's at the top somewhere—and then to a place called Bouzy, or something like that. This road," he says, pointing to a narrow walk which can only by the utmost courtesy be even called a bridle-path, "leads up to the pine-forest, but," he adds, indicating another on the right, "I fancy from what I recollect of the route—that this is the shortest."

"It looks more likely," I reply, by which I mean that, for my own personal comfort on Untaire, it seems to be less rocky and about two inches wider.

"All right!" cries the Colonel. "*Houp-là!*" and he is off again, up rocky mountain-path at full gallop. In another second, so am I, that is, so is Untaire. I can't be left behind and lost in a pine-forest on the mountains, so I give Untaire his head,—this is merely a matter of form so far as Untaire is concerned,—and away we go. In less than five minutes I have ascended half a mile, have gone breathlessly round some sharp angles, fought with stiff bushes, avoided whacks on the head from sturdy branches by lying along Untaire's neck, and am at last thoroughly rejoiced to see the Colonel and Risette actually walking along a fairish path between the trees.

The situation is magnificent : a perfect aisle of stately pine-trees on each hand—but the road is on the side of the mountain, and if Untaire doesn't overcome his partiality for leaning to the right, down he'll roll sideways, and be knocked from tree to tree, just as the marble is knocked from pin to pin—only this would be from pine to pine—at Chinese billiards, or in the old race game. But I don't want to play at any game of this sort, so am glad we are going quietly. I come up with the Colonel and hope, by engaging him in conversation, to keep him walking at his present easy pace.

"Is this the right road for Charrade?" I ask.

"Here we go up, up, up;
Here we go down, down, down O!"

"Yes! This is right! This is good going here! Whoop!" and before I can utter another word away he gallops, Untaire, breathing hard, but game to the last, after him. I wish to goodness that Untaire would not show such a decided predilection for leaning sideways, even when galloping, to the right. Either my knee will be severely injured by a tree, or with the slightest additional bias to the right down we go among the pines, and there's an end of one of us at all events, for I don't suppose that anything short of a sheer fall of a hundred feet on to sharp rocks would affect Untaire. I try to remember all the stories I've ever

Q

heard about slipping your foot out of the stirrup in time and throwing yourself off, and I only hope the occasion won't arise which will compel my attempting any of these wild-horse-of-the-prairie feats.

Light at last! . . . . End of the pine-forest—we are going always at a gallop, along a rocky road—and are approaching a little bit of open heath—we cross it—Untaire slithers (he is not so good on turf, as he is on rocks) but with his gaze fixed on Risette, he follows her without caring much where he puts his feet,—over the turf, more slithering,—down an incline of slippery grass, where we are prevented from coming down by a welcome bit of rock, which, in the ordinary course of things, would have damaged any civilised horses, whether in London or Leicestershire, for life,—and at last we are on a comparatively good road, where on a post is written "Charrade," and an arrow indicates the direction.

"What a view!" the Colonel calls out, pointing towards the plain below us—and the mountains far far away. We see towns spread out like toys with red-roofed houses—old church towers—those of Clermont-Ferrand Cathedral, standing out in the clear atmosphere—it is evidently a baking day in the valley,—and here we are being refreshed after our exertions by the most lovely air that comes to us over refrigerating mountain-streams, and filtered through the scented pines. Yes, the view alone is worth something,—and for the present the danger is forgotten.

"Ah," cries the Colonel, "when my wife drive up here and back she take two hours to come and one to return. The guide-book say cet is an affair of three hours, and here we are up to the top at Charrade in tirty-five minutes, and I do not know which way we come. I had forgot." And he beams upon me as if conscious of having done something extraordinarily clever. "We will write a guide-book for horseback. Now—*allons !*—cet ees all new to me."

A chill wind has arisen: I draw his attention to a black cloud obscuring the observatory on the Puy-de-Dome.

"It will be nutting," he says, setting off at a trot along the road, whereupon Untaire sets off too at the same pace, but before we have gone half a mile heavy drops begin to fall, and we take refuge among some bushes and young oak-trees.

I dismount. We are in a sort of natural arbour. Untaire exhibits a remarkable liking for acorns. What other animal is devoted to acorns? The pig. Has Untaire in the course of ages been evolved from an antediluvian pig? If so, that accounts for the obstinacy he displays under an assumed affection for Risette. The Colonel feeling inaction for five minutes somewhat irksome, observes that in this part of the world the storms are partial and local. I reply that I would rather they did not show a partiality for us. I have not taken an eight-franc ticket for Untaire in order to sit under a bush, while Untaire stuffs himself with acorns. The Colonel volunteers to reconnoitre. "Often it happens," he explains, "that while it is pouring just over your head, it is quite dry and fine a hundred yard further on." He will ride out and see : and he does so.

Untaire, intent on his acorn treat, does not notice the departure of Risette. After ten minutes or more, there being no signs of the Colonel's return, I determine to come out of my ambush and ride after him. This decision involves the summary interruption of Untaire's feast, and he reluctantly tears himself away from a young oak-tree, with his mouth full of green sprigs, which he suffers me to remove. I mount, and urge him into the open road. It is still raining : but only slightly. The Colonel having ridden off to the left, I pull Untaire's head in that direction. But Untaire having evidently formed his own theory on the subject, positively refuses to move towards the left, and sidles in a foolish sort of manner towards the right. I spur him with my right heel : I catch him a nasty one with my whip on the right shoulder : all to no purpose, the more I spur, and the more I whip, the more olunderingly and foolishly—it is a really foolish and crab-like movement—he sidles towards the edge of the road. The acorns must have got into his head. I never met with such an idiotic animal. As to his taking any notice of my tugging at the left rein, I might as well pull at a broken door-bell and expect an answer.

He is curving his body, and moving sideways towards the edge of the road, which being entirely unprotected by hedge or fence, discovers a precipice below. A precipice—simply a precipice. Untaire's piggish obstinacy will be his destruction and mine. I make one last desperate effort with whip and spur, to which Untaire only responds by intensifying his imitation of a crab. There's only one thing to be done—if Untaire is determined on suicide, he can go over by himself. I roll off somehow, and alight on my back, expecting to see the last of Untaire as he disappears into the abyss beneath. Nothing of the sort. Untaire pauses, his purpose is shaken,—so am I by the way, considerably;—just at this minute the sound of hoofs is heard, and the Colonel on

Untaire backing himself for a place.

Risette comes galloping back. Immediately a better spirit takes possession of Untaire. He consents to be led into the middle of the road, where he stands quiet as a lamb, and looking so gentle that you would think a child might guide him.

"It is lucky you were off," says the Colonel. "You are not 'urt! No? Good. Then come along! Ter rain is over. I have a short cut." And away he goes at a gallop down the road, then turns a corner and disappears. He is always turning corners and disappearing. I am compelled to follow. But my nerve is shaken, which, by the way, is a matter of not the slightest consideration to Untaire, who now seems to have made up his mind never again to lose sight of Risette. It is all down-hill. The path comes abruptly to an end at a meadow.

"Come along!" cries the Colonel, waving his whip as if it were a sword with which he were leading a charge of cavalry, and then he urges Risette down a steep mossy slope, which will lead us into a morass—I feel it will—where we shall stick in the mud, the horses will be up to their knees, and then what on earth shall we do? Besides it suddenly occurs to me, aren't we trespassing? And in a foreign country, too! Untaire slithers; he is not good on moss and damp meadow land. This place—this short cut the Colonel has chosen—is about as steep as the Devil's Dyke. Every

We part company. Untaire remains undecided.

minute I expect we shall roll over. Still, as the Colonel and Risette are now at the bottom of the meadow, Untaire and myself may be able to arrive there also. We should arrive there with sufficient rapidity if Untaire made one false step. Luckily he doesn't, and once landed on something like *terra firma*, I breathe again.

"There's the road home!" shouts the Colonel, pointing to a road up in the hills far above us, and more than a mile off, across fields and apparently through plantations where I am sure we have no right to ride. However we can't return; we must advance, and we must go together, or one of us will be lost, and that will be myself.

Hallo! Exactly what I had feared. A peasant, with a fierce dog, halloaing to us. Another peasant: more signalling and halloaing. They are running. We are galloping. The Colonel is making more cavalry charges, and waving his whip above his head frantically. We fly across a meadow. We hear shouts behind us. Before us is a running brook, rocky banks, and boulders. Can we jump it? The Colonel is off in a second. He takes Risette by the bridle, and jumps from rock to rock. I give Risette one sharp cut and she bounds over the brook like a stag, knocking down the Colonel. He is up again, quite pleased, and entirely unhurt. I adopt the same plan, without allowing Untaire a second for reflection, and he follows Risette, landing safely on the opposite rock. We mount and away, like a couple of Dick Turpins. Peasants and dogs in field halloaing: we ride full gallop up the next field. Peasants stopped by brook; perhaps the next field, where we are, isn't their property. Colonel sees a bank topped by a thick edge. He gesticulates to me, indicating that that is our short cut to the road and safety. We charge it, take it with a rush, and pull up desperately on the edge of a precipitous drop. No help for it; we have to dismount and climb down on foot the same way we came up; peasants below running round to circumvent us, dogs barking savagely. Luckily the Colonel strikes the right path, Risette breasts it gallantly; Untaire's powers are failing. He breathes hard, he blows, he heaves up and down . . . Now then, my gallant steed! think of Black Bess! only ten yards more of perpendicular rock, and we are saved!—Come up! He comes up—he makes a grand effort . . . and at last—we are safe and sound on the homeward road. We trot on quickly; the peasants and dogs are lost to view. "Colonel," I say, "let us ride the rest of the way quietly." For once the Colonel acquiesces, and it is only at the last, down-hill into Royat, that he cannot resist breaking into a canter.

"We will have another ride," he says, as we dismount. "Eet was first-rate. And I think I know a better road still." We shall see.

CHAPTER IX.

ONE MORE ON UNTAIRE.

Result of Untaire's Exploit—Separation of the body of the Boot from the Sole.

IF THE waters of Royat hadn't put plenty of iron into me, I don't think my nerves could have stood a second ride on Untaire. But the Colonel persuades me, and after a day's rest I am ready for the effort.

"It is the only way to know the country," says the Colonel, whose theory I admit is sound, but whose method of giving it practical effect is somewhat rough.

We start, and if the Colonel on Risette will only stick to road and rocks, I can follow him; but if he ventures on turf I feel that it is tempting the special Providence that has hitherto watched over Untaire. Every moment on grass with Untaire I expect to be off, and Untaire on me or on his back. And then?

Luckily the Colonel agrees with me, and prefers the rocky path. We descend through very wet bushes, the branches slapping our faces for our impudence. At last we are in a better road, a steep ascent, rather good going, and consequently any attempt at holding in Untaire being useless, away we go, I breathless, Untaire breathless too, but his head well forward, and his hoofs knocking the rocks like steel hammers. How his shoes stay on is a marvel! I catch a glimpse of the Colonel as he darts round a sharp corner, and I only devoutly trust that I may make no mistake as to the exact turning, or I shall be lost in the wood. Round to the right we go, at such an acute angle, and at such a tremendous pace, that the sudden change in the direction nearly upsets us both, and Untaire, who has been galloping right foot foremost, now suddenly substitutes the left, in order apparently to save himself from coming down on his side; but he executes the movement with

such a jerk, followed by such a heavy stumping action, that I
begin to fear he must have dislocated his shoulder, or otherwise
severely injured some portion of his frame.   He recovers himself,
however, and I become accustomed to the stumping movement,
which is just as if he had got a wooden foreleg.   No sign of the
Colonel.   Just as we reach the top I see the phantom Colonel
vanishing round another corner half-way down the descent.

THE START.

" From rock to rock,
With many a shock,
And bump and thump."
            " The Contrabandista," Act I.
            (Song in the Key of " Gee.")

Untaire has caught sight of Risette's tail, and hastens to rejoin
her.

Full pelt down hill, Risette kicking up the mud, and suddenly
stopping, reined in with a jerk by the Colonel, as Untaire, whom
I am unable to curb in his bold career, cannons against her.   No
injury done to men or beasts.   What's the matter?

" *V'là !* " shouts the colonel, roaring with laughter, as he points
to a notice-board.   " Ect ees La Pepinière.   We are trespassing.
In another moment will the gardener see us.   No dogs, no horses
allowed.   Come back, or it will be an *amende* if they catch us.

Houp là!" And without further parley he turns Risette and flies at a Dick-Turpin-to-York pace back again. Untaire doesn't wait to be guided, but goes round suddenly, as if on a pivot, and bolts after his favourite Risette. Sharp to the left, over some stumps of trees, across a small stream, over some rocks—up, up, up, until we find ourselves galloping on the hill above the beautifully-kept grounds of La Pepinière, where the gardeners and a *garde champetre* are now keeping a vigilant eye on our movements.

"Ah! we will take first road to right," cries the Colonel. "There must be a way down."

There is. Such a way! I don't believe any horses have ever

Untaire tries to see through a Stone Wall.

been on this trackless path before. It is all rock, and so steep, that even the Colonel is compelled to proceed at a careful walking pace. He has a plan for crossing by a wood below, and making for a village which he sees some way off, then round to Royat by a short cut,—always a short cut, as if we were in a desperate hurry on some matter of life and death, instead of being out for a quiet ride at four francs an hour.

After effecting our rocky descent, we have a treacherous bit of mossy grass, but, thank goodness, not much of it, and we issue on to a road which leads us by orchards and fruit trees, through a picturesque village, which is not the one the Colonel meant, but with which, as it is a village, he is equally delighted. Then we find ourselves on a high road, very white, very hot, and very hard.

This doesn't suit the Colonel, who instantly discovers a cross-country route, and exclaims, "See! there is a way by those vine-yards!" And before I can remonstrate, and point out that this is almost certain to be private property, he has urged Risette into a gallop and is half-way down a narrow path between two vineyards. I see in the distance the upper half of the Colonel above a low stone wall, which now borders the road. Untaire catches sight of Risette and impelled by his strong affection for her, it occurs

"Again he urges on his wild career."

Untaire Grazing—a Corner.

to him that he can break through all obstacles that separate them, and so, instead of waiting for the corner of the road, he makes straight for the wall in front of us on the other side of which as it seems to his limited intelligence, he sees Risette galloping away in the distance. I pull at him, but to no pur-pose, but he had not reckoned on a blind ditch, and into this he goes with a dash that brings his nose sharp up against the wall.

Like the wondrous wise man celebrated in verse for the feat of jumping into and out of a quickset hedge, Untaire no sooner finds his fore-legs in the ditch, than he extricates them, backs himself on to the road, perceives the right-angled corner of the wall, and

in order to rectify his error as soon as possible, makes for it at
such a pace, that, before I can do anything in the way of guiding
him, he has swerved round it so sharply as to bring my right boot
in contact with some projecting flints, which cut the sole as clean
away from the upper leather as if the operation had been performed by a machine specially invented for the purpose.

Luckily, Royat appears in sight, and I am no longer dependent
on following the Colonel's lead. This is my last performance on
Untaire, as the Colonel quits Royat next morning. Dr. Hammond Putteney and the others have all gone, and Cousin Jane
doesn't ride. Left to ourselves, we drive about the country,
visiting among other places the wonderfully well-preserved ruin,
the Chateau de Tournoel. Here, surveying the view from the top
of the Castle in the company of a strongly garlic-and-tobacco-
scented old guardian, I see Cousin Jane suddenly start back
from the ramparts with a terrified expression, as if she'd seen a
ghost.

"What is it?" I ask, anxiously. But by way of reply she can
only point towards the massive old stone wall. I look, but can see
nothing except the highly flavoured guide—one who comes under
the "Highly-Flavoured Nation" clause,—who is leaning his elbow
on the rampart.

"There! there!" she exclaims. "Don't you see those creatures!" If it had been a *viveur* who, after indulging rather too
freely, had exclaimed, "Look! those horrid creatures! See,
there they are again! popping up!" I should at once have
been able to trace his agitation to the probable cause. But
with Cousin Jane who is almost a teetotaler, whose general
health has been so much improved by the César baths, and her
nerves by the iron in the waters, it is another affair, and I am,
for the moment appalled as if in the presence of some frightful
calamity.

But the Highly Flavoured One hits on the right solution as he
points to some funny little yellow heads which are peeping up
between the crevices of the old stones in the blazing heat of this
tropical afternoon.

I am much relieved, and explain, as does the guide also, that they
are quite harmless, and that this hide-and-seek is only their play.

"What are they called?" I ask.

"*Lézardines,* answers the guide.

Cousin Jane is indignant. She gives a sniff in the air, and observes that the man must take us for fools to try and impose on us in this way.

I am mystified, and so I ask him again what is the name of hese creatures, and he makes the same answer, "*Lézardines.*"

"There! '*Les Sardines*'!" exclaims Cousin Jane. "As if we didn't know what sardines were. Nonsense!"

Cousin Jane has certainly been benefited considerably by the waters of Royat.

THE FINISH.

Riding quietly home.

CHAPTER X.

ASCENT OF THE PUY DE DÔME, AND GRAND FINALE.

"Salut, Mossieu' et Médame !"

WE ARE preparing for final retirement, and a wizened figure in black, like a rag-doll as a pen-wiper, presents us with our little bill for twenty-one days' washing, insists upon giving us sweet-scented flowers and unripe fruit, and then with her money in her pocket, shows herself out of the room, saying with plenty of bobs (and francs) and curtseys at the door, "*Salut, Mossieu' et Médame! Salut, Médame et Mossieu!*" and so ringing the changes on this formula, she disappears. We both took a great fancy to this old lady, who was full of chatter and gossip, but on subsequent consideration, Cousin Jane begins to question whether the work of the *Blanchisseuse* is quite the most reasonable of the charges, which as a rule are decidedly moderate at Royat. Afterwards, in driving about, we come upon the Grotto where the Nymphs wash and pummel the linen. If the amount of iron in the water is the same as that in the Source Eugénie or César, then the work of the *blanchisseuse* is an economy of time and labour, as in the Spring of the Grotto they do both the washing and the ironing at the same moment.

Coming on to the roof of our hotel, after a long drive, I hear a voice, exclaiming, "Hallo! What *you* here!"

Why is one Englishman always utterly astonished to meet another Englishman, and a friend, anywhere abroad? Wherever they meet it is "Hallo, old fellow! what on earth brings *you* here?" or, "Who'd ha' thought o' seeing *you* here?"—as if you had taken an unfair advantage of him somehow, or as if your presence anywhere was, in itself, a suspicious circumstance, and demanded instant explanation. In this case it is a Scotch friend, who has arrived for the benefit of his health. He is accompanied

by another friend, also a North Briton, who has come to see him
safely started in the Water Course, along which I have been sail-
ing pleasantly enough ; and after that he intends to return to the
Highlands, where, at the sporting season, his heart naturally is
and " not here ; " his heart, according to the old song, being
engaged in " Chasing the wild deer, the (something, I forget
what) and the roe. Oh ! my heart's in the Highlands wherever

A ROYAT-L ASCENT.

Happy Thought.—"I say, suppose we meet anything coming down !"

I go." This patriotic sportsman is the Chieftain of a Clan, at the
sound of whose pibroch (I am not sure of my Scotch terms, and
do not venture them in his presence) a thousand stalwart High-
landers, kilted and claymor'd, spring from the heather, and shout
something equivalent to " O ieroe ! " and then execute wild dances
by torchlight, in celebration of having killed something or other
on four legs, which must be considerably larger than a hare. I

mention four legs, because I do not think they have any midnight revels after killing a sixteen-pound salmon.

However, I admit my ignorance of Highland customs, and am glad to be instructed. Delighted also to partake of the savoury venison.

The Chieftain, who, with his friend the McInvalid, dines with us to night in the *salle à manger*, where the number of guests is daily diminishing, expresses his delight with Royat, at finding it so like Scotland. As a Chieftain who would have his foot on his native heath if he could, he is burning to climb a mountain, to ascend the steep and craggy rocks, and bound lightly from point to point like a gay chamois. " Can we not,"—he suggests, considerately turning towards the McInvalid,—" before you begin your baths and drinks, can we not ascend the Puy de Dôme ? "

Yes. Why not ? Nothing more simple. Order a carriage ; drive over there to-morrow morning ; " take luncheon with us," says the McInvalid. " By all means," returns the Chieftain, " and make the ascent." Though disliking climbings, and detesting, in a general way, going up any high places, whether a belfry, a tower. or a mountain merely for the sake of a view, I cannot refuse their friendly offer of a seat in the carriage and a share of the lunch. So I accept. The McInvalid has a guide-book, likewise the Chieftain has one. I tell them that I have a book which will be of service to me as a beginner in the act of going up mountains, but not to them as experts. " What is it ? " " Well—it is only a Grammar ; it is, in fact, Cardinal Newman's *Grammar of Assent.*"

Thus lightheartedly I prepare for the dangers of the morrow. I dismiss the excursion in two pictures which present a fair idea of the pleasant sensations we experienced in going up the mountain. The hardy mountaineers didn't like it. The Chieftain sat behind, and his chances of escape, in case of an accident, were somewhat better than ours in front, though we were all three boxed into the seats, and aprons tightly fixed. One comforting thought was, " How many have been up here before, and yet lived to tell the tale ! " But, on consideration, such a theory could only be supported by our having implicit faith in the word of anyone who told us that he had made the ascent

Unlike *Box* and *Cox* we did not meet anyone " Coming up-stairs,

us we were going down, or going down-stairs as we were coming
up." And it was fortunate for us that we didn't. When we
reached the top there was an Observatory, where we made several
observations,—strong ones too, some of them, on tumbling up and
down the stairs. Here the seamanlike Observer pointed out to
us all that was to be seen, and that didn't require pointing out,
and told us of a great deal more, including "Jerusalem and Mada-
gascar, and North and South Ameriky," which would have been
plainly visible to the naked eye had we only been up here yesterday, or the day before, or in fact at any time except the very day
we had selected. We saw the French soldiers practising firing in
the fields below—and that was all.

We had lunch previous to the ascent, which proceeding we
subsequently decided was a mistake; and the Chieftain chatted
freely and pleasantly with the peasants on our return. The
McInvalid was deeply interested in their habits and customs, and,
—his idea as to the dinner-hour being founded on the practice
of the London season,—he wished to know what time they
dined, and when they breakfasted, and was much exercised on
being informed by the chatty matron, that they had dinner at
eleven in the morning, and "soup" at about six or so in the
evening.

"*Et dites donc, Madame, s'il vous plaît,*" says he, regarding the
mother of the family with the deepest interest, "*ne prenez-vous pas
du thé à cinque heures alors ?*"

He couldn't understand that at the foot of the Puy de Dôme,
within reach of an Observatory, not more than a mile off perpendicularly, and within fifteen miles of Royat, this good lady should
not have her "day," and her "five o'clock tea."

It quite saddened him to think to what a state of ignorance a
peasantry might come, if only left out long enough in the
country. And to think that they shouldn't take tea at all, but
"*la soupe,*" before they went to bed! Such a derangement of a
menu !

This weighed on the McInvalid, and for some time after we had
started on our road home he was saddened and downcast. But
presently it began to mizzle, and fog swept over the heather, and
then both the North Britons revived.

"It *is* like Scotland," cried the Chieftain, beaming with pleasure as they both wrapped their plaidies about them, and revelled in waterproofs.

On our arrival at the hotel, a gigantic retainer, one of the Chieftain's Highland Body Guard, or Six-feet-three-Highlander, opens the carriage-door. Where has Donald been? He has just been up

Delightful Ascent of the Puy de Dôme. "So glad we came."

"what they call in these parts a mountain, but it's nae better than a hillock, ye ken, in Scotland."

"You got a good view, eh?" inquires the Chieftain.

Donald considers a second or two before answering, and then replies,—

"Aweel, when I got oop to the top o' the thing they ca' a mountain "——

"What did you see?" asks the Chieftain, cutting in quickly.

"Aweel," answers Donald, looking a bit puzzled, "I just saw a

R

Frenchman." And this seemed to have impressed the Highlander more than anything in the whole course of his journey abroad.

The next morning we bid Dr. Rem good-bye; Cousin Jane decidedly improved, myself undecidedly improved, and not yet out of the *traitement*, but looking forward to results to be hereafter apparent.

"You won't feel the benefit of the place all at once," says Dr. Rem. He is quite right—I don't. Perhaps I am getting it in bits, and I am what is expressively termed "mending."

I have seen the process of "mending." Even with the best housewife it's a slow business. But still, for anæmic persons who are overworked and weary, it would be difficult to find a better (and, mind you, a more moderate) place than Royat, with its vineyards, its lovely country, its magnificent air, its pine-forests, its picturesque environs, its amusements (they've stopped the *baccarat* and *petits chevaux*), its rides, drives, and walks, its *douches* of all sorts, and, in a general way, its Water Course.

The Nymphs of the Grotto.

SALUBRITIES ABROAD.

SALUBRITIES ABROAD.

CHAPTER I.

A RETURN VOYAGE.

"SALUBRITIES at Home" (*pace* Mr. Atlas, who will recognise this temporary adaptation of his world-renowned title) I should say are Buxton (for most people), Bath (for some), Harrogate (for others), and, —besides a variety of North, South, East and West, too numerous to be mentioned in these notes,—Ramsgate for nearly all.

"*Salubrities Abroad*" are Homburg, Aix-les-Bains, Carlsbad, &c., &c., and Royat, where I find myself again this year. "Scenes of my bath-hood, once more I behold ye!" There is "A Salubrity at Royat," which people of certain tendencies cannot easily find elsewhere. It is a cure for eminent persons of strong Conservative tendencies. Lord Salisbury was here last year, and my friend Monsieur Ondit, who is in everybody's confidence, tells me that his lordship will revisit a place where the *traitement* did him so much good. I believe he underwent the "Cherry-cure," at all events his lordship was seen in public constantly eating them out of a paper bag. *What did he do with the bag?* My answer is, "he popped it." Down went the cherries, and bang went the bag and fifty centimes. Well, did not Royat effect some change in his conservatism ? What has been the result ? But I am not here to talk politics.

*   *   *   *   *   *

Everybody is talking of the Boulanger-Ferry incident. This is Aug. 4, and nothing has happened.

> " Il n'y a pas de danger,"
> Dit Général Boulanger ;
> " Tout va, je crois, s'arranger,
> Chez Ferry, mes amis."

I haven't time to proceed with this, but, so far, the idea is at any poet's disposition to continue as he pleases, my only stipulation being that the air to which it is to be sung shall be "*Marlbrook.*"

My other friend, Benjamin Trovato, of Italian extraction, tells me that Boulanger is half English, and had an English education. Ben informs me that the General has never forgotten the rhythms he learnt in his happy English nursery; and that, when he read that M. Ferry had called him a "*St. Arnaud de Café-Concert,*" he sang out, recollecting the old catch,—

> A Note, a Note !
> Haste to the Ferry !

in which his friends were unable to join, owing to their ignorance of the words and tune.

When driving through Clermont-Ferrand from the Station up to Royat, we (three of us) had a small omnibus to ourselves. One of the party (a wag, of whom, and of the circumstances of our meeting, more "in my next") insisted on our calling out, "*Vive Boulanger!*" We did this several times in the most crowded parts, but the cry obtained no response, and aroused no excitement, as, being uttered with the greatest caution (at my instance), nobody heard it.

*   *   *   *   *   *

But what a thing to fight about ! If duelling were an English fashion, how fruitful of "incidents" this Session would have been. How often would Mr. Tim Healy have been "out"? And Mr. De Lisle's life would have hung upon a Lisle thread !

*   *   *   *   *   *

Note for strangers about to visit Royat.—The Continental Hotel has lost a little territory, as half of what was its terrace has been re-turned to the present proprietor of the hotel next door, with whom we Continentals have no connection, not even "on business," it not being "the same concern" and under one management as it was last year. But what the Continental Hotel has sacrificed in domain, Monsieur Hall, our obliging landlord, has more than made up in comfort and cooking. Dr. Brandt sees his patients in a charming Villa of Flowers. The weather is lovely.

＊　　＊　　＊　　＊　　＊　　＊

We are all surprised at seeing one another here. Each person for each couple or party) seems to think that he alone (or they alone) possess the secret of Royat's existence. We certainly are not a mutual admiration society at Royat. When we come upon one another suddenly, each exclaims, "Hallo! what are *you* here for?" as if the other were a convict "doing his time." Everyone thinks he knows what he is here for, but very few tell what he thinks he knows. And, by the way, the best-informed among us doesn't know very much about it.

＊　　＊　　＊　　＊　　＊

In the Reading-room of the *Cercle* there ought to be (as advertised in a local journal) at least three English newspapers daily. I have not seen them as yet. The only London paper arriving here regularly, and to be purchased every day early at the News-vendor's, is the *Morning Post*. *Vive* Sir Algernon! Can this be the attraction for Lord Salisbury? Why come out so far afield to read the *Morning Post?* Or wasn't it here, during Lord Salisbury's visit last year, and is he still ignorant of its having been subsequently demanded and supplied this season? And when he comes and finds it—"O what a surprise!"—no, thank goodness, we have escaped from this song—for a time, at least.

＊　　＊　　＊　　＊　　＊　　＊

Too hot to write any more journal. The hundredth bell is sounding for the fiftieth *déjeuner*. My *déjeuner* is finished. There are bells here perpetually. All day and all night. In vain would Mr. Irving as *Mathias*, put his hands to his ears and close the windows. The bells! The bells! Distant bells, near bells, sheep-bells, goat-bells, a man with pipe (not tobacco but tune, or what he and the goats consider a tune), dinner-bells, guests'-bells, servants'-bells, church-bells (not much), chapel-bells (early and occasionally), horse-bells, donkey-bells, breakfast-bells, supper-bells, arrival-bells, departure-bells, tramway-bells, crier's-bells, with variations on drum or trumpet, and several other bells that I shall notice in the course of the twenty-four hours, but have forgotten just now.

*　　　　*　　　　*　　　　*　　　　*　　　　*

The "*petits chevaux*" have not been stopped by the Government; they are running as fast as ever. There are two bands, playing morning, afternoon, and evening. The *Casino Samie* is as lively as ever, or, as my waggish acquaintance at once expressed it, in that vein of humour for which he is so specially distinguished, "The Samie old game," and to sit out in the garden, with a fragrant cigar and coffee, before retiring for the night, is indeed a calm pleasure, or would be but for the aforesaid waggishness, of which more anon.

*　　　　*　　　　*　　　　*　　　　*　　　　*

Soldiers about everywhere, Boulangering. Up in the hills is a splendid echo. This morning, having caught the very slightest cold, I went up into the mountains to get it blown away. Suddenly I sneezed. Such a sneeze! It reverberated all over the mountain like the firing of a battery. Again! again! These sneezes nearly shook me off the rock, and sent me staggering on to the *plateau* below. The effect must have been alarming, as the third sneeze fetched out the military, horse and foot, at full gallop, and the double. *L'ennemi? C'était moi!* They scoured the mountain sides, but I did not sneeze again. I have a sort of idea that my sneeze upset the entire preconcerted arrangements for a review. The Boulangerers retired—so did I.

*　　　　*　　　　*　　　　*　　　　*

'Tis the hour of *douche*. Richard, the attendant, will be there to give it me. *Douche-ment, douche-ment.* Gently does it! O Richard, O *Mon Roy-at!* . . . *Au revoir!*

CHAPTER II.

"AGAIN WE COME TO THEE,"—ROYAT!

TO THOSE *about to travel* viâ *Dover and Calais.*—Ask when *The Empress* makes the journey. Something like a boat, and the day our party went by her she did the crossing in the hour, and I won't positively swear it wasn't a minute or so under that time. There's a crossing - sweeper for you! The Empress of the Sea! Mind you it was a fine day, and what I should say would be considered a calm sea though there were several sufferers.

If not in a hurry—and who can hurry in such weather?—the easiest travelling is by the 11 A.M. from Victoria; admirable *Empress* for the crossing; and a good twenty-five minutes or more for one of the best buffet-luncheons in France. Stay the night in Paris, and off to your Royat, your Aix, or wherever it may be, as early as possible.

At the Paris-Lyon Station, en route for Royat.—Owing to the gentle influence of Colonel Waters, attached to the L. C. & D. corps in Paris, and to the indefatigable exertions of his lieutenant in uniform, Gustav Herlan, the P. L. & M. Company have consented to put a *lit-salon* carriage on to their day-train as quite an exceptional concession to an invalid, who might be supposed to have thus addressed them :—

> Pity the sorrows of a gouty man.
> Whose trembling limbs have brought him to your door,
> Who asks you to oblige him with—you can—
> A simple *lit-salon* and nothing more.

The perfect comfort of this arrangement for a long journey is worth the price including the *supplément*, which I am paying when a cheery voice cries "Hallo! old chap," and I recognise Puller, whom I haven't seen for some time.   I return his greeting heartily.   "You've got a *coupé reservé ?* " he exclaims gleefully, and literally skipping for joy.   I never saw a man in such spirits. He is not absolutely young, nearer forty than thirty for example, looking so wonderfully fresh, that turn-down collars and a jacket would suit him perfectly.   He is as clean-shaved as a Benedictine Monk or a Low Comedian.   He says of himself—he is the waggish companion to whom I alluded in my previous notes—" I am well preserved in high spirits."   He insists on paying the extra seat and *supplément.*   Cousin Jane (again going to Royat for the Cæsar Baths) says she shall be delighted, and so Puller is to come with us.   Certainly am delighted to see Puller.   Will he have his things brought here?   He will, "*à l'instant,*"—he pronounces it "*ar long stong,*" and roars with laughter as if he had delivered himself of the rarest witticism.   Then he skips off down the platform, waving an umbrella in one hand and a stick in the other. Suddenly Puller's social characteristics all flash across me.   I haven't seen him for years, and had forgotten them.   I recollect *now,* he is what they call " an inveterate punster," and loves when abroad (though an accomplished linguist) to speak the language of the country in which he may be temporarily sojourning with a strong English accent ; it is also a part of his humour to embellish his discourse with English idioms literally translated,—or, *vice versâ,* to give French idioms in colloquial English ; so that on the whole his conversational style, when in foreign parts, is peculiar. The impression left in my memory years ago of Puller, is that he is a wonderfully good-natured fellow unless a trifle puts him out, when he flares up suddenly into red heat ; but this is seldom, and he cools down directly if allowed to stand.   When he is not in the highest possible spirits he is an agreeable companion, as he can give some interesting, but utterly untrustworthy, information on most subjects, and, when this comes to an end, he falls asleep suddenly,—he does everything suddenly,—but, as I have since ascertained, does not snore.   When at his office in London he is the second partner of an eminent firm of Solicitors with a varied and extensive business.   For a safe and sound legal opinion in any difficult matter, specially on the Chancery side, there is no one to whom I would sooner go myself, or recommend a friend, than James Puller, of Horler, Puller, Puller (J.), Baker and Dayville. For the greater part of the year James Puller is hard at work, and is gravity itself, except on certain social and festive occasions. But in vacation-time he gives up Law and goes in for Lunacy. "I feel," he says, when he returns, still capering on the platform, this time with his stick in one hand and his hat in the other, "I feel like a school-boy out for a holiday," and, allowing for the difference of age and costume, he looks the character.

Travelling is very tiring; so is rising early in the morning (which is included in the process of travelling) after a night spent in fitful dozing, one's rest being broken by nervous anxiety as to whether the waiter will remember to call one at the cruel hour of 6·30, or not, and determining to be up at that time exactly, and if he doesn't appear punctually, to ring for him to bring the bath and the boots; then preternatural wakefulness, then the drowsiness, then the painful emptiness, then the necessity for extraordinary energy and bustle,—all this fatigues me so much, that when at last I find myself in a comfortable railway-carriage, I sink back, and prepare to make up for the lost sleep of the previous night.

Puller has been travelling all night right through, yet he is now as fresh as the proverbial lark. He is smoking. He came up smoking. I am a smoker, but at an early hour on a hot day, and comparatively unbreakfasted, I do not like the smell of the last half-inch of a strong and newish cigar such as Puller is now smoking. He is sucking at this last morsel of it as if it were the only one he should take (I wish it were) for another month, and as if it went to his heart to part with it.

"Don't you smoke your cigars rather short?" I ask, mildly, by way of a hint.

"No," he replies, quickly; "I smoke them rather long. Had him there, eh?" he says playfully, turning to Cousin Jane, who, I regret to say, encourages him with an appreciative smile. After his fit of chuckles has subsided (in which I do not join), he takes off his hat *à la française,* and addresses himself to Cousin Jane.

"If Madame does not oppose herself to that I shall smoke."

Jane graciously returns, "Oh dear no, I do not mind smoke," which isn't at all what I want her to say on this occasion. Puller throws away what is left of his cigar, and, producing an enormous case, offers me what he calls "a beauty,"—very big, very dark one, with a bit of red and gold paper wrapped round its middle, as if it were in a delicate state of health and might suffer from rheumatism,—but I decline it, saying pointedly, "I can't stand smoking so early, and before breakfast."

"Oh," he returns in an off hand manner, "can't you? I can smoke any time, it doesn't affect *me*. Besides, I had a first-rate breakfast at the fork, and spoon too, at the buffet,"—he pronounces this word as written in English—this is his fun (*i.e.*, the fun of a high-spirited Solicitor on a holiday), and forthwith he lights the big cigar, changes his seat so as to face us both, and then commences a conversation about all sorts of things, seasoned with his jokes and comic French, at which he laughs himself uproariously, and appeals to me to know if it, whatever the joke may be, "Wasn't bad, was it?" And when I beg him to spare some of his witticisms, as he'll want them for the friends he's going to meet at Royat—(thank Heaven, he *is* going to meet friends!)—he only says, "Oh, there's lots more where these came from," and off he goes again. Fortunately he turns to Cousin Jane, and instantly I close my eyes, and pretend to be overcome with fatigue. If Jane is wise she will do the same. Jane is tired, but tolerant.

Finding that neither of us is up to much talking (I have inadvertently opened an eye) he says, "Look here, I'll show you my travelling bag," as if it was something to amuse children. This delights him immensely. He opens it and explains its compartments, tells how he shaves, what soap he uses, how he invented a peculiar pomade for travelling, and how he had thought out this bag and had everything made to fit into its place. He takes out everything, brushes, combs, razors, glass-pots, knives, brushes, one after the other, expatiating on their excellence as if he were a pedlar anxious to do a deal, and we were his casual, but likely, customers. Then finding our interest waning, he shuts it up, and saying that the best of travelling in a *lit-salon* is that you can stretch your legs, he forthwith begins capering, asks Jane if he mayn't have the pleasure of the next waltz and so forth, until fortunately, he discovers the secret of the seat which pulls out and becomes a bed, and is so struck with the idea that he exclaims, "By Jove!

this is first-rate ! pillows, mattresses, everything ! I've never slept in one of these ! I haven't been to bed all night. You don't mind my taking forty winks—do you ?"

O dear no—take eighty if he likes.

"Ah, then," he says in broken English, "I go to couch myself. I salute you the good morning, Mister and Missis. I have well envy of to sleep." And thank goodness in another minute the high-spirited Solicitor is fast asleep, and *not* snoring.

Then we all drop off. At Montargis he awakes, breakfasts at the buffet : we breakfast in our *salon.* He returns, puffing another cigar, stronger and bigger than the previous one : but smoking yields to sleeping and his high spirits become less and less. After his second or third sleep he becomes hungry. The train is late. He becomes hungrier and hungrier. Again he smokes ; but his cigars are dwindling in size and growing paler in colour. He calculates when the hour of dinner will be. He foresees that it will not be till past eight and we breakfasted at eleven. Hunger has deprived him of all his jokes, all his high spirits ; he is hope-lessly depressed, and preserves an almost sullen silence till we reach Clermont-Ferrand, when the sight of the Commissionnaire of the Hôtel Continental slightly restores him, and as we get into the Omnibus he whispers to me feebly, " I say, let's cry '*Vive* Boulanger !' "

I beg him to hold his tongue, or the police will be down on him. I fancy this warning has its effect, in his present state of hunger, as he limits himself to whispering out of the window to any passer-by who happens to be in uniform, " *Vive* Boulanger !" but I am bound to say, nobody hears him, so finding the fun of the jest exhausted within the first ten minutes, he drops it, and once more collapses, shakes his head wearily over his wretched state, and expresses in pantomime how he is dying for something to eat. Jane and myself recognise Clermont-Ferrand and draw one another's attention to all points of interest, more or less incorrectly. Then, after noticing how familiar all the land-marks seem *en route*, we find we have been taken by a different road from the one we used to travel in order to avoid the dust.

Ha ! Here is Doctor Rem. Welcome to Royat ! Same rooms. New Proprietor, but same Hotel in effect, it is the Continental.

M. Hall, of what nationality I do not know, exerts himself to see that everything shall be right for everybody who has just arrived. There are several others by this train, all requiring special and individual attention, and all, somehow, getting it. New faces, but civility and readiness to oblige everywhere. The weather perfect!— perhaps a trifle too perfect. But Royat is high up, and, if it is hot here, what must it be down below at Vichy or at Aix! Dinner in the Restauration of the Hotel, where we pant for air because other visitors, chiefly French, of advanced years and in various stages of "The Cure," will not allow a door or window to be opened. We finish dinner, and hurry off for our coffee in the garden of the Casino Samie. End of first day.

P.S.—I said last week I could not find the English newspapers in the reading-room of the Cercle. I have since seen them, *Times* and *Telegraph*. But the only one sold outside is apparently the *Morning Post.* Lord Salisbury is coming.

CHAPTER III.

"PRESENT COMPANY."

HOTEL CON-TINENTAL, Royat.- Our party here (which, somehow or another, Puller has contrived to get together and introduce to each other by the simple means of induc-ing M. Hall to give us a room to ourselves for a small *table-d'hôte* at the un-Royat-like hour of 7·30) consists of La Contessa Casanova, the English wife of an Italian merchant, the head of a large house of business in London—she is Marchesa or

Contessa, I am not certain which, but Puller styles her *Miladi* and *Madame*. She is devoted to the serious Drama, and her pet subject is Salvini in *Othello*. Her daughter, an elegant young English girl, lively, amusing, and with a bias in favour of the very lightest forms of theatrical entertainment.

Then we have Madame Metterbrun and her daughters, Anglo-Germans, thorough musicians, with Wagner at their fingers' ends, —literally, as they are accomplished pianists. There is Mrs. Dinderlin, who was here last year, and is taking the waters seriously, and who knows when to put in the right word at the right moment. Cousin Jane who is taking the waters still more seriously and who is an excellent listener : myself an impartial referee : and Puller the Solicitor out for a holiday, who is alternately in the highest of spirits or the lowest depths of depression, according as the waters and weather affect him. Outside our party there are others whom I meet occasionally, consisting of the lady who finds fault with everything French, the gentleman who laughs at everything French, the grumbler whom nothing satisfies, the contented man who is pleased with everything, the man who after being here a day is intensely bored, the man who from the moment of his arrival is always studying Guide-books and *indicateurs* to see what is the best and easiest way of getting away again : the patient who has come all the way here to see the Doctor and then refuses to do anything he tells him : the patient who has come to find out what on earth is the matter with him : the man who doctors himself, and two or three ladies of my acquaintance of whom I only catch occasional glimpses as they issue from Sedan-chairs or muffled up like the Turkish women, merely recognise me with their eyes, incline their heads and pass on their way with a little drinking-glass in their hands.

To me Royat is an amusing place : it is certainly a pretty one, and its waters in most cases are decidedly of lasting benefit What those "most cases" are, the patients themselves best know.

* * * * * * *

For expanse there is nothing like the sea, and for grandeur the snow mountains. Unless I go up to the Puy de Dôme—which I do not mean to do, for I have been up there once, and never, never, never will go there again—I cannot see either. And even

from the top of the Puy you can only discern the sea, or Mont
Blanc, with a very good glass, on a very clear day.

*   *   *   *   *   *

M. Boisgobey's description of a Parisian Club in his latest
book (I delight in Boisgobey now that there is no Gaborian)
called *Grippe-Soleil* will amuse London Club members. The only
two Clubs in Paris I ever saw were not a bit like Boisgobey's
description.

*   *   *   *   *   *

When anyone who has been under treatment a week, unexpectedly meets a friend here, he stops short, stares at him,
examines him from head to foot, and then exclaims, in a tone of
utter astonishment, "What!! *you* here!!" as if the new arrival
were either an intruder or a lunatic. The person thus addressed
immediately retorts in an injured tone, "Well, what on earth are
you here for?" and then he adds maliciously, "there doesn't seem
to be much the matter with *you*." Now to say this is to utter
your deliberate opinion that the person you are addressing is at
Royat (or any other Salubrity Abroad wherever it may be) under
the false pretence of being an invalid, and is therefore, to put it
plainly, a shammer, an impostor.

*   *   *   *   *   *

After this greeting, explanations follow. The first man has to
prove his right to be at Royat, and the second man has to admit
the evidence to be incontestable, on the condition, implied but not
expressed, of his own case being taken as thoroughly warranting
his taking the baths and *traitement* generally at Royat.

*   *   *   *   *   *

Then comes the question of Doctors. "Who shall decide when
Doctors disagree?"—but who shall decide when patients disagree
about Doctors? "Whom do you go to?" asks the suffering Smith
of the invalid Brown. "Well," says Brown, apologetically,—
because he is not sure, this being his first visit, that he might not
have gone to a better man, "I go to Dr. Chose," and noticing the
astonishment depicted on his friend's face, he hastens to explain,
"Squills sent me to him." The suffering Smith professes himself
puzzled to know why on earth Squills always sends his patients to
Chose. "Dr. Rem's the man for you, my boy," says Smith. But

Brown feels that he is in the toils of Squills, and that it would not be fair to him or to Chose, if he suddenly left the latter and sought the advice of Dr. Rem, on the sole recommendation of Smith who, after all, is not a professional.

* * * * * *

Then two *habitués* meet. " I always go to Chose," says eczematic Jones, dogmatically ; " first-rate fellow, Chose. All the French go to him. *They* know." "Ah !" returns gouty Robinson, with conviction, "I never have been to anyone but Rem. He's the chap. All the English go to him. Best man in Royat." And if it weren't the hour for one of them to go and drink Eugénie water, and for the other to take his second glass of St. Mart, they would have a row and come to blows.

* * * * * *

Puller tells me that there's one London Doctor, describing himself as a Gynæcologist ("A guinea-cologist," parenthetically remarks Puller), who always sends his patients here. I think he says his name is Dr. Barnes. " He sends so many," says Puller, "that I propose changing the name of the place from Royat-les-Bains into Royat-les-Barnes." I see why he introduced the name of Barnes. Fortunately he is so delighted with this *jeu de mot*, which I fancy I've heard before, that he is off to tell his friends in the Parc, and, as I pass a group, I overhear him explaining the point of it to a French lady and her husband, with whom he has a speaking acquaintance. For Puller likes what he calls "airing his French," and is not a bit shy.

* * * * * *

The Band is performing another new tune ! How is this ? I can account for it. It rained nearly all yesterday, and so the musicians didn't come out. How did they occupy themselves ? In rehearsal. Well, here's one good effect of rain at Royat—it brings out the new tunes.

CHAPTER IV.

"THE OUT-FOR-A-LARK, ETC., SOCIETY."

A PROPOS of Puller "airing his French," Miss Louisa Metterbrun said something delightful to him the other day at dinner. Puller had been instructing us all in some French idioms until Madame Metterbrun set him right in his pronunciation. He owned that he had made a slip. "But," says he, wagging his head and pulling up his wristbands with the air of a man thoroughly well satisfied with himself generally, "but I think you'll allow that I can speak French better than most Englishmen, eh?"

Madame Metterbrun doesn't exactly know what to say, but Miss Louisa comes to the rescue. "O Mr. Puller"—he is frequently at their house in London, and they know him intimately—"I always say to Mamma, when we're abroad, that I do like to hear you talk French"—Puller smirks and thinks to himself that this is a girl of sense and rare appreciation—"because," she goes on quietly, and all at table are listening—"because your speaking French reminds me so of home." Her home is London. I think Puller won't ask Miss Louisa for an opinion on his French accent again in a hurry.

* * * * * *

I have just been reading Victor Hugo's *Choses Vues*. Admirable! *Fuite de Louis Philippe!* What a pitiful story. Then his account, marvellously told, and the whole point of the narrative given in two lines, of what became of the brain of Talleyrand. Graphically written is his visit to Thiers on behalf of Rochefort. Says Thiers to him, "*Cent journaux me traînent tous les matins dans la boue. Mais savez-vous mon procédé? Je ne les lis pas.*" To which Hugo rejoined, "*C'est précisément ce que je fais. Lire les diatribes, c'est respirer les latrines de sa renommée.*" Most public men, certainly most authors, artists, and actors, would do well to remember this advice, and act upon it.

* * * * * *

"*Choses Vues*," written "*Shows Vues*," would be a good heading for an all - round - about theatrical and entertainment article in *Mr. Punch's* pages. Patent this.

* * * * * *

Puller has recovered his high spirits. The temperature has changed: the waters are agreeing with him. So is the dinner hour, which M. Hall, our landlord, kindly permits us to have at the exceptional and un-Royat-like hour of 7:30. At dinner he is convivial. Madame Metterbrun and her two daughters are discussing music. Cousin Jane is deeply interested in listening to Madame Metterbrun on Wagner. The young ladies are thorough Wagnerites. La Contessa is unable to get a word in about Shakspeare and Salvini, and her daughter, who, in a quiet tone and with a most deliberate manner, announces herself as belonging to the "Take-everything-easy Society," is not at this particular moment interested in anything except the *menu*, which she is lazily scrutinising through her long-handled *pince-nez*.

Mrs. Dinderlin, having succumbed to the usual first attack of Royat depression, is leaning back in her chair, smelling salts and nodding assent to the Wagnerite theories, with which she entirely agrees. For my own part, I am neutral ; but as the Metterbruns are thorough musicians,—the mother being a magnificent pianist, and the eldest daughter a composer,—I am really interested in hearing all they have to say on the subject. Our bias is, temporarily, decidedly Wagnerian, for Cousin Jane, who is really in favour of "tune," and plenty of it,—being specially fond of Bellini and Donizetti,—in scientific musical society has not the courage of her opinions.

From composers the conversation travels to executants, and we name the favourite singers. After we have pretty well exhausted the list, and objected to this one as having a head voice, or to that as using the *vibrato*, or to the other as dwelling on an upper note ("queer sort of existence," says Puller, gradually coming up, as it were, to the surface to open his mouth for breath,—whereat Cousin Jane smiles, and Miss Casanova lazily nods approbation of the joke—while the rest of us ignore Puller, putting him aside as not wanted just now,—when down he goes again), we generally agree that Gayarré is about the best tenor we have had in London for some time ; that Santley is still unequalled as a baritone ; that there is no one now to play and sing *Mephistopheles* like Faure ; that M. Maurel is about the finest representative of *Don Giovanni ;* that Miss Arnoldson shows great promise ; that Albani is unrivalled ; that Marie Roze is difficult to beat as *Carmen ;* and that it is a pity that Patti's demands are so exorbitant ; and having exhausted the list of operatic artists,—Madame and her daughters holding that certain Germans, with whose names we, unfortunately for us, are not even acquainted, are far superior to any French or Italian singers that can be named— there ensues a pause in the conversation, of which the Countess Casanova takes advantage, and extending her right hand, which movement sharply jingles her bracelets, and so, as it were, sounds a bell to call us to attention, cuts in quickly with an emphatic, " Well, I don't profess to understand music as *you* do. I know what I like "—(" Hear ! hear ! " *sotto voce* from Puller, coming up again to the surface, which draws a languidly approving inclination of the head from Miss Casanova, and a smile, deprecating the interruption, from Cousin Jane),—" and I must say," continues the Countess, emphatically, " I would rather have one hour of Salvini in *Othello,* than a whole month of the best Operas by the best composers,—Wagner included," and down comes her hand on the table, all the bracelets ringing down the curtain on the first act.

We, the non-combatants, feel that the mailed gauntlet has been thrown down by the Countess as a challenge to the Metterbruns.

" O Mother ! " faintly remonstrates Miss Casanova, who loves a stall at the Opera. She fears that her mother's energetic declaration means war, and fans herself helplessly.

I am preparing to reconcile music and the drama, and am getting ready a supply of oil for what I foresee will be troubled waters, as the Metterbruns are beginning to rustle their feathers and flap their wings,—when Puller, leaning well forward, and stretching out an explanatory hand, with his elbow planted firmly on the table (" Very bad manners," says Cousin Jane afterwards

to me), says genially, " Well, *voyez-vous*, look here, you may talk
of your Wagners and Shakspeares, and Gayarrés, and Pattis,
but, for singing and acting, give me Arthur Roberts. Yes,"
he repeats pleasantly but defiantly, and taking up, as it were, the
Countess's gauntlet, " Salvini's not in it with Arthur Roberts."

The Countess's fan spreads out and works furiously. The
steam is getting up. The Metterbruns open their eyes, and
regard one another in consternation. They don't know who
Arthur Roberts is.

" Not know !" exclaims Puller, quite in his element. " Well,
when you come to London, you send to me, and I'll take you to
hear him."

" He's a Music-Hall singer," says the Countess, fanning herself
with an air of contemptuous indifference.

" Music-Hall Ar-*tiste !*" returns Puller, emphasising the second
syllable, which to his mind expresses a great deal, and makes all
the difference. " Now, Miladi," he goes on, imitating the manner
of one of his own favourite counsel, engaged by Puller & Co., con-
ducting a cross-examination, " have you ever seen him ?"

" Yes," she replies, shrugging her shoulders, " once. And," she
adds, making the bracelets jingle again, as with a tragedy-queen's
action of the right arm she sweeps away into space whole realms
of Music Halls and comic singers, " that was quite enough."

" Didn't he make you laugh ?" continues Puller, still in the
character of a stern cross-examiner.

" Laugh !" almost shrieks the Countess, extending her hands
so suddenly that I have only time to throw myself back to avoid a
sharp tap on the head from her fan. " Heavens ! not a bit ! not
the least bit in the world ! He made me sad ! I saw the people
in the stalls laughing, and I said,"—here she appeals with both
hands to the majority of sensible people at large—still at large—
" ' Am I stupid ? am I dull ? Do I not understand ?' "

" O Mother !" expostulates her daughter, in her most languid
manner, " he *was* funny ! "

" Funny !" ejaculates the Countess, tossing her head.

" I'd rather see Arthur Roberts than Salvini," says Puller,
waggishly, but with conviction.

" I think I would, for choice," says Miss Casanova, meditatively, but seeing the Countess's horrified expression of countenance, she takes care to add more languidly than ever, as if taking the smallest part in an argument were really too exhausting, "but then, you know, I really don't understand tragedy, and I love a laugh."

"Prefers Arthur Roberts to Salvini!" exclaims the Countess, and throws up her hands and eyes to the ceiling as if imploring Heaven not to visit on her the awful heresy of her child.

Here I interpose. Salvini, I say, is a great *Artiste*, no doubt of it, a marvellous Tragedian; and Arthur Roberts is not, in the true dramatic sense of the word, a genuine Comedian; but he is, in another sense, a true Comedian, though of the Music-Hall school.

"What a school!" murmurs the Countess, and with a pained expression of countenance as though she were suffering agonies.

The Metterbruns see the difference. Madame remembers a fat comic man in Berlin, at some garden, who used to wear a big hat and carry a large pipe, and make her laugh very much when she was a girl. Certainly, in his way, he was an artist. Is this Arthur Roberts anything like Max Splütterwessel? At this point, as we have finished coffee, and the Countess finds the room hot, I propose adjourning the debate to the Restaurant in the garden, as we are too late for the band at the Casino Samie.

The party is broken up in order to walk down to our rendez-vous.

Puller, whose idea of making things pleasant, and, as he expresses it, "sweetening everyone all round," is to order "drinks" for everybody, insists upon the party taking "*consommations*"—he loves saying this word—at his expense. The Countess at first objects, as also does Madame Metterbrun; but on Puller's explaining that he belongs to "The Two-with-you Society," they accept this explanation as utterly unintelligible but perfectly satisfactory; and so, accepting Puller's *al fresco* hospitality, we form a cheerful group round two tables put together for our accommodation. Puller's hospitality has taken the form of grenadines, chartreuses, and "sherry-gobblers,"—he loves this word too,—for us all round, and he has ordered for himself a strange mixture, which perfumes the night air as if some nauseous draught had been brought out of a chemist's shop, and which looks like green stagnant water in a big glass. It is called by Puller, with great glee, an "Absinthe gummy."

Anything nastier to look at or to smell I am not acquainted with in the way of drinks. However, he is our host, and I have a grenadine before me of his ordering, and between my lips an excellent cigar which is his gift. I can only say mildly, "It looks nasty;" and Cousin Jane expresses herself to the same effect, remarking also as she looks significantly towards me, that it is late, and that I am not keeping Royat hours. I promise to come away in ten minutes. Puller is in the highest possible spirits: surrounded by this company, all drinking his drinks, he as it were takes the chair and presides. He knocks on the table, which brings the waiter, to whom he says, holding up a couple of fingers, "Two with you,"—whereat the waiter only smiles upon the eccentric Englishman, shakes his head, and wisely retires.

"Ah, Miladi," says Puller, "you must take a course of Roberts. He's a rum 'un." Then he sings, "He's all right when you know him, but you've got to know him *first*."

His guests politely smile, all except the Countess. I preserve a discreet silence. Taking this on the whole for encouragement, Puller commences the song from which he has already quoted the chorus. What the words are I do not catch, but as Puller reproduces to the life the style and manner of a London Music-Hall singer, and cocks his hat on one side, it is no wonder that the French people at the other table turn towards us in amazement.

"For goodness sake, Mr. Puller!" cries the Countess, rising from her chair in consternation. Jane also rises, Miss Casanova is laughing nervously. The Metterbruns look utterly astonished. I feel I must stop this at once.

"My dear fellow," I say, magisterially, "you really mustn't do this sort of thing"—he is breaking out again with "*O what a surprise!*"—but I get up from my seat to reprove him gravely. "You would not do this if you were in a London restaurant."

"No," he replies, not in the least offended—"that's the lark of it. I belong to 'The-Out-for-a-lark-and-Two-with-you Society.' Don't you mind me," he adds; then turning with a pleasant wink to the ladies, who have been putting on their wraps and mantles, and are preparing to leave, he sings again,—

> "I'm all right when you know me—
> But——"

We leave him to finish the song by himself.

And to think that my friend Puller, with his hat cocked on one side, a big cigar in his mouth, a tumbler of "absinthe gummy" before him, a rakish expression in his eye, is the same Puller to whom, as partner in the firm of Horler, Puller, Puller (J.), Baker and Dayville, Solicitors, I would trust my dearest interests in any matter of property, of character, even of life itself! The strange story of *Hyde* and *Jekyll* is no fiction, after all.

CHAPTER V.

THIRTEENTH DAY OF CURE.

THE view from my window is charming, whether on a bright morning or a moonlight night. But I am not contented with it. There is within me an "Oliver, asking for more." Had I the faith which moves mountains, I would order that hill opposite to be removed, so as to give me a more extensive, and a grander view.

* * * *

The Beggars at Royat.—A nuisance and a disgrace to the place. Why are these wretched creatures allowed to trade on their fearful afflictions? Are there no free hospitals, no charitable institutions, where they can be taken care of? Of course there are. Is there no power to compel them to go in? Is there no "*traitement*" for them?

*   *   *   *   *   *

As for the little beggar boys and girls who are brought up to the trade and who waylay us all day, cannot they be put to some useful work and be forced into school? These able-bodied paupers should be employed in mending the footpaths leading up to Grave-noire and the environs, which are in a very bad condition.

*   *   *   *   *   *

I do not object, indeed by this time I take rather kindly to the *vin du pays*, but I detest what Mr. "Dumb-Crambo" would call—

The Whine of the Country.

*   *   *   *   *   *

À propos of walks in a wretched condition, why don't their Worships, the Maires of Royat and Chamalière, lay their heads together and mend the footpaths? In making the above sugges-tion, I do not contemplate wood-pavement. No: but I do think that these beggars might be utilised.

*   *   *   *   *   *

Pensées d'un Baigneur.—A bather has plenty of time to emulate the celebrated parrot. What can he do—the bather, not the parrot —in his bath, except think? He can talk, hum, or sing. He can recite: and exercise his voice and memory. But this would attract attention, and I fancy the talking, singing, or reciting bather would very soon be requested to keep quiet. Therefore he must think. He may not sleep: it is not permitted by the faculty. No: thinking is the thing. The time in a bath,—thirty-five minutes of it—passes as a dream, and the thoughts are as difficult to catch and fix as butterflies. Here are a few :—

It is absolutely necessary to please oneself even in things apparently indifferent. Out of politeness, I yielded yesterday to an invitation to take a drive of two hours. I was ill for nearly a couple of days afterwards. . . . . . So was the kind person who took me. I believe she meant it well, and intended it as an act of politeness. (N.B. This was written within the first seven days of the "*traitement.*" This sort of thing must come out of you. The waters bring out selfishness and ingratitude.)

*　　　*　　　*　　　*　　　*　　　*

Morning after morning I find myself staring at the notice on the wall at the foot of my bath. From that I gather that I am a "titulaire." My bath-cell is No. 17. So as Titulaire I am Number Seventeen,—like a convict. My Gaoler, the bathman, does not know me perhaps by any other name than "Monsieur &c., Dix-Sept." Ah, well, I never thought I should be seventeen again. But I am—at Royat. How it must be re-juvenising me !

*　　　*　　　*　　　*　　　*　　　*

I have been looking over a list of excursions to various "Salubrities Abroad." Among them I find this :—"*De Lyon en Savoie et en Dauphiné par Saint-André-le-Gaz, et retour.*"

"St. Andrew-the-Gas" sounds a novel name in a calendar. He was evidently a Saint much in advance of his time. An excellent man of course "according to his lights."

*　　　*　　　*　　　*　　　*　　　*

I saw a subject here for Mr. Marks, R.A. A bearded Franciscan Monk in his brown habit, with cord and rosary at his waist, sending a telegram at the telegraph office. Imagine the surroundings ! Mr. Marks might call it an Anachronism.

*　　　*　　　*　　　*　　　*　　　*

When abroad, I make notes of the names of any new dishes. The following one was new to me as a name, not as a dish, which was simple enough, "*Culottes de bœuf à la fermière.*" What next? "*Caleçons de veau à la baigneuse ?*" "*Gilets de mouton à la bergère?"* "*Culottes de veau à la Brian O'Lynn?*" "*Chapeau de volaille à la coq?*"

* * * * * * *

Music.—This morning, the fifteenth of my sojourn here, the band is playing something new. This is refreshing, as I am becoming a little tired of the overtures to *Zampa, Guillaume Tell, Italiano in Algeria,* selections from the *Huguenots* (highly popular as a good finish to any concert) and the dance music, waltzes and mazurkas, which have been popular for the last two years.

* * * * * * *

The clocks of Royat are still in an undecided state. The uninitiated person who takes his time—(*Note, en passant, for all baigneurs here*—Never be in a hurry, and always "take your time," no matter from where you take it)—from the Hotel, and starts at 7·30 in order to reach his bath by 8,—a walk of five minutes,— will find, on arriving at the *Établissement*, that it is just 8·5, so that he has taken a quarter of an hour to do the distance. If he starts from the *Établissement* at 8·30, to meet a friend at the station, on arriving there he will discover that it is 8·15 by the Railway Clock, so that he is at the end of his journey a quarter of an hour before he set out, having done the distance in considerably less than no time,—a record worth preserving. The Post Office Authorities, in despair, have put up a notice informing everybody that their clock has no connection with that of the *Établissement,* which may just do what it likes and be wound to it, and ignoring all church-clock authority and all municipal authority too, they (the Post Office Authorities aforesaid) announce that they intend to take their time from the Railway station, but even then will give themselves a margin of five minutes one way or the other, so that the public wishing to send letters must ascertain what the post times *ought* to be, and then give themselves another margin of at least ten minutes on the safe side. The calculation is not very complicated, when you are accustomed to it, and its uncertainty lends a gentle stimulus to the ordinary routine of the uneventful life at Royat.

* * * * * * *

For "Excursions from Royat by Rail or Road," see my Guide-Book, forthcoming.

     *   *   *   *   *   *   *

This advice, "*See my Guide,*" or "*See my History,*" is perpetually recurring as a friendly hint—it really being a most artful way of introducing an advertisement to your notice—in that invaluable publication, the *Guides Diamant, P. Joanne,* series, Hachette & Cie., without which no traveller's pocket or bag is completely furnished. Time for *siesta.*

CHAPTER VI.

SOMETHING ABOUT GUIDES.

I HAVE said Royat ought to be rebuilt. The Grand Hotel is of a sort of Doll's House order of architecture, splendid front, no depth to speak of, and built on so steep an ascent that it is hoisted up at the back like a lady's skirt by a dress-improver. *Beau site* all the same, and magnificent view.

     *   *   *   *   *   *

Last year the Hotel Continental formed part of a group of hotels —which seemed to have been the result of some violent volcanic eruption, when the mountain threw up several hotels, and left them there anyhow— it is at present separated from the Splendide and its other former companions by an impromptu wall, and from all its front windows it commands varied, beautiful, and, on the Clermont-Ferrand side, extensive views. It has a pleasant garden, a most enjoyable terrace, and it only wants to be in the hands of a firmly fixed and intelligent management to make it quite the best hotel in Royat. "Personally recommended," that is, as managed under the direction of M. Hall this year.

The service at the *Établissement de bains* is about as good as it can be. There are, however, no *bains de luxe.* A few of these would attract those " whom," as the appeals to the charitable used to have it, " Providence has blessed with affluence."

" La Compagnie Brocard," which manages Royat's bathing arrangements and undertakes a portion of the mild yet (to my mind as a serious bather) sufficient amusements, is not, unfortunately for the public, in accord with M. Samie, the spirited Proprietor of an opposition Casino, where there is a small theatre, in its way a perfect gem. Here all the " Stars" of any magnitude make their appearance on visiting Royat. As a " Baigneur de Royat" puts it, in a local journal, the Compagnie Brocard cannot consider their stuffy little room (" *le petit étouffoir* ") where theatrical performances are given as a real theatre. It is a pity that M. Samie and La Compagnie Brocard cannot, like the " birds in their little nests," agree. But as to Theatres and spectacles, my rule at Royat, or at any other Watercure place, would be this :—

"*Any baigneur found out of his hotel or lodgings after* 10·15, *p.m., shall be arrested, conducted back to his hotel, his number taken, and for the second offence he shall be fined. The fine to go to such objects as the Direction shall determine.*"

In short there should be introduced here the English University system of Proctors and Bull-dogs.

*   *   *   *   *   *

Another Rule.—No theatrical entertainment should last more than two hours with *entr'actes* of seven minutes each. The ventilation of the *salle de spectacle* should be assured.

*   *   *   *   *   *

If a company wanted to play a piece in four Acts, they must stop here two days ; and, if they couldn't do that, then they must begin their performance in the afternoon, have one *entr'acte* of an hour and a half to allow for dinner, and recommence at eight o'clock. I would discourage all evening indoor entertainments. Music, coffee, *petits chevaux*, M. Guignol's show, *ombres chinoises*, everything, in fact, that can be done *al fresco*—(and why not good plays *al fresco?* After the Laboucherian *Midsummer Night's Dream*, at Twickenham, which I am told was perfection)— *cafés chantants*, and so forth, including the " *consommation* devoutly to be wished," and all the lights out by 9·30. Lights in bedrooms to be extinguished same hour. This rule would mean, Early to bed, and early to rise, and the "*baigneurs*" would receive double the benefit they derive from these places as now constituted. Life in the open air should be the rule; plenty of exercise, riding and walking, and regular hours for everything for three weeks. The *baigneurs* to choose their own hours, and be kept to them strictly.

* * * * * *

But I have personally no sympathy with the *baigneurs* who find such a water-cure place as Royat dull. What do they want? If they cannot get on without a sort of continuation of the London Season, let them stay away altogether. Don't let them come and make night hideous with balls, suppers, dances, and won't-go home-till-morning parties.

* * * * * *

The above are my suggestions for the improvement of Royat; and now I go on to La Bourboule, and Mont Dore. By the way the waters at these places are all supplied, as I am credibly informed, from the same source; but the waters flowing towards La Bourboule and Mont Dore traverse certain *couches* on their way, and come out arsenical. It is strong drinking at La Bourboule and Mont Dore.

* * * * * *

One Joanne Guide introduces you to another Joanne Guide, or a history, you can't help yourself. The Joanne Guides are so united a family, that as soon as any member of it establishes itself on a friendly footing with you, your hand is always in your pocket while you are travelling on that *Guide Joanne's* account. An insidious tribe: and they make themselves absolutely essential to the traveller's existence and comfort.

* * * * * *

Each *Guide Joanne* tells you about his own country all that is requisite for you to know, and just so much more as inspires you with a thirst for further information. Say for example you see an old Château. Let us say *Le Château de Jean.* You want to know everything about it. Good. You inquire of the Guide

Joanne which professes to show you all over France, and which does it, mind you, in what would be an exhaustive style if it was not written with such an evident eye to the bookselling business. For example, suppose you are looking for information about the well-known ancient Château de Jean, here is a specimen of what Joanne would say on the subject :—

"*Sur la rive g.* (*V. ci-dessous B.*) *restes d'un château, style ogival, (mon. hist.,) bâti par le célèbre Jean Bienconnu-aux-enfants* (*V. mon. hist. x^e et xiie s.*), *beau portail, jolis détails d'architecture* (*mon. hist.*) *et en particulier l'appartement dit de la Donzelle toute désespéré (pour le visiter, s'adresser au gardien, pourboire), qui a conservé une grande partie de sa décoration originale et de sa peinture* (*mon. hist. xie*). *Le donjon renfermait une oubliette profonde nommée* DU RAT DÉ-VORANT, *qui autrefois servait de grenier au malt* (*V. mon. hist.*). *Ascension des Obélisques sur la terrasse (splendide panorama) et belles promenades autour de la petite chapelle dite* DU PRÊTRE CHAUVE. (*V. VI. L'Itinéraire du Pays-de-Bonnes, Guide Diamant.*)"

CHAPTER VII.

"ADVICE GRATIS."

Mees "O'Shocking!"

A T LAST I have seen him!—the travelling Englishman, the English Milord of the French Farce—"Oah, c'est moa!" of the *Journal Comique.*

*   *   *   *

But if the farce Milord is grotesque, the English "Mees" is equally ridiculous. I met, the other day, a lady of Albion, who was strutting about with an enormous "handled" *pince-nez* raised to her eyes, while she expressed her opinion "that those foreigners really *do* dress *so* absurdly!"

*   *   *   *

Diary of a Day.—At all these Stations Thermales the pleasantest hours of the day are sacrificed to the interests of the band, the casinos, the cercle, and the evening amusements. *Les Baigneurs sérieux* ought not to require any amusement after 9·30, and by ten they should be in bed. Their hours for walking and other exercise should be very early in the morning, or late in the evening before dinner. The remainder of the day should be given up to baths, to drinking waters, *déjeuner à la fourchette,* and rest.

*   *   *   *   *   *

By the way, at the top of the daily *menu* at the Continental Hotel the *déjeuner à la fourchette* at 11 A.M. is styled "LUNCH." Puller resents this as strongly as he does a waiter's answering him, "Yees, Sare," when he has given an order in his best French. Now this meal at 11 A.M. is not an English lunch, but *is* the French *déjeuner à la fourchette.* Is it becoming the common practice in hotels on the continent? If so, the English will soon remember that they don't come abroad for lunch—they can "lunch" well enough at home—but they do come abroad for *déjeuner à la fourchette*, and, if they do not get it, they will stay away.

"It's confoundedly insulting!" exclaims Puller, indignantly. "Do they think we don't know what a *déjeuner à la fourchette* means? But, dash it, you know," he goes on, in the tone of a man whom a very little more of this sort of treatment would disgust with life generally, "they're making everybody abroad so English." Then he repeats, "So English, you know," in imitation of some American burlesque actor, and this has the effect of restoring his good humour. He thinks the quotation so apt and so humorous, that he expands in chuckles, and goes out of the *salle-à-manger* doing a step, and repeating, "So English, you know!" The French, Spanish, and the visitors of various nationalities, shake their heads, shrug their shoulders, and evidently hope he is harmless. The waiters smile, and this reassures the guests.

* * * * * *

The special merit of the Royat Drinking Waters and Baths consists in the large amount of iron contained in them. Over the gates of the Park at Royat, where the *Établissement* and *Buvettes* are situated, should be inscribed, for the benefit of English visitors, "Washing and Ironing done here."

* * * * * *

The Uncertain Bather.—My acquaintance Mordel is another variety of the genus *Baigneur*. He is dissatisfied only with himself. He is perpetually having a row with himself. The Hotel is good enough, he says; the Doctor is all that can be desired. The baths and waters are managed very well; but the question is, he says to himself, "Was I right in coming here at all? Ought I not to have gone to Aix? or to Vichy? or to Homburg? or to Mont Dore, or to La Bourboule?" "Well, but"—I say to him, with a view to reconciling him to himself—"are the waters doing you good?" He reluctantly admits that they are not doing him any harm—as yet. In this state of uncertainty he remains during the whole course of treatment, and to the last, he is of the opinion that he ought to have gone to some other place, no matter where.

* * * * * *

T

It is a real pleasure to see Smith, of the Colosseum Club, meet
Brown, also a member of the same sociable institution. He greets
Brown heartily,—never was so glad to see anybody. Yet they are
anything but inseparables in London; and it certainly was not
owing to Smith's good offices that Brown was elected to the Colosseum. Brown has just arrived at Royat, and is not so effusive at
the sight of Smith, as Smith, who has been here ten days, is on
beholding Brown. "Thompson's here, so's Jones," Smith tells

"L'Anglais pour rire."

Brown, beamingly. "Are they?" returns Brown, who recognises
the names as those of eminent Colosseum men. "And now,"
exclaims Smith heartily, "in the evening we can have a rubber!"
This was why Smith was so overjoyed at meeting Brown; not
because he was an old friend, not even because he was a member
of the same social set, but because *he would make a fourth!*
"You'll want a rubber," adds Smith, cajolingly. "If he does,"
interposes Puller, in excellent spirits this morning, "he'll have to
go to Aix-les-Bains. They don't do the *massage* here. Aix is the
place for Rubbers." The joke falls among us like a bombshell and

the group disperses, each wondering how long Puller is going to remain at Royat. His movements may govern our own !

* * * * * *

Uneventful ! General Boulanger has called here to-day. No, not on me, but on a noble English poet, who is staying at the Continental. From the portrait in the *Salon* I should have expected a fine fellow of six feet high, rather Saxon and swaggery. Had he resembled his portrait I should not have believed in him. Now I do. There is hope for Boulanger. He is a short man. Napoleon was a short man. *" Il grandira ! "*

The Cravate au Moulin.

* * * * * *

Encore des Pensées.—" There is a time to talk, and a time to be silent." The first occasion is, when I have something to say, and an audience to say it to ; the other is, when I don't feel well, and hate everybody equally. Puller, when high-spirited, cannot understand this. Undergoing these Royat Waters, Puller and myself are on a see-saw. When he is up, I am down, and *vice versâ*. After trying to breakfast together, and to be mutually accommodating, which is done in the most disagreeable manner possible, we separate, on account of incompatibility of temper. Temporarily our relations are strained. This only applies to the morning. I want to be quiet in the morning, and detest early liveliness. Jane and myself, in future, breakfast together at our own time, and at our own table, in a corner. (And this is also within the first seven days of the *traitement*.)

*　　*　　*　　*　　*　　*

By the way, what a chance of *réclame* I lost on the occasion of Boulanger's visit. It never occurred to me till too late. I ought to have been at the front door, awaiting his departure. At the moment of his leaving, I should have left too. Then the report could have been spread about that I had "gone out with" General Boulanger. How astonished M. Ferry would have been. "Quite a Fairy tale for him," says Puller, who wishes to exhibit his acquaintance with the proper French pronunciation of M. Ferry's name.

*　　*　　*　　*　　*　　*

The Twenty-Second Morning.—I shall give myself three days leave of absence, and revisit La Bourboule and Le Mont Dore. These two places are higher up in the mountains of Auvergne.

*　　*　　*　　*　　*　　*

La Bourboule Revisited.—Very beautiful the line of country between Royat and La Bourboule. But the latter is an out-of-the-way place compared with Royat, which has the great advantage of being within a quarter of an hour's ride, or walk, of such a real good town as Clermont-Ferrand, whereas La Bourboule and Mont Dore are an hour-and-a-half's drive each of them from their own station, Laqueuille, which is nothing more than a mere country railway station, with a simple buffet, and four hours from Clermont-Ferrand, which I suppose is the market town, and certainly the only place of any importance to which one can go, "there and back again," in a long day.

Of course the descendants of Balbus, who "*murum ædificavit*" in our old Latin Grammar—(Are Balbus and Caius still at it in the Grammars of the present day?)—could not leave La Bourboule alone, and villas have been springing up in every direction. Shops, too. Already one side of a Boulevard has been commenced, represented by half-a-dozen superior shops, one of which, it is needless to say, is a sweet-stuff emporium, and another a Tabac. Then they've a Hotel de Ville at La Bourboule. In our time there was only a solitary Gendarme, in full cocked-hat and sword, who, as an official, was a failure, but, as a playmate of the children, and a friend of the *bonnes*, was a decided success. He looked well, and inspired the stranger on his arrival. But the feeling of awe soon wore off. Perhaps he, also, was a *baigneur*. Invalid Gendarmes might be usefully employed in this manner, their imposing appearance at various watering-places would inspire confidence, while they might be benefiting their physique. Policemen could be also

The dear Old Things who won't have a Door or Window open in our small Salle-à-manger.

effectively used in this way. " Recruiting Sergeants-de-ville " they might be called, engaged in recruiting their own health.

* * * * * *

A storm of rain and wind swept us out of La Bourboule—we subsequently heard that there was snow at Mont Dore—and drove us post-haste back to Royat warmth—comparative warmth, that is, for they were having two or three cold, rainy, and gusty days at Royat, too, preceding the day fixed for the Eclipse. But such weather is bearable at Royat, if you have once experienced it at La Bourboule. The valley of Royat is fairly high up, and well sheltered ; but as to the situation of La Bourboule and Mont Dore one may say, reversing the quotation, " And in the highest heights a higher still ! " " Only not by any means still," says Puller, who knows the country, and whom no inducement will lead away from Royat.

*   *   *   *   *   *

I have mapped out a short tour by way of return from Royat, which is at the disposition of anyone who is preparing to make himself a *baigneur* and a *titulaire* next season.

*   *   *   *   *   *

My *itinéraire* is this: London to Paris, taking care to travel by the *Empress* from Dover to Calais. Inquire beforehand at the L. C. & Dover Station. Victoria. Go by the A.M. Dine in Paris at 8·30. In a forthcoming little work I contemplate benefiting the travelling public generally with a few useful details, of which these are only hints. Paris next morning, to Clermont-Ferrand, for Royat. At Royat, I should naturally recommend the Hotel I know best. This is the Continental. It may change hands next year; if it changes hands it changes heads at the same time, and my advice may or may not be useful.

*   *   *   *   *   *

Stay at Royat for cure; visit—as excursions easily done in a day, when you're in fettle—La Bourboule and Mont Dore. For all information, ask the most civil of men, and the most obliging, the agent, who has an office in a line with the few shops situated on the upper terrace of the Parc. He will tell you everything— and be delighted to do it.

*   *   *   *   *   *

By the way, when once you've settled your tour, take my advice, and visit Messrs. Cook, of Ludgate Circus. Provide yourself with all your tickets beforehand. It will save you a heap of trouble afterwards. Too many Cooks can't spoil your journey, as you will take them on the "play or pay" system, and it binds you to nothing, except, in case of not using them, a slight discount ; whereas, on the other hand, it helps the person who is at all "infirm of purpose" to make up his mind, and keeps him to his original plan, which any experienced traveller will agree with me in saying, is, nine times out of ten, the wisest and best course to pursue. Of this more anon in my forthcoming *parvum opus* on this and cognate subjects.

*   *   *   *   *   *

Royat (if you are a *baigneur*, recommended here by your Doctor) is an easy place to get to, and to get away from. My friend Skurrie, who, immediately he has arrived at any place, passes all his time there in consulting guide-books, maps, *Bradshaws*, Cook's tourist books, and local *indicateurs*, with a view to see how he can best get away, comes to me with a paper full of closely-written details, and says, " Here's my plan :—Royat, Lyon (why do we put an 's' on to it, and make it ' Lyons ?' it would be as sensible for the French to call Liverpool ' Liverpools,' or Manchester ' Manchesters.' And why can't the French call London ' London,' instead of ' Londres ?')—then Aix-les-Bains (for a *massage*, and an excursion or two) . . then Geneva. This is, if you've got time to spare. If not, in a week you can make a really refreshing tour by pushing on from Lyon to Geneva, to Bâle, to Heidelberg, to Mainz, down the Rhine to Cologne, then Antwerp, Flushing, Queenborough. This will complete your week, and you will return to England with a store of variety to last you a year."

CHAPTER VIII.

EN ROUTE FOR HOME AFTER THE ROYAT TREATMENT.

AT GENEVA I met an old friend, one of the heartiest men I've ever known, and one of the best. He is delighted, really delighted, at our accidental meeting. I am for going on, but he will not hear of it.

"I know the place," says he, cheerily, with a wink and a nudge, "and I'll take you about."

What a wink it is! and what a nudge! So full of humorous appreciation of life and character. Such a knowing not-to-be-done-by-anyone sort of wink. And the nudge is intended to draw your attention to the wink and emphasize it. John Birley is the frankest, openest, freest-and-easiest of men, with a boundless capacity for enjoyment, the strongest sympathies with suffering, and a reverential grateful spirit that thanks Heaven for all bounties, and accepts misfortunes and sorrows as kindly reminders from Providence that the misfortunes and sorrows of others have to be considered and relieved, and again he thanks Heaven for having put it into his power to relieve them. His chief enjoyment is in giving pleasure to others. The most selfish would gain some good from contact with John Birley; and the craftiest, to whom it might occur to make John Birley's acquaintance for the sake of what he could make out of him or by him, would soon discover his error, and would be informed that he stood detected, very clearly, plainly, and straightly, not by anything that John Birley would say, but he would have it intimated to him beyond possibility of mistake by John Birley's wink and a playful nudge from John Birley's elbow in his left or right side, for John speaks with both elbows. The crafty rogue would there and then know—if he were not too fatally crafty for himself as are so many rogues, or too conceited to realise the humour of the situation,—that his little game, whatever it might have been with John Birley, was up, that his schemes were upset, and that to "try it on" any further with John Birley would be utter waste of time and trouble. That is what John Birley's wink would convey to the rogue. But to the honest man, to the friend, the wink and nudge assure good comradeship and something rare in store for him. To the unfortunate and suffering there is another tone to the wink and nudge, and to these they are full of promise of hope and help, and act as a fine invigorating tonic.

Such is John Birley, whom I meet *en route* and who insists upon my stopping with him and showing me the place. He travels a great deal, he knows everybody, and everybody knows him. No matter what the language of the country may be, no matter whether he is in France, Germany, Russia, Egypt, India, or Africa, among cultivated peers, outlandish peasants, or uncouth savages, John Birley invariably makes himself thoroughly understood, for any deficiency in his acquaintance with the language he ekes out with a wink and a nudge adapted to the occasion, and he is sure to obtain exactly what he wants, or an excellent substitute for it, if the thing itself is not to be had. And this has always been so. It so happens that he has retired from business and is now very rich, but long ago when he was working hard, and struggling too, his manner and method were just the same ; he has never been discouraged, never been discontented, always energetic, always sanguine, and has elbowed his path for himself through the crowd, politely, pleasantly, apologising sympathetically for any toes he may have accidentally trod upon in his onward course, and working himself well into the front rank by the magic charm of his wink and nudge. He has pulled some others after him who have clung on to his coat-tails, and brought out of the ruck not a few of those on whose toes, as I have already said, he had pressed rather heavily in passing.

I know I cannot be in better hands, and he is going to show me about everywhere within the very few days I can absolutely spare, now that my cure is finished, my Royat time over, and that I am on my way back to England, home, and beauty.

He maps out a few excursions. He has taken them all before,

long ago. But, delighted to go over old ground, the greater part of his pleasure will be found in my enjoyment; for to revisit places associated with pleasant memories, or with nothing but the remembrance of their loveliness, their grandeur, or their solemnity, is to him, in some way like welcoming old friends. All John Birley's friends are old ones; he has no new ones, he never had. Some men of the world discussing him, aver that it is a sort of proof to themselves of there being something good still left in them, that they can reckon themselves among John Birley's friends. They are of all shades and colours are his friends, and they will analyse each other's characters behind each other's backs in the presence of John Birley, and afterwards they will be more inclined towards each other, more sympathetic, and more charitably disposed, in consequence of each other's good points having been brought out into strong relief by John Birley's kindly light. So it is with seeing the beauties of nature or art in his company; and so it is that I consider myself to have alighted on my legs in having come across him in this, the lovely playground of Europe, the home of the Merry Swiss Boys and Girls.

There is the Lake to be done; there is Nyon, Thonon, Rolle, Lausanne, Ouchy, Evian-les-Bains, Vevey, and then there are the heights above, including the ascent to St. Gergues, and to wherever can be obtained the best views of Mont Blanc, the Dent du Midi, and the other well-known "objects of interest." Were Puller here, he would say that "the best views of these mountains can be obtained at the photographers"—but he is not here, he is finishing his treatment at Royat. So it is all arranged, and we dine together, as a commencement.

"You don't mind a third party present?" says Birley to me, apologetically, "as I have just found old Sir Alec McQuincey, wandering about without a companion. Wretched to be alone, eh! and not well, eh? Suffering from liver—nasty that—gives jaundiced view of life. So must cheer the old boy up. He's off for a cure to Evian-les-Bains; so I said to him, 'Dine with us to-night, and we'll land you there to-morrow, eh?' —that's right, isn't it?"—and he gives me a cheery wink and nudge, taking me, as it were, into partnership with him in his scheme for entertaining Sir Alec McQuincey, and for keeping up the latter's spirits, previous to seeing him off to-morrow to the place across the Lake where he is to undergo his treatment, which I trust may enable him to "live happily ever after," and enjoy any amount of City dinners ("He is a City magnate," says Birley, with a nudge, "and that's not good for liver complaint, eh?") till the end of next Season.

Sir Alec is a capital companion, hearty, cheery, and full of anecdotes. He has got an excellent listener in John Birley, whereat I am rather astonished, as John generally has a lot to say for himself, and a good story from one man invariably draws out another from J. B. But on this occasion he is so unusually silent that I am puzzled. It is true that Sir Alec commences most of his anecdotes with an apology to Birley in this shape, "I've told this to Birley before, but," turning to me, "you haven't heard it, and it may interest *you*," whereupon Birley nods approval, and I politely assure Sir Alec that I am already deeply interested by anticipation, and in the words of the ancient drama, now obsolete, I feel inclined to add, "Proceed, sweet warbler, your story interests me much ; proceed."

The sweet warbler, who, by the way, is a trifle hoarse and occasionally a little indistinct, tells several of these narratives—they are narratives, and I cut in with occasional observations more or less to the point, which are silently acknowledged by Birley, but not by Sir Alec, who seems bent upon getting on with his series, interspersed with anecdotes, to the exclusion of all other conversation. He begins with the fish, and his first story about somebody who rose from nothing and arrived at being something, lasts, with the assistance of several discursive but illustrative anecdotes, till we reach the merry Swiss cream and stewed fruit. With the coffee and cigars he opens volume two of his interesting and remarkable stories of great men—each biographical monologue being really interesting by itself, only taken together they ought to be spread over a considerable period, like the *Arabian Nights' Entertainments*, and still Birley contentedly listens, gently inhaling his cigarette, and, when referred to, nodding corroboration. It occurs to me that as Sir Alec has told all these before to John Birley, so the latter may have told most of his to Sir Alec and myself, and that that is why he is now so silent. At all events, he only rarely makes observations, and these of the curtest. I fancy he wants me to come out and amuse Sir Alec, in return for Sir Alec interesting me ; and it occurs to me that I shall be ungrateful if I do not cut in with something new, just to save Birley from hearing Sir Alec's stories all over again, and Sir Alec from hearing Birley's, with which I presume, as they are such very old and intimate friends, he must be acquainted.

So I rouse myself, with a strong determination to shine or perish in the attempt. I make a sharp and apposite remark on some portions of the story which Sir Alec is now recounting, whereat Birley smiles, and Sir Alec smiles too, but resumes his narrative at once, as if he were afraid of losing the thread in consequence of my interruption. I am conscious of having only glimmered; I have not yet shone. On he goes again ; he is telling us of a wonderful silver tea-pot, how it was lost in a cart, how some one saw it outside the Old Bailey, how some one came up at that moment and a Judge said to an Alderman, "That's the tea-pot!" Now at this moment I remember that I have a story which neither of these two has ever heard, of a Judge and an Alderman which will come in capitally here, and so as I am quite certain that if I keep it to myself and allow the opportune moment to pass, I shall forget it entirely, and so lose a magnificent chance of shining brilliantly in the presence of Sir Alec (who if favourably impressed can be, I am aware, of the greatest possible service to me), I take advantage of Sir Alec drawing strenuously at the last half-inch (he is a thrifty man evidently) of his expiring cigar, to say briskly, "By the way—excuse my interrupting you—but that reminds me," and then I give my story of the Judge and the Alderman, which makes Birley laugh, and brings a smile to Sir Alec's lips, though it seems to me there is a puzzled expression on his countenance, as though he couldn't quite understand the point, and was appearing to be amused chiefly out of politeness to me as being a friend of John Birley's.

However, Sir Alec does smile, and then forthwith resumes his narrative. When he has finished, as he has mentioned the names of some persons with whom I am acquainted, I ask him if they are so and so, and he replies, "Yes," and adds something which elicits from me a sharp remark that gets a roar from Birley, and produces on Sir Alec's countenance another smile and the same sort of puzzled expression I had noticed before. I feel that I have shone, but that somehow I have not turned my light strongly enough on to Sir Alec. I question him as to the identity of some other celebrated persons he has been mentioning, and he replies with something about them which doesn't seem to exactly correspond with my question; but once more—being in the happiest vein, and shining in a manner that positively astonishes myself, I let off another brilliant jest, which is received in precisely the same manner by my audience as were my previous conversational fireworks. I think to myself, " I am ingratiating myself with Sir Alec. This will be a first-rate thing for me and for several members of my family, as a man in Sir Alec's influential position," &c.

Sir Alec now starts another subject, and as I foresee that if he sticks to it, I have something which will cap everything, I at once question him as to something he has just uttered. He replies, but, as before, I am bothered by his reply, which seems to me utterly inconsequent. So I repeat my question. And he smiles, nods and says, " Well—yes—" doubtfully. But my question required quite a different sort of answer. It had been, " How many times did you say Lord Grangemore sneezed on that occasion ?" To which it is evident that a doubtful " Well—um—yes," is not a satisfactory answer. So I repeat the question, whereupon he turns towards me confidentially and says, " No, I don't think so. It was her sister he married." I look at him inquiringly to see if this is his fun, but at that moment I catch a wink from Birley, who is putting up his hand to his ear and intimating in the clearest possible pantomime for my private and particular benefit, that our entertaining friend Sir Alec McQuincey is uncommonly deaf!

Now I comprehend Birley's silence. Now I comprehend why Sir Alec goes on talking, and why he looks puzzled at any interruption, and why he could only smile when he got the cue, as it were, from his companion, and was made aware that there had been something said which required to be smiled at.

I relapse into silence. I accept an excellent cigar from Sir Alec, and I let him talk for the rest of the evening uninterruptedly, until he looks at his watch, says that nine-thirty is late enough for him, that he has enjoyed his evening with us amazingly, and goes off to bed.

"Agreeable old chap," says Birley, stretching out his legs, preparatory to taking a short stroll. "Seen a lot of life has old Alec. He's a capital Chairman at a Board-meeting. Just deaf enough when he doesn't want to hear any arguments. I let him talk on."

"So I see," I say, and we walk out to bid good-night to Mont Blanc.

"The Mons looks like a warrior taking his rest—his last rest," says Birley, gravely, giving me a subdued nudge. "Napoleon the Great, and his cocked hat, carved out of white stone. Ah!" and, meditatively we linger, and then walk slowly back to the Hotel.

"We'll take old Alec to his warm bath at Evian-les-Bains to-morrow," says Birley. "Good night." Then he pauses on the stairs, as with a wink full of fun, and last playful nudge, he says, "I suppose you'll let him have all the talk to himself, eh? Won't you? Ha! ha! I shall."

*   *   *   *   *   *

My friend Skurrie, to whom his own Plan of Return, which I have accepted, is as the law of the Medes and Persians, says he will give me three days more for Geneva and Birley, and that then we must emphatically start homewards, as he insists on Jane and myself seeing Heidelberg *en route*, and every half hour of our time from Wednesday to Monday is so carefully adjusted that to miss one train will upset all the plans he has taken such pains and trouble to arrange for us. I am closeted with him for two hours, when he explains it all to me, gives me, so to speak, the key of the puzzle, insists on my verifying the items by *Cook's Tourist Train-Book* (an invaluable work), and then reducing it to writing. After this I am headachey, and exhausted.

[P.S.—Revising this, long after the event, I say, "Beware of Skurrie and his fixed plan of sight-seeing against time."]

CHAPTER IX.

"Is this the Hend?"—Miss Squeers.

SKURRIE puts us in the train, gives us our Cook's tickets all ready stamped and dated. No trouble. Then he insists on comparing his notes of our route with mine, to see that all is correct.

"Wednesday," he says, "that's to-day. Geneva *dep.* 12, Bâle *arr.* 7·45." He speaks a *Bradshaw* abbreviated language. "Change twice, perhaps three times, Lausanne, Brienne, Olten. Not quite sure; but you must look out." Oh, the trouble and anxiety of looking out for where you change! "Then," he goes on, "Thursday, Bâle *dep.* 9·2 A.M., Heidelberg *arr.* 1·55."

"Any change?" I ask, as if I wanted twopence out of a shilling.

"No, at least I don't think so. But you had better ask," he replies. Ah! this asking! if you are not quite well, and don't understand the language (which I do not in German Switzerland), and get hold of an austere military station-master, or an imbecile porter, and then have to carry that most inconvenient article of all baggage, a hand-bag, which you have brought as "so convenient to hold everything you want for a night," and which is light to carry until it is packed! "Then," goes on the imperturbable Skurrie, "you'll 'do' Heidelberg, dine there, sleep there, and on Friday Heidelberg *dep.* 6 A.M.——"

Here I interrupt with a groan—"Can't we go later?"

"No," says Skurrie, sternly. "Impossible. You'll upset all the calculations if you do."

Jane says, meekly, that when one is travelling, and going to bed early, it is not so difficult to get up very early, and, for her part, she knows she shall be awake all night. Ah! so shall I, I feel, and already the journey begins to weigh heavily on me, and I do not bless Skurrie and his plan. "But," I say aloud, knowing he has done it all for the best, and that I cannot now recede, "go on."

He does so, at railroad pace :—"Heidelberg *dep.* 6. Mannheim *arr.* 7·5, *dep.* 7·15. Mayence *arr.* 8·22, in time for boat down the Rhine 8·55. Cologne *arr.* 4·30. And there you are."

"Yes," I rejoin, rather liking the idea of Cologne, "there we are—and then ?"

"Well, you'll have a longish morning at Cologne ; rest, see Cathedral, breakfast," and here he refers to his notes, "Cologne *dep.* 1·13 P.M., and Antwerp *arr.* 6·34."

"Change anywhere ?" I inquire, helplessly. "Yes," he answers, meditatively. "At this moment I forget where, but you've got examination of baggage on the Belgian frontier, and you have two changes, I think. However, it's all easy enough."

"I'm glad of that," I say, trying to cheer up a bit, only somehow I am depressed : and Cousin Jane isn't much better, though she tries to put everything in the pleasantest possible light, and remarks that at all events "the travelling will soon be over."

Skurrie continues reading off his paper and comparing the details with my notes, "Sunday—Antwerp *dep.* 6·34 P.M. Rosendael *arr.* 7·45—yes—then Rosendael *dep.* 8·44, and catch the 10·10 P.M. boat at Flushing. Queenborough *arr.* 5·50, fresh as a lark, and up to town by 7·55."

"But we don't want to go up to town, we want to go to Ramsgate."

"Ha !" he says slowly, giving this idea as just sprung upon him his full consideration. "Ha !—let me see—" Then, as if by inspiration, he continues quickly—"sacrifice your London tickets, book luggage for Flushing, only then at Flushing re-book it for Queenborough, and once you're there you catch an early train to Ramsgate, and you'll be there nearly as soon as you would have arrived in London. Train just off. Wish you *bon voyage.*"

I thank him for all his trouble, and ask, with some astonishment, if he is not going to accompany us ?

"Can't—wish I could," returns Skurrie. "But I've got to go off

to Peterborough by night mail. Business. Should have been delighted to have looked after you and seen you through, but you've
got it all down and can't make any mistake. *Au plaisir!*"

And he is off. So are we.

Oh, this journey!! Everything changes. My health, the
scenery, the weather, all becoming worse and worse. Poor Cousin
Jane, too.

Oh, the changes of carriage! The rushing about from platform
to platform, carrying that confounded bag, and sticks, and
umbrellas, and small things, of which Jane—poor Jane!—has her
share, and, but for her sticking to every basket and package, I
should, in despair, have surrendered to chance, left them behind
me somewhere, and should have never seen them again. All aches
and pains, and weariness! At last at Bâle, rattled over stones and
bridge in a jolting omnibus, through pouring rain to the hotel of
" The Three Kings."

Our treatment in the *salle-à-manger* of that Monarchical
Hostelric is enough to make the most loyal turn republican. A
willing head-waiter with insubordinate assistants—and we are
miserable.

Off early to Heidelberg. Delighted, at all events, to bid farewell to the worthy Monarchs. This trip seemed to invigorate us
and if civility, polite attention, good rooms, and an excellent
cuisine could make any invalid temporarily better, then our short
stay at the Prinz Karl Hotel—a really perfectly managed establishment—ought to have revived us both considerably. And so
it did. A lovely drive to the heights among the pine-woods and
in the purest air went for something, but alas the knowledge that
we had to rise at 5 A.M., to be off by six—it turned out to be a
6.30 train—drove slumber from our eyes, and only by means of
a cold bath, the first thing on tumbling out of bed, could I brace
myself for the effort. Then on we went, taking Skurrie's pre-
arranged tour.

Let the remainder be a blank.

When abroad I had bought a French one-volume novel which I
had seen praised in the *Figaro*. I will not give its name, nor that
of its author. If it indeed portrays persons really living in Paris
and if these persons are not wholly exceptional (but, if so why

this novel, which implies the contrary and denounces them ?) then
is the latest state of Republican Paris worse than its former state
in the days of the *dégringolade* of the Empire, and Paris must
undergo a fearful purgation before she will once again possess
mens sana in corpore sano.   I read this disgusting novel half-way
through until its meaning became quite clear to me, and then I
proceeded by leaps and bounds, landing on dry places and
skipping over the filth in order to see how the author worked
out a moral and punished his infamous scoundrel of a chief
personage.   No.   Moral there was none, except an eloquent
appeal to Paris to rise and crush these reptiles and their brood.
On the wretched night when feverish, ill, and sleepless, I lay
miserably in the saloon of the Flemish steamer crossing to Queenborough, I opened the porthole above me and threw this infernal
book into the sea.   After this I bore the sufferings of that night
with a lighter heart.

*   *   *   *   *   *

Suffice it that I arrived at home—and how glad I was to get
there—broken down, prostrate and only fit for bed——where
with railways running round and round my head, steamboats
dashing and thumping about my brain, the shrieks of German
and Flemish porters ringing in my ears, Skurrie always forcing
me to travel on, on, on, against my will, I remained for about
three weeks.

Advice gratis to all Drinkers of Waters.—"The story shows," as
the Moral to the fables of Æsop used to put it, that when you
have finished your cure, make straight by the easiest stages for
the seaside at home.   Avoid all exertion ; and ask your medical
man before leaving to tell you exactly what to eat, drink, and
avoid, for the next three weeks at least after the completion of
your cure.

*   *   *   *   *   *

While ill, but when beginning to crave for some amusement or
distraction, I asked that my dear old Boz's *Sketches* should be read
to me, to which in years gone by I had been indebted for many a
hearty laugh.   Alas ! what a disappointment !   Except for a little
descriptive bit here and there, the fun of these *Sketches* sounded as

wearisome and old-fashioned as the humours of the now forgotten "Adelphi screamers" in which Messrs. Wright and Paul Bedford used to perform, and at which, as a boy, I used to scream with delight, when the strong-minded mistress of the house, speaking while the comic servant was laying the cloth for dinner, would say of her husband, "When I see him I'll give him——" "Pepper," says the comic servant, accidentally placing that condiment on the table. "He shan't," resumes the irate lady, "come over me with any——" "Butter," interrupts the comic servant quite unconsciously, of course, as he deposits a pat of Dorset on the table. And so on. Later on, I tried Thackeray's *Esmond*. How tedious, how involved, and full of repetitions! It is enlivened here and there by the introduction of such real characters as *Dick Steele*, *Lord Mohun*, *Dean Atterbury*, and others, and by the mysterious melodramatic appearances and disappearances of *Father Holt*, a typical Jesuit of the "penny dreadful" style of literature. But the work had lost whatever charm it ever possessed for me, and, indeed, I had always considered it an overrated book, not by any means to be compared with *Vanity Fair*, *Pendennis*, or even with *Barry Lyndon*, which last is repulsively clever.

*　　*　　*　　*　　*　　*

Then I asked for a book that I never yet could get through, and to which I thought that now, with leisure and a craving for distraction, I might take a liking. This was *Little Dorrit*. I tried hard, but it made my head ache even more than *Esmond* had done, and I laid it down, utterly unable to comprehend the mystery which takes such an amount of dreary, broken-up, tedious dialogue in the closing chapters to unravel.

*　　*　　*　　*　　*

I took down Washington Irving's *Sketch-book*, and read it with delight. Fresh as ever! It did me good. So did Charles Lamb's Essays. And then guess what moved me to laughter, to tears, and to real heartfelt gratitude that we should have had a writer who could leave us such an immortal work? What? It is a gem. It is very small, but to my mind, and not excepting any one of all he ever wrote, the most precious in every way for its true humour, for its natural pathos, and for its large-hearted Christian teaching, is *The Christmas Carol,* by Charles Dickens. Had this been his only book, it would have sufficed for his imperishable fame.

＊　　　＊　　　＊　　　＊　　　＊　　　＊

And then what made me chuckle and laugh? Why, Thackeray's *Sultan Stork*, which, somehow or other, I never remembered having read before this time of convalescent leisure. It is Thackeray in his most frolicsome humour, and, therefore, Thackeray at his best.

＊　　　＊　　　＊　　　＊　　　＊　　　＊

I am almost recovered, and am finding my "Salubrity at Home."

DUE SOUTH.

DUE SOUTH.

CHAPTER I.

MONTE CARLO—VILLA ROUGE-GAGNE—THE CASINO.

HERE at 9·30 A.M., having just finished my early chocolate and my fragrant cigaretto *per esser felice* — the adjective reminds me of what Mrs. Ramsbotham said when, after telling her nephew not to smoke in the dining-room, she found him with what he called "a fragrant weed" in his mouth, so that, as she said, "I caught him in *fragrante delicto*"—but this quite "*en parson*," as the waiter said when he saw his white tie reflected in a looking-glass—here I am, sitting out amid the orange and lemon trees, feeling myself making part of a Burne-Jones picture, in summerish attire, under a sunshade, looking out on to the blue Mediterranean, down on to the hot and dusty road to Nice, and up at the saffron-coloured tiles and pale white-and-yellow walls of the Citadel of Monaco. It is too hot to walk much—except, presently, down hill, as far as the terrace of the Casino—so I prefer to bask beneath the pleasant verandah while I read the day before yesterday's *Times*, which recounts how London is in difficulties, as usual, with the snow, how the sun has shone fitfully, for a few minutes at a time, during the day, and, in a general way, how beastly the weather is everywhere but here.

On Monday we had our share of wind, for there was what
Mrs. Ram terms "a Minstrel," which raised blinding clouds of
dust, and one minute you were hot, and the next you were cold,
the whole entertainment "presenting," as the dear old lady
above-mentioned says, "a complete illustration of one of Allsop's
Fables about the Sun, the Wind, and the Traveller." But to-day
life is worth living,—and it would be still more so if one could
look back without regret to the result of last night's *roulette*, when
I lost quite fifteen francs, or could anticipate with certainty the
successful issue of planking down the maximum on a single
number,—and, at the present moment, life would be perfectly
enjoyable, if two dirty rattish-looking troubadours, with a couple
of guitars, had not invaded the gardens, and commenced a serenade.
Where are the police? Where is the army of Monaco? They
don't expect police, but they do expect "coppers." And *I* shan't
be happy till *they* get them. Their style and manner reminds me
of the Derby Day, and of the itinerant musicians whom one sees
outside public-houses in London, pursuing their calling, or rather,
their bawling. I fancy under the influence of a Franco-Italian
sky I am dropping into poetry. "It's the fine weather brings
them out," says our confidential waiter at the Hôtel Windsor,
"*Comme les oiseaux au printemps,*" which is small compliment to
the birds.

Everybody here, in this wonderful Casino! Many who, I
imagine, must be neglecting their professional duties "to serve
tables." Some excellent people would like to see each of these
tables a "*tabula rasa*," but where's the special and particular
harm, any more, that is, than in horse-racing, card-playing, Stock
Exchange speculation, or any other form of gambling?

Perhaps all gambling is bad,—I don't say it isn't, and I certainly
am far from saying it is,—but why is this particular form of it at
Monte Carlo to be denounced as so utterly monstrous?

"Why," says some one to me, "notice the faces round the
tables! Look at the people! Did you ever see such a set?
Look at the women, regard the men! The Demon of Play has
seized them all! It is a Pandemonium!"

"Quite so," I reply, "and by the way I observe several distinguished English Statesmen and highly respectable English

ladies in that crowd—and—and—as the red hasn't turned up
for the last four times, I shall put on *les quatre premiers,* and on
red—excuse me." And turning to apologise to my companion for
interrupting his flow of moral conversation, I find I am addressing
myself to a perfect stranger, and that my virtuous friend has contrived to get a seat, and has his money on in four different places.
The Mediterranean is blue, the oranges and lemons are yellow, the
sun shines brightly, the air is exhilarating—health before everything by all means. But at Monte Carlo—as in Denmark where
there was something rotten in the state *tempore Hamletto*—" the
play's the thing"—*il n'y a que ça—rien ne va plus*—and so I
finish my brief correspondence just to let you know where I am.
Well, I am on the four first, the middle dozen, and red. I sign
myself yours truly, singing—

> "MONTE CARLO IS MY NAME!"

P.S.—I have returned from the Casino. Yes. The gambling
ought to be stopped. The weather is chilly. I will have the fire
lighted. Such a fire! Only wood—no coals. Bah! Why come
here for health and change of climate? Isn't good honest snow
and muck in England, and no sun, better than losing 500 francs
in three-quarters of an hour? And to think that if I *had* only
put on the *quatre derniers,* instead of the *quatre premiers* (as I did),
I might have won something fabulous. I shall send for my bill.
Where's a cheap restaurant? Shall I have one turn more at the
tables? Well, just one. To-night.

P.S. No. 2.—Lovely night! Beautiful moon! Stars magnificent! Such an atmosphere! Who would stop in England,
and, above all, in smoky London, if they could only get out here!
Let me see; I'll just empty out my pockets—750 francs; that
leaves me 250 to the good. After all, there's no harm in
gambling; merely *pour passer le temps.* And then the place is
so healthy! Why, one can be up till two in the morning, and
take anything and everything, and smoke any amount, without
feeling the effect. The air is so exhilarating. Shall stay here a
few days more. Shall I play again? that is the question. At
present I am inclined to say, *Monsieur, faites votre jeu! J'y suis!*
I send you this as a sort of diary just to show you what good the
climate here is doing to   Yours truly,   M. C.

CHAPTER II.

MONTE CARLO—THE ENGLISH BAR—CHEZ "PETERS."

EVENING *of the Fifth Day.* — Beautiful night for walking home. Moon bright. Air fresh. Charming place! Lovely weather! After many ups and downs at the tables, I have come off a winner of ten francs. Had I lost ten francs I do not think the night would appear to me so lovely as it does. It is a long way up to the Villa Rouge Gagne, so my companion, who says he is out to "see life," purposes taking light refreshment *en route*. Among the many light refreshment-places here, one of the most successful seems to be an English Bar, on a small scale. Here distinguished compatriots stroll in after the tables, to take a "John Collins"—I believe this is the name of the harmless beverage—or a few oysters and stout, or a glass of beer, or spirits and water. Odd to come all the way from London merely to play *roulette* in a hot and crowded room, and afterwards to sit at the bar of a small public-house overlooking the blue Mediterranean. But I do—and so do very many others. In front of this bar, within the last few minutes, the policy of an empire could have been quietly arranged over a "John Collins" or glass of whiskey-and-water and a cigar. We stroll out into the moonlight, and just look in "*Chez* Peters." Here, while the dignified but obliging and industrious Monsieur Peters serves behind the bar, sportsmen gather round the simple marble-topped tables, discussing pigeon-shooting, and strange stories of the chances of war, at *trente et quarante* and *roulette*. One very big man, with a loud voice, is energetically recounting to a small circle of admirers some wonderful *coups* that he had made at the tables. Thirty thousand francs at one go is the lowest amount he will condescend to talk about.

"I put down, Sir," says he, emphatically thumping the marble table with his fist, and addressing no one in particular, "four times I put down a thousand francs at each corner, and one of the numbers came up every turn."

"No!" exclaim some young men who are listening, open-mouthed.

"Very odd!" drily remarks a shrewd-looking person, with the cynical air of an elderly Mephistopheles.

"Yes, Gentlemen, I did," says the big man, emphasising his narrative with more thumps on the marble table, "and then I put forty on *passe*, a hundred on *six premiers*, and another forty on 22. They all turned up, and so I went on, and that evening made just eighty thousand francs, in something under an hour."

"No!" again murmur the younger portion of his audience, while the elderly Mephistopheles, lighting a cigarette as he raises his eyebrows, and observes, "Did you really? Very strange!"

I certainly became interested in his stories. They made me thirsty. Some one suggests oysters and stout. I think, hearing of all these vast sums of money being won, has given me a strong inclination for oysters and stout, as suggested. Though I had not thought of them before, I now feel that I can't possibly go on for another five minutes without them. An additional incentive is, that the friend who has joined us, and who suggested this form of nourishment, is in excellent spirits, having unexpectedly won forty francs, and offers to provide the entertainment at his own expense. Offer immediately accepted. And so we sit down to oysters and stout, and bread and butter "*Chez* Peters," at Monte Carlo, and for all that we see the Southern sky, the brilliant moon, and the blue Mediterranean, we might as well be at Rule's, in Maiden Lane, or Wilton's, in King Street, St. James's. But when we leave "Peters," and walk up the hill, then we feel the effects, not of the supper, but of the invigorating air, and the clear atmosphere ; and as we look upwards at the deep blue sky, and the brilliant moon, we say to one another, Shakspearianly, " ' On such a night' we could stay out for any length of time, and walk any-where, without fatigue"—which sentiment may be more poetically expressed in the words of the immortal bard, who sang, "We won't go home till morning, Till daylight doth appear." As a matter of fact, it is 12·30, and we retire now, one of the party to Villa Rouge Gagne, and the other two to the Hôtel Windsor.

CHAPTER III.

MONTE CARLO—THE TABLES—CHANGE—BYNGLEIGH.

ON MY road to the Casino at Monte Carlo I meet Hodgkins, Peterson, and Flickmore. "How have you done?" I ask, as I am collecting all the information I can about the country, so to speak, in which I am about to try my fortune.

"Pretty fair," answers Hodgkins. "Not bad," says Peterson. "Might have been worse," observes Flickmore.

"Lost five hundred louis first day," says Hodgkins, looking sharply at his two friends.

I smile sympathetically. Five hundred! Dear me, a large sum to lose. And I began to think that I'd better reflect before I tempt the hazard of *roulette*.

"We picked it up next day, though," puts in Peterson, also looking round at his companions, and smiling.

"And the second day were two thousand to the good," says Flickmore. "Not pounds—louis; but not bad business even in that."

Bad business, indeed! I wish it would happen to *me* even in francs—or half francs, for the matter of that. I am eager to know the system.

"Well," answers Hodgkins, "you see it's a little difficult to explain and to carry out, unless you're really going in for it. Perhaps you'd hardly understand it."

Well, I think my powers of comprehension are quite up to this; I mean that, if these three chaps, who are mere *flâneurs* on the face of the earth (except when they are in their business in the City) can master the system, I'm pretty sure that *I* can.

"Can't you give me an idea of it?" I ask, almost piteously.

"Well," says Flickmore, "it takes a day to carry it out properly, even with luck, and it requires three fellows to play it. We're a Syndicate, and we bring in five hundred apiece. Lose *that*, we stop."

Thank you. Much obliged. I needn't trouble them for their system, as I am not "three single gentlemen rolled into one," and so can't be a Syndicate.

They are going in to the Casino, and pass me on the steps. Now what shall I do? While I am meditating on my plan of campaign, Lord Arthur Stonebroke, passing me hurriedly, cries, "Halloa, old chap, going in to break the bank, eh?" I reply, as he halts for a second by the door, as carelessly as I can, as if I hadn't quite decided whether I should let the Bank have another day's grace or not,—"Well, I don't know." And then I pay him the compliment of asking "what *he* is going to do," as if to imply that my movements shall be decided by *his*.

"Oh," says he, in an off-hand manner, "I'm just going in for a flutter before dinner. Only taking in five hundred louis."

I nod to him pleasantly, and he passes in, and disappears. "Only five hundred louis to play with before dinner!" I am debating with myself whether I shall put on three five-franc pieces all at once, or extend the operation as they used to do the torture of the rack by doing it in three turns. Shall I stop at three five-franc pieces, or shall I go on to six? Let me see—five five-franc pieces are a sovereign, and therefore ten make two sovereigns. I wish *one* could make two sovereigns—and that one be myself.

First Decision.—I settle that it is better to have the ten five-franc pieces in my pocket, *in case* I want to play.

Second Decision.—The number of my coat is 200. I've often heard that a man backing the number of his coat, or multiple of it, or some division of it, makes a heap of money. *Happy Thought.* Try it. I ask Smithson, who has been an *habitué* for years, how he would divide 200 so as to make it into playable numbers. Smithson, with an air that inspires me with confidence, says offhand, "Put on the *six premiers*—that includes the two— on the middle dozen, so does that—on the *pair*, which includes the 20, and on zero, that's your game." And, nodding knowingly, to me, he walks away with the satisfied air of a man who has done the best he can for a friend, and who, throwing off the responsibility there and then, leaves the friend to do the best he can for himself. I note it down, and determine to act upon it. It is, one fiver—I mean one five-franc piece—that is, four-and-twopence, only it sounds more sporting to speak of them as "fivers"—one fiver on the first six numbers, another on the middle dozen, another on "even," and another on *zero.* Good. Stay—that makes four all at once, and I only intended to put on three. If I lose these, then on go four more—that's eight—and I shall only have two left.

I decide to change a third sovereign—just as well to have fifteen "fivers" (silver fivers) in my pocket as ten.

I enter the room. I walk up to the Changers' bureau, and get my fifteen French five-franc pieces in exchange for three beautiful golden English sovereigns. It doesn't seem fair, to begin with. I look upon them as counters, and three sovereigns seems a lot of money to pay for fifteen counters. I go to a *roulette*-table in first room. Crowd. No getting near it. I see Peterson with a pile of gold before him, looking very serious; behind him stand Hodgkins and Flickmore. Their eyes are on the table. They don't see me. Next moment the *croupier* cries out something that I don't catch, and the effect of it is that a lot of money is swept off one way, a lot another, and then Hodgkins and Flickmore seem to breathe again as Peterson has notes and gold pushed towards him with the *croupier's* rake. Somehow I don't like this table. I leave it. I don't even visit the one opposite, and enter the middle room. Here the table at the lower end has an attraction for me. Some one standing by one of the *croupiers* just moves out, and leaves a momentary vacancy, which fate seems to point out to me as the very place for me. It is almost opposite *pair,* which just suits my plan, the only difficulty being to get at the other end of the table, and deposit my five-franc piece on the middle dozen, and to get it back again, with the companion which it ought to win, from that distance in safety. At the tables I have often heard of old French women collaring what doesn't belong to them; and then indignantly protesting that the expostulating Englishman had tried to rob them.

This rather sets me against the middle dozen. Also somehow I

don't fancy zero. If I snub the middle dozen and zero, then I only
need risk two fivers each time, and this will give me more sport for
my money. And, after all, on the middle dozen you only get two
to one, and the odds against zero turning up are greater than
against anything else on the table. Besides, instead of losing four
each time I should only lose two. For all these excellent reasons
I decide to follow only half of my friend's advice, and I select the
six premiers and *pair*. When shall I begin? No time like the
present. Now: this next turn. I brace up my nerves, I give a
nod that the Duke of Wellington, at Waterloo, might have
copied, when he shut up his telescope with a snap and gave
the word to charge, and producing two five-franc pieces, I lean
over the man in front, and with a polite " Pardon, M'sieur," I take
his rake from him, and push my piece on to *pair*, nearly jobbing
him in the eye with the handle as I draw the instrument back
again. Elderly Frenchman looks up angrily. I feel hot and
awkward : I foresee a duel, and so give him a smiling apology to
turn away his wrath (which it doesn't), and then catching the
croupier's eye—not with the rake this time, but figuratively with
my eye—I ask him to shove my other five-franc piece on to *six
premiers*, which he does with a careless air, as if it didn't matter
twopence to him (and it doesn't) or to anybody (no more it does
except to myself and family), what becomes of this absurd stake.

Then I draw back, fold my arms, try to appear utterly indifferent,
look round the table to see if I can spot a friend to nod to, fail, and
then I keep my eye on my pieces, and stoically await the issue.
" *Rien ne va plus !* "—click !—it is over. *Vingt-cinq*—middle
dozen and uneven. Thank you—five-franc pieces, fare ye well !

Two more on the same. Same business of jobbing Frenchman's
eye with rake, catching *croupier's* eye, folding arms, awaiting
verdict—which . . . . *nineteen!*

Thank you. Exeunt second supply. Upon my word, I think
I'll try the whole lot at once. *Six premiers*—zero (hate zero)—
pair—and middle dozen. I do. Middleton comes up at the
minute. " Doing any good?" he asks. I shrug my shoulders.
As I turn round, the number is called—I don't see what it is—
but whatever it was, I find that it was neither zero, nor *pair*, nor
middle dozen, nor *six premiers*, and all my pretty chicks are gone

at one fell swoop. No, I'll limit myself to two. It's quite enough
to lose at a time. And those two shall be—stay . . . . shall I
change my plan—evidently I'm not in luck. Wish I hadn't asked
Smithson how to divide 200. Also wish I'd never heard that some
gamblers choose the number of the ticket given them for their
coat, and have immense luck with it. Stupid story : it's stories
like this that lead one so astray.

My last two. I object to zero. The first six have played
me false. The middle dozen can no longer be trusted. *Impair*
has once stood my friend. Suddenly the number 19, which has
nothing whatever to do with my calculations, seems to stand out
from the rest, and invite me. It absolutely seems to say, "Put
five francs on me, and one on the red." My whole plans are
deranged. Nineteen is staring at me. "You'll regret not planking
down on me," it says. "*Messieurs, faites le jeu !*" "*Faites !*" Fate
it is. Once more "pardon," and I job the irate Monsieur in the eye
with the end of the rake. On to the 19 plump, *en plein.* Already
I see the *croupier* preparing to pay me thirty-five times my stake.
Shall I put another, *the* other—and the last—on something? If so,
on what? The ball is whizzing round ! The second—shall I on
zero ? Smithson said *zero*—it was part of his original plan—as
I catch the *croupier's* eye—an inspiration. "*Six premiers, s'il vous
plaît* "—he pushes it on just where I would give any amount—
another five francs to recall it. The *croupier* opposite says,
inexorably, "*Rien ne va plus !*" and—click ! . . . zero ! ! Ha ! ha !
and I was within an ace of putting on zero. O Smithson ! When
I tell you that, after asking your advice, I've not acted on it, you
will think I've been making a fool of you—and of myself.

Shall I change another sovereign ? And try another table? I
will. I go to the magician, who warily examines and changes the
gold into silver behind the pigeon-hole of the bureau, and get my
five-franc pieces. Odd ! this time as I slip them into my pocket,
I feel as if I'd won them from the man behind the pigeon-hole, and
somehow, I experience the pleasant sensation of having somehow
or another got the best of him in a bargain. To which table shall
I go ? What plan shall I pursue ? With Smithson's I can only
play once with four francs, and if I lose, then once with one. At
this moment up comes Byngleigh.

CHAPTER IV.

NICE—THE BATTLE OF FLOWERS—RESTAURANT FRANÇOIS—
BEFORE THE BATTLE—AFTER—EVENING.

WHAT I did with Byngleigh, who came up after I had lost my little all, and had changed some more gold into five-franc pieces, I will recount on a future occasion. At present a day must intervene, a *fête* day, which removes me away from the tables, and takes me over to Nice.

Certainly, being at Monte Carlo, let us go to the second day of the " Battle of Flowers." This is March the 4th, and the Battle of Flowers does sound such a summery proceeding.

" Mrs. Grayling and her niece Mabel want to see it," says Mrs. Grayling's brother-in-law, the generous Taplin, who, when out for a holiday, likes to do the thing well ; " and so, if you'll come," this to me, " I'll take the lot of you. One more or less makes no difference."

Being delighted to hear that my presence will make no difference, I embrace the offer.

The carriage is at the door. There are two baskets of flowers and two bouquets. This looks like the First of May, old " Chimney-sweepers' Day." It may " look like " the First of May ; but with a cutting North wind, with just a touch of East in it, it *feels* like the time of year it is ; namely, the fourth day of March, at Monte Carlo and elsewhere. At all events there is no fog, as there probably is in London at this moment. The sky is clear, the Mediterranean is blue, the sun is bright, the view is lovely ; the wind is cutting. We take rugs, wraps, and overcoats, but out of compliment to the appearance of the place, with its hedges of geraniums, its red roses on the walls, the spreading palm-trees, the cactuses, the olive-trees, and the prickly pears, " all a-growing" and looking tropical—(how they do it is a wonder to me. I am

x

inclined to think they're most of them sham, the deception being connived at by the authorities, and kept up by the hotel-keepers and the Casino officials at an enormous cost)—so, as I say, out of compliment to the tropical "scenery and properties," we decide on *not* having foot-warmers in the carriage.

Taplin, huddled up in rugs, with only the upper part of his head under a pot-hat, appearing above (so to speak) the bed-clothes, exclaims, from time to time, "There's a beautiful view!"—nodding at it, for he won't take his hands out from under the coverings,— "Lovely, isn't it?" to which we all assent, the pair on the back seat not turning their heads to look at it, for fear of getting a stiff neck and being "struck so;" and then Taplin, wriggling down lower than ever under his counterpane and blankets, murmurs, with conviction, "But, *I say*, it *is* cold!" And so say all of us, and all snuggle down under the rugs. For all this, we are going to the celebrated Battle of Flowers at Nice.

Nice.—We pull up at the *Restaurant Français.* Descend. Nice is *en fête.* Flower-baskets everywhere. Fans for sale. Ragged urchins with baskets of flowers. Everybody moving about. Fortunately we find one table unoccupied. We swoop down on it, and occupy it bodily. We are here for the Battle of Flowers; so *à la guerre comme à la guerre.*

Restaurant doing enormous business. Crowd too big for the small room. Prices up probably in consequence. It will be "breakfast at the fork out." Head-waiter imposing personage, but with his wits about him. Good breakfast and good wine. We begin to feel warm and comfortable.

"Amusing scene," says Mrs. Grayling, patronisingly. Miss Mabel is delighted with everything. Taplin says, "I don't see anything very Carnivalish about the place." Miss Mabel exclaims, 'Oh, don't you think so!" She is evidently afraid that if Uncle Taplin begins to be disappointed with it, he may suddenly decide to return without seeing any more. So she continues, "Why, Uncle, look at all the people! And then, you remember, we saw that figure of King Carnival sitting in a ship as we drove in!" "Ah, yes, so we did," replied Uncle Taplin, brightening up. Whereat we all brighten up too, and Uncle Taplin insists on our having some old Burgundy, whereupon we brighten up still more,

and become warm and genial. We expand like the flowers, and
by two o'clock, when we get into the carriage again,—this time
with the rugs concealed, and only the flowers displayed,—we are
all in full bloom. The North wind has blown itself out,—at its
own luncheon, perhaps,—at all events, we don't feel it so much in
the town, and the sun is shining.

Everybody is now *en fête.* Shops are closed, all business suspended for the rest of the afternoon. It is the Flower Derby Day.
All sorts of Tom-fools among the populace in false noses, dominoes,

Going to the Battle of Flowers at Nice.

as Pierrots, and in a variety of shabby fancy costumes, the odds
and ends of costumiers' old clothes. A carriage comes along, being
one mass of flowers, wheels and all. It is Jack-in-the-Green on
wheels. These faded costumes, and ruddled cheeks, these clowns,
and harlequins, and columbines, do certainly recall my boyish
recollections of Chimney Sweeper's Festival in London, with My
Lord and My Lady, Pantaloon, the Swell, and Clown, with the
ladle collecting the coppers.

It is a great day for the *Niçois* 'Arry and 'Arriet. It is a great
day for every one who has anything in the way of a fan or a bouquet
to sell. Any price. How much for that fan ? "Fifteen francs."
Bah ! "Then how much will Monsieur give ?" Monsieur will
give a third of the price. "Oh, impossible." Monsieur passes on,
and purchases two fans (with which the ladies are to protect their

faces), for one franc each. "Let's have two good bouquets," says Uncle Taplin, becoming enthusiastic; and the ladies exclaim, "Oh yes, do! Let's!" So Uncle Tap purchases two bouquets, and our coachman, being an ingenious creature, and a bit of an artist in colour,—having already decorated his horses' heads with small nosegays, now takes the carriage-lamps out of their sockets, deposits them in a shop (I hope with a trusty friend), and in half a minute, the two bouquets have replaced the lamps, and give quite a gay and festive appearance to our equipage.

Basket after basket of flowers is offered to us. Ten francs, nine francs, any francs, down to one franc, according to size. Here's a good basket-full. How much Madame? Madame replies readily, hazarding a likely price, "Monsieur shall have it for nine francs." Monsieur, who is hard at a bargain this morning, won't hear of it. What, then, will Monsieur give? Monsieur will give five francs. "*Tenez!*" she exclaims, shoving it into my hands, "*prenez-le, prenez-le!*" She won't wait—the bargain is concluded—she is afraid I shall change my mind. I take the basket, and, my hands being full, I ask Uncle Tap for the money. "*Et encore un franc pour le corbeille!*" shrieks the lady, who is a type of a *Niçoise* as an outside-Covent-Garden market-woman.

"Hey, what's that?" asks Uncle Taplin, suspiciously, under the impression that something has gone wrong with the bargain.

"One franc more for the basket," I say, carrying it off to the ladies.

"All right!" says Uncle Tap, much relieved, and pays up.

Boys surrounding us, begging to be taken as *ramasseurs.* Fortunately someone has told me beforehand that a *ramasseur*, at two francs for the afternoon, is necessary as a sort of running footman, to pick up the nosegays, and return them to the carriage. I select a sickly-looking chap, who really does seem in want of a job. Five francs he wants. No. Three. Very good, he'll undertake it for three,—and will Monsieur pay before-hand? No, Monsieur won't. This engagement being made, our successful *ramasseur* shows that he is not quite the sickly creature he appears, by kicking and cuffing all the smaller and unsuccessful candidates for our *ramasseurship*, and then he mounts by the side of the coachman, and we are off to the *Promenade des Anglais.*

At the entrance we are stopped, and a louis is demanded.

"Halloa!" says Uncle Taplin, induced to resent the demand as an imposition on confiding foreigners, "What's this for?" I remember the Derby Day, and remind him that even in free England we have to pay a guinea to take our place among the coaches on the hill. "Ah, so we do!" says Uncle Taplin, and seeing the matter in a different light, and rather pleased that this price of admission should be an imitation of an English custom, he pays it with cheerful alacrity, and the coachman receives a yellow ticket, while for one franc more, our consumptive *ramasseur* has purchased a Carnival fool's cap, which is the badge of his connection with our carriage, and so we enter the rank as combatants in the Battle of Flowers.

The Drive is not crowded at first. It is railed in on both sides. There are mounted *gendarmes* keeping the course, and occasionally, when tired of standing still, taking short sharp gallops from one point to another, on the evident pretence of giving each other orders, or delivering official messages. There are important personages, stewards of the course, on foot, wearing red rosettes, who are very ill-tempered, cross, and fussy. By the *Hôtel de la Méditerranée* the crowd is really dense,—but never at any one point, or at any part all along the course, does it ever exceed the crowd to be seen in Hyde Park by the Serpentine on a fine day at the first meet of the Four-in-hand, or Coaching, Club. Here are the Tomfools and clowns, and other professional gentry going about just as the acrobats, and the conjuror, and the strong man, and so forth, do on the Derby Day. There are very few good turn-outs, and the presence of *voitures*, hired traps, and vans, are rather suggestive (to the Englisher of Cockney experience) of a "day out" with the Foresters, 'Appy 'Ampton, or Odd Fellows. There is a band playing somewhere which is to be heard occasionally.

"When is the battle going to begin?" asks Mrs. Grayling, who is a trifle nervous.

"O Aunt!" exclaims Mabel, "look—they're throwing already." And scarcely are the words out of her mouth than three small nosegays fall lightly into our carriage, and a fourth drops outside, which is immediately picked up and given to us by our *ramasseur*, who from this moment has his work cut out for him. A gaily-dressed lady drives by, and throws a bouquet at Uncle Taplin.

" Ha ! " he exclaims, his eyes sparkling with delight at the compliment thus paid him by the fair stranger, and he discharges one at her, which misses.   Mrs. Grayling receives nice little nosegays on her bonnet or her face, and returns them with a graceful sort of movement, as if she were curtseying on her seat.   Miss Mabel becomes energetic, and goes in for rapid pelting, keeping the consumptive *ramasseur* hard at work.

" Really," says Uncle Taplin, chuckling, " this is capital fun." Here comes at him, a small bunch of violets, which he returns so quickly that it gently hits his assailant—a very pretty woman—

Before the Battle.

on the corner of her ear.   " Aha ! " laughs Uncle Tap—" and all done with such good humour !   Oh ! " he cries, suddenly, " who the deuce did *that ?*" as a heavy-handled bouquet bound with wire, gives him a stinger on the cheek.   I can't help laughing.   " That was a nasty one," I say, and, seeing a big man, in a white hat, pass, I hurl the heavy bouquet at him.   Bang goes his hat, and there is a shout of laughter.   It is too late to retaliate,—he has been driven off one way, our carriage another.

" Capital ! " I exclaim.   I'm really getting quite warm with the exertion of throwing.   I select prominent personages, on coach boxes, or sitting up at the backs of the carriages.

" Now look here," I say to Uncle Tap, " see me catch that chap on—Ha ! conf——." A heavy blow, as if from a tennis-ball, catches me behind the ear, another whack in my eye, and a third bang on the cheek—"*en plein*"—as we say at *roulette*. Shouts of laughter from the bystanders. My cheek is smarting painfully, and my eye is watering. This is horse-play. This is not good-humoured. That blow on my ear—my, how it tingles! was vicious, distinctly vicious. I prepare a heavy, well-wired bouquet. If I could only catch the confounded fellow who——Ah! bang on my hat. I turn sharply, and discharge, savagely, my life-preserver bouquet,—"as an olive-branch out of a catapult,"—whack, on to the nearest Tom-fool's head. He flinches and goes down to avoid, whereupon, my life-preserver bouquet catches an entirely

After the Battle.

innocent person, standing just behind him. A laugh—and a whack at me—right on the tip of my nose—which feels smashed in. Nosegay indeed! I feel my nose is anything but a nose-gay now. Shouts of laughter, in which Uncle Taplin joins. This reminds me suddenly, that I must keep my temper, or at all events, keep up appearances of being in the best possible humour; otherwise, if the crowd becomes nasty, vegetables might follow. So I take my punishment smiling.

Mrs. Grayling and Mabel have recognised lots of friends, and have been pelting and pelted right and left. Once Mabel gets rather a nasty one, and retaliates with all her might and main. Mrs. Grayling has her hat knocked on one side, which gives her a momentarily dissipated appearance; but she only smiles, and tosses back upon her fierce assailant a pretty little bouquet, making her usual half-curtsey on the seat, and then puts her hat to-rights.

Happy Thought.—As our baskets of ammunition may be soon exhausted, let us attract the fire of others upon ourselves by feigning to be preparing to throw. This succeeds admirably, and in a few minutes our baskets are choke-full again.

Some one cries out, "There's the Prince of Wales!" and in the distance we hear the band playing our National Anthem, but I am unable to catch sight of His Royal Highness, as, just when I am raising my hat to receive him, I salute a heavy bouquet full in the face,—" *en plein* " again,—and can't distinguish even the most distinguished persons for the next couple of minutes.

Having driven up and down the promenade three times, and having, all of us, received " nasty ones," more or less, in the eyes, nose, mouth, and ears, isn't the amusement becoming a trifle monotonous? Isn't the fun a little forced? Isn't it rather devoid of " life " and " go "? " Is there anything else to do or to see?" I ask the driver when we get into a quiet part of the promenade where there is only a single line of carriages. The coachman shrugs his shoulders; no, this is all. " *Tout ce qu'il y a à faire, ou à voir.*" When does it finish? Well, about 4·30, the coachman says, naming an early hour, as he probably is becoming tired of it, and wants to get home to tea.

"It's not well arranged," says Uncle Taplin, with his hat smashed in, and one side of his face as red as a rose from a recent violent blow.

"No," I reply, feeling very hot and very angry, because with a swollen cheek, a burning ear, and a partially discoloured eye, I have not been able to be revenged on "The Man who struck O'Hara"—(Oh, if I had only been near him with a thick stick! I'd have shown him what a Battle of Flowers ought to be, and be blowed to him for a coward!) "Let's turn back and cut it," I suggest. Yes—the ladies have had enough of it. We are not vanquished. We do not retreat. No; we simply don't want to play any more—and—ha!—a drop of rain! Rain it is! and rain it will be, when it once begins. So hurry back, Coachman. Out with the bouquets, in again with the lamps, lighted this time, for the gloom is coming on, all the forces are routed, and in full retreat we drive along the road to Monte Carlo, arriving in time to vaseline our wounds, and prepare for dinner.

It has been a glorious fight, this Battle of Flowers. Not quite so lively as we expected, and yet a little too lively occasionally. We all agree that it is a pretty sight. But Uncle Taplin and myself are of opinion that it is badly managed, and the horse-play spoils it.

In excellent form for dinner. The very evening for a glass of real good champagne. Now in France, as a rule, this is just what you can't get, pay what you will for it. But, to the eternal praise of Signor Zucchi (of our Hotel) be it recorded, that he is able to produce for our benefit Pommery and Greno '80, and very soon we are all unanimous in our expression of opinion that the Battle of Flowers at Nice is well worth seeing, that we wouldn't have missed it for anything, that all the pelting was most good-tempered, and that if there were, now and then, a little horse-play, it must be expected from a crowd ; and—after all—didn't we join in it as heartily (and as fiercely) as any one ? Certainly. Another bottle of Pommery, '80 or '84, and here's the health of the Battle of Flowers at Nice.

"Sauve qui peut!"

CHAPTER V.

STILL AT MONTE CARLO—AFTER THE BATTLE OF FLOWERS—RETURN TO
THE CASINO.

BYNGLEIGH comes up to me at the table. He is a small man with a sharp shrewd manner, and a glittering eye,—strictly speaking, two glittering eyes. He is building a villa at Monte Carlo—that is, he is building it with the assistance of an architect and gangs of workmen, and from being accustomed to deal, in his London house of business, with a large number of *employés*, to whom his every word is law, and with chiefs of various departments who do not attempt even to discuss his suggestions, he has acquired the habit of excogitating complicated problems of trade in half a second, seeing all the pros and cons of a scheme at a glance like a First Napoleon, and of giving his orders with the same promptitude and decision that characterised the commands of the Iron Duke. His word, nay, even his opinion, is as the very concentrated essence of the spirits of the law of the Medes and Persians. He stands behind me and closely follows the progress of the game.

"Well," he says in his crisp chirrupy manner, with his head a little on one side, addressing me, while he never takes his eyes off the board, "Well, what are you doing?" Now at this minute I am hesitating whether I shall put on the *six premiers* or the sixteen *en plein.* "No good going on numbers," remarks Byngleigh, curtly ; "you won't do anything at that. Go on red." But I point out to him that on red you can win only the amount you stake.

"Well," he returns, "if you do that often enough, you'll make a good lot."

"No," I reply, with dogged determination, "I've made up my mind to go on the first six."

"I shouldn't," he says, decisively. But I do. "*Messieurs, faites le jeu! . . . Rien ne va plus!*" and I've lost.

"Told you so," says Byngleigh, with a dry laugh, and shrugging his shoulders as much as to say, "if you will insist on running contrary to my advice, you know what to expect."

I quote to him the authority of Smithson, an old hand. Smithson, I remind him, advised me to put on the first six, the last dozen, and zero. "Oh, Smithson doesn't know everything," retorts Byngleigh.

This I admit is true ; but still, having trusted to Smithson, and Smithson having been right,—and if I had only stuck to what he told me, I should have been by now a richer and a gayer man,—I am a little hurt to hear Smithson's advice so contemptuously treated by Byngleigh. I can't help telling him that Smithson has played here for years over and over again, and that——

Here Byngleigh cuts me short by saying authoritatively,

"It's no use dodging about the table. You put on the red,—that's the best game."

No, I beg his pardon, I will put on the 16 to 21 "*transversal,*" and also back the middle dozen.

It turns up "three, red," which is neither in my transversal nor in the middle dozen, and I lose on both. If I had stuck to my "*six premiers*" I should have won five times my stake, and only lost the middle dozen one.

"But it was red," says Byngleigh, persistently.

Yes, it was ; but I shall stick to the numbers. I like transversal. I like the *quatre premiers*, which includes zero, for which you get, as I explain to him, eight times your stake, and this time I shall go on the four first and the middle dozen.

"*I* wouldn't," says Byngleigh, shortly. "*I* should go on the red."

I put my five-franc piece on the middle dozen, then, by an inspiration, on "*impair,*" and finally I am just saying to the croupier, in my sweetest and politest manner,—nay, the words are actually on the tip of my tongue—"*Les quatre premiers, s'il vous plait,*" when Byngleigh jogs my elbow and draws my attention to a large amount which somebody is putting on the red, and, by an otherwise utterly unaccountable *lapsus linguæ,* I suddenly say

"*Six premiers*" instead of "*quatre*," and before I can correct the mistake, the magic words, "*Rien ne va plus!*" are uttered, click goes the ball, and "Zero" turns up! Zero counts for *quatre premiers*, but not for *six premiers*, and I've lost again.

"Red's put in prison!" says Byngleigh. I mentally wish that he was sharing red's fate, that is while I am playing. "It'll win you'll see."

It has been red so often, that I feel confident it can't come off this time. I tell Byngleigh it was his fault that I didn't win just now, because he jogged my elbow, and distracted me just at the critical moment.

"Oh nonsense," he replies, with an irritating chuckle. "You go on the red."

No, I don't care about colour. I feel an inspiration to try the middle dozen, and *impair*. It is 16 (red) which is in the first dozen. Lost again !

"You would do it," says Byngleigh, shrugging his shoulders with an air of supreme disgust at my inconceivable obstinacy. "It's no use your going on numbers. Stick to a colour."

"Which ?" I ask, in despair.

"Ah," he replies, with another shrug, and a short cynical laugh —I hate a short cynical laugh— "I haven't been watching, but I should say black for choice."

Savagely I throw down one piece on black, and another I place *en transversal* 16 to 21, and, just as I am doing it, I feel a strong impulse to put it on 13—18. By a sudden impulse, and begging somebody's pardon for rubbing his ear the wrong way as I lean energetically over towards the *croupier* at the end of the table, I place a piece on the last dozen. "*Messieurs ! faites le jeu ! . . . Rien ne va plus !*"—it will soon be *rien ne va plus* with me—and— click !—up comes 14 red. Lost on all !

"Ah," says Byngleigh, smiling sardonically, "you oughtn't to have gone on the black."

"But you said black," I retort, annoyed at his perversity.

"Oh," he replies, with the same irritating cut-and-dried laugh, and the usual shrug, "you mustn't go by me."

"Look here," I say to him, in a manner which is described in the "business" of an operatic *libretto* as "with concentrated emotion,"—"look here, you bring me bad luck. I wish to goodness you'd go away." I feel that this is childish superstition. But, if you begin gambling, you'll find yourself giving in to all sorts of superstitions,—and you can't help it.

Byngleigh shrugs his shoulders again, and saunters off. I remain, and go on losing. Then I stop playing, just to see if I should have had any luck. I say to myself, "This time I should have put a five-franc piece on 13 and black." I stand calmly watching the table. No one puts on 13. "*Messieurs,*" &c. Somebody suddenly stretches out his hand and puts a pile of gold coins on 13. "*Rien ne va plus!*" 13 by Jove!!! Now, that's worse luck than anything else. I turn away. "*Rien ne va plus!*" I retire into a corner and reckon. Bang has gone one hundred and seventy-five francs. "*Rien ne va plus!*"

"Messieurs, faites le jeu!"

It is just on eleven, and I stop at the last table. Byngleigh is here. He shows me five pieces he has just won. "I went only on red," he says, smiling triumphantly. His manner implies that I am an idiot for not having done the same as he has. "Now," he cries, "look here!" and he chuckles in anticipation of good luck, as he puts his money on red and even. It turns up black and uneven. Bang have gone two out of his five. "The black's turn now," he says, and reaching out his hand deposits his three pieces on black. In a second it is raked up and disappears with all the other stakes, the *croupiers* descend from their perches, the servants are covering up the table, the players are dispersing, and Byngleigh is left grabbing at the cloth, and exclaiming,

"Here! Hi! I hadn't any go for my money!"

But no one attends to him, the rules are inexorable, and Byngleigh has lost all his hard-earned gains, and a trifle more into the bargain.

"My dear fellow," I say, not so much to console him as to

rebuke him for having previously lectured me on my method of playing, and for his irritating style to me in the hour of my adversity, "there is no rule in this sort of thing. It is all luck."

"Yes," he mutters, bitterly, "and bad luck too."

"Let's go to 'Zero's,'" suggests Johnnie Spofferd, coming up in a great-coat and muffler, for it is uncommonly cold. We visit "Ciro's"—popularly known as "Zero's," which is a small American-English drinking-bar, where very soon some fifty persons crowd into a small space calculated to accommodate, with careful adjustment, about thirty-five. And here we are, on a balmy moonlight night, balmy but freshish, within a stone's-throw of the blue Mediterranean (which we can't see) in the land of the Sunny South, sitting in a small bar, drinking Scotch whiskey-and-water hot, gin-sling, "John Collins," stout-and-bitter, all of which beverages are, as is well known, peculiarly characteristic of the Sunny South of Europe.

CHAPTER VI.

LAST FEW DAYS AT MONTE CARLO—FINANCE.

Going "A cheval."

THE winning of one five-franc piece brightens existence. The loss of sixty sours it. Such is life at Monte Carlo.

Once more Attempt.—At first table on the left. "Good business," says Tom Whiffler, showing me a handful of notes, "just played three *coups.* Two thousand francs. Not bad, in five minutes, eh?"

"What did you go on!" I inquire earnestly.

"I went on the dozens. First dozen, then middle dozen. Middle dozen," he adds, "was first-rate," which sounds as if he were talking of oysters. And off he goes, the lucky chap, nodding airily to me, and "chortling in his joy."

Think I'll try the "middle dozen." Difficult to find a place, so crowded. I notice several people here, whom I had always understood were "anything but well-off," playing with piles of notes and heaps of gold. How do they do it?

"Oh," Johnnie Spofferd explains, "they're playing with the Bank's money." Yes, but how did they get the Bank's money? *I* can't. On the contrary, the Bank gets mine.

Squeezing myself in close to a *croupier,* I present him with two five-franc pieces, and request him in the sweetest possible tone,— all novices address the *croupiers* in the sweetest tone, possibly with the idea of ingratiating themselves with them, and so squaring it somehow, as if being on speaking terms with a *croupier* could assist you to win,—to put one on the "*six derniers,*" and the other on "*douze premiers.*" Fifteen turns up, and I've lost. Then I try 19 *en plein,* and the first six, and again I lose, whereupon I change to a *transversal,* which includes 19 (I've a fancy for 19), and *impair. Trente-trois* turns up. Out of it again. Whereupon I give up my fancy for 19 and leave it. Immediately up it comes! and this happens also with *trente-trois.*

Lost sixty francs. Time to go and dress for dinner. Chilly air. They cover up all the flowers and shrubs at 4 P.M. So the beauty of the place is artificially kept up. North-east wind. Queer sort of sunset. Seen sunsets twice as good as this in England, when I *hadn't* lost sixty francs. Meet Dordly Tapp going to his hotel, "The Paris," to dinner. How has he done to-day? Any good? No, Dordly has lost.

"Beastly place," he says, " and so cold too, eh?"

I remark that there is an odd sort of sunset.

"Ah!" replies Dordly, "that *is* a queer sunset. Rum colour I remember a sunset exactly like that the night before the earth-quake. I shouldn't be in the least surprised if there wasn't a *tremblement de terre* to-night. There's one comfort, this place felt it less last time than any other on the Riviera. Still it's not pleasant. If I'd won, I should be off to-night, but I must have another turn at the tables. Ugh! Horribly cold!" and he shivers—he has a *tremblement* all over him—and hurries off.

One more Attempt at the Tables, after Dinner.—Luck turns. I say to Mrs. Wetherby (who has had wonderful luck and made £1500), "Shall I put *en plein* on 32?" She replies quickly, "Yes!" It turns up. 32! by all that's lucky!

" I told you I should bring you luck," she says, as I receive thirty-five times my stake, which was only five francs—(ah, why didn't she tell me to put on eight louis?)—and so pocket one hundred and seventy-five francs, that's seven pounds, in a second, merely for risking four shillings and twopence. This is exhila-rating. This is the air of Monaco. I ask Mrs. Wetherby, as she is so lucky, to stand by me, and give me some more tips.

"Ah!" she replies, smiling, "I'm afraid my luck has gone. I don't feel as if I could advise you correctly again."

"Shall I leave it on?" I ask, alluding to my five-franc piece, which is still lying on the 32.

"I think I should," she answers. "You may as well leave it on." But though her tone no longer inspires me with confidence, yet I leave it on; but, *rein ne va plus,* and the *croupier* takes it

off. I'll take myself off. I'll be satisfied with this for to-night.
Let us regale ourselves. Really nothing is so easy as winning.
I meet friends. I tell them seriously, as if it were a feat of
dexterity or a well-calculated stroke of business, requiring great
acumen and shrewd, sharp clear-headedness, how, without any
system, I put *en plein* on 32, and it turned up.

"Had you got the maximum on?" asks Dordly Tapp, who has
had a fair evening of it.

"No," I reply, carelessly; "no, I hadn't got the maximum on.
Only a small stake." I don't tell
him it was merely a five-franc piece.
Probably my one bit of luck will be
magnified into thousands, as any one,
who subsequently tells the story,
may credit me with having put on
any stake that suits his fancy.

Eight louis in my purse, and a
lot of five-franc cart-wheels in my
pocket. We regale. Dordly has
won, he says, a hundred. Johnnie
Stofferd at once decides that Dordly
shall stand treat.

"How about the earthquake?"
I ask Dordly.

He has forgotten all about it.
"Earthquakes?" he asks, "What

Cooks Tourists.

earthquakes?" I remind him of the melancholy forecast he made
only a few hours since. "Oh!" he exclaims, there's not a chance
of one. I thought over it again, and now I remember it was quite
a different sunset when we had the last earthquake. Besides,
with such a lovely night! What stars! what a moon!"

We agree—Johnnie Stofferd, too, who has won a trifle—that Monte
Carlo is a beautiful place, and that the nights are magnificent.

"I like this place," says Johnnie Stofferd—"it's so foreign.
One couldn't do this sort of thing in London." It is half-past
midnight, and Johnnie, wearing a soft felt hat, cocked very much
on one side, is perched on a high stool in front of the bar,—not at
Zero's," but "*chez* Peters." He has just finished a plate of devilled

Y

oysters, and is now drinking stout, and enjoying a pipe. No, certainly, *we*—when we come abroad—manage these things better in France, in the Sunny South. But why travel all the way to Monte Carlo, in order to sit on a high stool in a public-house, to eat devilled oysters, to drink stout, and to smoke a pipe? We discuss this walking back to the hotel (1 A.M.), and Johnnie Stofferd's opinion, freely expressed, is that "he's blowed if he don't think that the nights at Monte Carlo are about the best part of the amusement."

I find out that whenever Dordly Tapp has had a bad time at the tables, he becomes an alarmist. I meet him next day with the longest face possible. What's the matter?

"Matter, my dear fellow? Haven't you heard?"

"No, I haven't. What is it?"

"My dear fellow, there's measles and scarlet fever all over the place. We're going to pack up and be off at once."

"Really? It's very sudden. How did you hear all about it?"

"Oh, everyone's talking of it. Two or three persons died yesterday. And the place has no drainage. It's really too bad. I shall be off. Good-bye."

I confess I can hardly believe it, but I can't help repeating to several people what Dordly Tapp has told me. No; they've not heard anything about it, but nothing is more likely. Johnnie Stofferd remembers to have heard a whisper about it before he arrived. Uncle Tamplin can't recall where he also has heard some rumour of the sort. And so within an hour or so there will be a scare sufficient to clear Monte Carlo.

"Well," I inform Uncle Tamplin, "Dordly Tapp and his wife have packed up and are going off." And this I subsequently hear him repeating to his sister and niece, who at once commence the study of *Bradshaw*, with a view to as speedy a return as possible.

Next afternoon, going down to the Casino, I meet Mr. and Mrs. Dordly Tapp. He and his wife are beaming with joy. "Halloa, not gone!"

"Gone!" he cries, "No; why should I go? Bless you, I've just been and won two thousand louis. Shall stay here any length of time."

"Well," I say, "but the measles or scarlet fever——"

"Oh, yes," he returns, in an off hand manner, "I did hear something about it, but my wife inquired and found it wasn't true." Mrs. Dordly confirms this statement with an emphatic nod. "Oh," continues Dordly, "it's all right. Monte Carlo's the healthiest place in the world."

"But you said yesterday that there was no drainage?"

"Did I! Ah, yes, so I did."

"But I asked two Doctors," interposes Mrs. Dordly, coming to her husband's relief, "and they both say that where there are smells there is no danger, and there are lots of smells here; so it's all right. They explained about the gases, but I don't understand it. And," she goes on, "wasn't I lucky, while Dordly was winning his two thousand, I made a hundred louis, all out of a poor little five-franc piece to start with! I *do* like Monte Carlo! *Au revoir!*"

"En plein."

"Ta! Ta! *au plaisir!*" says Dordly, jauntily, as they go into the Grand, where they have a dinner-party.

I return to Uncle Tamplin and explain. The ladies call on Mrs. Dordly Tapp, and hear from her the Doctors' account of the salubrity of Monte Carlo, and in another hour or two the scare will be heard of no more—that is, not until some one has lost heavily, and is in a general way disgusted with everything and everybody.

CHAPTER VII.

LAST NOTES AT MONTE CARLO—ON TO ROME.

EVERYONE has a System which is almost infallible. I note down a few "Systems" for the economical and timorous Monte-Carlist:—

First System—The Imaginative Player.—To all those whom Providence has not blessed with opulence, and who wish to play at Monte Carlo, I recommend the following system:—Go to every table in turn. Think of a number. Imagine you've got a five-franc piece on it. Watch it. If it turns up, you have the satis-faction of knowing that your judgment was correct. If it doesn't turn up, you can congratulate yourself on not having been such a fool as to put on that particular number. This can be repeated as long as you like, varying from colour to number, and *vice versâ*, and visiting every table in the room. You'll have most of the fun, and none of the risk. When friends and acquaintances meet you and ask " how you're doing ?" you can say, " You're about as you were," or any other formula.

Second System.—If you like to hear the jingle of the five-franc pieces, when you've won them, in your pocket—and it *is* fascinat-ing, I admit—go to the *bureau*, change a sovereign into five " cart-wheels," and walk about jingling them. Visit the tables, act on the Imaginative Player's plan (*First System*), and when your opinion is correct rattle your five-franc pieces forcibly, and smile as if you'd won a big *coup*. When your opinion is wrong,—don't rattle them, but purse up your lips, frown desperately and shake your head. When the question is put to you, " Doing any good, eh ?" you can jingle your coins, replying, " I've got a few left," and pass on.

Third System. How to reduce the Loss to a Minimum.—Put one five-franc piece on *pair* and another on *impair*. Then your only chance of losing is when *zero* turns up. But, when this happens, as your pieces are imprisoned for a second turn, depending upon which colour comes up, you can then only lose one piece and must gain on the other. This system includes a certain amount of ex-citement, and leaves you quits at the end of the evening. Even with the safest of safe Systems it is possible for you to lose both pieces ; that is, if dishonest persons are sitting near you, bold enough to declare that your five-franc pieces belong to them, and to pocket them accordingly.

Last System. How not to Lose at all !—Don't play. This is too evident to need explanation

When you have resolved not to go into the Casino, the next best thing is to stay outside, and watch the people going in at any time during the day, and coming out at eleven at night. The life and soul of Monte Carlo is the Casino. The whole of Monte

Carlo is really the Casino. All its word is *trente et quarante* and *roulette*, and, as Shakspeare says, who was of course writing of Monte Carlo,

"All the men and women merely players."

They go in like lions, they come out like lambs; in many cases, like shorn lambs.

It is midday or any time you please in the afternoon. Look at the gamblers entering. They arrive by train, or by carriage, or in a *fiacre*, or on foot, and up they go, like men of business bustling towards "the House" in Capel Court, or with that air of preoccupation which marks a new Member of Parliament who has come determined to catch the Speaker's eye, ascending the steps at Westminster. A few among them saunter in, assuming listless-ness, and a very few smartly-dressed men and women chatter and laugh as they pause on the top step to finish their conversation, evidently wishing to draw the line sharply between pleasure and business. See them leaving between half-past ten and eleven, when the Casino shuts for the night, not separately, but in groups. Some chatting, very few laughing, but all most decorously, as if they were coming out of Church after a sermon, and their good name depended on keeping up appearances.

After a time, whether winning or losing, life even at Monte Carlo becomes monotonous, and, taking for granted that you have ex-hausted all the usual excursions, your amusements are limited to the following programme :—

1. The reading-room, where a couple of hours may be fully occupied by waiting for the paper you particularly want to see. Here also you can write letters.

2. Watching the pigeon-shooting from the terrace. This is gratis.

3. The Concert (admission free), every afternoon.

4. Watch the people entering and leaving the gambling-rooms.

5. Walking up and down the *atrium*, talking to friends and acquaintances, and, once a day, trying to feign some curiosity as to the contents of the latest telegram posted up in the hall.

6. See trains arrive; see them depart.

7. To walk down several times a day from your hotel to the Casino with a view to consulting the clock over the portico, and

then, comparing its information with the two Railway clocks, and then with that given by your Hotel clock : finally to regulate your own watch by striking a fair balance.

8. Walk up to Monaco Gardens (lovely !) and back. Wonder at the variety of smells. Try to arrive at a satisfactory solution as to their cause, whether drainage, or harbour, or gas-works, or a combination of any two or of all three.

Private Opinion of Monte Carlo in the Season.—For the robust,—lovely, delightful. But beware the Mistral, the Wandering Mistral. For the invalid,—lovely, seductive, treacherous !

Uncle Taplin's niece, Mabel, has been attacked by the Wandering Mistral. She is temporarily disabled. Uncle Tap decides not to go to Rome. Offers me his ticket there and back. I accept. Can I refuse ? if only to see St. Peter's ? My holiday is finishing.

"You will zee," says our worthy Italian Hotel-keeper, "ze carnival. Do not go for ze *confetti*—no—for zey jomp you in ze eye. He 'urt." I promise him that having had quite enough of "jumping in the eye" at the Battle of Flowers, I shall not go in for *confetti*-throwing at Rome. I complain to him that last night it was actually snowing. He reluctantly admits the incontrovertible fact ; "but," he goes on in his own peculiar English, for which he has a patent, "ze snow," here a contemptuous shrug, "he was nozing,—he did not lay on the floor." Beautiful expression this. But, whether the snow "lies on the floor" or not, off I go. To Rome ! O Riviera !

CHAPTER VIII.

FROM MONTE CARLO TO ROME, VIÂ VINTIMILLE, GENOA,
AND PISA.

FIRST nuisance. — change of time, from French to Roman time. Second nuisance,—examination of baggage at the frontier, which I am bound to say, Italian officials make as easy as possible. It may be exceptional; I hope not. We are not in a particularly good humour.—I forgot to mention that Johnnie Spofferd is my travelling companion, in consequence of the tables having turned against him, which makes him fancy that a little change will do him good,—and therefore, any railway rudeness would jar upon us.

The eighteen-hour journey is pleasant enough; and then we both exclaim, "Now we are approaching Rome!! The City of the Cæsars and the Popes!!" We approach it very slowly, through a dreary, low, marshy country.

"Is that the Tiber?" I ask, on catching sight of a muddy stream.

"S'pose so," replies Johnnie. "Beastly dirty, isn't it? Worse than the Thames. P'raps," says Johnnie, after a pause, "P'raps it's the Rubicon. Where was the Rubicon?"

I can't exactly say. "Cæsar crossed it," I observe.

"Oh, I know that!" replies Johnnie, pettishly. He is not in a good humour.

Nothing of Rome can I see from the windows. It is raining heavily, and all is fog and vapour in the distance. Some peasants are out under big umbrellas.

"But," says Johnnie, grumbling, "not a single Roman nose among them. As far as I've seen, those that ain't turned up or Grecian, are as flat as the surrounding country. Bah!" he says, with an air of the deepest disgust, throwing himself back in his seat, "I believe the whole thing's a swindle. P'raps there's no such place as Rome after all."

The other day in the *Times* I saw advertised a book entitled *Some Features of Modern Romanism.* I can confidently assert that Roman noses won't be prominent among these "features." Not a Roman nose at the station, among the Roman legions of guards and porters.

The Roman Noses we expected to see.

Pouring with rain. "City of the Popes and Cæsars be blowed!" growls Johnnie, as we sit in the small omnibus that is to take us to the hotel. Everything about us looks as muddy, damp, murky, and miserable as if we were waiting for our luggage on a thorough wet day outside Fenchurch Street Station, instead of being in the metropolis of Christendom, Rome.

We arrive at the Albergo Bristolini, Piazza Bristolini, which looks clean and comfortable enough, even on such a day as this. It is, I have been informed, the best-drained Hotel in Rome. Our room, a double one, for the hotel is full, is large and, we hope, comfortable. There is no prospect from the window, which "gives" on to a narrow, noisy street. This, after the beautiful view and the quiet of our Monte Carlo home, is most depressing. It is raining *canes felesque*—("Must be classic in Rome," says Johnnie, trying to cheer up a bit)—which does not tend to enliven us. We descend to the Restaurant Department. Considered as a Restaurant, it is the dreariest room possible.

"What a place!" exclaims Johnnie. "Why," the commercial room of an old-established provincial hotel in England is quite Parisian in its gaiety compared with this. City of the Cæsars! I should think this place was started when Caligula was on the throne. Ugh!"

I am too depressed to contradict him. Let us breakfast. Let us have a Roman breakfast. Not a Roman dish on the *menu!* We order a good French *déjeuner.* "At all events," I say, brightening up a bit, "we can have some Italian wine."

"Let's have some Montepulciano," says Johnnie, regarding the waiter severely, as though warning him beforehand not to attempt passing off any Italian wine of an inferior quality upon him.

The waiter, in perfect English (I having addressed him in French, and Johnnie in Italian), wishes to know what wine it was the gentleman demanded?

The Roman Noses we actually did see.

"Montepulciano," Johnnie repeats, only this time in a less certain tone, being evidently a trifle distrustful of his pronunciation, and his eye falters before the waiter's calm, but not unsympathetic, gaze. The waiter has never heard of it. "What!" exclaims Johnnie, "never heard of Montepulciano? Why, in Horace's time——" But the waiter was not here in Horace's time.

"Wasn't that Falernian?" I ask, rather siding with the waiter, who, as an Italian, at least so I suppose, ought to know.

"Well," returns Johnnie, ceding the point, "let's have Falernian."

No; we cannot have Falernian; we can have some *chianti,* which the waiter can highly recommend, or some Barolo, of which, he tells us, they have a remarkably fine specimen.

We decide on *chianti.*

It is some time before Johnnie can get over the waiter's never having heard of Montepulciano.

"Of course," he says to me, "*you*'ve heard of it." Yes, I fancy I have; but, trying to recall it, I cannot quote my authority unless it's somewhere in the *Bon Gualtier Ballads* The line, I fancy, is "Regal Montepulciano drained beneath its native rock." This is unsatisfactory to Johnnie, who is just beginning to express his doubt as to whether Montepulciano is in Italy or Spain, when the breakfast arrives, and we cheer up a bit.

CHAPTER IX.

ROME—NO SMOKE—DARK AGES—JUPITER PLUVIUS –MORNING CALL
—ST. PETER'S.

BREAKFAST restores us to fairly good spirits. If it were not muggy and close indoors, and raining and generally filthy outside, we should be rollicking. "However," says Johnnie, leaning back and pulling out his cigar-case, as the waiter brings in the coffee, "the great charm of a foreign hotel is that you can smoke your cigar immediately you've finished, without leaving the table." And he strikes a light. "Beg pardon, Sir," interposes the civil Waiter, "but smoking is not allowed here. Only in the smoking-room."

"What!" exclaims Johnnie, in a voice of thunder. The Waiter shrugs his shoulders; such is the case; he, the Waiter, personally would wish it otherwise, but Monsieur the gentleman will understand that *he*, as only Waiter, is not responsible for it. "But——" Johnnie restrains himself, and, with suppressed fury, requests to be shown to the smoking-room. The Waiter, coffee in

hand, motions us to follow him. "Of all the, &c.," I hear Johnnie
muttering as he walks along, anathemas not loud but deep, and I
perfectly agree with him. We enter a small room, commanding a
view of the Piazza, which is something, but in all other respects a
mere repetition of any old-fashioned smoking-room in the hotel of
an old-world English cathedral town, with the usual "writing-
materials," consisting of half a sheet of measly-looking blotting-paper,
a small cheap inkstand, with very little ink in it, and a steel
pen that looks as if it had been used as a pipe-picker, the
inevitable *Bradshaw* of a date long past, one or two advertising
books on the table, and some advertising pictures on the walls.
"And this," exclaims Johnnie, "is civilization in Rome!! Not

smoke in the Res-
taurant after din-
ner!! Bah! I've
got a precious good
mind to chuck the
whole thing up,
and go straight
back to Monte
Carlo." And so
great is the upset
to his habits and
ideas of social en-

First View of Rome from Triumphal Roman Car.

joyment, that, but for my undertaking to interview the landlord
on the subject and obtain some concession, he would, as he
expresses it, chuck up the whole bag of tricks, which includes
St. Peter's, the Vatican, the Coliseum, and all that makes Rome
Rome, and go back *hic et nunc* to Monte Carlo, "Where," as
e says, "at all events a fellow is in a civilised place, and can
smoke at his own table, in his own hotel, and take his ease at his
inn."

I promise further, on condition of his remaining, to undertake
all the ciceroning trouble, and to personally conduct him everywhere. "And first of all," I say, "as it's raining, let's drive to
St. Peter's, where we can spend the afternoon." Agreed. Is *this*
Rome, as seen from the Roman Car, under a hood, on a pouring
wet day? If it is, the streets are scarcely wider than Chancery

Lane, and the slush and mud are far worse. But for the prospect of seeing St. Peter's, we—both of us being in the same sweet humour—would pack up our things and return to Monte Carlo.

En route it occurs to me that I have to leave a card on a distinguished Monsignore dwelling within the precincts of St. Peter's. As Johnnie speaks Italian, limited, but apparently intelligible, I propose that he shall accompany me. He will, with pleasure. We ascend the steps on the Vatican side. We are challenged by one of the Swiss Guards. The Merry Swiss Boy, in canary-coloured uniform with zebra stripes over it, is six foot two and very courteous. He indicates where we may find the Monsignore's door. Ascending the stairs, we encounter a gorgeous officer in a mediæval costume. Johnnie is of opinion that he is a "noble guard." The "Nobil Signor"—(I remember this from the Page's Song in *Gli Ugonotti*—"*didicisse fideliter Italianas Operas*"—making "Opera" feminine—is evidently of some use to a stranger in Rome)—the Nobil Signor cannot be too courteous. The Monsignore, he informs us, lives on the "*primo piano*"—sounds as if he were a music-teacher—and thither we go. We are admitted by Monsignore's *concierge*, a little snuffy man in threadbare black, like a second-rate lawyer's clerk, into a comparatively unfurnished apartment, where he is keeping himself warm with snuff and a small charcoal fire in a *brasero*,—at least, such Johnnie tells me is the name of the large frying-pan without a handle, filled with charcoal at a white heat. I intrust the letter for Monsignore to him, and am rather relieved at being informed that Monsignore is not at home. We leave the *primo piano*, and descend the steps. After passing with great politeness the last of the Merry Swiss Guards, we once more breathe freely, and having so far done our duty, we turn towards St. Peter's.

"Nobil Signor!"

Grand! Then we mount the steps. Then timidly and cautiously we push at a door, and in another second we are in St. Peter's. For a minute or so we can only look about us, dazed, then we regard each other, curiously, as if we had expected some transformation of our personal appearance. No; here we are, the same that we were outside—and yet . . . well . . . awestruck is the word. Overpowering! I have been told I should be disappointed. Disappointed! If it were only to have come here for this one short visit that I had travelled from London, I should have been more than repaid by the *coup d'œil* on first entering this marvellous temple.

CHAPTER X.

ST. PETER'S—SOLVITUR AMBULANDO—MASONRY—WAYS AND MEANS
"BOCK AGEN"—MONTE CARLO—LONDON.

Balbus and Caius, A.U.C. 89.

THE SIZE of St. Peter's! I mentally compare it with everything big I have ever seen. Johnnie, having partially recovered his self-possession and the use of his voice, says, "Look here, I'll step it. I measured my back drawing-room for a billiard table by stepping it, and so I can easily get an idea of its size." He at once sets to work in order to give practical effect to his theory of measurement, and he sets about it with as much care, caution, and "strict attention to business," as if he were giving an imitation of a man walking on a tight-rope without a balancing-pole. After three attempts, each of which signally fails, on account of his inability to preserve a straight line, when he, as it were, topples off his imaginary rope, comes to the ground, and loses his reckoning up to that point, he gives it up, shakes his head solemnly, and says, "Oh, it's enormous! Why, St. Paul's is nowhere compared with this!" I recall to mind the monumental effigies in St. Paul's, any one of which is a doll by the side of any one of the figures in St. Peter's. And then the London grubbiness of St. Paul's, its dinginess, its lecture-room benches crowding the centre, and its chilly dreariness; whereas here all is space, colour, light and life. Glorious! Everyone knows, by hearsay at all events, about the size of those chubby little boys who support the holy-water stoups at the entrance. Come up close, and though you are perfectly prepared for a surprise, yet your astonishment is not a whit the less at finding the stoups baths, and the little boys a couple of giants. I can scarcely believe my eyes, but so it is, and Johnnie and myself are never tired of walking up to these deceptive full-grown cherubs, coming on them unexpectedly as it were, and patting them on the hands and arms to ascertain whether they are playing us any trick, and whether they are the Anakim they seem. Yes, there *is* a deception; it is the deception of perfect proportion. Every day we go into St. Peter's, but these happy - looking baby - giants exercise an unaccountable fascination over us, and on our last visit we are quite sad at the idea of leaving them behind, but being unable to take them with us, we pat the backs of these chubby Brobdingnagians, and bid them affectionately good-bye. And the last *souvenir* of St. Peter's that will remain indelibly in my memory, is the sweet-tempered smile on the faces of the two giant-babies—the holy-"water Babies"—nearest our door of exit craning towards us, saying as plainly as dumb action can speak, "We should so like to come with you, only we can't leave this great big heavy basin, or it would tumble down. But mind you come and see us again; you'll find us here, always on duty,—don't forget."

Pouring rain. The streets of London not "in it" with those of Rome for slosh and mud. Here in this museum of antiquities, the home of classic Art and ancient frescoes, the principal mural decoration that catches my eye at almost every turn is that charming picture of a fine and fascinating *décolletée* female, with yellow hair streaming down her back,—the fair one with the golden locks,—so well known to all Londoners as the pictorial advertisement of Mrs. Somebody's Hair Restorer. This, apparently, is the most striking fresco in the City of the Popes and Cæsars, but as the Cæsars are defunct, they can't interfere;

and, as the Pope's daily constitutional is unconstitutionally limited to the Vatican grounds, His Holiness possibly is not aware how the city is being vulgarised. Yet the obtrusive presence of this leering woman representing Mrs. Somebody's Hair Restorer on the walls of the Eternal City, does recall to my mind a proverbial saying, which seems peculiarly applicable in this instance, namely, "See Rome and dye."

The truth of another proverb, that "Rome was not built in a day," is borne in upon us with irresistible force at every turn. "Rome built in a day!" cries Johnnie. "Why, they're at it now!" Balbus and Caius, who were always building walls, by way of Latin exercise, in our youth, are still at it, still building Rome in A.U.C. 2640. They're making quite a new Rome—a Haussmannish Rome—of it. In another ten years Rome will possess splendid streets (at least I am inartistic enough to hope so), and ample pavement (also my sincere wish), and in its main thoroughfares it will be as like Paris as the Balbi and Caii, carrying out their orders and contracts, can make it.

"' Masonry ' is condemned at Rome," says Johnnie, "and so it ought to be, until the streets are widened, and pavement-makers have been set to work."

"It's wonderfully picturesque, though," I say, referring to the old gate, old streets, old walls, and old houses.

"Very," returns Johnnie, coming cautiously out of a dark hole in a wall where a small Roman greengrocer carries on his trade, and in which Johnnie has taken refuge from the dangerous proximity of a recklessly-driven cab; "only I do object to there being no pavement for foot-passengers."

As to the environs, on a pouring day like this, we might as well be walking in a ploughed field. Fortunately we don't attempt it, and having hired a Roman car with a hood and apron, we are driven to "St. Paul's outside the Walls,"—("I thought it couldn't be 'without the Walls,'" says Johnnie, "or how on earth could it stand up?")—which is almost as great a wonder as St. Peter's.

During our short stay, we see everything that is possible to be seen in the time; but Johnnie is thoroughly upset by the fact of not being permitted to smoke after breakfast and dinner in the restaurant of the hotel, and what with the heat of our bed-room, which is next to the kitchen chimney, the noise of the street at night, and the almost incessant rain, he is dissatisfied with every-thing—except a dinner at the *Caffè di Roma*, and the *chianti* in a magnum flask—and anxious to return as soon as possible to Monte Carlo, and so home.

We take a walk on the Pincio, and delight in a view. In these gardens there are so many ecclesiastics of all sorts, sizes, and ages, and such a large proportion of them evidently only students, that I am forcibly reminded of the College grounds of Cambridge or Oxford in term time. The youths are enjoying themselves with all the soberness that characterises such reading men at either

Balbus and Caius, A.D. 1889.

University as affect their cap and gown at all times, even when taking their con-stitutional. I suppose if one of these Roman students is out without his acade-micals, there is no Roman Proctor and Bulldogs to stop him and ask him for his name and college, and then fine him six-and-eightpence.

Cabs are wonderfully cheap in Rome. In order to compete with the recently-introduced omnibuses and tram-cars, the cab-proprietors have reduced their tariff to half-a-franc for a course, " but," says Johnnie, cheering up a bit, " no one gives less than a franc as a matter of course." No *pour-boire* is expected, and if given, it is received with gratitude. The price for driving about is two francs the hour, their pace is generally good, and if the thoroughfare be crowded with pedestrians and the street more than usually dirty and narrow, then you may rely upon his going at full speed merely for the humour of the thing, and you'll have plenty of excitement for your money.

On our last morning we go to see the pictures and the statuary in the Vatican. We have no catalogue.

" Don't want one," says Johnnie. " All the names are on the things, and I can make mems as I go along."

So, with a big note-book and pencil, he walks through the

galleries, as if the Pope had been sold up, and he, Johnnie Spofferd, were the man in possession taking an inventory of the plate, ornaments, and fixtures. "Look here!" he says, suddenly drawing my attention to a small bust in the Hall of Philosophers and Muses. "Fancy this being Socrates!" Yes, fancy! "And yet," says Johnnie, "I seem to know the face. Yes. It's uncommonly like the bust of Darwin in one of the Kensington Museums."

In the Sistine Chapel we see several tourists lying supinely at full length on the seats. "So irreverent, in a chapel, too! Just as if they were resting after a Turkish bath," says Johnnie. "Though," he adds, as he glances round, "it isn't much like a chapel to look at." No, it is not. More like a decorated Concert Hall. We gradually become aware of the fact that the sprawling tourists are only deeply interested in the work of Michael Angelo on the ceiling, and have discovered that the only way of studying it satisfactorily is on their backs. Johnnie is tired, and pines for Monte Carlo. I rather think that a telegram which he receives on re-entering our hotel is a bogus one, only intended to give him a fair excuse

ΣΩΚΡΑΤΗΣ

for saying he must return at once "on business." As I must make the best of my way to London, I decide to accompany him, hoping for another opportunity of seeing Rome at my leisure, and having a month to do it in. We start.

Monte Carlo Revisited.—"Great attraction!! For one night only!!!" That is as far as I am concerned, only a day and a half and one night. Lovely weather. Beautiful N.E. wind. Johnnie, who has recovered his spirits, says jocosely, "Rather have had N.E. other wind. But better than Rome. One can breathe here," and he disappears into that unhealthy hot-house the Casino. At dinner, he tells me he has met a man who has been awfully lucky playing only on the thirties. That's his system. Meeting subsequently at Zero's, Johnnie is looking weary and worn. Anything the matter? Yes, his system is upset. He

z

wishes he had never met the man who told him about the "thirties." He will leave Monte Carlo with me to-morrow morning. After all, no place like London.

London.—Black Fog. Certainly no place like London. We lose sight of each other in the fog. Johnnie goes due East. I due South once more, only not farther than South Kent Coast. End of holiday.

HOW, WHEN, AND WHERE.

z 2

HOW, WHEN, AND WHERE.

CHAPTER I.

HOW, WHEN, AND WHERE—FIRST SKELETON ROUTE—GENERAL
DIRECTIONS.

NE thousand questions having been daily put to us just before the vacation season of the year, as to "when to go, how to go it, where to go to, and what to wear where you go;" we drawing largely upon our own travelling experience, are now about to give a full and sufficient answer. The third point is the one to which we must first give our serious attention, and therefore let it be our cheerful task, before entering into the details of expense and so forth, to suggest a few pleasant routes for the consideration of the still dubitating tourist. Home circuits will not of course come under our present notice.

Let us suppose then that you want to be away for ever such a long time : very good ; then we will commence by reducing that period to three weeks at the outside. This phrase "at the outside," will fairly exhaust the first part of our subject ; while, "at the inside" will relate merely to the pocket, and we shall soon exhaust that.

Now then, Ladies and Gentlemen, for our

GRAND PATENT THREE WEEKS' TOUR ON THE CONTINENT,
CONDUCTED ON THE MOST ECONOMICAL PRINCIPLES.

Let us begin at the beginning ; alphabetical order of places by all means. Let us say you want to go to Antwerp. By the way, you must say you don't, or else we're done, and won't play any more.

Very good ; then you do want to go to Antwerp. Now here is a nice little three weeks' jaunt for you :

Antwerp. Athens. Berlin (where the wool is). Copenhagen. Dresden (calling at China). Ems. Florence. Göttingen and back again, *viâ* Leipsic, Hong Kong (if time), Madeira, Paris and the Margin of Fair Zurich's Waters *Tullaliety*, and so home.

This will suffice for the first journey. You can start from anywhere you like, say Brunswick Square by Moonlight.

While we feel inclined, permit us to make three observations :—

1. The Tourist's Best Pocket Companion is,—MONEY.

2. Bank clerks and others (specially "others"), should not leave England without their employers' permission, lest they be caught tripping.

3. Don't be extravagant ; but if you're going very far, it is, perhaps, as well to be "a little near."

If, in the course of these directions, any abbreviations are used, let it be understood, once for all, that *r* means rail, and that *s* doesn't ; that *o* means nothing, *p* means something, *q* anything, and so on.

First, catch your Passport. This must be signed by all the Crowned Heads of Europe. On being asked your name, reply "N. or M. as the case may be."

Having procured this necessary document, packing up before packing off is the order of the day. So now we must consider—

What to take?—The simple answer to this regular puzzle is, "Take time ;" don't flurry yourself or "take on" if you find matters going unsatisfactorily, and take off your coat and waistcoat, if filling a portmanteau be warm work ; and, finally, end by taking yourself off altogether. If you take this idea, you'll commence excellently well.

Another important question is, " *What quantity of Luggage shall I require ?* " We are prepared for this or any other emergency :—

Necessary Luggage.—One portmanteau, full ; another empty, in case you lose the first. A hat-box, with hat *inside*. A bag containing "Things." A large sandwich-box to hold muffins, strawberries, and slices of roast beef, which you can't get abroad. A packet of collars, silk neckties, and an Alpine stock, much worn among the mountaineers. Don't bother yourself about taking soap ; if you were to spend much money in this article, you'd soon be cleaned out. Carefully provide yourself with blankets, table napkins, sheets, candlesticks, snuffers, and panes of glass, in case any of the windows in your bedroom at the hotel are broken. A knife, fork, and spoon are indispensable. A barrel organ will amuse you on the road, but we scarcely recommend your carrying it, unless there's a donkey to take it about, which, by the way, there probably would be.

Glasses, &c.—You can always obtain plenty of glasses on the journey, at the various refreshment rooms ; some people can, however, see better without them. Carry a telescope about the size of Lord Ross's ; or hire it for your tour. If you can get on fast with a walking-stick, take two, and then you'll get on faster. Umbrellas, belonging chiefly to other people, you will be able to pick up on the road. Perhaps, however, it is better to carry one, as when hungry you will always have a spread ready.

So far, so good. The next point is money. Procure this from a banker, before four o'clock. The best time, however, is when he's not looking. If this is impracticable, ask him to sing a Round, and then catch some of his circular notes.

So much for the present ; there remains quite as much for the future. We ourselves have not travelled for nothing ; and, by the way, on referring to that admirable publication, "Our Banker's Book," we devoutly wish that we had.

CHAPTER II.

TRAPS FOR TRAVELLERS—RAILLERY FOR THE RAIL.

ORTHY of the gravest consideration to the tourist is the subject of Dress. The choice of costume, especially as regards the adoption of old clothes, must depend a great deal upon previous habits. Provide yourself, however, with—

A Reversible coat, black one side and white the other, with tails to hook on, in case you want to go to an evening party.

Reversible Boots, so that you may be able to retrace your steps with ease. Let them be very neat, for it always is a point to turn out your toes well.

Travelling is dull work, sociably speaking, or, we

Hooky Walker.

should say, *not* sociably speaking. Take our advice, and break through any bashfulness and awkward reserve in opening a conversation with a chance companion.

Before you step into the train, a carriage must be selected. Choose one where the only available seat is filled with the boxes, rugs, sticks, &c., belonging to the occupants. Insist upon these being immediately removed. When this operation has been performed, and everyone is more or less uncomfortable, say you've changed your mind, and sha'n't come in. Walk a little way from the door, then return to request them to keep the seat for you. Wait until three minutes before the train starts, then lose no time in shoving your fishing-rod, desks with unpleasantly sharp corners, telescopes, sticks, umbrellas, and curiously impracticable hat-boxes, under the seats. You must be very careful in looking after your luggage ; therefore, at frequent intervals during the journey, rummage about among the passengers' legs with your stick, in order to ascertain the safety of the various articles. If you miss anything, at once charge your travelling companions, individually and collectively, with the theft. Even if they haven't stolen it, 'twill serve as a pleasant little *ruse* for breaking the ice, and navigating a north-west passage to conversation-point. If they won't second you in your laudable endeavours, whistle, hum, sing, eat oranges, and let the window perpetually up and down, in order to dispose of the peel. Should you happen to be shut in with a solitary companion, say, for instance, an elderly gentleman, sleepily inclined, the following will be found an excellent

Scheme for a Railway Conversation with an entire stranger (elderly, First Class) :—

How do you do, Sir? I hope you are pretty well? It is a very fine day, a very wet day, a queer day, a tooral-li-day, &c., as the case may be. Seen the new *Hamlet?*—[*Here give a succinct account of the plot, finishing with, of course, an imitation of* Mr. Fechter *as Hamlet.*

Been to the Opera? Heard Lucca and Patti?—[*Here give imitations of* Lucca *and* Patti: *this is the way to get on in the world, and to make yourself a pleasant companion.*

Of course you've travelled by the Underground Railway? No? Dear me! well then, &c., &c.—[*Here give imitations of the Underground Railway : say* sssssssssssssh, *to imitate steam, and shriek when representing the passage through a Tunnel ; these embellishments to your discourse will render the account graphic and life-like.*

Seen Pepper's Ghost, I mean Dircks' and Pepper's Ghost? No! I have. Look here, this is the way it's done.—[*Here show him the way it's done.*

Been up in a Balloon? No! Dear me! What, never been up in a Balloon? Not with Glaisher? Lor', Glaisher goes up in a Balloon with Coxwell, and when they've reached an altitude of 300,000,000,000 feet, their breath is taken away, and, &c., &c.—[*Here show him how* Coxwell *and* Glaisher *reach an altitude of* 300,000,000,000 *feet, and take his breath away.*

Ah! Stopping at a station! Hungry, eh? No—dear me. Thirsty? No?—What are you going to stand?—[*It will now be* his *turn to show you what he's going to stand; only, if he stands this sort of thing much longer, he will be a greater muff than we take him for.*

Adapt yourself to your company; if your fellow traveller be a Bishop or Archdeacon, the following scheme will serve your turn :—

How are you, eh? Like wearing Gaiters and Shovel Hats? I saw you at Ascot. You old doo, you!—[*Here dig him in the ribs.*

I'll write to the Archbishop, you sly dog, I will. I say, did you see the last Fight for the Belt? You didn't—my eye!—well, you must know that when Jem's Novice drew the claret from the Dustman's smeller, &c.—[*Here illustrate the action of drawing claret from smellers, and so on through the several rounds.*

Good Ballet at Her Majesty's this year! fine gals—rather. I say, do you know that capital story about——[*Here tell him that capital story about——*

I'm told the Bishop of London isn't going to shoot this year—eh, why?—because he was seen drawing his Charge—ha! ha! ha! had you there, &c., *ad libitum.*

All this is very cheerful, sociable, and sprightly, and will carry you down* to Dover, Newhaven, or S'thampton Water as pleasantly as possible.

---

* " *Carry you down,*" a mere *façon de parler*, in no way depreciative of the advantages of steam locomotion. N.B.—If you wish to obtain your journey gratis, talk in a flippant and insulting manner before your assembled fellow-travellers in any waiting-room; some one will be pretty sure to " take you down." Do not forget this.

CHAPTER III.

TWO FEET FOR THE POETRY OF MOTION—SECOND
SKELETON ROUTE.

Visit to Spa.

N OW is the time to give Pedestrians a few little hints and advice to go upon when travelling. We therefore obligingly inform—

Pedestrians that they should not go upon our hints, but follow our advice, and go upon their own Legs.

Our readers must not be frightened when we speak of "Skeleton Tours;" we have merely appropriated one of Murray's phrases, or, so to speak, *boned* it for our own purposes.

The first projector of Skeleton Tours was the Original Bones.

Before proceeding any further, we must advise the reader as to more abbreviations and certain signs to be used in this work, which have been rendered necessary in order to save repetition, and to increase the already generally acknowledged usefulness of the only really successful competition with Murray and Black. Therefore let it be remembered, that you mustn't be frightened when you see a Dark Line thus ▬▬▬ for it doesn't mean anything like what it does in a transpontine playbill, where you read—

AWFUL DÉNOUEMENT!

THE DYING VILLAIN—REMORSE—THE COMPACT—FEARFUL APPEAR-
ANCE OF THE ————————, WHO COMES TO CLAIM HIS PREY!

Which he does, with a lot of red and blue fire, that makes you
sneeze for at least five minutes after his disappearance. If you
ask what the line means when it occurs in our type, suffice it to
say that we don't intend any harm, but we're not going to answer
merely impertinent questions.

Y. and N. will mean yes and no; that is to say, if you like, but
we don't insist upon it.

In all ground-plans of towns, cities, and public buildings, R. H.
will mean right hand, R. standing for right, and H. for hand, and
H.R.H. means the Prince of Wales, who knows all about travelling
by this time: L. H. means left hand: O. L. H. means Over the
Left; and in every instance the reader is supposed to be on the
stage or diligence, as the case may be, facing the audience. In
paying a bill, where the R. and L. hands are used, the reader of
the little account will merely have to face the landlord.

Once more, if X. occurs suddenly in the middle of a sentence,
you will be as much astonished as we shall.

Now for our second Skeleton Route. This series provides you
with a skeleton key to the Continent, so look out for the Police.
Now Away! Away!

Amsterdam. Boulogne, of course. Strasbourg, stopping to see
Patti. Le Mans, where the celebrated City b'scuits are made.
O. L. H. Lyons, stop to see the Lady. Montargis, one day for
the Performing Dog. Up the Rhine to the Tyrol. Bacharach,
Balancez, Hands across and back to your places.

Now then, adopting this scheme, let us say you land at
Amsterdam.

The Language.—On disembarking at any Foreign quay, you
will first of all be struck by the language, which is, generally,
Bad. Do not therefore attempt to learn it. And at this point, it
will be as well to draw your attention (what a subject for an artist,
by the way!) to

Foreign Tongues.—There's the Russian tongue, the R{ɔ}indeer's

tongue, the Ox tongue, and so forth. But this is not exactly what
you want, is it? No. Very good : then as a beginning let us
remark that *je suis* means " I ham," which is the French tongue,
and that's as much as you can swallow for the present.

Now let us see where we are, Boulogne, or Amsterdam ?
Wherever you like, my little dear, so we'll make a few more
general observations.

There are a certain number of objects of interest in every
Foreign town. The first being—

The Banker's or Change-the-money Office, where you'll cash a
circular note in order to square matters. The generic name for
the clerk at these places is Billy de Bank ; so be careful to address
him by his Christian, which in this case, is his proper name. If
you want to get full change, don't go to the nearest banker ; the
nearest is invariably the dearest. The Clerk (Billy) will ask you
" How will you have it ? " Don't be bullied, square up and say,
" Now, *where*'ll you have it ? " Billy will subside, and probably
alter his question to " What'll you take ? " When immediately
choose the light wine of the country. Their light wine is better
than their light money. If Billy further inquire, *Dans quelle de
monnaie désireriez vous recevoir la somme !* which means, " What'll
you take it in ? " say " A glass of course, and a good large one
too," whereupon you'll receive your draught in due form.

The next, or, when you are either expecting a remittance, or to
hear from *Her* (ahem !), the *first* object of interest is in every
town—

The Post Office.—Doors R. H. L. H. Window in flat ; and
when you happen to look out, flat in Window. If you've any
brains, now's the time to get a head ; you're certain to require
one. If you don't know how to ask for it in the language of the
country, or of the town, adopt a system of expressive pantomime,
thus :—Take an envelope, wet a corner, put your own head on it,
and stamp your foot ; you will get what you want, unless you are
at once taken to a *Maison de santé*, where you'll get a great deal
more than you want.

We should advise the tourist to go straight to Boulogne. This
is a capital starting point, because from Boulogne you can go any-

where, as of course you can from any other place. And again, from anywhere you can go to Boulogne; this is another point in its favour, though on second thoughts the advantage is equally shared by Ramsgate, Scarborough, and other spots on the English coast. We must here caution the reader, that whenever in the course of this work the word "spot" is used, we do not mean that the place so indicated is any blemish to its particular situation. Do we make ourselves understood? Clearly so; then on we go, which is a rhyme, but it can't be helped, and so let us not say another word about it.

"Nice piece o' biled mutton, sir?"

CHAPTER IV.

FRANCE—LANGUAGE—DOGS AND DOUANIERS.

IN FRANCE the French language is chiefly spoken; and this, on consideration, is not surprising. At first you will be astonished to hear the smallest, dirtiest, little boys in the gutter addressing one another in French gutterals; and the thoughtful traveller will immediately note down in his pocket-book that the education of the lower classes on the Continent is very much superior to that in England. The traveller, however, on becoming more thoughtful, will probably erase the note soon after it has been made. Now, we must at once ask you *Parlez-vous Français?* Your answer may be, "What's that to you?" But that's rude: so you will politely reply to the interrogator, "I can read and write it, but don't understand a word of it." If a Frenchman makes the inquiry, be ready to say "*Bang poo, may john tong,*" which means, "I don't speak it much, but I know what you are talking about," and after having thus delivered yourself, walk off quickly in the opposite direction. Let us here pause to make one remark about—

Comfort.—Always make yourself quite at home, remembering that, by pursuing this course, you have the advantage of the poor ignorant foreigners, who are always "abroad."

Choice of Hotels.—At Boulogne there is very little choice. They are mostly kept by an English proprietor of the name of *Bains;* at least, we so gathered from having seen *Hôtel de Bains* inscribed over the doors of several large houses. The best hotel is the *Hôtel de Ville.* To be taken in here, however, requires a certain amount of personal interest with the native police. They will sometimes show you the inside of this building for nothing. On the occasion of our visit, in company with a gendarme, we were obliged to make several complaints, to which no attention was paid; and we cannot, therefore, recommend the place to our friends.

While upon the subject of complaints, it would be as well to mention that any communication about faults in the *cuisine* must be made by letter to the Minister of the Interior. This General Regulation applies to every part of France.

Walks.—Your first Walk at Boulogne will be from the steamboat to the Custom House, and during these few steps you will have great opportunities of noticing the physiology of the Lower French Classes, who speak a very different language to the youth of both sexes who are ranked under the same title in our English schools. The voyage will probably have improved neither your personal appearance nor your temper. In case the observations made as you pass between the two lines of the Mob thus assembled to welcome you, should be unintelligible, we will translate them for the benefit of the traveller, who is supposed to be walking along feebly and wretchedly, as after a bad passage.

Our cheery lively neighbours are assembled to greet you :—

First Lively Neighbour (addressing himself generally to lots of lively neighbours). "Oh! look there! There's a white roast beef!" (*This means you, you know*).

All (laughing). "He! he! he! he! he!" (*Ad lib., till they think of something else to say*).

More Lively Neighbour. "I say, Mister, ain't yer well?"

All (laughing at you again, you know). "He, he, he, he!" (*Ad lib.*)

Small Neighbour (livelier than ever, pointing distinctly at you, with a very dirty finger). "He wants some 'portare beer.'"

All (immensely tickled by this witty homethrust). "He! he! he! he! he! he!" &c., &c. (*Ad lib.*)

Somebody in the Crowd (who has a slight acquaintance with our language, says in French-English. "He's a grrrreat long strrrrong." (*The mother tongue attracts your attention, and you turn round, and the speaker arrives at the end of his limited vocabulary with*) "Oh, ye-ees!"

All (highly relishing the joke, which the traveller cannot of course at first be expected to see). "Oh, ye-ees! Oh, ye-ees! He! he! he!" &c., &c. Which will be continued, until the last *voyageur* has disappeared within the doors of the Douane.

The Custom House.—You will be asked if you've anything to

declare. Now's the time for the traveller to assert himself. If it
is a lady, let her say, "Well, I declare!" and then refuse to utter
another syllable. If a gentleman, let him declare that he'll write
to the *Times*. Don't give up your keys. *They've no right to ask
you*, at least they would not dare do it if they were in England,
the cowards! Mind you say all this, adding the line about what

Prevention better than cure.- A sketch at Milan.

your native country is in the habit of expecting the conduct of
everyone to be with regard to Duty. They will want to inspect
your hat-box; always make a difficulty about your hat-box, and
then take good care that there is nothing inside when you open
it. A hat-box lined with red has a deep political signification;
so has black and white; blue and yellow are also the signs in
constant use among the *carbonari;* * so take care. The punish-

---

* *Carbonari*, Italian name for the Secret Society of Coal Heavers; so
called from the carbon in the coals.—*Vide* " Black's Guide."

ments, even now in vogue in France, are hanging, drawing, quartering, whipping, scourging with fish-hooks, branding on the nose; hot-ironing and mangling are still done here. For a minor offence, say, for instance, a smaller hat-box with a less deep lining you will render yourself liable to be loaded with chains, and blown up by a magistrate. Do not tremble, be sweetly polite, address each of the Douaniers as "Milor," and all will be well.

Precautions.—To save *all* the above mentioned trouble, and any further annoyance, write over to Boulogne generally some days before and say you're coming. If you can't write, get somebody to go over instead of you, or Don't Go. The observance of this last precaution will, at some future time, lead us to give some advice as to what is to be done by the Traveller who stays at home. At present we are on the Continent.

Geographical Position of the Continent.—The Continent is a neck of land, divided from every other place by something or other which is not surrounded on all sides by water. To bring the definition nearer home is impossible, as it would involve moving France, Russia, Spain, Austria, &c.; however, the reader may be sure, that, whenever there is a movement in any one of these places, we will take advantage of it.

The Continent then is not simply Boulogne, howbeit, many to this day are of that opinion. What then is the Continent? It is a Tract of Land; and being a Tract, is imagined by a few to belong to some proselytising society. This idea has no foundation in fact. After these few but useful remarks we will proceed.

CHAPTER V.

FRANCE CONTINUED—JOHN BULL AT BOULOGNE—PLACES OF
AMUSEMENT.

St. Barbara.—Taken from life.

N REFERRING to our skeleton route No. 2, the tourist, staying at Boulogne, will find that he ought to have commenced with Amsterdam. If, however, there be ladies in his party, he will have acted with touching delicacy, in avoiding a place, whose name possesses so profane a termination. We will therefore, for the present, remain at Boulogne, and give a few broad pieces of advice, upon which the Traveller may, or may not, act, as he thinks proper.

Never go to a foreign barber's in order to get shaved. The very evident reason for this is, that, when abroad, it is always remarkably unpleasant to get into a scrape.

You will, of course, frequent a *Café* during the daytime. Now these places are of two sorts: there is the *Café Gnaw*, which is, as the name implies (very like English by the way, eh?) entirely for eating; and the *Café oh Lay*, where, as may be gathered

---

* The Female Barbers in this place form a Religious Sisterhood, under the patronage of St. Barbara, who was taken from Life many years ago: they are known as the Lather-day Saints.

from the title, you lay yourself down and devote the time to singing. The proprietors of either place do not interfere with one another, and business is thus carried on upon the most amicable principles.

If you do not understand the language, always on taking your seat at a *Café*, amuse yourself with the contents of a French newspaper. In this case, no article however bitter will disturb you, and you have the advantage over other people, in being able to read it sideways, or upside down, with equal gratification.

You will notice, that when foreigners have finished their little cup of coffee, they invariably empty the contents of the sugar-basin into their pockets. As it is always well for a visitor to be more French than a native, you should not confine yourself to the sugar, but appropriate the spoon, cup, saucer, or plate, or anything else that suits your fancy, and is adapted to the meanest capacity of the pocket. Always go to the best hotel; of course you will be obliged to try several, before ascertaining which is the one that can fairly claim the honourable distinction.

In many places you will be told that the waiters " speak English." So they may, but they probably don't understand it.

We once heard a damp tourist, on arriving in steaming haste at an hotel where "English was spoken," cry out to the waiter as he was hurrying to his room, " Waiter bring me some hot water;" whereupon the intelligent *garçon* readily answered, " Leg of mut-ton, yaas sare,"—and smiled cheerfully, being evidently highly pleased with this ingenious interpretation of the visitor's wish. You should have a few sentences always in stock; first, for instance, on entering the hotel : *Avay voo day shombrr ;* this means " Got any rooms?" But mind you *do* say this, before the Landlord or Boots, or anyone else has the chance of addressing you ; as they may make some remark which you don't understand, and which will utterly upset any scheme for a French dialogue that you may have previously formed. In order not to be thrown out you must force his reply with your question, and should the former not be the one required, pretend to blow your nose, feign a sneeze, or a cough, which would of course prevent your catching what he said, and then return to your own pre-arranged conversation.

On entering your apartment immediately take up your carpet, if there is one, and order the dust to be swept away.

To avoid the repetition of that useless form of regret, commencing with the phrase, "I wish I'd brought (whatever-it-may-be) with me," we will here give a list of actual necessaries, which you should have about you, as few rooms abroad possess them. Seldom, for instance, will you find shutters to the windows: provide yourself with these. See also that you do not travel without—

20 Pegs for coats, dressing-gowns, Ladies' gowns, &c.

2 Venetian blinds.

1 Wardrobe.

1 Chamber-pail for slops.

1 Cheval glass.

2 Pairs of Snuffers.

1 Bell.

Several different kinds of soap, and baths for hot or cold water, which you can turn to account by letting out to brother or sister Tourists who have forgotten to bring them. You will find the beds small and comfortable; and if otherwise, they will do for a mere night shift very well. A couch three feet wide may sometimes serve your turn, but when you do turn, you should, like the late Duke of Wellington, turn out.

Now let us say that you've prepared your sentences, according to the plan contained in this Guide, and you ring your bell in order to summon the *garçon.* You must ring as a rule several times, but do not be afraid of a multitude of servants being attracted thereby; though it would probably follow, that if the ringing of one bell resulted in one servant, the consequence of two bells would be two servants, three bells three, and so on. Such, however, is not the case. The servants will be a long time before they reply to your summons. This you must expect, remembering that as—*Time is made for Slaves,* they of course, have a perfect right to as much of it as they like.

Take plenty of exercise in order to get up an appetite for the pleasures of the table. With a view to real gastronomic enjoyment, it is well to study beforehand the bill of fare. Unite the occupations, thus :—Some time previous to the appointed dinner-hour, ask the waiter for the *Carte*, and go out with it.

Now let the Tourist open his eyes and be taken aback, almost aback to England by the information, that, in nearly all parts of France, every chambermaid is a man. The only place where we ever heard of anything like a real English chambermaid, was at the Railway Station, when a guard directed us to the *Salle d'Attente*, which so many travellers, in common with ourselves, have mistaken for "Sarah or Sal the Attentive," but which turns out to be the Waiting Room ! Yet it is to such impositions that the English uncomplainingly subject themselves upon the Continent. The word Continent must, when you are travelling, be pronounced *Continong*, or you'll display an amount of ignorance not to be tolerated in an enlightened Briton. Do not forget this, but you need not give your authority.

What shall we do to-day ? Why, you must look at some list of entertainments, and you will probably find that the places of amusement for day visitors are the Burial Grounds, the Hospital for Incurables, the Maison de Santé, the Prison, and the Police Station, &c., &c.

There is always a Church and a Church Tower to be seen. From top of the latter you will have a splendid view ; but before the aspiring sight-seer can go up lightly, he will be forced to come down pretty heavily.

Before quitting Boulogne, we would remind our readers not to forget to ask after the notorious *Bore de Boulogne*. He became such a social nuisance as to be ultimately sent to Paris, where he is now located.

CHAPTER VI.

BELGIUM—ANTWERP—FIRST SIGHT OF THE LAND OF GROSCHEN—
FINANCIAL HINTS—VERY DISTANT VIEW OF THE RHINE—
DARMSTADT—RULES OF THE ROAD.

A view from the boxes.

STANDS for Antwerp, and therefore We starts for that place.

As of course you will have arrived at the quay, per steamer, one or two hints will save you a vast amount of trouble. You will be requested to remunerate the Steward for the sustenance that you've consumed during the voyage. Economy, mind, is the first thing to be considered; reply, therefore, to this demand by telling them confidentially "that you'll look in another time," or 'you'll be coming that way again in a few days, and then you'll settle your little account." If, after getting over the sea passage, you can also get over the boat's crew, you will be a happy and a fortunate man. The vessels where, of all others, very high prices are charged for a very low sort of diet, are, as their name implies, the *Screw* Steamers. The British stranger will now cast his eyes (he must not throw his glances

away, as they will be wanted subsequently for several parts of the
journey, where you must keep your eyes about you) upon several
distinguished military-looking gentlemen, to whom the untutored
impulse would take off its hat, deeming them to be at least second
cousins to general officers. It at first appears that these exalted
personages have come on board to welcome the Little Stranger,
and the Enthusiastic Tourist should, if he have the heart of a man
and a brother in his breast, rush forward and give way to his
feelings. Such conduct will mollify the otherwise obdurate hearts
of these Superb Foreigners, and, on being safely escorted from the
ship to the land, as, under the circumstances, you would doubt-
lessly be, you will find that you have executed that marvellous
gymnastic feat known to travellers as Clearing the Custom-house
Officers.

Porterage.—Your first care must be to procure a fly, cab,
hackney-coach or omnibus, wherein to take yourself and luggage
to an hotel. Stand on the noisy quay, and in a much noisier key
shout for a vehicle. You may shout as long as you like. *There
are none.* Now then, say, " Hi! Here! you fellow!" to one of
the gentry idling about the place in the dress of a Continental
butcher out of work. These be the porters: and if your porter
has anything like a head, he will tell you the best hotel to go to;
and thereupon he will put your baggage on to a truck and wheel
it away, and you on it into the bargain, if you approve of that
mode of entering the town.

You will probably be taken to the Hotel of St. Antony (not
because, as a feeble creature might say, there "*an't any* other," but
because it is the best), and, in order to save all discussion about
the fare, hold out to the conscientious porter a handful of coins,
consisting of groschen, kreutzers, francs, sixpences, florins, dollars,
and thalers, and let him select as many of them as may suit his
fancy. Don't begin your journey by quarrelling; but regard, with
feelings of unmixed pleasure, the gratification of this humble son
of toil on leaving you, at the door of your hostelrie, with one
silver groschen in your hand.

Before we proceed further, it would be well to offer a few
remarks upon the rate of exchange in the various towns and
countries.

The rate of exchange in a fashionable Continental town is very rapid. You are always purchasing something as a keep-sake to take home to Fanny, or somebody else whose name isn't Fanny, as of course there is no reason why it should be.

Fourpenny-bits will pass as threepenny-pieces anywhere. This is useful and important. Threepenny pieces may, among a

Clearing the Custom-House Officers.

quantity of other money (when naturally one expects a reduction on taking a quantity), pass for fourpenny-bits; but this is only successful, as a rule, when you are actually, and at the very moment of disbursement, quitting the place.

A farthing, well polished and brightened, may, among the very simple mountaineers of Switzerland, the Tullaliety and Hilliho sort of people pass for a sovereign; but most of these mountain passes are attended with a certain amount of difficulty.

On board ship, or when travelling by tidal service boat, always pay for your passage with the current coin of the river.

Should you pass through the kingdom of Bohemia (celebrated for the beautiful tea called Bohea, whence the name), the following coins are at present in circulation :—

Bohemia.	Bohemian Relative Value.	Germany.	English.	French.
Joeys	= one Kick =	3⅜ Groschen =	Four pennies	= 31³⁄₁₂ cts.
Tizzies	= one Bender =	5 Groschen =	Six pennies	= 52¹⁄₁₂ cts.
Bobs	= two Tizzies =	10 Groschen =	One shilling	= 1 fr. 20 cts.
Benders	= one Tizzy =	5 Groschen =	One sixpence	= 52¹⁄₁₂ cts.
Kicks	= one Joey =	3⅜ Groschen =	One fourpence	= 31³⁄₁₂ cts.
Tanners	= one Tizzy =	5 Groschen =	One sixpence	= 52¹⁄₁₂ cts.*

If you carry any change, be careful to take more kicks than halfpence. You'll always get them for the asking. In Cologne the cent is chiefly used. As, however, these are not punctually paid, the Owe de Cologne cent has passed into a proverb, so as to make the place smell in the nostrils of Tourists. Paper money, known as Flimsies and Bitsostiff, are seldom seen in Bohemia; while sous and straw-papers are common. When a *Billet de Banque* is unnegotiable everywhere, it is called a Billet *Doo*.

Rhino is the general term for all species of coin passing up and down the romantic river between Cologne and Mayence, and may be termed the floating capital of Rhenish Prussia. Another example of this existing fund may be found in the South, where Venice is the floating capital of Europe. This, however, by the way, and rather out of our way at present. In many places, Tourists have found brass an excellent substitute for tin. The Cosmopolite should always carry a plentiful supply of coppers with him, and then he can do all his "washing" in his own room.

Another point is the computation of distance, and the application of correct measurement to the hiring of vehicles. Mind; when you hire a *voiturier*, lower his price. Now, it must be

---

* *Time is Money.* True: but this will scarcely warrant the Tourist in using the above as a Time Table for Railways, &c. We mention this to prevent disappointment.

taken as a general rule, to which there are but very few exceptions, that **every** object, when divided from the traveller by an interval of several miles, is further removed from his particular locality, than is another object which is within a few feet of his touch. Very good. In the latter case a carriage will not be required. In the former, let us suppose you're going to drive to Darmstadt, which is ten miles off from anywhere you like. Well. if you know this, all you've got to ask is, "How much a mile?" and, when the coachman has given you the information, you will have added to the stock of knowledge which you already possess. You can thank him for the information, and retire. If, however, you are uncertain of the distance, rise early in the morning, procure a short, or long piece of tape, go over the ground, cheerfully reflecting the while, that one day you'll have to go under it, and measure carefully : this will give you a nice walk before breakfast, of course to Darmstadt, and then you'll be in a position to withstand all attempts at extortion. To enable you to measure correctly, provide yourself with a TWO FOOT RULE OF THE ROAD.

Consideration for those millionnaires who can afford to be carried, shall not prevent us from turning our attention to the poor pedestrians.

General Precautions to be observed by Pedestrians and Others :—

When it rains, let the traveller stop at some inn on his road, so as not to get wet ;

And, when the warm Sun is shining, let the traveller stop at several inns on his road, so as not to get dry.

CHAPTER VII.

ANTWERP—THE CATHEDRAL—A LOOK AT ST. LUKE'S—VISIT TO THE
CONSUL.

WHAT with our driving and our walking tours, we find ourselves rapidly leaving Antwerp. We therefore, if you
please, and if you don't please it can't be helped, will return to
the Hotel of St. Antony.

On your arrival, let it be your first endeavour to prove to the
as- regards - English- manners- benighted -and-totally - uninstructed
citizens, that *you*, at all events, have none of that phlegmatic reserve and dulness of spirits which are the characteristics, we hear,
of so many of our travelled countrymen.

Proceed thus : never leave off whistling or singing, except
when you're shouting, speaking, laughing, eating, or drinking ;
this will show lightness of heart and head, innocence of disposition, and cheeriness of manner not to be surpassed by the most
volatile of our liveliest neighbours. Get rid of your *vigilant*
that means a cabman, when there is one, by giving his horse a
sharp cut with the whip and saying, "Hoop ! tchk ! come up !"
and off he will set, as hard as he can lay legs to the ground,
down the street, and, of course, his owner after him. Now then
for a good old practical joke, which, however, being quite new
here, will establish your reputation for hilarity from the very
minute of its execution.

Begin thus :—Tell the crowd who are looking on that you're
going to "play at Pantomimes." They won't know what you
mean, but that is of no consequence ; and, by the way, this fact
is equally true as regards the majority of people who, during the
season, are intensely interested in listening to the poetical
libretti of Italian operas. Commence humming, "*Rum tum tiddle
tiddle*," any words you like here, to give the idea of the never-
ceasing music in the orchestra at Christmas. Knock with your
open hand three times at the door of the hotel, and then lie
down flat on your face in front of it. If the proprietor is up to
the business (and if not, why is he in that situation, we'd like

to know?) he will wait until after the third knock; when he will open the door, look straight before him, smile blandly, rub his hands, and at the first step of his advance fall over your prostrate form. You yourself must be up on your legs as nimbly as possible, and lose no time in belabouring the weak-minded tradesman with one of his own advertisement boards. When he *does* rise, he will only shake his fist at you, and will immediately allow himself to be mollified by your putting your hand on your heart, bowing politely, assuring him that "*you* didn't do it," and then intimating that "you are willing to pay for accommodation in his house."

"Business" with shopkeeper.

You will be shown to your bedroom, when it will be as well at once to ask for a tallow candle to rub the floor with, and make a slide, on which the proprietor will be the first to fall; then ring for a warming-pan, a kettle, a large box labelled Pills, concluding the performance by jumping into bed with your clothes on. You may now consider that you have done enough to prove yourself several degrees removed from those proud, cold, say-nothing-to-nobody sort of Englishmen, who are so generally to be met upon the Continent.

In the morning, and also during the entire day, you will hear the Chimes of Antwerp Cathedral. The ambitious Tourist may seat himself upon his portmanteau, and interpret the language of the bells as "Turn again, Robinson" (Jones and Smith are out of the question), "Lord Mayor of Antwerp." They don't of course say anything of the kind, and there is no Lord Mayor.

The name of this town is, as we have said before, Antwerp; but the French, with their usual perversity, *will* call it *Anvers.* The pronunciation of this name reminds us, that the tune, which the Cathedral clock plays, may possibly be

" Anvers and Anvers is my Hieland Laddie gone ? "

However, this is simply interesting to the man who winds up the works: on second thoughts we remember, that the economical authorities have provided themselves with a permanent winding staircase in the Church Tower, which saves the expense of employing a clockmaker.

There is an ancient society in Antwerp called St. Luke's, to which the artists belong : it corresponds, we believe, to St. Luke's in London, of which several Royal Academicians might be distinguished members.

Be the weather fine or wet, the Tourist may walk about the streets of Antwerp all day *free of charge.*

Gratis Exhibitions.—The Exterior of the Cathedral can be well seen from earliest dawn till quite dark ; also, the outside of several Churches ; and from the same side, an excellent view can be obtained of the Museum.

The Theatre, we are informed, is only open for a part of the year ; and that part is always well filled.

The British Consul may be seen for twopence a head through a glass-door. Feeding time at one o'clock, when the price of admission is raised. No one is admitted after the Consul is once quite full. There is no deception, he is alive, and will shake hands, talk affably, and answer any questions that may be put to him. Sticks and umbrellas must be left in the hall.

The Post Office in this town is not the same as the Post Office in another town, and is, on this account alone, worth the trouble of a visit.

We now consider that the time has arrived when, previous to quitting Antwerp, we may give a few more—

General Hints for the Tourists.—Always *shout* out your English sentences at foreigners. They're all deaf. Your only other chance of being understood is by talking broken English to them. For what is the good of speaking your perfect mother-tongue to those who cannot understand it? It's simply a waste of words.

A pushing acquaintance.—An Anglo Gallican sketch.

Take it for granted that every one is trying to cheat and impose upon you.

Dispute every item in every bill separately.

To ensure civility and respect, see that all your portmanteaus, bags, and hat-boxes be labelled MURRAY in the largest capitals.

CHAPTER VIII.

GERMANY—LANGUAGE—COIN—THE BUREAU—MEYERBEER—KANT—
HARZ MOUNTAINS—WESTPHALIA—POLICE!

The tourist's glass.

HE Tourist will now leave Antwerp with a view (which can be purchased at any stationer's shop) of going up the Rhine. He probably will have determined upon walking up several mountains, and so, by way of practice, he should have begun by running up a considerable bill at his Hotel.

Now, if you are a mere machine in the hands of Murray, your attention will be attracted by the name of the next place, *Turnhout;* but if you'll take our advice, you will not turn out of your way to go there. There is merely a monastery to be seen, where dwell the Monks of La Trappe. The chief of the order resides in Paris, and is called Père la Chaise. As may be gathered from these titles, their occupation is to let out flys, broughams and saddle-horses.

Cologne is to be our next point? Yes? very good. Then Cologne be it. For Germany! Away! away! Music, and scene changes to.

GERMANY.—This country is bounded on every side by a lot of places, but that it has any connection with the German Ocean is a mere German notion that must be at once dispelled. The male population are called Germans, the female, of course, Gerwomans; the rest of the family Ger-boys, Ger-girls, Ger-babbies, and so on.

The natives call their country Fatherland, and it therefore follows that the Mother-tongue is never spoken. The enterprising Tourist having to reach many farther lands than Ger-many Father-

The official in his bureau.

land, must not be stopped too long by etymological considerations.

The money of the country is simply divided into good and bad. To the former description, however, belongs the current coin.

As a General Rule for Economical Travellers the ordinary English Sixpence will go a very long way if, for instance, you carry it with you from London to Constantinople, or any other distant spot. The Prussian dollar was, some time ago, of so little value as to be merely *nix* in the market. Hence the proverb, musically expressed by that ri-tooral Tourist, Mr. Paul Bedford, in the words, "*Nix my dollar!*"

All Germans have long or short light-hair, to which natural ornament you will often hear them make allusion by saying "Yah, mine hair."

Their habits are simple, being coat, waistcoat, and continuations, as worn in England.

The use of a parry-pluie.

Their language possesses only one word of any importance, and that is "zo," which monosyllable, according to the tonic inflexion given to it, means everything and anything you like.

Passports.—The traveller in Germany must have a passport, that is, an Order to see the place. No orders are admitted after seven. Evening dress is not now rigidly insisted upon, unless you're going to stop the night in a city or village; when, of course, you would adopt it for your own comfort. If you are a member of Oxford or Cambridge, it is considered a graceful compliment on entering such a town as Heidelberg at eleven o'clock P.M. to appear before the authorities in your University nightcap and gown. The official who sits in his Bureau (you'll find him in the top drawer, left-hand side) will ask you if you're going to sleep there, to which you can reply by going to sleep there and then. English ladies travelling need not be in the least degree shocked at the mention of the officer in the drawers of his Bureau. There is no

Carrying out your directions.

breach of decorum here, and everything is conducted with due regard to propriety.

German Hotels.—If you are going to stop, and if you are not *going*, you will, of course, *stop*, it will be as well to come to some understanding with the landlord. If *he* doesn't speak English, and *you* do not speak German, and neither know French, an understanding will be a difficult matter. There is some legend attached to almost every old house in Germany, and all the ancient hostelries are full of long storeys. See that your bed-room window commands a pretty view, which is invariably an object with *us*: if you fail to get such a prospect, that's your look out, not ours.

Beds.—" The German bed is only made for one." This is what Murray says, and consequently the simple Tourist, acting correctly as he imagined, upon this information, has, on arriving at a German town, immediately ordered a bed to be made for him. This is, we need hardly point out, an unnecessary expense ; as, even after the bed has been actually made for you, you cannot take it away. This rule does not in any part of Germany or Prussia apply to a hat or coat, which article, once made to order, becomes your own property.

Drinks.—You will find that the Germans are far ahead of the English in the point or pint of beer. *We* have hop gardens, such as those of Cremorne and Highbury. *They* get a step beyond this and encourage Beer-gardens. The beer, of which they are most justly proud, is Meyerbeer. The pedestrian journeying along the high roads will encounter a number of beggars who will address him in canting tones : this is the worst specimen of the whine of the country. These mendicants, by the way, are generally Philosophers, and disciples of Kant.

Geography.—The celebrated Harz Mountains are *not* in Germany, as is the common supposition. These heights are in Scotland ; and, in proof of this, every one will recollect the words of the national melody

" My Harz in the Highlands."

The natives in the eastern districts are known as a race highly successful in everything they undertake. In the west, however, the reverse of this is the case, and from the unhappy results which have attended all their efforts at an improved cultivation, the district has long been known as that of " West-failure."

Manners and Customs.—If five Germans are walking in a row, and meet a lady with whom only one of the party is acquainted, all the five take off their hats. If you meet five Germans you will raise your hat five times. The Englishman must take his politeness with him to the uttermost parts of the earth ; he can never, in our opinion, carry it too far. If you ever refuse to take your hat off to German strangers, you had better take yourself off immediately afterwards. As a stranger you will be expected to fight all the German students, who may be residing in the same town with yourself: if you do not conform to this rule, you will find every one for whom you have any regard turn away from you; and surely 'tis better to be cut by a few students than by many friends. At dinner you will be careful to convey peas, beans, and gravy to your mouth by means of your knife. The feat requires some practice, and for some time your meals will have the dangerous

The "slips."

character of a "Sensation" entertainment so popular now-a-days.

Now then on we goes to Cologne. Your luggage, mind, must be weighed, to send that baggage on its weigh as speedily as possible.

At railway stations every one, except the railway guard, is uncivil, and though there are plenty of porters, you will find it necessary to carry your boxes yourself. Take them all at once, as you must never on any account part with your luggage. Supposing that you are not well up in the language, keep on shouting out the name of your ultimate destination : this will attract the guard's attention, and he will put you into the proper compart. ment. Wherever you are going, you will have to change carriages three times at least on the road. Take this for granted, and change carriages at every station. · Show your passport and railway-ticket to everybody, so that there may be no mistake. If you can't smoke, always travel second-class, and you'll soon get in the way of it.

Be careful to observe all police regulations. On your arrival at any place, you, being widely suspected, are narrowly watched. Two policemen in plain clothes dog your steps day and night. The man who attends you as a *laquais de place* is a Government ·spy, who, unless you fee him well, reports everything you say, and plenty that you do not say, to his employers. If you want to go out for a walk by yourself for more than two hours, you must procure a "permit" from the police. The charge for a walk by yourself is seven-and-sixpence for the first hour, five shillings for the second, half-a-crown the third and the rest. The Rest would of course naturally come after the third hour's walk, If you wish to take an umbrella with you, notice must be given two days beforehand.

Very good. Now having got your ticket, you've taken your seat in the carriage by the kind permission of the police, and in a few hours you will be at Cologne.

CHAPTER IX.

COLOGNE ON THE DEUTZ SIDE—THE GARDENS—THE INTERIOR OF
THE CATHEDRAL—ARTISTIC NOTE—NOTICE TO QUIT—THE
BILL—QUITS—THERE AND BACK FOR NOTHING!—TRINKGELD
—EISENBAHN TELEGRAPH.

The railway belle.

ERE we are at Cologne, a German Cologney. You will stay a short time; let us say that you will stop for the space of a semi-Cologne. Cross the bridge, taking care however not to go over it, and take up your abode at Belle-vue the Hotel, Deutz side.

It is said to be the "largest and wealthiest city on the Rhine." So far Murray; but if this is so, what does he mean by saying "*Pop.* 100,000?" "Pop" is, of course, a delicate way of hinting at the existence, in this place, of that number of Pawnbrokers.

You will dine at the *table d'hôte*, unless for privacy's sake you like to order the *table d'hôte* all to yourself in a separate apartment, in which case the hungry visitors will be rather astonished. You would probably fill yourself, but you would empty the hotel, and very soon there would be—

"No one in de house wid Diner."

Howbeit, you must remember that he who stops to eat, remains to pay.

In the evening, sit out in the garden overlooking the moonlit Rhine, and become poetical. "Wine" rhymes to "Rhine;" and in the mouth of any affected demi-swell, the roll of whose pedigree is probably as slight as the roll of his R, the word is precisely the same. You have seen the *tableau* n the opening of an Opera. Here you have the original. Peasants, priests, soldiers, and travellers, grouped about the grounds, drinking, laughing, and talking while the band is playing. Mark your time, and by way of showing your appreciation of the scene, come forward to the lights, cup in hand, and give them a tune. The libretto might be, for instance—

> Wine! Wine! Wine!
> Liquor of Rhine.
> Ichor divine.
> Mine! Mine! Mine! } and
> Thine! Thine! Thine! }
> Oh, it is pleasant, 'tis pleasant,
> At present, at present,
> To drink THE Wine.
> Spar-ar-ar-kling Wine! Spar-ha !-klingwine !

This may be followed by a short dance, very short, and you will then be, probably, kicked out. This will not prevent your returning in order to show that you bear no malice, and can enter into the fun of the thing.

Sights in the City.—The best sight is unfortunately hidden from view. It is the sight upon which the City of Cologne stands. After this, the Cathedral. Cologne Cathedral is older than the Nelson Column, but is even in a less finished state. The order of architecture to which this noble pile belongs was probably "Building by contract," and one of the parties failed. To describe it minutely would be tedious; we will therefore say that the doors have a good deal of open work about them, and great panes have been taken with the windows. The only *pointed* style in the Cathedral to attract the Tourist's notice, will be that of his Cicerone, by whom everything inside will be pointed out to him.

Caution.—Beware of the Suisse, that magnificient Esquire-

Bedell in the Cathedral. For all he looks so grandly harmless, his hat is cocked, and may, by way of a salute, *go off*. Beware!

The *Choir* is about 161 feet high; more than a hundred treble octaves above the level of the C. The Base of the Cathedral assists on Sundays, and tones down what would otherwise rise into a screech.

In one of the side Chapels, where you'd naturally expect a

"Spar-ar-ar-kling Wine! Spar-ha l-klingwine!

piece of sculpture by Chantrey, you will find an old painting in Distemper. The Society for the Prevention of Cruelty to Animals ought to remonstrate with the Foreign Ecclesiastical Authorities on the subject of this picture. Poor thing! in Distemper since 1410!

There's plenty more to be seen, but you've got a pair of eyes we suppose, and we really cannot stop here talking all day. We saw everything in the place, why shouldn't you? Do you give it

up ? If you do, come along somewhere else. As we suppose that
you have, of course, lost your luggage, it is not necessary that
you should return to your hotel, where you'd only have to pay
your bill, and thus make yourself uncomfortable on that score.

Notice.—There are many books published now-a-days informing
the tourist how to see the Continent for five or ten pounds in as
many weeks. We can tell him how to see it for nothing. Insist
that the steamboat brought you by mistake while you were saying
good bye to a friend ; go away saying you'll bring an action
against them, and they'll offer to take you back again ; disdain
their proffered courtesy ; they'll be frightened and offer you money
not to tell ; if they do, take it ; if not, they'll be only too glad to
put you on shore and get rid of you. After this, unencumbered
by packages, your course is easy. The hotel is not built that can
hold *you* for any length of time. You can tell the various landlords that you are going out to look for your luggage, and this
search may reasonably take you many miles away from the place
where your last little bill was run up. The trains go so slow,
that, with very little practice, you can easily get out during the
journey and thus avoid all those absurd forms and ceremonies
attendant upon rendering up the ticket, which, as you, when
travelling economically do not possess it, would simply waste time,
and would materially retard an otherwise rapid progress. Your
foreign fellow-travellers, will, if asleep, not see you ; for they have
a way of closing their eyes when in a somnolent state, and, in this
particular, resemble Englishmen. If their eyes are open, the
fumes of tobacco will be an effectual cloak for your exit. Should,
however, any one of them see you and tell, the chances are that
the rest won't believe him : and if they do, they'll merely laugh
at the eccentricities of the English, and consider your conduct as
the ordinary mode of travelling adopted in your own country.
The railway carriage is your only difficulty, and we've shown you
the way to get out of it. In this manner a great deal more of
the country will be seen than if you were shut up in a close compartment.

The man who prodigally pays his way and tips the servants, is
sometimes remembered ; but the man who doesn't is never for-

gotten. They will be looking out for you everywhere, they will be even anxious about your health, and be desirous of seeing you again as soon as possible. This is affecting, but don't stop for it. Hire some conveyance that will gallop past the well-remembered windows, whence are peering the old familiar faces. Be open-handed with them as befits your generous nature, and wave adieux

A cocked hat going off.

from your fast disappearing vehicle. You can always get rid of the driver by asking him to get down and pick up that parcel you've dropped in the road. When he has retraced about three hundred feet of the road, jump into the box-seat, crack your whip, cry "Tchk!" and then once more urge on your wild career. You can sell the carriage and ride the horse, which, after carrying you some distance, will fetch a sum that will enable you to travel like a gentleman when you get back to England. If any Economical

Tourist's Companion can show us a better method than this, we should be glad to know it. We will tell you *How to go to Cologne for Nothing !* Well, you see, if you've nothing to go for, why, there you are. This advice is only applicable to a minority of loungers.

Now we've seen everything that can be seen, and we're going to quit Cologne. Let us turn our attention to post-travelling and payments appertaining thereto.

German miles are different to English or Irish miles. In olden times there was a league of barons, counts, and dukes, which must have had as queer an effect as seven-miles' worth of the aristocracy would have in England. By this league all other distances were measured; and the greatest distance was between the last baron and the first shopkeeper. Leave your card upon the Chief Baron before the long vacation commences, and he will tell you all about it.

Postmasters are empowered by Government to compel their passengers to carry the horses and drag the carriages up all the hilly places. When you hear and see a high hill you will doubtless exclaim "Hillo!"

Trinkgeld, drink-money, is the sum given by way of liquidating your debt to the postilion.

Before journeying by carriage take the number of your horses : this ensures civility.

Purchase, for your own private reading, all the back numbers of the *Eisenbahn Telegraph* which is a *German Bradshaw !* With a very slight knowledge of the language you may derive considerable pleasure from the daily study of this delightful work. The only man who ever attempted it, was ultimately found all alone in his room at the hotel, trying to set the railway guide to music, marking each bar with the time of the different trains. He is now quite harmless, and passes his days in playing elaborate fantasias from *Bradshaw's Railway Guide* for the current month, on the bassoon or violoncello.

CHAPTER X.

UP THE RHINE—OBERWESEL—STEAMERS—ST. GOAR—TO THE LURLEI
BERG—TO LUR-LI-ETY—BEATE MARTINE!—ASSMANHAUSEN—
BINGEN—RUDESHEIM—STOLZENFELS—RAT'S CASTLE—LEGEND—
MAYENCE.

"Now I'm Comfortable!"

P AND down the River
Rhine, In and out the vessel,
that's the way the money
goes. Stop! Oberwesel! and
there we are at a half-way
house on the Rhine. We
may call one of the inns by
this name, as it is partly
hotel, partly dairy or as it
may be termed, half-beer
half-whey house.

While *bateau-à-vapeur*-ing
up the Rhine, we will make
a few observations on Steamboat travelling.

The one general rule that
governs all voyagers by
steamboat is, "No one
must *speak* to the Man at the Wheel;" but you may
whistle at him, howl at him, shout at him, or dance before him as
much as you like. It is the part of genius to break through rules;
therefore, if you would not be set down for a mere commonplace
Tourist, take pity upon his isolated condition, and commence an
animated conversation with the steerer. Whisper soft nothings in
his ear; tell him that "good thing you heard the other day," and
point your jokes with your forefinger under his fifth rib.

You may wave your hat and halloa in front of him; this is
a very good way of cheering him upon his lonely voyage.

An you understand not his language, nor he yours, make faces
at him until he roars with laughter, and finish by singing to him

in your best style, "*O Wheellie, we have missed you!*" when he, being of a sympathetic soul, will join you in the melody, playing rhapsodically upon the spokes of his wheel. Others on board may laugh and be jolly, but he remains throughout the one stern passenger, unless, as we have suggested, you can overcome his unnatural reserve. He seldom moves from his position, yet is he perpetually taking a turn on deck. We never

IT IS NOT
PERMITTED TO
WITH THE HELMSMAN
SPEAK.

ES IST VERBOTEN
MIT DEM STOVERMAN
ZU SPECHEN

"O Wheellie, we have missed you!"

met anybody who knew one of these men "at home." We cannot help thinking that they have run away from the domestic circle. Maybe, for some dark crime, they are undergoing a self-enforced silent system, rendered all the more difficult of endurance by the opportunities of communication with their fellow-men which their situation offers. In consequence of the Helm obeying the will of this roving recluse, the Germans have but one generic name for the class, every individual member of which they address as Will-Helm Meister.

Steamboat travelling differs from Railroad travelling, inasmuch as the authorities of the former take you on trust, not demanding your fare until they have carried you for some distance upon the voyage. The first feeling produced by this system in the breast of an honest Englishman is gratitude to the beneficent beings who, apparently, are going to give you a trip for nothing. On the approach of the inevitable money collector, this sentiment is entirely superseded by a desire to avail yourself of those facilities of personal locomotion which a deck affords, to dodge the official, and avoid that mutual unpleasantness and misunderstanding which must result from one person demanding as a right that which another person is unwilling to concede of his own free will.

The Collector, you will notice, is closely followed by another wary official, who is doubtless set as a watch upon his superior officer, lest that individual, having collected the money, should suddenly collect himself for a spring and violently abscond by leaping over the side of the vessel, and by a bold stroke of genius swimming to shore.

Here we come alongside of the bank, and for a minute or two we must touch upon this point.

It is a dear, or rather cheap, at least we found it so, old place called St. Goar. You will perhaps smile at any of the Rhine show-places being cheap, and will say, ironically, "Go-ar-long!" but nevertheless such is the fact.

Hereabout there is a whirlpool which tumultuously eddies round a horrid rock. Hence the proverb, "'Tis the Lurlei Berg catches the Whirl." We heard a Cockney drop an H and a remark, to the effect, that, it "made him quite 'eddy to look at it."

The Church of St. Martin is a specimen of one of the very earliest churches, in consequence of the service commencing every morning at 4 A.M. The ancient and well-known legend can, we believe, be found here, if you look very carefully for it, commencing "*O mihi, Beate Martine,*" &c.

Then you come to Assmanhausen, so called because the donkey-man has his house in this place, whose animals can be hired by day or hour, by your or our party, as the case may be, for the sake of making excursions into the vineyard country. The public conveyance, in this part of the world, is called the *Van* Ordinaire.

"Don't be offended with the captain if he tells you to "get out" at Bingen. You'll want to go to Rüdesheim. There is a regular charge for donkeys at this place, so you had better keep out of the way; or, if in your own country you are a Volunteer, prepare to receive the charge with your umbrella. It was at this place, that we saw the heart-rending spectacle of a French tourist arriving too late by a minute and a half for the departure of his steamboat. An Englishman in a similar position, after a few words of very old Saxon, would have inquired for the time of the next boat, and would have waited at the nearest Hostelrie for its arrival. Not so Mossoo; he anathematised his hard fortune and the day of his birth. He dashed his hat on the ground, and danced on it: he tore his hair, and at length in a passionate burst of tears he sat down on his portmanteau, and consented to listen to the voice of reason issuing from the mouth of a stolid Prussian porter.

" Paddle on all," and away we go again.

To keep and find your place in " Murray," and at the same time find the corresponding places on the Right and Left Banks of the River, is a feat of no ordinary difficulty. You should read it thoroughly before starting, and you will then be able to enjoy yourself and benefit your companions.

" What is that place ?" inquires a fellow-tourist without a Guide Book, attracting your attention to Stolzenfels.

" That ?" you reply, pretending that you haven't been cramming up the Rhine history over-night. " That is Bishop Ratto's Castle, so called because when he was refused by the Fair Guda, he made the child Werner eat all the rats in his barn, while every one was shouting out ' the Rhine ! the Rhine !' as with the voice of one man. For this barbarous deed he was thrown into the river, where he was subsequently interred and canonised."

The only newspapers published in the Vineyard Country, are issued from the Wine Press. In the fruitful season, which is also the shooting season, you will often see a poor peasant, who is unable to buy a gun in order to keep off the small birds, watching for the tiny depredators of the vines, having previously loaded himself with grape.

In Steamboat travelling, a rug, a great coat, a portable bath, a carpet-bag, a hatbox, a portable writing-case, race-glasses, an umbrella, a camp stool artfully compressed into a peculiarly inconvenient walking-stick, are absolutely necessary to the tourist who wishes to make himself thoroughly uncomfortable. He sits on his camp-stool, wraps himself up in his rug and great coat, places his portable bath on his hatbox, and his feet on the portable bath, settles his writing-desk on his knees, puts his umbrella up to protect him from the sun, and saying to himself, " Now I'm comfortable !" vainly tries to read his " Murray." Whenever he would

turn over a page, down must go the umbrella, and on getting the
race-glasses out of the case in order to look at the scenery which
can probably be seen a great deal better with the unclothed eye,
down goes umbrella and "Murray." If you leave the things, and
walk up and down the deck, you will be nervously suspicious
about every one who goes near them, and will keep on returning
to the spot, until finding them on every fresh occasion in their
original position, you will say to yourself, "Away, base suspicion!
Hence, fear!" and giving yourself up to the allurements of the
Nymphs of the Rhine, will gradually cease to remember your en-
cumbrances, and upon disembarking, in the anxiety for the safety
of your trunk or portmanteau, will forget the lesser properties altogether. In this state we get out of the boat at Mayence, and not
having as yet found out the loss, proceed in ignorant bliss to the
Rheinischer Hof, Hof which you have probably heard a very good
account, and will certainly, on leaving, receive at the hands of
the disinterested landlord, a very moderate account indeed

The juice is in it.

CHAPTER XI.

THE RHEINISCHER HOF—ARRIVAL AT AN HOTEL WITHOUT BOOTS—
OPERATIC—MONEY-LENDERS' OFFICES AND OTHER OBJECTS OF
INTEREST IN MAYENCE—MANNHEIM—SPIRES.

"Now I'm'appy."

THE serenely happy Tourist will now remember that he has just arrived at Mayence, without his rug, hatbox, umbrella, carpet-bag, portable bath, race-glasses, walking-stick-campstool, and writing-desk, all of which he has accidentally left on board the steamer that is now bearing his treasures to Mannheim. As he reaches the door of the Rheinischer Hof, the sense of the fearful loss comes upon him like a flash of lightning. He claps his hands to his pockets, not meaning as it were to applaud them for having done something clever, but with a vague idea that the portable bath, campstool, and carpet-bag may not be so far off after all. What before were luxuries, now assume an importance that makes them appear absolutely indispensable. " Everything," he cries, " was in my carpet-bag ! I can't get on without a rug ! and what the dash can I do at Baden-Baden if I haven't got a hatbox ? My soap's in my carpet-bag, so's my brush, and comb and—and —my other boots ! " By the way, those other boots, always carried and not required, or if not carried, invariably wanted, are sure to be lost during the trip. *A propos de Boots*, however, we will just stop for one minute to say that, if any traveller, fond of grandly romantic scenery, wishes to make certain of seeing a good *fall of water* he had better *trip up the Rhine with his boots.*

To return to the missing articles.

As landlords and waiters everywhere are supposed to know everything, the obvious course will be at at once to question them on the subject.

"Were the articles directed?" asks the host.

"O-o-h his portable bath!"

The Tourist patiently explains that he doesn't generally label a rug, great-coat, and an umbrella, but inwardly regrets that he had allowed the direction, "Mr. Smith, Passenger to Bristol," to remain upon his portable bath.

"Monsieur knows the name of his *bateau à vapeur?*" the landlord suggests, mixing a little French and English, in order to show that he is prepared for his customer whatever he may say.

Monsieur however hasn't got the slightest notion what was the name of the "battue a vampire," and prides himself upon having pronounced the name right *that* time, anyhow.

"Ah!" says the landlord, "Monsieur knew the Captain?"

"Good heavens! No: nor the Stoker, nor Boiler, nor Man at the Wheel, nor anybody connected with the steamer."

"Did they see where you got out?" asks the landlord.

The tourist had been so engaged with his large luggage, that he had not noticed if, in stage phrase, "he had been observed."

"The boat stops at Mannheim," the landlord remarks.

"Well, there, I suppose," suggests the traveller, "they take out all the luggage."

"Yes," replies the proprietor of the Rheinischer Hof, "and if the things are not claimed at once——"

"Well?" inquires our friend, anxiously noting a slight hesitation on the speaker's part in arriving at the catastrophe.

"Well," resumes Rheinischer Hof, slowly, "if they are not claimed at once—they sell them."

> "Tourist! a blight is on thy path—
> What'll become of the portable bath!"

Whistle the air of the "*Mistletoe Bough*" and sing,—

> "Oh, my portable bath!
> O-o-h! My por-tar-blebath!"

Chorus, in which the sympathising landlord and waiters will (if not otherwise engaged, and if conversant with the air,) join,—

> "O-o-h his portable bath!
> O-o-oh his port-tar-blebath!"

After this, order dinner, see your room, shake hands with the landlord, and determine to let byegones be byegones.

The most remarkable object in Mayence will be, of course, yourself. Do not let the knowledge of this importance prevent you from visiting the Cathedral. Protestant though you may be, you will be here received into the Church by the Suisse, who is generally a fine handsome-looking man, of whom the ladies say in Suisse-whispers, "Do look at his Suisse-whiskers!" The French, ever attached to the lightest possible literature, once converted this Cathedral into a Magazine. It soon, however, fell to the ground, and now-a-days very little that is original remains, as the people subsequently took all their articles from the French.

Even though you, or any other tourist, may have given up all idea of lying hands upon the lost baggage, yet should you, as a pedestrian, walk to Mannheim. At this place you'll halt, and probably begin to limp as one maimed by the unwonted exercise, unless you have been previously accustomed to do the same thing, or as the French call it, *maim*-chose, or shoes, as in this case.

A pleasant wet day may be spent at Mannheim, by trying to find out, by the aid of the Mannheim Directory, the address of your old friend who has performed the Samson-like gymnastic feat known as "Taking up his Residence," in this ancient town. We've often heard of Dramatic critics being able to "give a theatre a lift with their pens," and we suppose that these expressions are the results of a strong muscular creed.

But to the Directory.

Mannheim houses are not as other houses. They are arranged in blocks, chiefly blocks of stone. The streets intersect one another at right angles wherever they can, and at wrong angles wherever they can't, and by generally interfering with one another in the most unaccountable manner, produce upon the mind of the stranger the feeling that he might as well be in Fair Rosamond's Bower, or the Maze at Hampton Court, without the sweet little cherub who sits up aloft and sings out "To your right —To your left," and other intelligible instructions to help him on his way.

The streets have no names, though they will have, and pretty hard ones too, after you've been puzzling and meandering about them.

The simple direction for finding out where anybody lives is, ask him himself on the first opportunity; but if you can't see him, and haven't got time to write, take the Directory, and observe that all the blocks are arranged alphabetically, that the house are numbered, and that there are many blocks more than the Alphabet has letters, and that then you begin again and make the best you can of it. That's plain so far, isn't it? Well, let's

say you want to call on Mr. B. Very good. Mr. B. you find
lives at A., now on this point you will not be at Sea. Then A.
being a block, you find the number; now, we forgot to mention
that each block is numbered as well as every house, so that when
you've ascertained the number of the house, you must take care
not to confuse it with the number of the block, and when you've
carefully arrived at a knowledge of both numbers, your next step

"Lightest possible literature!"

will be to retrace your former ones, and see whether you were
correct in the first instance. After this, take care that the block
is the block in the Alphabet and not one out of the Alphabet;
then see that the number is the same as the one you had fixed
upon, and finally learn whether or no B. lives at this number or
not. After this it will be time for you to brush your hair and go
to bed.

Visit the Theatre, which was once reduced to a mere shell by the Austrian bombs. Ever since then all the Pieces have gone off well.

The Cathedral was pretty considerably knocked about by the French, who chipped and clipped pillars and statues and sepulchral monuments. Here some Margraves are buried; the iconoclastic French, however, appear to have been the principal mar-graves. They compelled the ecclesiastics to fly for their lives, and each one of the good monks was forced to take up his breviary and mizzle.

There is no inducement for the traveller to follow the Rhine above Mannheim, and the Rhine might look upon such a proceeding as going rather too far. You're not Grant and you're not Speke, so none of your sourcey observations, if you please. Come move on! will you, and just drop in at Spires. This place was built by the same ingenious architect who raised the one spire in Langham Place, Regent Street, of which this town is merely (as the name implies) an ample development. Keep your eyes open and you will be Spyers too. Mind you ask for the celebrated Diet of Spires at the *table d'hôte*. Don't be put down by the unseemly jests of the landlord, or the gibing of the *Kellners*. Very interesting place, Spires, full of historical reminiscences, so on we go to Heidelberg.

CHAPTER XII.

HEIDELBERG—THE UNIVERSITY—THE CASTLE—A TUN AND A HALF
—TOXICOLOGY—BADEN-BADEN—THE BOARD OF GREEN CLOTH.

Pique and re-pique.

EIDELBERG, or the Bridge, the Town, and the Tower! This is our next point. A lazy old place, sure enough, with all the H'Idle burghers lounging in their shop doors, if there's nothing doing.

Every one here seems to have suddenly, in printers' phrase, been set up in small caps, for caps of all sorts, sizes, and colours, ornament the heads of the University youths. They are very free with their swords, and the following University rules are found necessary :—

1. Any Student refusing to give his name to the Proctor in the streets, may be immediately cut down by the bulldogs.

2. That in cramming for examinations, the armed Students *in statu pupillari* shall run through several authors.

3. That every candidate at Matriculation shall be able to translate Arnold's *Roman Sword Exercises.*

You will be considered a great man among them if you appear as a Professor of the Noble Art of Self Defence, and give Lectures on the New Cut, Lambeth.

Of course, the first thing you'll want to go and see is the Castle. Well, you'll have to go up a hill. This Castle was taken once by the French, and once by Mr. Turner, the celebrated artist. The

Electors Palatine, who used to live here, were people of *bon Tun*, as may be seen if you visit the cellar, where stands the celebrated Tun, on the top of which the peasants, when they were very jolly, used to dance. This was when the vintage had been a good one, and the happy rustics were living on the vat of the land. There is some trick connected with a fox's brush, that starts out of some-where suddenly, and hits you anywhere when you pull a string, of which we have some vague and unpleasant recollection ; if you don't want to know anything about it don't pull any string, and you'll be safe. This is of course the jest or rather the Butt of the place ; the good folks ought to get a second like it, on the excellent principle that " one good TUN deserves another."

Cold Steel!

Of course, while you are at Heidelberg you will stop at an Hotel. Now the mention of an hotel naturally leads us to the subject of pickles. You will be in a hurry to see the sights of the town, and desirous of making a rapid act of feeding. No more rapid act can be made than an attack upon cold beef and pickles. Tourist, beware in every place of pickles. Few and far between are the instances of jars of these luxuries being unadulterated. Avoid them as you would Jars in your own family. As a rule, these pickles *are* adulterated, and specially in Germany, with copper. Now copper in this form is first cousin to poison, and it is admitted on all hands that it is unpleasant to be poisoned anywhere, but specially in Germany, and more particularly in Heidelberg. Now then the question is, do you understand the science of Toxicology? If you can't pronounce this word, use any other you like; such names are but arbitrary; but bear in mind that this science has nothing to do with bows and arrows. On arriving therefore at your inn, immediately inquire of your landlord if he is a Toxicologist; the word may be sung or said, according to fancy, powers of vocalisation, or special opportunity. He may stammer out a reply, or he may not understand you : in either case, Tourist, beware, and having ordered at once your cold collation, immediately attempt to detect the presence of copper.

Tullaliety!

Now, the first way to detect the presence of copper, is to offer the lowest silver coin in your possession, and to ask for change for that amount. If they are unable to give it you, be on your guard, lest all the available copper may have been invested in pickles. If the sum in the metal is given you, remember that it may be but the residue of what has already been sunk in pickles. Cold steel will always attract copper : and a celebrated Italian brigand, when in a genial and communicative mood, once informed us that he had been able to detect the presence of copper in a landlord's pocket by introducing a small and exquisitely shaped dagger into the corporeal vicinity of that region. This is a method which we would hardly advise the ordinary Tourist to adopt, but as he loves his health, and would avoid dyspepsia, let him study Toxicology, or whatever he likes to call it, and give his earnest consideration to the subject of pickles. *Experientia docet*, and he who doesn't take warning by our *experientia*, will have to "dose it" pretty considerably. After this we need hardly say that you'll leave this romantic town as quickly as possible. For ourselves, having found that we were treading upon this mine of copper, we, nearly exploding with indignation, took a light luncheon, and then went off with our present report. Away to

Baden-Baden, merely observing that the railway by which you travel has all its seats ("Murray" says) "comfortably stuffed full," and therefore it must be very difficult to procure a place to yourself. Be careful to say "That's the Ticket" to the railway clerk, when you take your billet for Baden-Baden. You know the reputation of this place for gambling, of course, and therefore you will not be surprised on entering the town, at once to be asked by the Inspector of Police, "How much you'll stake on the black?" or, "What are the odds against red turning up three times running?"

Whether you look black or turn red upon being thus addressed the surrounding natives will call at your hotel, leave their cards upon you, and subsequently give you their hands. Beware of such friendship. Baden-Baden is a very damp place, and one of the chief residents, the man who keeps the Bank at the Tables, suffers with the croup all the year round, and is therefore known as the Croupier. You will see plenty of Rakes on and about this Board of green cloth. When you have lost more than two florins, go away, take a pocket-pistol, and

Merry Swiss Boy!

treat yourself to a "blow out" at the nearest restaurant's. When we visited the Tables there were plenty of Americans playing at Rouge et Noir, and, we suppose out of compliment to their prejudices, the Croupier so managed the colours that the Black was invariably beaten. Whether you back Noir or not, you must be prepared with sufficient Ready. Having finished all your gamb'ling in the town, you can leave the valley and gambol on the hills. There are some very pretty walks about the place and some nice runs, the best being a good run of Luck in the Conversationshaus.

The excursionist, although personally objecting to the monastic system, should not refuse to take the vale of the Murg. Here you get a foretaste, or rather a one taste, of the coming Switzerland. Sing *Tullaliety, Tulla li-he-ho,* and prepare to be marching to the *Margin of fair Zurich's waters, Tullaliety, da capo.* By the way, the first *Merry Swiss Boy* we ever saw had taken a great deal more fruit than was good for him, and was bemoaning his sad fate at the hands of a peculiarly grim Swiss, or as she appeared in this instance, Swish matron.

CHAPTER XIII.

SWITZERLAND—DIET—MONEY—CONVEYANCES—ARTH—BASLE—BERNE —BY THE MARGIN OF FAIR ZURICH'S WATERS—SCHAFFHAUSEN FALLS—A PRETTY PASS.

The face of the Country.

OW here we are going into Switzerland as quick as possible, if you please, seeing that there's not much time to be lost, for the Vacation is just coming to a close, and some of us must be back to our griefs and briefs in the Classic *Aula Pumpeii,* otherwise known as Pump Court, Temple, or elsewhere.

An air of repose characterises the face of Switzerland, and the observant traveller may gather that the country is rather inclined to sleep, from the fact that he will continually see ranges of mountains rising and stretching away in the distance.

The Tourist intends to ascend the steeps? Does he, indeed?

then, once for all, we don't; albeit we may give some good advice; and first and foremost, as the unaccustomed traveller may possibly catch cold in the Alpine heights, he should be careful to provide himself with an Alpenstock to wrap round his easily-affected throat.* Beside this, you should carry a Swiss pipe, whereon to play as you walk lightly o'er the eternal snow, and a good collection of magic-lantern slides, to take you rapidly over the seas of ice.

Talking of ice, you must not be disappointed at not finding much of the Wenham Lake material up here. The Railway will, of course, make some difference in this respect after a time, and Mr. Gunter may be inclined to speculate. A Lake or Tarn of Fresh Strawberry Water, by Sunset, would be a fine subject for Mr. Telbin's brush, and, as every spoon of a Tourist is accompanied by a Tourist's glass, we want but some pretty girls to hand wafers and sponge-cakes to us, and the thing is done.

In regard to dress, adopt a gentlemanly evening suit : you will never require a change of boots ; as after an hour's walk over the ice, they will of their own accord become slippers. A false nose and burnt cork, wherewith to make moustachios, and playfully frighten the mountaineers, as usual.

Diet.—For Breakfast, ask for stewed zwanzigers and *cotelettes à la pommade.* There is no other meal during the day, but you can repeat this one as often as you feel disposed. During the repast, the good-natured waiter will read to you, sing one of the songs, or dance one of the enlivening dances of his own native land. You must, unless you would be accused of rudeness, *encore* every one of his performances separately.

Money. Swiss Batz.—This coin is no longer a legal tender, in consequence of so many Swiss Batz having been given in exchange for the English Kites, which had been flown by certain of our unprincipled compatriots in the neighbourhood.

Conveyances.—Recollect that your driver being a poor boor of a fellow, always requires some *pour boire* money, by way of a parting

---

* As you are apt to be tender with yourself, get some vicious friend to wrap the Alpen-stock smartly about your head. As a homœopathic cure for headache this can be recommended.

gift. The travelling lawyer will observe that, in all countries, an intimate connection exists between a conveyancer and his draughts.

One of the first places to which you will be taken, will probably be Arth. So rare is the stranger's visit in this quarter, that even the most civil officer, meeting the Tourist in the street, will start back with astonishment, and ask, " What on Arth he's doing there?" Being a man of spirit, you will at once quit the place, and proceed to Basle. The distance of Basle from anywhere is just three Basley-corns and a half. At the hotel called the Three Kings, you will find the servants very attentive, so don't say anything before them that you do not wish them to hear. They are so attentive, that it will be well for the visitor to blow through the keyhole of his bed-room door every five minutes, to see if the waiter is listening outside ; then to search well the chest of drawers, rattle his umbrella up the chimney, and look in every corner for these attentive inn-dependents. Of course, you do not want to follow the regular route, but intend to go backwards and forwards, and round and round, as suits your fancy. While on the subject it would be as well to state, that no steamer ever sailed round Switzerland in six hours. Berne is the quaintest of places. There was not much to be seen when we were there ; but this fact was probably owing to our arriving at eleven o'clock on a very dark night. Go early, and you'll be delighted. The clock is the most striking object in the town. As the Tourist cannot possibly be satisfied with anything until he has seen Zurich, let him hasten there at once, and put up at the hotel on the Lake.

One of the curiosities of this spot is the garden attached to the hotel ; it is so much attached, that, although for years it has been perpetually going down to the water, it has never yet been able to take the last steps necessary for the separation. A touching site this, touching the Lake ; and, by the way, touching the Lake, words are wanting to convey to the absent traveller any idea of its beauty. Let us see ; you know the Serpentine, or the ornamental water in St. James's Park? Well—no, it won't do ; our powers of description fail us.

Now is the time and place for a romantic adventure. There are plenty of Zurich's fair daughters living on the borders of the Lake. This mode of existence is, however, not exclusively confined to

these delightful creatures, but is also adopted by two or three
landlords and lodging-house keepers, who also live on the boarders.
By the way, here is a curious phenomenon for our astronomers.
Late at night the fair damsels come out to look at *the moon on the
water in a boat.* All you've got to do is to hide under a ripple,
and gently rise from the stream, like a river-god decked with

Zurich's fair daughters!

weeds, with a short-pipe in your mouth, whence shall issue sounds
most dulcet; and the fair ones must be a most dull set indeed if
they do not at once yield themselves captive to the fascinations of
your voice.

In a charitable spirit visit Schaffhausen, but do not make any
severe observations on The Fall, remembering that we are all
liable to err; and also recollecting that, if the landlady of the
Falls Hotel provide luncheon, you will be liable to *her.* We did

not think much of the food here, but this isn't the place to cut it up. Go back to Zurich. In the morning patronise the bath in the hotel garden. Plunge bravely in, headforemost, but you must be able to swim, for there is a depth of at least four feet of water.

Your next point will be the Righi, if you want to "do" the Righilar thing; if you do not, you will cross the lake and try to get over the mountains to Interlachen. The mountains are not to be got over by soft words, persuasion being, in this case, less useful than force with a good thick stick.

Do you want to see one of the great beauties of mountain scenery without much trouble? You do? Very well, then; lose all your luggage, ready money, clothes, and circular notes, and you'll then commence by being brought to a very Pretty Pass.

"The Righilar thing."

CHAPTER XIV.

THE RIGHI—HINTS TO MOUNTAINEERS—THE ALPINE CLUB—THE GHOST—HOTEL RIGHI CULM—A BRUSH WITH THE GUESTS.

Having a blow on the mountain.

UR own experience, which has led us to give the foregoing invaluable advice for going as far as the Righi, will now furnish the Tourist with a rule to be observed by every one who seeks this usually sunny climb. A great deal has been written at divers times, and in divers places, concerning the actual necessaries to be taken during an ascent. One thing, and only one, is it necessary for even the hardiest mountaineer to take while toiling up the precipitous steep; let his pace be slow, or let his pace be fast, walk he with tottering steps or firmly-planted feet; the Tourist, be he high or low, tall or short, *who goes up the Righi must take*—Breath.

Sit down awhile, and behold above you the broad expanse of sky; this will exalt your mind to the contemplation of the lark; and what says the Poet,—

> "Hark, hark, the dogs do bark,
> For the lark at Billingsgate sings."

Open your heart to your friend, if one be near you, but forget not to open your chest, and carp the vital airs. Ah! If you know any of the musical compositions of Dr. Blow, now is the occasion for whistling them. Walk up! walk up! walk up! To your left you'll see the black-beetling crags; these will remind you of the

D D

strange creatures that came up to look at you, and followed in
your wake, when you paid an unwilling nocturnal visit to the
kitchen, under the impression that you were about to bring a
couple of burglars to account for a wrong double entry. To your
right you'll see ever so many things that did not meet your vision
on your left, whereupon you will exclaim, "Beautiful! Beautiful!" somewhat after the well-known, time-honoured manner of
the talented German *siffleur*, Von Joel, evergreen, ever Green's!
Walk up! Walk up!

The agile admirer of the "beautiful for ever" (this line is not
meant by way of a toast or sentiment, though, apart from the
context, it may be adopted by members of the Alpine Club for
that purpose) will probably take a short cut, in order to reach the
bird's-eye view sooner than his fellow-travellers. Our own personal
remembrance of the short cut that we chose, is, that it began very
pleasantly, during which gentle progress and halcyon time we
congratulated ourselves upon our superior cunning; that, after
half an hour, the ascent became more decided, and we, being in a
broiling sun, jokingly comforted each other "that we shouldn't
have much of this;" that, in the course of an hour, the inclination
of the ascent increased inversely as our inclination *for* the ascent;
that, in an hour and a half's time, we sat down helplessly and
bemoaned our happy childhood: that, being parched with thirst,
we induced a little peasant boy to give us a drink; that he
brought us *kirschwasser* of such a strength and old shoe-leathery
state that we couldn't drink it, save when qualified with water,
which water he, for a few small coins, procured for us; our grateful remembrance of this boy is that he was a wonderful boy, the
most wonderful boy we'd ever seen; that, despite the fact of the
descent to the limpid stream being of the very early perpendicular
style of mountain architecture, this boy, this wonderful boy,
holding in his hand the broad-mouthed shallow wooden bowl of
kirschwasser, executed, after the manner of his English brethren in
the London streets, "three catherine wheels a penny," without
spilling a single drop (was he not a wooooonderful boy?), and in this
way arrived safely at the running stream. Here he filled the bowl,
and safely ascended to our place of session, walking or jumping,
as far as our memory serves us, upon his head. We rewarded

him handsomely, and he disappeared down somewhere as suddenly as he had risen before us ; a grin, a kick, a leap into the air—and he was gone ! There was no smell of brimstone ! Could he have been the lubber fiend ? The Kobbold of this country ? A Brownie, maybe ; and, now we recall the colour of his skin, we hesitate no longer to decide that we on that occasion did see a veritable Brownie.

Perpendicular becomes the ascent of the short cut, and he who takes this road will never use his feet as the sole mode of progression, until within a few yards of the Righi Culm.

Think you, O Tourist of the nineteenth century, that in Switzerland you can be free from——The Ghost ! * * *

Not a bit of it. If you're in luck's way, you'll see the spectre of the Righi. Of course it is patented. Give the waiter at the Righi Culm Hotel a noble gratuity, and he'll tell you all about it. Albeit, the only spectre we came across was the landlord of the above-mentioned hostelrie with his little bill, which shook our nerves fearfully. We were nearly running away, but were prevented by——no matter what.

Joyful is the moment when the golden spire of the Inn, effulgent, shines on the sun-scorched face of the weary travellers. Let us stop here to remark that, when we arrived at the top, we found that our short cut had taken us exactly two hours longer than going round by the ordinary route. This discovery at such a moment is calculated to act upon the temper even of the most angelic. You come late and can't get a room. Ha ! ha ! (*Stage direction, laughs sardonically.*) "Waiter !" "Yes, Sir." (*Exit waiter in the opposite direction.*) You turn and find him gone, or rather don't find him, because he *has* gone. Another menial in a blouse. Ha ! "Waiter ?" 'tisn't the waiter, but no matter. "*Garçon !*" "*Ouim'sieu.*" (*Exit second waiter, hurriedly, through a small door in the passage.*) In desperation, you open it in order to follow him. The door leads apparently nowhere, or to fifteen other doors, which means the same thing. "*Garçon ! Kellner ! Waiter !* Hi ! Here ! anybody—I want to wash. Hot water—*donney more o show.* No, I mean *eau sucrée*— no, that's swearing—I mean——." Never mind what you mean, the *table d'hôte* is nearly ready. Rush into the kitchen regard not the screams of the men-servants or maid-servants, nor the stricken cook, but wrench the boiling kettle from its brooding o'er the coals, and make for the first dressing-room at hand; stand not upon the order of your going, but go it! Should Kellner interfere, cry, "This to decide!" One, two, three, four, under: one, two, three, four, over—thrust, and he falls. You reach a chamber. Lots of queer-patterned crockery about, seize and take

"Donney more o show!"

anything to wash your hands in. Soap and nail-brush in your pocket of course. "*Garçon! Femme de Chambre! Hi donc! ici towels.* What's towels in French? *Donney more assets*—my assets, you know." Go through the pantomime of rubbing your hands, and the attendant will probably say, "*Oui, M'sieu, c'est très bien froid,*" or something equally to the point, and leave you, which isn't exactly what you wanted. You want to get a glimpse of the view before going to dinner. Rush out. Nothing but mist. Wonderful! Beautiful! A friend tells you that you should have

been up there two hours ago and seen "the voo" *then.* "Ha!"
you return, "we had much better voos coming up here. We came
by an unusual path; not in the common track; so hackneyed.
You should try it, it's worth going down again, merely to come up
by it." Here's an opportunity for romancing—but now the dinner.
Ha! soup. Carried in triumphantly. Take off the cover; a thin
steam ascends. The landlord commences ladling. Consternation
is on his face, horror on the waiters' countenances! What is it?
The guests tremble. They are in a foreign land: and one crusty
old gentleman already pulls out his note-book, and commences a
letter to the *Times.* Poison? *A pint of very dirty lukewarm soap
and water, with a nail-brush in it.* Tourist, be careful where thou
dost in future wash thy hands.

Dropping in for a nice thing.

CHAPTER XV.

ZURICH TO INTERLACHEN—THE RIGHI AGAIN—THE GOLDAU SIDE—
GUIDES—AMUSEMENTS—WILD SPORTS—NEEDÉLPIN CRAG.

The Ascent.

WHERE are we now? Just about to start from Zurich to Interlachen.

The Tourist can, if sufficiently strong, take the Righi on the road. He mustn't take it very far, or it will be missed; as it happens, the top part of this mount has been mist more than once, but has never been entirely lost.

You intend to make the ascent from the Goldau side. Now, the question is, how do you get there? Take the first turning to the right on leaving Zurich, the second to the left, and then anyone will tell you; if they won't, implore the sulky peasant to reply; taking care to offer him a *sou*, or you will *sou* in vain.

Guides.—Always take a guide with you. One who knows the way is to be preferred.

The best guides, who move in the very highest society, have a speaking acquaintance with all the principal mountains, and invariably obtain very civil answers from the most distant echoes. They also address themselves to their journey in a manner that makes the journey answer. They are very straightforward and honest on the road; at all events, whatever wrong they do, during the excursion, is kept secret, as the steeps and heights never seem to tell upon them.

If you go without a guide choose the safest path.

Amusements in the mountains.—If you want money, and can

draw, now is the time to turn the art to account: thus, make friends with a Foreign Banker, take him up into a lonely spot, then, when nobody's looking, take out your snicker-snee, and draw upon him for any amount.

Never be unprovided with pencils, brushes, and paints; if you can execute light rapid sketches, you can do what our travelling artist did, and turn your tour into a carica-tour.

Maps.—Never travel in Switzerland without a Map; never mind what map, any one you've got by you will do. Don't forget a *knapsack* to serve, as the name implies, for a *sac de nuit* to sleep in.

Carry a flask made on the principle of Houdin's inexhaustible bottle. How's it done? Mustn't tell; it would be Robbin' Houdin the Conjuror of his secret. Come along, will yer!

Away! Tourist! Away!

Hire a mule that will leap lightly up the perpendiculars; if you don't fancy a mule, you'll find lots of crev-asses all about the mountain.

Light your pipe and show the

The bold muleteer.

donkey boys how to go up a mountain. A pipe is the most independent companion that a traveller can have; it goes out with him, and it goes out without him. If you're a great smoker it becomes a nuisance when you're riding, as, though you want to keep on the mule's back, yet must you be perpetually a-lighting. Gee up!

Now for some sport. A shrill cry from a neighbouring bush apprises you of the approach of the Wild Strawberry. Strike spurs into your mule. Over! Oh the pleasures of the chase! If you allow the Wild Strawberry to run to seed, you will lose it. Stole away! For'ard! Yoicks! As when hunting in Devonshire, so here you will have to get off your horse and proceed on foot.

In rushing at your jumps, grasp your Alpen-stock, 'twill save you from the Russian, or Rushing, proceeding of falling on your Pole. Here you are at the Needelpin Crag, an ascent of some little difficulty; yet while you, the bold hunter, are shivering on the apex, the Wild Strawberry has sprung up on the opposite of the precipice.

The Polar regions.

CHAPTER XVI.

TOP OF THE RIGHI—THE LAUGHABLE FARCE OF SUNRISE, OR FOUR
IN THE MORNING—VARIATIONS OF DESCENT—THE CAUTIOUS
CROCODILE—THE WEGGIS SIDE—WILLIAM TELL—MOUNT PILATUS
—LEGEND—LUCERNE—THE LION OF THE PLACE—GRUTLI—TOKO
THE DANE.

AT FOUR o'clock in the morning the happy peasants on
the top of the Righi blow their cow's-horns, and the

Cold without.

miserable visitors, who are just dropping gently into their first
sleep (for anything beyond a feverish snooze has been utterly
impracticable up to this hour), will doubtless "blow those horns"
too, but nevertheless they will grumble and get up to look at
the sunrise; not because they like it, but because it is the proper

thing to do, and is in fact the aim and end they've had in view all along.

Swaddled in rugs and blankets the shivering Tourist appears in front of the hotel. As a rule, the sunrise is an utter failure, though it ought not to be, considering how many times it has gone through the part before. Like almost all theatrical *artistes*, Glorious Apollo gets very careless. Stars are not free from fault, and the Sun is suffering from the force of bad example.

No. I.—"Merrily, oh!"

We believe that he has lately got into a very low Sun set. Unless they've improved their arrangements with new scenery, decorations, and appointments since we've been there, you must not expect anything more than a confused mass of clouds and mist; and the only rise you're likely to see, is the rise which is pretty certain to be taken out of the angry audience, who, however, if they are free Britons, may use their privilege as such, and hiss the entire performance.

The cow-horn players actually have the impudence to go round and ask for money from the assembled Tourists. Of course you will simply say that "you never give to people in the streets," and should they artfully suggest that "you can give it them *in the House*," you can pretend not to understand; or, should you feel yourself sufficiently strong for the occasion, you can literally "take them in," and "pay them out" in a novel and unexpected manner.

The next movement is to get some breakfast, and then ask for your bill. When you've got your bill, do not at once cut your stick, which would be, what a low-bred woodman might call, a specimen of bill-hooking it.

The Young Jack and Jill having gone up the hill must now come down; and here will be an opportunity for Jack to show his a-Jill-ity. It takes about two hours and a half to ascend the Righi, and it takes a quarter of an hour to descend. There are several modes of downward progression: which would probably be described by any Orthodox Churchman as the Variations of Descent. No. 1 is called —

The Flying Fluteplayer.— Hold your Alpen-stock like a flute, and whistle a tune, if you can, to assist the illusion. Stretch out one leg, whichever you like; march, quick time, don't stop playing the flute, and away you go.— N.B. Paper, pens, ink, and the usual forms for making your will, can be obtained at the Righi Culm, and the obliging landlord will, for a consideration, be a witness to anything. No. 2 is termed

No. 2. – Coming down on the Weggis side.

The Venturesome V.—Sit down in the shape of a V, keeping your hands disengaged, so as to save yourself from bumping against the sharp projections, which would otherwise annoy the unwary traveller. No. 3 is known as —

The Cautious Crocodile, and is, perhaps, better adapted for the progress of invalids and elderly gentlemen than either of the above.

We advise the Tourist to descend on the Weggis side, where the Lake of Lucerne is. Here you are in the land of William Tell, as the boatman will tell you, and where also you will be toll'd for your boat. The traveller, who understands German, should take Schiller's *Wilhelm Tell* in his pocket; and the traveller, who doesn't understand it, will, if he take it, keep it there. Here you will see the giant mountain, Mount Pilatus. There is an old legend concerning the derivation of the name which everybody knows, and according to some, the title is only a corruption of Pileatus, which means "Capped," in allusion to the ceremony always observed by the superstitious peasantry on looking in that direction. Be the derivation from the story of Pilatus or the fact of being Pileatus, one thing is certain, that, as the mountain can always give certain

No. 3.—"Again he urges on his wild career."

prophetic signs of a coming storm, surer even than those of Admiral Fitzroy, he, the mountain, not the Admiral, may be considered as the safest Pilot on the lake.

Land at Lucerne, and heartily admire the memorial Lion. Think of Sir Edwin Landseer, the Nelson Column, the Squirts of Trafalgar Square, the Lowther Arcade, and rejoice in your proud birthright.

Visit Tell's Chapel on the lake; then, to his memory drink with spirit in the waters of freedom at Grütli; but be cautious as to the amount of spirit mixed with the waters, lest, in keeping the patriot's memory, you lose your own. There have been fierce disputes as to the existence of Tell, who is, some captious Prigs assert, a Swiss *Mrs. Harris.* The same story, they urge, was told of one Toko in Denmark. It is within our province to set them right. The story of the Danish gentleman was promulgated by the friends of Gessler, the oppressive Governor, who, as we all know, got Toko from Tell. Hence the mistake.

The Tourist in Switzerland who wishes always to be a dandy in dress, should be provided with Murray's invaluable *Handbook for Bucks.*

Now then, let us get to Thun, and if we have time, visit Interlachen, which will bring us to the last scene of all that will end this strange eventful history.

CHAPTER XVII.

INTERLACHEN—SWISS VILLAGES — VISITORS— THE JUNGFRAU—MIN-
STREL BOYS — HOTELS—RIFLE CLUBS— DANGER SIGNALS—
NATURAL HISTORY—SIR E. G. LYTTON-BULWER.

"I'm monarch of all I survey."

NTERLACHEN is of that picturesque order of Swiss villages contained in a child's toy-box. The plan in its most original construction, is, as is the work of every truly great mind, of the very simplest description; consisting in fact of one side of a street and a row of trees, and is in consequence admirably adapted for obviating the necessity of a voluminous guide-book, as there is not the smallest chance of losing your way. The residents are hotel-keepers, lodging-house keepers, and purveyors of the necessaries of life. During the season they are busy enough, but when the Tourists have departed, it is supposed that, to keep themselves in good practice, they stop at one another's houses, going through the pantomime of paying money, and the laughable farce of making out the bill, in the most Inn-correct manner. The visitors in the summer are Americans, English, and waiters. We begin to think that somewhere or other, Heaven only knows where, there is a Cosmopolitan Canton populated entirely by waiters, possessing no nationality in particu lar; where the children are born waiters, and from the moment of their beginning to talk at all, speak five languages with equal incorrectness and facility. Perhaps 'tis this mysterious spot that the retired waiter seeks, when the familiar " Coming " is about to change into the sure and certain " Going." Perhaps 'tis here that there is an Asylum for Dumb Waiters ; a charitable Institution presided over, may be, by a Side-board of Directors. But we are wandering : let us return to Interlachen. Every window in front commands some sort of view of the Jungfrau, and from the back you can gaze upon the swift-running waters of the Aar, and the steep hill on the opposite bank, called the *Harder ;* a name evidently given to it by the many English pedestrians, who have found the meadow bank on the Interlachen side the *Easier.* There is one street-musical nuisance, that comes out in the evening in the shape of a band of five Swiss Minstrels in the national costume who favour the company with what they are pleased to call a song. Despite the accuracy of the " get up," we have our

Shooting the Beaver.

doubts as to the genuineness of these minstrels' nationality, for, coming upon them at an unguarded moment, we couldn't help fancying that we heard the chief singer talking with just the least taste in life of a brogue ; and, but for the assurance of a learned philologist, that there is a close affinity between the two languages, we could have sworn that the speaker was from the County Tip.

The gardens of the two principal hotels, we forget their names, adjoin one another, which is a very pleasant discovery for Jones, who had purposely gone to the one in order to avoid those Browns

who are putting up at the other—Jones' reason for this being that
he cannot put up with the Browns. How charmed then is he to
find that there is nothing to divide them ! May be he has
whispered soft nothings in Miss Letitia's finely chiselled, in this
instance very finely chiselled, ear, or pressed her younger sister's
hand, or done both impartially, which is embarrassing ; or there
may be that little matter of a few pounds still standing 'twixt

The grasshopper monstroserus.

Jones and Old Brown, which causes Brown to be very glad to
meet Jones, but occasions no reciprocity of sentiment in the latter
gentleman's breast. The gardens form the stage for the performance of many little comic dramas of every-day life.

The Tourist who is fond of shooting, or who takes an interest
in the Volunteer Movement in his own country, will do well to
walk along the banks of the Aar, when the members of the Swiss
Rifle Club are practising. The Switzers take up position in a hut
about a hundred yards from the river, on the Interlachen side :

the Target is fixed upon the opposite bank of the Aar. The
happy and unsuspecting Tourist cannot be too noisy during this
walk. We advise him to be constantly shouting out " Hi !" or
" Ho !" or " Hiho !" or " Hilliho !" or in fact anything he likes,
and as loud as he can, in order to attract the attention of the
marksmen, who, from their guarded position, cannot see anybody
coming, and the pedestrian will be lucky if the first inkling that
he gets of his proximity to the rifles, is hearing a whirr, and then

"Strange things come up to look at us."
The Admiral

the sharp report at no great distance from him. We say he will
be lucky, as the ball may be through your hat or your head before
you know where you are.

One middle-aged Englishman of nervous temperament held up
his new hat, and shouted to the riflemen to show that he was
there. The Switzers mistook this for a challenge to their skill
in hitting a new kind of target, and in less than five seconds as
many bullets riddled his bran-new gossamer. To go upon all-fours
is no protection, as they might take you for a beast, and though
their firing at you under these circumstances would be pardonable,

nay, even commendable, yet it is admitted on all hands, that whether you are killed by mistake for somebody or something else, or on purpose, the result to yourself is equally unpleasant. Perhaps, after this, the conclusion to which you will come, if you do not come to any other unfortunately premature conclusion as above mentioned, will be the sensible one of not walking on the banks of the river Aar.

If the Tourist is fond of Natural History, and for the matter of that, if he isn't, he will come across some curious specimens of the Insect tribe, and some too curious specimens of the insect tribe will come across him. We never realised Spiders until we saw them in this neighbourhood; neither could we have imagined to what a Grasshopper might come at last, if it once had its own way. There was once upon a time a Pantomime called the *Butterfly's Ball*, where all the insects were as big as men, but even in those early days of oranges in the boxes to keep us quiet, we knew that they *were* men, because we saw their legs, and consequently did not cry after making that discovery; and there used to be at the Polytechnic a lecturer of cruel tendencies, who was wont to frighten children under the shallow pretence of instruction, by showing them a drop of Thames water magnified. Do you recollect those black, crawling, swimming, darting, jerking, unpleasant animalculæ? They were not nice to look at; but we swallowed them then, and do now, in spite of a patent filter and the Thames Commissioners. Well, these awful beings are nothing to the sweet creatures inhabiting the fields on the Harder Bank of the Aar.

In the heat of the day you go to sleep among the long grass, and are dreaming that HER dear face is beaming upon you with love and tenderness, when suddenly you are awakened to a dread reality, to which, in our terrified opinion, the *Dweller on the Threshold*, in Sir E. Lytton-Bulwer's *Zanoni*, is not for one instant to be compared.

E E

CHAPTER XVIII.

THE LAUTER-BRÜNNEN ROAD—UNSPUNNEN—THE LEGEND.

THE Poetical Tourist will make a point of walking along the Lauter-brünnen Road, only stopping at the Castle of Unspunnen, the reputed residence of the amiable but mistakenly impulsive *Manfred*, to call for Mr. Phelps.* Somebody writing concerning this castle has observed, that, "from its position in front of the high Alps, Lord Byron must have had it in his eye." That the noble Poet, not being exempted from the ills to which all flesh is heir, might have had, at some time or another, a stye in his eye, is probable ; that he ever had a castle in it, is simply impossible. A gifted Cockney Tourist however, actually observed, that, " If Lord Byron 'ad a stye in the heye, he might 'ave 'ad a castle in the 'air." The Legend of the Castle of Unspunnen is a very touching one, and will be sung to you by any peasant for a mere song. The following is a translation, adapted to the well-known and once exceedingly popular air, *Villikins and his Dinah :*—

THE LEGEND OF IDA, THE BOLD BARON'S CHILD.

The Baron.   Old Buskard the Baron, the last of his race,
    Had a very big body, and very red face,
    That he came of a right Royal Stock, some suppose,
His nose,   From the purple he constantly wore on his nose.
And Chorus.   Singing : tooral li, tooral, &c.

His domici-   In Unspunnen Castle this Baron did dwell,
* lium.* He had but one daughter, a werry fine Swiss gal,
The Heiress.   Her name it was Ida, with a fortune that seems
With air   A whole heap o' money when told in *centimes.*
and chorus.   Singing : tooral I, tooral I, tooral *I da.*

---

 * Who took the part of this Immoral Philosopher at Drury Lane Theatre, 1863.

What He said. Said the Baron one day, in a very stern voice,
"I want you to marry the man of my choice."

What She said. Says she, "I can't do it ;" says the Baron, "For why ?"
"'Cos,' says she, "I love Rudolph," says the Baron, "My I—
—da," tooral I, tooral I , tooral I da.

"I love Rudolph."

His Wrath. When the Baron heard this he was furious and riled,
And he bullied his daughter, who patiently smiled,
Which annoyed him so much, that he hit at her crown,

Eider down. And u-pon a feather bed he knocked Ida down.
Tooral I, tooral I, tooral I da.

Hisswallow. Then he bolted the door and he locked it outside,
"You shall *never* come out to be that Rudolph's bride ;"
Then he kicked all his servants impartial*lee,*

The Menials Till the menials each felt like a vassal at sea.
Tooral I, tooral I, tooral I da.

Rash Oath.　While the Baron was a-swearing just like anythink,
A Wink.　　Rudolph, at her window, saw Miss Ida wink,
　　　　　He squeezed through the iron bars, being but thin ;
A Lovier.　While the Baron " let out," *he* was being let in.
　　　　　　Tooral I, tooral I, tooral I da.

"The Loviers."

What They did.　To Zähringen the fond loviers ran away,
　　　　　And the Baron waged war upon Rudolph next day,
Tactics.　It lasted some time, as they went on this plan,
　　　　　Each alternately fought and alternately ran.
　　　　　　Tooral I, tooral I, tooral I da.

　　　　　At the end of two years, p'raps, or rather before,
The Door.　The Baron one night heard a knock at his door,
　　　　　Sharp as hit with the stick that the Scotch use at " Golf,"
　　　　　It was Mister and Missis and Master Rudolph.
Chorus as be-fore.　　　Tooral I, tooral I, tooral I da.

Then his daughter knelt down, and said she, " I'm a Ma' ; "

Baby.   Then held up an infant, " so like Grandpapa ! "

And the Baron, who had of real feeling no lack,

Emotion and Felt *hysterica passio* all up his back.
Chorus.   Tooral I, tooral I, tooral I da.

The Blessing.

" Oh, bless you, my Ida, my Rudolph and Boy ! "

Said the Baron ; and all from that moment was Joy !

And they wrote 'neath the crest that belongs to their kin,

Moral.   " Love locked out of doors by the window gets in."

     Tooral I, tooral I, tooral I da.

So much for the Baron and his fair daughter Ida.

CHAPTER XIX.

INTERLACHEN CONTINUED—LAUTER-BRÜNNEN ROAD DISCONTINUED—
HÔTEL EN PENSION—EGGS IS EGGS—LAKE OF BRIENZ—
GIESSBACH FALLS—THE FAULHORN—POPULAR ORNITHOLOGY—
NATIONAL PHYSIOGNOMY AND PHYSIOLOGY.

"I'm a-looking at you."

UNLESS the Tourist is going to somewhere else, he will not pursue the Lauter-brünnen Road any farther. On his return to the hotel at Interlachen, the pedestrian will probably be inclined to walk into his dinner. The real economist, by the way, will never live *en pension*. It sounds very nice; only six francs a day for *everything!* You agree, and commence, let us say, with breakfast. Being an Englishman, and accustomed to make rather a substantial affair of your first meal in the day, you are somewhat surprised when the waiter brings you a small coffee-pot holding about a cup and a half, a diminutive and aërial-looking French roll, one small thin pat of butter, and a kind of large earthenware salt-cellar filled with lump sugar. It is true that whatever is deficient in bread and butter is certainly made up to you in saccharine nutriment ; but, eke it out as you will, this is hardly a substitute for the fish, meat, and eggs of the domestic table. The guileless traveller will probably call the waiter, and order a couple of eggs, and some more bread. At midday, the simple Simon will further command a light repast, and, while enjoying himself with a cold collation, will say to a friend, "Capital idea this, you know; I'm living *en pension;* only six francs a day, and it includes *everything.*" The friend, being perhaps unwilling to disturb this blissful state of ignorance, will perhaps say, in a tone of surprise, "Oh, does it?" If the Tourist be of a fidgety turn, he will repeat these words to himself in his friend's absence in the form of an inquiry as to "what's he mean by 'oh, does it?'" The explanation, which will be given in the bill at the end of the week, will probably cause the simple one to lengthen his face and shorten his stay. "Why," says the indignant gentleman, "I thought *en pension* included *everything,* and here (*emphatically slapping the little account*) I find eggs charged extra."

"Yes, M'sieu," explains the polite *garçon,* "but M'sieu must understand that everything in an *en pension* sense means only the regulation breakfast provided by the hotel. Some coffee, a little bread, some milk, some sugar, is everything that——"

"But—surely—Eggs—you know ——" gasps the Tourist.

"Ah! M'sieu, eggs are not everything."

And so the Tourist having learnt that, as at home so abroad, "Eggs is eggs," and that the comprehensive

"Over!"

Everything often means almost Nothing, packs up his portmanteau and returns to England a wiser and a sadder man. But he mustn't pack, and he mustn't go back, until he has seen the sights round about Interlachen; unless indeed his economical living *en pension* has rendered his departure an inevitable necessity. Seek then the Lake of Brienz and the Giessbach Falls. If you are a member of the Alpine Club, you will take your way to the Lake of Brienz by ascending the Faulhorn, and walking along a pleasant footpath which cannot be attempted without a guide; so take this Work with you, and there'll be nothing to fear. When on a dizzy height, or a dangerous pass, such as the one first mentioned, *never look down at the depths below you*—such a proceeding is fraught with danger; on the other hand, you will find that the method practised by some, of invariably keeping your eyes steadfastly fixed on the sky, is not entirely without its own peculiar disadvantages. The woods about the Giessbach Falls offer many charms to the naturalist. Here the rare hen Cockeyolly Bird pipes her tuneful lay; a peculiar note it is, and specimens of this Ornithological curiosity may be seen in the Lowther Arcade, the Pantheon, and the German Bazaar.

In Switzerland the Physiologist will notice the glorious type of Face, immortalised by the carvers of wooden match-boxes, nutmeg-graters, and ornamental paper-knives. The searcher after Physical Facts may try to ascertain if their heads come off; but we believe they do not, as a rule; still there's no harm in making the experiment, if agreeable to the peasant.

CHAPTER XX.

HOW TO WINTER AT ROME—JESUITS—FRIARS—ROMEWARDS AND HOMEWARDS—"BOCK AGEN"—BUBBLES, TOILS, AND TROUBLES—FLEXIBLE BATH—ITS ADVANTAGES—ST. GOARSHAUSEN—ALL A-BLOWING—A MUSICAL MANIAC.

THE Tour is finished. From Antwerp to Interlachen has been done, and nothing now remains but to quit. "To those whom Providence has blessed with affluence," we say, winter at Rome; and as, in that case, the present Guide must unfortunately be absent, let one general piece of advice be given and acted upon; namely, "'Do' at Rome; as they 'do' at Rome."

If an intelligent and enlightened Protestant, be on your guard: such is the ecclesiastical tyranny in this ancient city, that every waiter in your hotel is obliged to take Orders, and you may look upon each one of them as a Jesuit in disguise. Visit the hotel kitchen, and in the man-cook behold a Friar. Being accustomed to see the notice, "You are requested to take off your hat," stuck up in your own St. Paul's, you will make a point of keeping it on, there being no such requirement expressed in St. Peter's.

Pooh-pooh everything that is not strictly English, and show your own superiority over the poor superstitious Italians by talking loudly in the churches, and criticising in any terms of artistic slang with which you may be acquainted, the paintings that adorn the interiors. The truth of the ancient Proverb will strike any one after a walk round the City, viz., that "Rome was *not* built in a day." We must not, however, forestall a future trip; so, if you be bound Romewards, our paths lie in opposite directions. Farewell. Homewards, to the coast; and we have nearly reached the end, at all events the Ost-end, of our journey. And now, to occupy the time taken up in retracing much of the old ground, we will request the Traveller's attention to a few parting remarks, the result of our own personal experience, which we will call—

BUBBLES FROM THE BRÜNNEN ; OR, CONTINENTAL BATHS.

The order of the Bath is peculiarly English. None but the cleanliest of nations would possess such an honourable decoration. The terms arising out of the constant use of the bath enter largely into our ordinary converse. A needy Toady, we are accustomed to hear, "Sponges" upon his patron. The sour crab-apple-disposition'd man "throws cold water" upon every jovial proposition. "How are you off for Soap?" is an inquiry supposed to relate to the financial resources of the party interrogated. The moral teaching of those excellent institutions, "Baths and Wash-'uses," is conveyed in the dingy chambers of a "Sponging House;" and many other instances will, we doubt not, occur to the careful observer. Let us not be misunderstood. Foreigners enjoy a *bathe* as much, nay perhaps more, than we ourselves: but the domestic matutinal "Tubbing" is, on the Continent, comparatively unknown. The Tourist need not trouble himself to con the French, Italian, or German, for "Bring us a hip-bath or saucer-bath," as the case may be, because he won't get one, at least not what he wants. To remedy this great inconvenience, a certain cunning artificer in india-rubber, invented a portable bath of that flexible material.

It was capable of being reduced to the size of an ordinary table-napkin when folded up, and might be carried in the coat-tail pocket with as much facility as a pocket-handkerchief. There were, and ever will be, a few disadvantages accompanying this ingenious contrivance. The first is, that supposing you've got it with you, every one in the carriage begins sniffing and observing that there is "a strong smell of india-rubber somewhere." If you are nervous or bashful, this is unpleasant. If you are neither one nor the other, you will say, "Dear me, yes—these carriages are not well ventilated," and will insist, homœopathically, upon smoking a cigar. Again, its receptacle in your coat becomes for ever after a very Pariah of pockets, and impregnates every article that may be placed in it with a faint sickly smell of india-rubber.

This bath was fitted up with a brazen mouth-piece, which rendered it a somewhat unpleasant companion in the hinder pockets of any traveller, who, forgetful of his treasure, was in the habit of impulsively jumping into railway carriages and sitting down sharply. When required for use, you had to sit down on the floor of your room, cross-legged like a tailor, and applying your lips to the aforesaid mouth-piece, blow into it with the vigour of at least three professional players sustaining a note upon the gay bassoon. When we first travelled, we purchased one of these curiosities, intending to go over the wide world like a cleanly Diogenes. The tale of our tub was brought to a sudden and unexpected conclusion. It was, if we recollect right, at St. Goarshausen, that, while we, orientally squatting as above mentioned, were engaged in filling our bath with air, the intelligent waiter entered our room, and on seeing our undignified occupation, paused, stuttered out an apology, and quickly retired, leaving the door partly open. Now to get up and shut this door would have been, under the circumstances, a waste of breath, and therefore, as we had still a cheerful half hour's "blow" before us, we preferred keeping our seat. In a few minutes a shuffling of feet in the passage and a sort of "hush-hush-hushing" chorus, made us aware of the presence of the landlord, landlady, his two daughters, and other members of the establishment, not being otherwise engaged, who were stealthily peeping into the room. Our host, on observing that we stopped and probably appeared somewhat angry, stepped forward, and by way of apology informed us, that "he and his family were very musical : and so, hearing that the English gentleman was just going to play a tune upon quite a

"A Tale of the Tub."

new kind of instrument, they had taken the liberty of being present at the performance." This had evidently been the report of the imaginative and artistic waiter. "My daughters," continued the landlord, "have a piano in the house, and would accompany you with pleasure. Does the English gentleman play by ear or from notes?" After an explanation of the real use of the machine, we were evidently considered as a harmless lunatic; an opinion shared in by everybody except the Boots, upon whose shoulders was thrown the onerous duty of regularly, every morning during our week's stay, bringing two buckets full of water up to our room, six flights of stairs above the level of the first landing. He went through the work for three days, but on the fourth morning, he, for we have no moral doubt that he it was, wreaked his miserable vengeance upon us. On the previous afternoon he had cut a hole in the bottom of the bath. Of course there was no one who could, or if they could, *would*, mend it. His vengeance was complete; for as a bath of some sort was a necessity, we had to take those at the bottom of the house, fitted up in its foundations, to which we had to descend exactly eight flights of stairs. But we were fertile in expedients for torturing the malicious menial : so we made him come up the usual six flights to fetch our sponge, soap, towels, and hair-brushes; descend eight flights following us on our way to the bath ; and finally, when we had finished our ablutions, he was summoned to ascend the eight flights, bearing the aforesaid requisites back again to our chamber. We had lost our pet luxury, and now began our travels in search of a tub, with what success shall be hereafter shown.

CHAPTER XXI.

DIOGENES IN SEARCH OF A TUB—PARIS—HYDRAULIC PRESSURE—
SPIRITUALISM—HOME AND ABROAD—INFERNAL MACHINERY—
NOBS—TUB THE FIRST—NUMBER TWO—LYONS—A CURIOSITY—
MARSEILLES—STUDY FROM THE ANTIQUE—FAMILY JAR.

"Pneumatic Dispatch."

THE travelling Diogenes commences his search for a tub, let us say at the Great and Grand Hotel, Paris. This hostelrie is furnished with all sorts of luxurious contrivances. For instance, the room that falls to your lot is number one hundred and sixty-five, at the top of the house, ten storeys high: an objection is upon the tip of your tongue concerning the number of stairs which you'll have to encounter, when,

hey presto! up goes the room in which you are sitting, and before you can say Jack Robinson (we contend, by the way, that this is far from being a natural exclamation for any one when startled or surprised), you are landed at the door of your lofty chamber. Thus it is that the visitor is conveyed to his apartment by means of Hydraulic pressure, and whenever he wants to descend, he is taken down again by a Pneumatic Dispatch Pipe. Mr. Home, the Medium, might be utilised here, if he could only carry weight, and go up in the air with the Tourist's luggage, whenever required. Your boxes are unpacked by steam, and everything laid neatly in the chest of drawers by a similar agency: in short, as far as our

"Oh, blow it."

memory serves us, you are washed, combed, brushed, dressed, put to bed and called in the morning, all by machinery. Those who hear that there is a small Nob in every room will set this place down for a very aristocratic establishment.

The knob, however, is of brass, and, in lieu of a bell, communicates with a battery that sends an electric spark into the waiter,

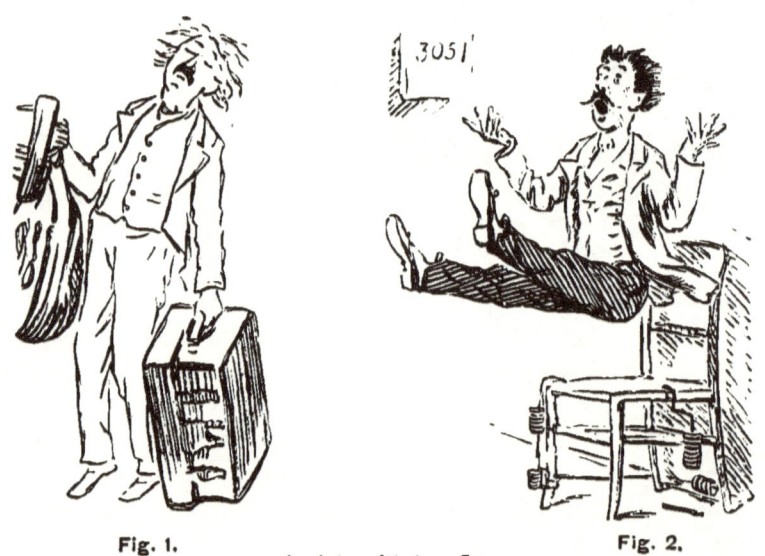

Fig. 1.

A plate with two figs.

Fig. 2.

who is calmly sitting—it may be, perchance, dozing—at the end of the passage. Another wire jerks the number of your room out of its place on the wall and suddenly obtrudes itself upon his notice. The poor creature's attention being drawn to your requirements by this really shocking process, he steps upon a sliding board and glides into your apartment like an amiable Corsican brother's ghost with his coat on. Give your order while the waiter's in the

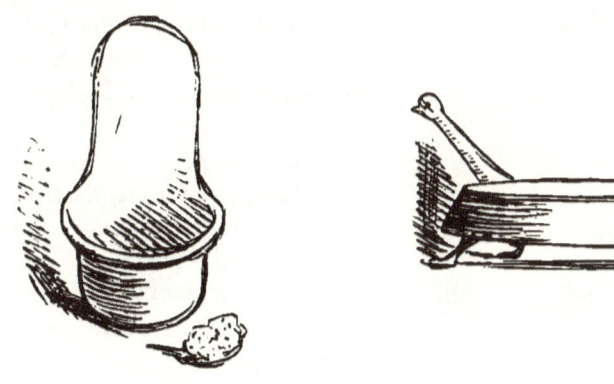

Another Plate.

room; with all these electric forces about, there's no knowing where he will be in another minute. The menial does not go down-stairs to execute your commands: he knows a trick worth two of that; he sends a telegram to the cook, housekeeper,

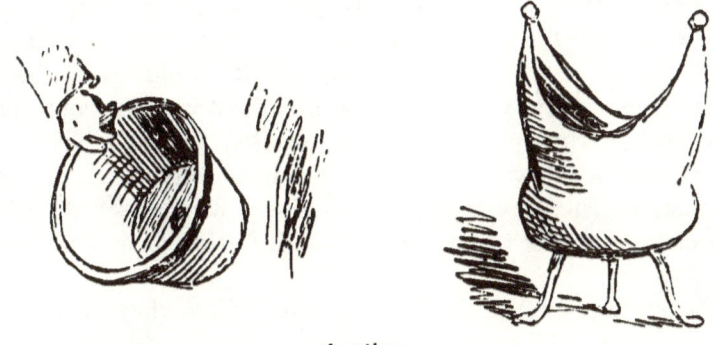

Another.

boots, or whomsoever it may concern. Such are a few of the improvements with which you will meet in the Great and Grand Hotel, Paris. Surely here Diogenes will obtain his matutinal Tub? Let him try. We did, and this is what they sent us. Nothing earthly did it resemble save a tin perambulator without its wheels. This curiosity was a tight fit for one, and held, if you could have wedged yourself into it, about three teaspoonfuls of water; being also of Nautilus' shell shape, it laboured under the disadvantage of not possessing, of itself, any power of remaining in an upright position. We explained (by the Hotel Telegraph) that what we required was a hip-bath, and the master of the hotel returned us the polite answer, also by telegraph, that he had sent us the only hip-bath in the house.

We changed our quarters, and experimentalised at a smaller hotel. An intelligent waiter listened to what we had to say, inquired what amount of water we wished the machine to hold, and the time when we should want it, as it was so often in use. This sounded well, so we told him our usual hour, and went to bed looking forward to the joys of the morning. Punctually came the *Garçon* and brought us a nondescript copper vessel; it might have been a saucepan, and it might have served for a frying-pan; for our part, judging from its grimy state, we believe that it had been used in both capacities; but whatever it *might* have been,

"A Hip Bath?"

there was one thing which it most certainly was *not*, and that was, a bath. The waiter informed us that it was what they *called* a bath, and would we make haste, as there was another gentleman, an Englishman, waiting for it. We generously gave up our claim, in order to send it on to him forthwith, and we hope he liked it.

Our next inquiry was made at Lyons. Here they gave us a large flower-pot. This might have served for one foot at a time, had the aperture common to these articles been stuffed up with some more durable substance than mud.

At Marseilles we were introduced to a very remarkable specimen of the antique. At first sight we set it down for a petrified mitre; but the bowl and three legs rendered this position untenable.

Being brazen, it occurred to us that it was not very far removed from an inverted helmet; but here again the legs came in our way and floored us. As to using it for the ablutionary purposes of a sponging bath, that was simply impossible. There was no sitting or standing room in it. We passed about half-an-hour in trying to invent some method of adapting this vessel to our needs. We failed to devise a plan, and ended as usual by either going to the bath-room or taking a dip in the river.

A "Mentone" Bath.

At Nice all trouble of exercising our ingenuity was saved us by the production of an article which the waiter evidently regarded as an un-equalled work of art. He showed it to us with some pride. "M'sieu wants a bath for his apartment; here it is, see!" We *did* see: the thing would have been nothing more nor less than a fishing-can, had it not borne an equal resemblance to a slop-pail, and was like neither one nor the other, inasmuch as it possessed four up-right handles, which, as far as we could make out, rendered it useless for any object save that of ornament, for which, seeing that it was a dirty old green tin, it was perhaps scarcely qualified.

At Genoa they brought us a tea-urn, with the heater in it complete.

At Mentone, after a very great deal of trouble, the politest of landlords with much delight, flattered himself that *he* at all events had succeeded in suiting the English taste, in the way of tubs, to a nicety, and assisted by three civil and obliging waiters, entered our room in great triumph, lugging in a gigantic Oil Jar. Had he wished to put us quietly out of the way, by the landlady playing *Morgiana* to our *Forty Thieves*, this would not have been a bad method of accomplishing his design. So far, the tub was not yet discovered.

CHAPTER XXII.

STILL IN SEARCH OF A TUB—ZERMATT—CASUS JELLY—ST. NICHOLAS
—"A FLORENTINE JOKE"—BOLOGNA—TURIN—SORROW—RESO-
LUTION—ACTION—THE CLIFFS OF ALBION—THE DISCOVERY—
"REST AND BE THANKFUL"—AT HOME.

The Bill !

HE little village of Zermatt is now a place of popular resort for Tourists, of whom no small proportion are pedestrians. Each of these gentlemen who foot it merrily, is himself a Diogenes in search of a Tub; and therefore we sincerely trust that in the course of the next century the supply of sponging baths may equal the demand. The waiter placed no difficulty in the way of furnishing us with our tub, and, after a delay of some twenty minutes, passed by us in the dreamy anticipation of coming pleasure, the good-natured server entered our apartment carrying a Zermatt sponging bath. It was a jelly mould ! Considered as a jelly mould, it was undoubtedly a fine specimen of its kind, and would turn out a grand angularly-peaked shape, enough to satisfy the requirements of sixteen sweet-toothed people; but, regarding it, as we did, in the light of a substitute for a hip-bath or tub, we couldn't honestly say very much in its favour. We explained our wants to the landlord, who forthwith upbraided the waiter pretty freely for his stupidity, and finished by bringing us a gold-fish bowl, with the live stock swimming about in it.

At St. Nicholas they gave us a vase, of the same shape as that one, which every one knows, with the two birds perched *vis-à-vis* on the two handles, and evidently bent upon taking the first opportunity of drinking whatever may be poured into it. Well, this was just the same as the one above mentioned, only without the birds.

At Florence, we, still as Diogenes, were introduced to a most startling pantomime trick in the shape of a castellated washing-tub. It was shallow, but its width compensated for want of depth, and though a sitting position in consequence of the pointed corners was impracticable, yet we really hoped that here at last we should be able to obtain a good sponging bath in our own room. Alas! the tub was made up of ever so many separate bits of wood, like a puzzle, held together with a belt of the thinnest wood, which, just as we had poured in the contents of our can, even to the very last drop, suddenly snapped asunder, and in another second, boots, stockings, slippers, and hastily thrown-down clothes were a prey to the wild unbounded waters.

Bologna became memorable in our annals by reason of their having been very indignant at our denying the properties of a sponging bath to a gigantic bread-basket, with a stiff wooden handle.

T. stands for Turin and tea-pot. 'Twas a curious old specimen, and an interesting object to us at any other time. But when you want a good substantial cut from the Roast Beef of old England, the sight of a Pompeian dish-cover will scarcely afford you an equal amount of satisfaction.

No, we could bear it no longer; fairly broken down by so many trials and disappointments, we sat down and wept. At that sad moment the strains of music—soft, soothing music—fell upon our ears; and, upon the evening draught, which came up through the long hotel passage, in at the chinks of our door, daintily flavoured from the kitchen, there was wafted to us a melody divinely soporific. We have got some ear for music, and this air reminded us strongly of "*Home, Sweet Home*," though, for the matter of that, it wasn't a bit like it.

Dover! Hurrah! We would stop nowhere until in the comforts of our own old home, our own dear warm bedroom, we indulged in OUR TUB.

Arrived! Ring the bell! down with the luggage! How much, Cabman? Six shillings. Too much, but the rascal thinks I'm a foreigner. Ha! ha! ha! good that. Here you are; off he goes, without a sign of gratitude. Ha! Mary—all well at home? That's good. Didn't expect us so soon? Oh! no fire in our bed-room? Then light one — quick. No dinner? Then get a steak, bachelor's resource; or chops; or—anything. Here we are in our own bedroom : neat and cosy; fire blazing up. Travelling *does* make one so dirty and mucky. Large tin hip-bath in the corner—out with it. We are all alone; and drag it from its recess; then proceed to unpack our sponges. Mary, the towels! Here they are; and the hairgloves. Now for a rubber before dinner. Bring two cans of water, Mary—quick.

"Go to Bath."

What's that she says? Eh! Can't have a bath? What does the girl mean? Why, here it is. Eh! what's that? Something the matter with the cistern; no water come in to-day. No water! Do we pay rates, taxes—pooh! What do you say? Man *has* been here; says there's something wrong with the ball-cock, does he? Hang the ball-cock! Oh! you have got some water from next door? Enough for my hands—ha! ha! But not enough for a bath! Doesn't Britannia rule the waves? And this, this is England! This, this is Home!!

BRADBURY, AGNEW, & CO. LIMD., PRINTERS, WHITEFRIARS.

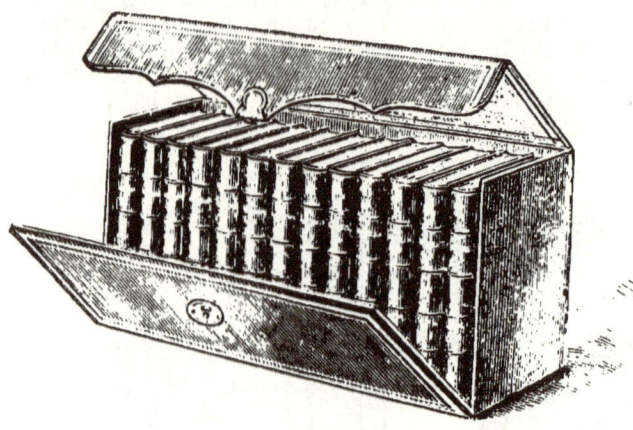

www.ingramcontent.com/pod-product-compliance
Lightning Source LLC
Chambersburg PA
CBHW030938110726
47900CB00004B/1045